Behold .

A magical
secrets, inside himself that could threaten
kingdom.

A photographer finds he has the power to open gateways to alternate universes, which is the key to everything he has lost in his life.

A skilled artist uses his mind to control and shape countless insects into beautiful works of art, but only if he can control his own fears.

Explore . . .

A pair of explorers on Mars unravels a fantastic mystery of an ancient galaxy-spanning civilization . . . but not everyone wants the answers to be found.

The flotsam and jetsam of humanity eke out a living on floating garbage islands; they have the key to saving the world, unless they tear themselves apart first.

A vast network of imprisoned, unconscious humans begin a revolution using the powers of their minds.

Discover . . .

A loyal golem learns to understand love and humanity, even as the people around him forget. . . .

When a clone obtains her soul, she learns the joys—
and dark consequences—of being human.

In a post-apocalyptic world, a young man and woman
work desperately to keep their isolated home safe,
until protection degenerates into paranoia.

Artificial intelligence and nanotechnology recreate
Irish literary figures—with a vengeance.

Journey . . .

The only way for a soldier to penetrate an incomprehensible alien infestation is to stop her own heart and
die—repeatedly.

Humans responsible for bringing a new race into a
galactic alliance learn that one mistake can mean the
annihilation of both races.

In the hyper-accelerated world of an augmented
human, life and death—and all the decisions in
between—can happen in a fraction of a second.

*These stories from the freshest, most talented new voices
in science fiction and fantasy, are individually illustrated
by the best new artists in the genre. You will definitely
encounter these names again in the future—but you saw
them first in L. Ron Hubbard Presents Writers of the
Future Volume XXVIII.*

What Has Been Said About the
L. RON HUBBARD
Presents
Writers of the Future
Anthologies

"Always a glimpse of tomorrow's stars . . ."
— *Publishers Weekly* starred review

"An anthology of the best of the best original science fiction short stories and illustrations from the annual Writers of the Future and Illustrators of the Future international programs."
— *The Midwest Book Review*

"Not only is the writing excellent . . . it is also extremely varied. There's a lot of hot new talent in it."
— *Locus* magazine

"A first rate collection of stories and illustrations."
— *Booklist* magazine

"Where can an aspiring sci-fi artist go to get discovered? . . . Fortunately, there's one opportunity— the Illustrators of the Future Contest—that offers up-and-coming artists an honest-to-goodness shot at science fiction stardom."
— *Sci Fi* magazine

"That phone call telling me I had won was the first time in my life that it seemed possible I would achieve my long-cherished dream of having a career as a writer."
— K. D. Wentworth
Writers of the Future Contest winner 1989
and Contest Coordinating Judge

"The Writers of the Future Contest was definitely an accelerator to my writing development. I learned so much, and it came at just the right moment for me."
— Jo Beverley
Writers of the Future Contest winner 1988

"I only wish that there had been an Illustrators of the Future competition forty-five years ago. What a blessing it would have been to a young artist with a little bit of talent, a Dutch name and a heart full of desire."
— H. R. Van Dongen, Artist
Illustrators of the Future Contest judge

"The Writers of the Future Contest played a critical role in the early stages of my career as a writer."
— Eric Flint
Writers of the Future Contest winner 1993
and Contest judge

"The Contest kept the spark and life of my science-fictional imagination going. I might have had little confidence before, but after the workshops, I received the great start that the Contest's visionary founder always hoped and knew that it could provide."
— Amy Sterling Casil
Writers of the Future Contest winner 1999

"It's hard to say enough about how unique and powerful this Contest can be for any writer who's ready to take the next step."

— Jeff Carlson
Writers of the Future Contest winner 2007

"The Writers of the Future Contest sowed the seeds of my success. . . . So many people say a writing career is impossible, but WotF says, 'Dreams are worth following.'"

— Scott Nicholson
Writers of the Future Contest winner 1999

"The Illustrators of the Future Contest is more than a contest. It is truly a great opportunity that could very well change your life. The Contest gives you the tools to think outside the box and create a niche for yourself."

— Robert Castillo, Artist
Illustrators of the Future Contest winner 2008
and Contest judge

"You have to ask yourself, 'Do I really have what it takes, or am I just fooling myself?' That pat on the back from Writers of the Future told me not to give up. . . . All in all, the Contest was a fine finishing step from amateur to pro, and I'm grateful to all those involved."

— James Alan Gardner
Writers of the Future Contest winner 1990

"Knowing that such great authors as the WotF judges felt my stories were worth publishing encouraged me to write more and submit more."

— Eric James Stone
Writers of the Future Contest winner 2005

"The Writers of the Future experience played a pivotal role during a most impressionable time in my writing career. Everyone was so welcoming. And afterwards, the WotF folks were always around when I had questions or needed help. It was all far more than a mere writing contest."

— Nnedi Okorafor
Writers of the Future Contest
published finalist 2002

"Illustrators of the Future offered a channel through which to direct my ambitions. The competition made me realize that genre illustration is actually a valued profession, and here was a rare opportunity for a possible entry point into that world."

— Shaun Tan, Artist
Illustrators of the Future Contest winner 1993
and Contest judge

"The generosity of the people involved with the Contest is amazing, and frankly humbling. It's no exaggeration to say I wouldn't be where I am today without it, and that means I wouldn't be going where I am tomorrow, either. So, in a way Writers of the Future shaped my future, and continues to shape it."

— Steven Savile
Writers of the Future Contest winner 2003

"These Contests provide a wonderful safety net of professionals for young artists and writers. And it's due to the fact that L. Ron Hubbard was willing to lend a hand."

— Judith Miller, Artist
Illustrators of the Future Contest judge

L. Ron Hubbard PRESENTS
Writers of the Future

VOLUME XXVIII

L. Ron Hubbard PRESENTS

Writers of the Future

VOLUME XXVIII

The year's thirteen best tales from

the Writers of the Future

international writers' program

Illustrated by winners in

the Illustrators of the Future

international illustrators' program

With essays on writing & illustration by

L. Ron Hubbard / Kristine Kathryn Rusch /

Shaun Tan

Edited by K. D. Wentworth

GALAXY PRESS, LLC

Of Woven Wood: © 2012 Marie Croke
The Rings of Mars: © 2012 William Ledbetter
The Paradise Aperture: © 2012 David Carani
Story Vitality: © 2010 L. Ron Hubbard Library
Fast Draw: © 2012 Roy Hardin
The Siren: © 2012 M. O. Muriel
Contact Authority: © 2012 William Mitchell
The Command for Love: © 2012 Nick T. Chan
My Name Is Angela: © 2012 Harry Lang
Lost Pine: © 2012 Jacob A. Boyd
Advice for a New Illustrator: © 2012 Shaun Tan
Shutdown: © 2012 Corry L. Lee
While Ireland Holds These Graves: © 2012 Tom Doyle
The Poly Islands: © 2012 Gerald Warfield
Insect Sculptor: © 2012 Scott T. Barnes
Illustration on page 14: © 2012 Emily Grandin
Illustration on page 53: © 2012 J. F. Smith
Illustrations on pages 93 & 138: © 2012 Paul Pederson
Illustration on page 195: © 2012 Hunter Bonyun
Illustration on page 255: © 2012 Rhiannon Taylor
Illustration on page 314: © 2012 Carly Trowbridge
Illustration on page 329: © 2012 Mago Huang
Illustration on page 413: © 2012 Pat R. Steiner
Illustration on page 439: © 2012 Greg Opalinski
Illustration on page 486: © 2012 Fiona Meng
Illustration on page 530: © 2012 Jay Richard
Illustration on page 553: © 2012 John W. Haverty Jr.

Cover Artwork: Beyond Babylon © 2012 Stephen Youll

Interior Design: Jerry Kelly

ISBN-10 1-61986-076-7
ISBN-13 978-1-61986-076-6
Library of Congress Control Number: 2012933271
First Edition Paperback
Printed in the United States of America

CONTENTS

Introduction

BY K. D. WENTWORTH

K. D. Wentworth has sold more than eighty pieces of short fiction to such markets as F&SF, Alfred Hitchcock's Mystery Magazine, Realms of Fantasy, Weird Tales, Witch Way to the Mall *and* Return to the Twilight Zone. *Four of her stories have been finalists for the Nebula Award for Short Fiction. Currently, she has eight novels in print, the most recent being* The Crucible of Empire, *written with Eric Flint and published by Baen.*

K. D. won the Writers of the Future Contest in 1989 (WotF 5). She later served as the Contest's First Reader, and in 2008 became the Coordinating Judge as well as the Editor for the Writers of the Future anthology.

She lives in Tulsa with her husband and a combined total of one hundred and sixty pounds of dog (Akita + Siberian "Hussy") and is working on another new novel with Flint.

Introduction

Another year. Another crop of wonderful stories and promising writers! Why has the L. Ron Hubbard Writers of the Future Contest remained such an on-going success year after year now for twenty-eight years?

The answer to that is twofold: First, the contest is set up to find writers just on the edge of breaking out as professionals and has done an exemplary job of it now for a very long time. Entries are anonymous so that the new writers are competing only with others in the same phase of their developing career. Pay levels are professional and competitive so that we can attract the best of the new writers' submissions.

Then, second, the winners are not only given monetary prizes, they are published, so that their efforts can be read, and are transported to a professional-level workshop where they are instructed by our well-known panel of judges. The money and chance for publication are the initial big draws here, but it's being treated as a professional, the chance to network with other writers and the workshop instructors and the workshop training that are the real prizes here, just as Hubbard knew they would be. Money is nice, but it's soon spent and gone. Knowledge and experience will be with them forever.

This is in the grand tradition of the science fiction/ fantasy field of "paying it forward." When a seasoned professional writer helps someone at the beginning of their writing career, you cannot pay them back in any meaningful way. They don't need anything that you can give them, but you can, when it's time, pay it *forward* by helping someone else who is just starting out.

When L. Ron Hubbard set up the Writers of the Future Contest, he was paying it forward in a big way. The scale is unprecedented. Most authors can help only a few new writers over the course of their career. But that is the sole focus of the Contest. It consistently seeks out and promotes at least twelve writers a year, not counting those just on the edge of breaking out who were encouraged to write more stories just so they would have something to enter.

That means over the last twenty-eight years, we have published and trained more than four hundred new writers and more than 250 illustrators. Not all of them have gone on to lucrative careers, but an impressive portion has. Even many of those who have not yet become household names are selling regularly and their bylines appear in anthology and magazine tables of contents throughout the year. At least twice a month, I get a note from one of our winners who has just sold a first novel. Kristine Kathyrn Rusch, Dean Wesley Smith, Eric Flint, Robert Reed, Jay Lake,

Steve Savile, Sean Williams, Nina Kiriki Hoffman, Bruce Holland Rogers, David Farland, Jo Beverley and Patrick Rothfuss are just a few of the wonderful writers who came out of the Contest.

L. Ron Hubbard knew that by helping new writers he was also helping fans everywhere. He believed that to function properly, society needed a healthy creative life. He said, "A culture is as rich and capable of surviving as it has imaginative artists . . . It was with this in mind that I initiated a means for new and budding writers to have a chance for their creative efforts to be seen and acknowledged." He knew that, if we do not provide a forum for new writers' work, many of them will give up and then we will all lose.

In 1988, the L. Ron Hubbard Illustrators of the Future Contest was created as a companion to Writers of the Future. Again, the purpose is to find talented artists just on the edge of breaking out, recognize and commend their abilities, publish their creative efforts and instruct them on how to move up to the next level in their career. Their talent must be nurtured and given a chance to grow, like a tiny flame that builds into a full roaring fire. Again, the meme is paying it forward, assisting those who need just a small break at the moment when it can do the most good.

Quarterly winners are assigned to illustrate one of the anthology's stories, then transported to the annual illustrators' workshop taught by seasoned professionals Cliff Nielsen, Ron Lindahn and Val Lakey Lindahn, among others. They dispense invaluable advice about how to develop and manage a career as an artist and keep inspiration coming. Unfortunately, as rare as it is,

4

it is not enough to just have talent. Emerging artists must learn how to develop a portfolio and professional contacts, market their work and make it pay.

The workshop/anthology/prize money format is a combo that has been working well for an impressive number of years, both for writers and artists. Hubbard knew what he was doing when he set all this in motion. Now, aspiring writers and artists just have to send in their work so that we can give them what they need to rise to the next level.

That old adage "You can't win if you don't enter!" has never been truer. We want to see your story or novel win the Hugo or the Nebula in a few years. We want to see your art win an Oscar as Illustrators' judge and former winner Shaun Tan did last year.

So send in those stories and illustrations! The future is just within your grasp.

Of Woven Wood

written by

Marie Croke

illustrated by

EMILY GRANDIN

ABOUT THE AUTHOR

Marie Croke was born and raised in southern Maryland. Being the sixth child out of nine, she watched the rest of her family go to bed with books, so she would sit in bed with a miniature dictionary.

By the time she could read, the basement had been turned into a library, shoved full of books of every genre imaginable on account of the number of people in her family and their very different tastes. Many science fiction and fantasy authors introduced themselves to her in that basement. Eventually, she did start having to buy her own books.

The two authors she credits with shaping her love of otherworldly stories are L. Frank Baum and Anne McCaffrey. In fact, the only childhood birthday she can remember with any clarity is the one on which she received the entire Oz series. She hopes to one day inspire other children to dream big the way these authors inspired her.

In 2008, Marie began following her own dreams. Her Writers of the Future win is her first professional sale and she has since sold two more stories, one to Daily Science Fiction *and another to* Beneath Ceaseless Skies.

Marie graduated from St. Mary's College of Maryland with a degree in economics and she currently lives in Maryland with her fiancé and their two children.

ABOUT THE ILLUSTRATOR

Emily Grandin was born April 2nd, 1978, in Hong Kong. She first circumvented the earth at nine months old, and has been an avid traveler ever since. Growing up in the Canadian suburbs of Montreal, she was a typical tomboy with a strong distaste for the color pink. When asked what her favorite color was, she would answer that it was a tie between green and black. To this day she still gets annoyed when people point out that black is not technically a color.

She spent her younger years climbing trees, casing out the local haunted mansion, devouring books and playing by the river. At school her favorite subject was, of course, art class.

As she got older, she came to terms with the color pink, sort of, stopped climbing trees as much, but her love for the arts endured.

In her mid-teens she moved with her family to Stockholm, Sweden, where she finished her university-preparatory school in the science program. She proceeded to study geology at the University of Stockholm, where she entertained her classmates with the post-apocalyptic graphic novel she would draw during lectures. She later realized one of her dreams when she was accepted into the architecture program at the Royal Institute of Technology.

Emily lives with her longtime partner and professional cartoonist, Axl. She aims at doing what she has been told is impossible, to scratch out a living drawing sci-fi themes and bunnies.

Of Woven Wood

His head hurt. Now that was odd. His head never hurt. His head never felt much of anything, generally speaking. Well, there was that one time when the top shelf had fallen upon him. Then it'd been more of a . . . flat feeling, but Haigh had fixed him right up. Re-wove him a whole new face, much better than the first. And bigger. Big enough to hold a larger set of shears, among other things.

This was different.

He could sense something was completely out of place. No, not out of place, just . . . out. An incredibly *empty* feeling.

Lan sat up and felt over the top of his head. Nothing. Oh, no, Haigh would be furious if he'd lost tools. Then a thought occurred to him. What if his other . . .

He dropped his hands to his chest, checking each opening, his waist, his legs, then dropped his hands in relief. Nothing else seemed missing. Everything was settled firmly in its home. Even the dead rat that Haigh had embalmed was still sitting in its basket, its tail sticking out under the loose lid.

So it was just his head that was missing its contents. Maybe that's why it hurt. Lan nodded to himself. Yes, that seemed reasonable. If he'd find everything and put it back, then things would be as they'd been and the pain would fade.

That seemed to be how Haigh's body worked. He'd curse, then bleed, then the part would cause him pain until its skin had finally grown back. Although, for him, it'd take days for his body to bother creating such miniscule pieces of himself. And that one time when his side had been burned open, that one had taken weeks.

At the time, Lan had been less than half the size he was now, his body barely holding a third of what Haigh gave him. He'd figured that the pieces needed to be found and woven back in and that Haigh was just in too much pain to even manage to crawl around looking for his pieces. So Lan had tried to help, searching for them everywhere, but to no avail.

He smiled slightly at the memory, then cradled his pounding head for a moment. He wasn't used to feeling this frustrating pain, and besides, if he didn't find the tools, then they'd be missing when Haigh needed them. And if he couldn't even be counted on to hold things for people, what good was he?

He sighed. Or as good a sigh as he could make with his woven mouth. Then he gathered himself up to start his search. The shears would be large, too large to miss.

He cast about upon the ground, stopping when he saw Haigh. That was odd. . . .

No. Not so odd now that Lan thought about it. He pulled himself closer to the Apothecary and leaned over, staring into glassy eyes. There'd been shouts, and the vibrations of many feet. Haigh had been nervous and rushing about, shoving new things into Lan's parts. He'd been so proud that Haigh was trusting him with such important ingredients. So proud.

"Haigh, please don't be angry. I will find the shears and to make up for losing them I'll gather Night Irises all week while you sleep." He stopped when Haigh didn't blink.

He started to reach out, to touch Haigh's face, to beg him awake, then froze. His fingers had cracked and shredded. Only two of them, but those two looked awful. Just as his foot had looked after that stray mutt had nibbled on him. He couldn't touch Haigh with those fingers. He'd be sure to strip skin.

A sound at the door startled him. Jaddi stood right inside the room, her frock covered in ash and her face streaked with tears. He'd seen her once before like that. The night of the fire that had torn up Haigh's side. She'd been much younger.

Jaddi stepped carefully among the shards of broken glass about the room, coming closer and crouching beside Lan.

"Haigh will have a fit," said Lan. "You're not allowed in the workroom, Jaddi."

She didn't look at him. Then, after a moment, she reached out and ran her hand across Haigh's eyes, closing off the glassy stare he'd been giving Lan. She reached out to Lan and squeezed his shoulder. "It's all right now, Lan. Haigh won't be needing the room any more." She paused and sniffled quietly, then threw her hands around Lan's neck. "I'm glad you're all right."

He patted her back, with three fingers since Jaddi's

11

skin could tear just as easily as Haigh's. "Is he dead then?" The words felt wooden in his mouth. Most words felt that way, but these ones felt stronger, harder to form. And that had nothing to do with his baskety body.

She nodded, rubbing her cheek against his woven chest, her ear catching on one of his lids, tilting it, but not removing it. She couldn't remove it, not even Haigh could remove it, but the lids occasionally shifted, and if not watched carefully could come open if they thought Lan was wanting their contents.

When she pulled away, he straightened it. That one held tiny frog eggs, the hole enchanted to not leak, but that didn't mean they couldn't slip out if the lid wasn't fastened. Haigh had made it very clear when Lan was only a few baskets old that the enchantments were useless if he didn't keep the lids in place.

That thought brought him back to his empty head. He reached up and felt again, hoping maybe he'd just missed the tools. No, his lid was still hanging over the back of his head. Empty.

He looked up when Jaddi gasped. She'd stood while he'd been searching and now leaned over him, a concerned expression upon her face. "Oh, Lan. This is horrible."

Blanching, he bowed his head. "Yes, I know. I lost the tools. He will be so an . . ." He trailed off, staring at Haigh, noting there was nothing wrong. No pieces missing, no torn holes. But he was still dead. Even Jaddi thought so, so it wasn't his own failure to miss something. "Jaddi, what happened to Haigh?"

She had her hand in his head, feeling the emptiness, he was sure. She shook her head. "Not now, Lan."

Right. She would be angry with him too. He was useless, so useless. He wanted to cry at his failure and began searching the room again. It seemed fruitless though. The room was such a mess. Haigh just *could* not work in these conditions. Lan would have to help clean it up, and maybe find the shears and the needles and the prongs. He began to brush the glass shards and their dumped contents away from Haigh and into a pile when Jaddi grabbed at his arm.

"No, *not now,* Lan." Her voice was firm, as firm as Haigh's had always been. "Right now, you need to come with me before they come back."

"Before who comes back?" He glanced about the room. Of course, he'd *known* someone else was responsible for the mess. *He'd* not done it, and Haigh would never have done such a thing, no matter how much he'd cursed when things went wrong. But it just hadn't seemed important. They weren't here right now, after all, and there was a mess to clean. And then there was his empty head. "But I've lost some tools, Jaddi. I must find them."

"Never mind that; come."

Lan took a last look at Haigh laid out upon the floor, then followed Jaddi, wondering if she would help him look later. As she led him out of the house, he noticed the blackened walls and curled books. A sharp scent hung in the air, of fire and . . . herbs. Lan frowned. That meant the herbs must have been burned too. And he'd spent many hours hanging his findings to dry for Haigh. But the fires must have been contained, whether by enchantment or an expert hand, for they had burned what was important, then stopped before burning down any part of the house itself.

EMILY GRANDIN

Outside, he looked back. There was no telling that anything had happened inside at all. The burned spots had been localized, the workroom a wreck, Haigh upon the floor, quite dead, but with no obvious wound that could be put back together, and yet the house looked as tranquil as it normally did.

Jaddi sighed and he turned to see her with her hands upon her hips, waiting. It was never good to keep others waiting, that's what Haigh had always said. Usually it was about his customers, but he'd told Lan that it was a good practice for all things one day when Lan had fumbled with the latch to one of his baskets. He ran a hand down his back as he caught up with Jaddi, making sure each of those lids was secure. They were.

All of him was secure, his outside smooth, with only the little latches to show where each new basket had been woven inside of him to make him grow in both size and use. And when he closed his eyes, he could sense that each was full, the fluids sloshing as he walked, the bark shavings and petals rustling, the hummingbird fluttering her wings (chest, center-left column, sixth down). All full— except his head, that was.

They didn't walk far, just to Jaddi's own house down the lane. Haigh lived—had lived—on the outskirts of the little town of Otaor. Far enough away he didn't feel as if eyes were on him on a constant basis. People had to go at least a little bit out of their way to come see him, which was exactly how he liked it. Lan hadn't minded either way, but at least that way the forest was closer and he knew he did not frustrate any neighbors when he came and went during his night collections.

In Jaddi's kitchen, overly warm from a small fire where she'd been cooking, she made Lan sit. "Now, let's see if we can fix that gaping hole in your head."

He sat up straighter. "Yes, please. I hate having an empty space, especially my head."

She laughed, though it came out strangled and did not reach her eyes. "That's not quite what I had in mind. Somehow you've managed to rip a hole in the bottom of your head. You couldn't hold anything right now if you wanted to."

"Really?" Maybe that was why it hurt then? But, no, he looked at his fingers again. They were shredded and they didn't hurt. Not one bit.

Jaddi must have noticed his gaze for she grasped his two fingers in her hand. They were bigger than hers, each at least the size of two of her fingers. Haigh had said it was so they could hold something bigger than dried mouse droppings—though one of his fingers had been relegated for that as well.

"Hmm, I'll have to soak your hand to fix those; don't want any more of you breaking." She made him sit with his hand soaking until the wood was more easily bent and woven back into shape, while she went about working on his head. She used new sticks, after snipping off the broken ends. It was slow going, each new branch being woven in all the way around his head so that it would be as strong as it'd been before. Lan appreciated that.

"You take longer than Haigh did fixing me," he noted.

"Well." Jaddi paused and straightened her back.

16

Lan heard a distinct snap as something popped, then she leaned back over to continue working. "Haigh generally didn't care much what something looked like as long as it got the job done. I take pride in the way my work is presented."

Lan turned to look at her, feeling her fingers fumble to hold on to what they were doing. "Haigh took pride in his work as well. He was a great Apothecary, knowledgeable in much more than simple tonics and antibodies."

Jaddi laughed again, though this time it seemed she'd actually found something funny in what he'd said. He'd not meant it as funny, though. "That sounds like Haigh." Then she patted his shoulder once. "I'd not been knocking his knowledge and abilities, but you have to admit, the man was much more interested in *what* a thing did than how it looked when it did it."

"That *is* what is important."

"We each have our priorities, of course, but I'd like to think the package is just as important as what's *in* the package." She gave Lan a kiss upon his head, then her lips froze upon his wooden skin.

A pounding came upon her door a moment later, followed by a shout. Jaddi grabbed the rest of the branches she'd been using and tossed them on top of her woodpile, then poured the bowl where he'd been soaking his hand into a bucket upon the counter.

"Jaddi, I don't think those are fire worthy—"

"Shush." She pulled him into the next room and made him face the wall with his hands outstretched, then threw a blanket over each and placed a vase of flowers in his head. "Don't say a word and don't move a muscle." She went into the kitchen, then poked her head back out to add, "And you better not break that vase. It was my mother's and worth a lot more than anything you've got in your pockets."

The pounding knock came again and she was gone to the front door, shouting, "I'm coming, I'm coming," before Lan could respond.

"They are *not* pockets," he muttered under his breath. Then he was very aware of how heavy the vase truly was and how his head had just gotten worse under the weight of it.

He could hear the other woman's voice, annoyed, and a man's voice, that was too low to make out. "I've been told that you were a friend of Apothecary Haigh." Then the man added something Lan couldn't hear.

"We *were* neighbors," said Jaddi. "It stands to reason I would get to know him. The man never washed his own clothes so I volunteered to take care of them for him."

Volunteered? She'd run a hard bargain on that, demanding that Haigh always leave her a fresh bottle of medicinal cream for her hands every week when she dropped off his clothes, holding them hostage until he did. There'd been that one month Haigh had tried to resist, wearing the same two sets of trousers and shirts until an accident in his workroom set one on fire and the other became so sticky with resin it started to contaminate his work.

Lan started to open his mouth to correct her, then remembered what she'd said and closed it again.

"I see." The woman sounded skeptical.

The man said something again. A question by the lilt at the end of his sentence.

Jaddi snorted in response. "Ha, you must never have met the man. He kept that workroom so secret no one's ever set foot in it. I have never, at least. Only caught a glimpse once when he was slow to shut it."

That wasn't true either. It *had been,* up until today.

"Nope, he was a secretive sort. We get them now and then, but we don't complain at all here in Otaor when it means we have someone as useful as he was."

"You obviously knew him better than most." There was an awkward silence that filled the air. Even where Lan was standing on the opposite side of the wall he could almost see Jaddi's stern face, her mouth a slight line as when she'd been displeased with Haigh.

"And you obviously must not have found what you were looking for to be banging upon my door as you are."

"And you have it?"

"I have no idea what it even is. But I do know that Haigh is dead, and I could only assume that it was because of you."

"That's a strong accusation," said the man, his voice snappy and defensive, and for the first time loud enough to be heard.

There was a hard step and a creak on the kitchen floor and a sharp sound that echoed faintly, just as when Haigh slid metal prongs against a boiling beaker. Then the woman spoke again, quietly at first, "That's fine, Mart. She can think however she wishes. This whole town can think how they please." Then she spoke louder, "We did not kill him, though I doubt you will believe us. We wanted him alive, to speak with him about something he took from Queen Yula when he was sent from the court."

19

That was something Lan had known, sort of. Haigh had mentioned it once or twice, mostly in passing when describing something, or comparing the availability (or lack thereof) of things he needed. But it hadn't truly *meant* anything. At least not until now.

"The court?" asked Jaddi. "You've got to be joking." She let out a long drawn-out sigh. "I knew he came from a good background to get the learning he possessed, but that seems a bit farfetched, if you ask me."

"We weren't asking. We are telling," said the woman. "He was once greatly admired until he angered the queen."

"She as fickle as the stories say?"

"You don't talk about the queen. Ever." Mart's voice sounded as if he were snapping each word out.

"Not at all," added the woman. "I think anyone would have been rightly upset as she was, but it is beside the point. Haigh simply took something with him that didn't belong to him."

"And it took, what? Almost fifteen years to figure that out?"

Crickets. Lan turned his head to the window as if he'd be able to see the bugs.

Instead, he saw his home. An odd feeling crept over him, as if he were just here on an errand, bringing Jaddi something from Haigh, staying to talk for a few moments, before heading further into town with other deliveries. He'd do that every week, enjoying the sun warming his wooden body, knowing everything he held was safe under their enchanted lids. Most of the people here always greeted him in a friendly way and there were some children he'd play with. Not everyone, but enough that he'd been happy.

"Irrelevant."

The woman's voice brought Lan back. His thoughts dropped. There'd be no more Haigh to hand tools to, no reason to be holding all of the things he had stored. And his head still pounded, worse now that the vase was pressing on the freshly woven branches.

He felt tired, though he never slept. And sad. Tears leaked out of his eyes and dripped down his face, no doubt leaving dark paths in the grain of the wood. They were talking some more, but Lan paid no attention to it.

Haigh was gone. Lan could still see those glassy eyes staring out at him. They'd been calm and gentle, as Haigh had never really been. The man had had a fire inside that spurred him on, a passion that Lan loved to see when he'd worked. But now Lan would never lean over an experiment again, hands outstretched with anticipated tools or ingredients. He'd never hold anything steady or put details in Haigh's journals.

He knew exactly where everything was in himself, would be unfastening latches before Haigh could even ask for what he needed. And now? What would he do with himself? There was no point in even going back and searching for what was missing from his head. Not when there was no one to hold them for.

A hand upon his arm made him turn unconsciously, only afterwards wondering what would have happened if it hadn't been Jaddi who'd touched him.

"They're gone. Oh, Lan." She brushed the dark tracks his tears had made, then removed the vase and blankets. The pain in his head eased slightly. "Did you hear all of that?"

"Most," he said, following her back into the kitchen.

"Do you know what they were looking for?" she asked. "Did he hide it in . . . one of your baskets?" She glanced down his body as if she could see beyond the lids, her eyes lingering on the dead rat tail sticking out at his waist (front waist, rightmost) and the feathers protruding from a lid upon his leg (right leg, center column, sixth down).

Relinquishing his hand again to her ministrations, he started to say he didn't know, then stopped. He remembered Haigh rushing about, shoving more things into Lan's hands, insisting he find places for them in his already stuffed body.

There'd been expensive and rare ingredients: a diamond beaker (back, leftmost column, second down) and an emerald hummingbird (chest, center-left column, sixth down); that one was tickling his insides every time it decided to hover. Flowers hardened and coated with blood-dyed amber. He remembered contemplating whether he could remove the embalmed rat, but he'd helped make that rat, Haigh handing him the tools and letting him fill the miniature stoppered urns. He'd been so excited. No, the rat stayed and the ambered flowers were shoved in with a basket of seeds.

So he shrugged. "It is possible. He didn't say anything about most of what he gave me today."

She lifted his hand up. "Looks good. Just be careful until it dries all the way. You don't want anything to misform."

"How is my head?"

"It looks all right, but I wouldn't put anything in it just yet." She didn't mention the vase, so Lan didn't mention it either. Nor did he know what he would put in it if he couldn't find the shears, the needles, the prongs and there was something else, but his head hurt too much to really think about it. Probably one of those pestles; yes, that seemed right. It surprised him that he was having so much trouble remembering.

"But it still hurts."

"It hurts?"

He nodded.

"Hmm." She looked into his head again and felt around, pushing against some of the newly woven branches. "It looks good now. Everything looks fine, Lan. I don't know why it'd be hurting. Maybe it'll get better as the wood settles." She kissed his cheek, then turned to peek out the window.

"I'm sure he probably gave whatever it was to you. He trusted you."

"But I don't even know what it is."

She shook her head, her eyes growing dark, and he heard her mutter under her breath. He caught only the tail end, ". . . enough to get him killed. Stupid man." Then louder, she said, "He certainly loved his toys. I just wish they hadn't gotten him killed." She glanced over at Lan's body again, her eyes lingering on some of the lids, making him squirm uncomfortably.

Lan nodded. He didn't know what else to do. She was right; Haigh had loved that workshop, had rapped Lan's knuckles many a time when he'd tried to touch things, some of which were now, oddly, inhabiting his body. It never hurt, but he'd always been chastened and would look on in awe as Haigh finished something else. It'd only been during the last ten to twenty basket additions that Haigh had finally let Lan do things himself. Mostly simple tonics for people in town and the creams for Jaddi, but it'd still been exhilarating.

"They're gone; come." Jaddi didn't wait for a response before starting out her front door.

"Why?"

"I'm not going to just leave him up there. You're fixed and those queen's guards are gone. I doubt they'll be back again today, if ever. Maybe we can bury him right inside the forest or under the eaves of those tall trees in his backyard." She rattled off a few more options, her voice soothing the pounding in Lan's head. His own thoughts turned back to the workshop. He'd be able to find the things for his head in there, certainly. That should make the headache disappear. He hoped.

They ended up burying Haigh at the base of a large maple tree halfway between the house and the start of the forest. The wildflowers grew like crazy outside the shadow of the tree, ringing the grave and dancing in the wind as the spring turned to summer.

Lan searched himself, finding bits and pieces of things Haigh had loved, and immortalized them in colored glass, glazing each piece with enchanted paint (left leg, front-left column, third down) and stringing them up into a wind chime to hang in the tree. It took a bit of time, but was easy to do while Jaddi slept at night.

Once it was finished, he took the next evening to search for what was missing from his head. But when he got there, the workroom had been swept clean, probably by a few souls from town who'd been looking for their last deliveries. It was a kind thought, but it frustrated Lan that so many had been in such a place that'd been only his and Haigh's for so long.

Most of the shelves were empty and the desk had nothing but a small oil burner and a cracked clay pot sitting upon it. Nothing, absolutely nothing to fill his head.

He dragged himself back to Jaddi's house that night, dejected and overly lonely, where she promptly told him he wasn't allowed to go back if it made him so upset.

Instead, she had him help her around her house. Taught him stitch work so he could help patch the clothes she mended, since he couldn't very well wash them. He helped clean as well, finding things to do to make her life a bit easier. He knew she didn't need his help, but it felt good to be doing things for someone now that he could no longer help Haigh.

His baskets gathered dust—not on the inside; that would be impossible with the enchantments. And not on the outside either since he was very much active. But around the lids and underneath the latches, a slight coating of dust always began to gather. When Lan noticed, he would spend hours unlatching and relatching each and every basket, pretending that they were still in use. Though that did nothing for his empty head.

They were outside, Jaddi weeding her garden and Lan gathering what she'd pulled out to later throw into the forest, when a thought occurred to him. "Jaddi, is there anything you need me to hold for you? I've got space, and I can make more now that I don't need most of what is stored within me." That last sentence almost choked him up, though he had no real throat to be closing up on him.

She stretched and sat back on her heels to rest for a moment while she considered him. "I don't really need you to hold anything. Most everything has homes in my house and those that don't usually don't stay long. But thank you for the offer."

She massaged her hands, plucking a piece of dried skin off before she bent back over. "Granted, if I were going somewhere that might be a different story, but I'm content here." She paused in her work and stared out at Haigh's empty house, a sad expression passing over her face, but it was gone almost as soon as it appeared and she was back at her work.

Lan felt his shoulders sag in disappointment. That'd been a perfect plan, exchanging Haigh's things for Jaddi's. It would have been bittersweet as he missed Haigh fiercely, more with each day, always hearing the man's words in his ears despite him no longer being around. But it would have cured the constant headache he bore and helped Jaddi. He'd thought.

"So what should I put in my head? It's been empty since Haigh died."

Jaddi didn't look up as she was busy working a long weed out. "Whatever you want, I guess."

He stared at her, a little angry that she'd be so dismissive. And completely unhelpful. It wasn't so much to ask for something—anything—to be given a home in his head.

His headache became almost unbearable for a few moments, then eased as his eyes began to water. This was unnatural. He'd never felt any pain at all, at least not physically, before Haigh had died, and now he was stuck with an empty head that refused to be pacified.

Jaddi thought it was emotional pain finding a bodily way out, but she was also a believer that if one thought something often enough it became reality. Not that, Lan privately admitted, he'd never given that one a try.

It was another week after that conversation, in the dead of night, that he decided to take another look about his house. With a mostly full moon in the sky, Lan walked down the lane, now partially overgrown from disuse.

The house was untouched, dusty and empty. He could see decently well with the light coming in from the windows, but it wasn't the same as it'd been the many years he'd spent growing from a few tiny baskets to the hundred he had now. He sat heavily in a chair in the workroom, staring at the bare shelves and workbench.

His night went by no faster here than it did at Jaddi's house. Time seemed to slow when he had nothing to do, no one to help, until it felt as if it stopped altogether. The moon's light shining upon the floor didn't even seem to move at all.

Wandering further in the house, he stared sadly at the drying room. He'd spent a good bulk of his time here, hanging flowers and stems, crushing them later, draining sap into pots. All of which were now either burned or broken. *This* room had not been cleaned as the other had. Not as interesting, he supposed.

So he set to work, mostly unconsciously. Cleaning off the tables and dusting off the hooks. He swept the floor clean, taking bucket after bucket full of debris outside. Then he set about scrubbing with a long-handled brush, not realizing morning had arrived until the sun was already long in the sky.

He hurried back to Jaddi's house, glad for the quick night, and glad again for her company. She didn't ask where'd he been, merely greeted him warmly when he arrived.

The next night, and every night after that, he went back to Haigh's house, wiping soot from the walls, mending broken furniture, scouring burned books for pages still legible. There were quite a few, as the fires had been quick work, not thorough.

That thought gave Lan pause. The queen's guards would have had plenty of time to burn anything they'd wished. Then again, it could have been out of spite that they had ruined things, angry that Haigh had not given them what they needed. Or the queen needed. Or whoever.

He spread out the pages worth keeping, carefully scraping off the burned pieces. The rest he scanned. Most were notes from experiments, many of which Lan remembered. Some were even in Lan's hand. Those were the newer ones when Haigh had trusted him enough to keep track of things. A few, a very few, were from Haigh's private journals. They had been rarely updated, and when done so, with little emotion. He only wrote factually, as in one page "Finished updating experiment G-kpo4."

Lan could read Haigh's coding easily enough, the

first capitalized letter signifying the original recipe, lowercase letters standing for which ingredients were changed and the symbol between standing for how those ingredients were changed—reduced, in this case, with a zero meaning they were taken out completely. A double line with more letters, but before the number, meant there was a substitute. And the number was simply how many experiments in he was. Always at least five of the same. Couldn't run the risk of bad data.

The page crinkled under his sudden tight grip and a tear plopped upon the page, blurring some of the letters. Lan quickly dabbed it dry, struggling to remain gentle with the fragile paper. It was all he had left.

No, that wasn't true. Lan pressed his wooden fingers against his chest, feeling the hummingbird (chest, center-left column, sixth down) take flight and flutter her wings against her little cage. It tickled, giving Lan a slight smile. There was much Haigh had left, but it was within Lan. Then Lan sighed. Maybe he should put that silly little hummingbird in his head so she'd have more room to fly about. No, he'd as likely lose her while trying to do so, and then he'd have two places aching instead of one. Besides, Haigh had always told him not to put anything breakable up there, for it was impossible for Lan to see what he was taking out.

There were hundreds of books to go though, most of which had at the very least a few legible pages, some with whole sections that'd not been burned. It took Lan weeks of working every night to collect them all as he cleared out the ash.

It was midsummer when the house was finally back in order. Nothing like it'd been before Haigh had died. Too empty for that. But it was clean, as if ready for a new Apothecary to take up residence. Lan walked the rooms for a few nights dusting shelves that didn't need dusting, finding imaginary specks of dirt that required cleaning, until he realized the dull feeling rising up inside of him was an echo of how his head felt on a daily basis. Empty. Hollow.

Lonely.

He mentioned the feeling once to Jaddi, who didn't look up from where she was easing a layer of skin off the back of her hand, a grimace upon her face. "Were you feeling that all along?"

He thought for a moment, then said, "No. Not at all. Just recently when the house became clean and there's nothing left for me to do."

"Nothing? Maybe that's the problem." She looked up at him and raised her hands. "Don't you know how to make that cream he was always giving me every week?"

Lan shrugged. "Sure." He knew it better than Haigh probably did these last few years, considering he'd been the one making it.

"Well, why didn't you say so before?" She looked almost cross. "Would have saved me a bit of frustration. This—" She waved a hand in front of his face again— "runs in the family."

It took all of an hour, spread out over a few nights as he had to dry a few things and grind them down, but it was an hour where the headache eased and the loneliness slipped away. Worth every second he spent.

So thanking Jaddi profusely, he filled the dead of nights with collecting and drying. He found the old trees he'd been collecting sap from and hung new buckets, preparing for when it started running. There was no recreating some of the things Haigh had stored around his workroom, many of which had been ordered from out of country, with some, Lan suspected, on the underground market. Though, those that hadn't been bought illegally were just as expensive. But he took to stocking what he knew he could find.

Despite that not being very much, he still quickly ran out of jars and had to walk farther into town to visit the potter about more.

"It's been a long while since you've stopped by asking after those," he said. Kiag was a short man, with a straight face and quiet disposition, one of those who always had Lan wondering what it was he thought about a man made entirely of woven wood and baskets.

"Yes." Lan bobbed his head as he spoke. "But many of Haigh's things had been broken, and I'd like to replace them."

Kiag raised his eyebrows just enough for Lan to be able to tell they'd actually moved. "Have you found out what happened to him? Losing him was a blow to this town. Anyone who'd been his client has had to either send from the next town, costing at least three times as much, or suffer in silence."

Lan shook his head slowly. "I don't know."

The potter *hmm*ed to himself. "I'm not one for gossip. I can assure you I'd been letting the things being whispered about him wash over my back. However, if you're taking up his mantle, I'll be sure to spread the word."

Stuttering a thanks, Lan quickly put down a payment

to get the potter started on his order and backed out of the shop, too flustered at the thought of doing half of what Haigh had. It was only after he'd walked halfway back to Jaddi's house and had noticed a few people dodging his glances that he remembered the other half of what Kiag had said and wished he'd thought to ask.

He started to ask Miss Amain when he saw her. Then, feeling all his baskets turn a notch and their contents shifting inside him uncomfortably at her bright smile, he ducked his head and shuffled off, concentrating upon his feet so that he wouldn't fall.

Jaddi laughed when he asked her later. "Don't worry about them. There're some folks who'd talk even if the world were collapsing beneath their feet."

"But what do they *say*?" Lan insisted.

She pursed her lips and narrowed her eyes. "It's nothing, Lan, nothing true, at least."

When he didn't look or move away, she finally relented.

"Some think that he had it coming, is all. Think that he might have had a hidden treasure somewhere."

Lan nodded and said quietly, "Somewhere. You mean they think *I* have it."

She shrugged. "It's probably crossed everyone's minds, Lan. But you're the only one who can open those latches of yours, so you keep whatever it was safe from their greedy fingers. That's obviously what Haigh wanted, after all." She smiled sadly. He followed her gaze out to Haigh's house. "He was a pretty impressive man, regardless of what he might have done." She bowed her head and sighed. "I miss him a whole lot."

"But," she continued with a happy lilt in her voice, "I have you still. So glad they didn't burn you up like they did with the rest of his things."

He almost mentioned how he didn't think they'd done that, but stopped short, not wanting the questions that might follow.

With the jars from the potter, he began to truly fill the shelves in the workshop. He didn't need to label them, not as Haigh had (though his labeling had been mostly haphazard and usually wrong after the jar had been emptied and refilled a few times). Perhaps it came from a life of memorizing what was contained in each part of his own body, but he knew at a glance where everything was upon each shelf.

Upon the completion of the second order of jars from the potter, Kiag mentioned his wife's monthly pains, sighing wistfully of the much-too-expensive prices of buying from the random merchant traveling through.

"They have a tendency to throw their prices at the moon, knowing that if we need it we'll have to find a way to buy it. My wife grins and bears it though, saying she'd rather not have that kind of money spent just to keep her comfortable. I married right, I know that much, though I wish I could take some of that pain away."

"I could take care of that for you," said Lan. "I didn't know it was such a problem."

"Great!" said Kiag. "I'll have your payment ready upon delivery; looking forward to seeing you next week." Then he shouted at one of his sons to be careful as he followed the boy into the back room.

Lan left feeling as if he'd had no control during the whole exchange.

But he still did as he'd promised and brought the man a painkiller for his wife's tea the following week. And that was just the start.

A few people caught him on his way back to Jaddi's house that same afternoon, mentioning their own deliveries that had long ago ceased being brought. And more stopped by and left orders with Jaddi in the evenings during the following weeks.

"You know you don't have to stay here during the day," she said one morning when she was reciting a cosmetic order from one of the young women in town. "You seem to be getting plenty of work, and I've no doubt when word spreads the neighboring towns will be sending orders."

"Are you sure? I really don't mind helping you as well."

"I lived alone for quite a few years, Lan, ever since . . ." Her face darkened, but only for a brief moment. "You can come and visit whenever you like. I'm not telling you to leave, but you seem bored here during the day." She winked.

Lan nodded, knowing what she didn't say. Ever since that fire, the one that'd hurt Haigh when he'd gone to put it out. The fire that had covered Jaddi black with ash and done much worse to her parents and older brother. Haigh had carried her out in his arms, the fire waning in his wake. Lan had been screamed at that night, for daring to get so close. He raised his hands, remembering the heat, but he'd ignored it in his fear that Haigh would never come back out.

"You really think other towns will want my work as well?"

Jaddi shrugged. "They did with Haigh." As if that meant anything.

But in the following days as a mild autumn kicked up cool winds that tugged upon his latches, he found himself lost in work that included towns close enough to Otaor to hear the news that the Apothecary was back up and running. He became happier in his work, though much busier than he'd ever been with Haigh, and the ache in his head was forgotten more often than not.

When he wasn't mixing or cooking, he delved into Haigh's journal pages, painstakingly going through each and copying them into new journals where he added all the details he remembered from the experiments. He surprised even himself with as much as he did remember, noting even how many baskets he'd had during most of the experiments.

There were a few that baffled him, using a coding system he didn't recognize at all. Until he stumbled across one with what had obviously been a bright red seal stuck to the bottom of the page. A lopsided sigil pressed into the wax, drooping from where it had been reheated, much of it trying to escape from the page.

The queen's seal. Her royal approval of his work.

Lan stared at that seal for a long time before going back through some of the experiments he'd found with the odd coding and reclassifying them under a new pile. Those he'd have to go over later. Right now he needed the pieces he could actually read and understand if he was going to continue going forward with Haigh's work, taking the results of the experiments and creating his own recipes.

So, lost as he was normally, and perhaps just a bit too trusting, he didn't even pause when the workroom door opened one day. "Jaddi, I think I've managed to figure out how to take away the side effects of this . . ." He trailed off when he turned around.

Jaddi did stand there, her eyes wide with worry and her mouth a thin line, but next to her stood a woman in a regal traveling robe, her arms crossed and a scowl affixed upon her face. Before and behind the woman stood four guards, all with the same sigil Lan had seen in Haigh's notes stitched into the shoulder of their uniforms.

Suddenly he felt as if he were only one or two baskets big, and feeling his distress, anything even remotely alive within him became quite agitated. "Can I help you?" His words came out stuttering, sounding childish to even his own ears.

The woman strode forward, her cloak grazing the floor. He was suddenly glad he always kept up on the cleaning.

"I hear you have something of mine," she stated, stopping about a foot in front of him. She was shorter than him, by about a head, not even as tall as Jaddi. Despite that, Lan felt as if she was standing twice as tall and it was *he* looking up at her. The queen. Queen Yula was standing in his workshop. It made his baskets shrink slightly thinking about it.

"I don't think so," he said. He glanced about the room. "I have never even been beyond Otaor. How could I have taken anything from you?"

"Were you Haigh's . . . assistant?" She said the word as if it wasn't the one she wanted to say. Lan recognized the tone well enough. It hadn't happened much as he got older, but when his baskets had been fewer and people less accepting, he'd heard that tone well enough conjoined with much worse descriptions for himself.

"I guess."

"His created assistant with enchanted woven baskets where only it can remove the contents?" At his hesitant nod, she added, "A perfect hiding place, don't you think, for something a man wishes to never see the light of day as proof of his betrayal."

"I . . ." Lan couldn't think of a good response that either didn't insult the queen or incriminate Haigh, so he shut the tiny hole of his mouth as much as possible.

"I wish you to remove all the contents of every . . . cavity. Now."

"But . . ."

"But?" She took another step forward. "Do you have any idea what that cretin stole from me?" Not waiting for a response, she continued, "When I gave birth to my second child, he was perfect and wonderful, destined to serve my daughter in a ranking position when it came time to rule. But my son sickened quickly with disease, his body becoming a frail husk, him unable to even turn his own head to suckle and swallow.

"Haigh promised he could save him."

Lan glanced over at Jaddi, but she wasn't looking at him, her eyes instead upon the floor and the thin line of her mouth turned down as when she was upset. His breathing was steady, from having a woven body and a throat that could never constrict, but his mind was racing despite the dull ever-present ache.

"And did he?" asked Lan, when it became obvious that was what Yula wished.

She stepped back a pace and her voice dropped some of its fierceness. "He took my son from his body, coercing my child into a trinket. A filthy bauble, not even fit for my child to play with, let alone *live* in. And then had the gall to tell me he could put my son into another's body, if a boy of his age was brought to him.

"Naturally, I refused. How could I, though I am a queen, ever force that pain on another mother? So, instead I banished him, thinking he'd given me the correct trinket he'd placed my son into. I treasured it, sang to it, as if it held my son's soul, only to find it was empty when we finally found a boy who had a body, but no soul to use it."

"And you think I have it now?"

"When my guards arrived, they found him already dead and most everything ruined, so I can only assume he anticipated that I would discover his betrayal and hid my son in you."

Jaddi gave a strangled cry from behind Yula. "You don't mean . . . he couldn't have!" She covered her mouth, swallowing whatever else she was thinking and Lan saw her shoulders shake. He wanted to comfort her, though he didn't know how he could as he knew what Yula said to be a dreaded truth he'd not wanted to admit to before. It was easier to think Haigh had left them unwillingly than of his own accord.

Yula glanced from Jaddi to Lan, then back again.

"So, I guess that makes a sort of sense. I'd probably not have let him off as easy as he let himself."

Lan glowered at the side of the queen's head, hating how she could dismiss his death as the act of a coward. "You think he was scared of what you would do to him?"

"I know he was," said Yula, casting a dangerous eye at him. "He was my Apothecary long before he'd brought a bunch of crappy intertwined *baskets* to life."

He bowed his head, a part of him whispering that Haigh really had no other reason but fear to do as he'd done. Lan shook the thought away, refusing to dwell upon it. "Fine, you can have your son back."

Behind Yula, Jaddi passed Lan a horrified expression through her tears. "Don't . . . Lan. He—"

One of the guards moved to drag Jaddi from the room. She gasped, but the frightened look in her eyes didn't speak of pain.

"Stop . . . just leave her alone. Just leave us all alone." The guard stopped and glanced to Yula, who nodded tightly. Lan asked, "So what was he in?"

"We don't know," said Yula, "But I'm sure I'll know it when I see it."

Lan doubted that, not if she'd been singing to an empty bauble for over fifteen years before this, but he began to unlatch a lid (chest, leftmost column, first). Jaddi suddenly became calm in the guard's grasp, watching with a closed expression.

He put the vials of butterfly innards upon the workbench and began on the next latch as Yula stared in shock. Then basket, after basket he unlatched and opened and placed its contents next to those vials.

The workbench overflowed onto the chair. The chair overflowed onto the floor. Broken flower petals and seeds were underfoot, crystallized tonics and the diamond beaker glinted in the sunlight. The emerald hummingbird ducked her head, hiding behind much larger things Lan pulled out and hopping away from the embalmed rat when it plopped beside her.

He expected his body to slowly fill with aches and pains as he emptied himself, but the empty, lonely feeling of those baskets never came. Maybe the anger staved it off, or maybe it was the way Jaddi calmly watched him or the truth that was buzzing about his mind.

Maybe it was because he knew Queen Yula to be wrong about Haigh. He'd run through a burning building to rescue Jaddi once, after all. Had then yelled at Lan in a crazed voice, in fear that Lan would come too close and become kindling. No, Haigh was not afraid of a painful death. But he had been afraid of losing something dear.

Yula searched among the things he'd spread out, mumbling occasionally to herself. "This would have been easier had Haigh been still alive. Which do you think it is?" she asked finally.

"I have no idea. Why don't you take it all?" He shoved the mess forward upon the workbench, startling the little hummingbird, who shot into the air, her wings flashing. Yula jumped back, and to her credit, swallowed any shout that'd risen to her throat.

"Catch him," she commanded. The guards moved, but too slow. The hummingbird dashed about the room for a moment, then dove over a guard's hand and slipped through the crack in the window.

40

Yula sighed angrily. "That had to be him. Go after it." Two of the guards disappeared out the door chasing down the emerald hummingbird. "And collect the rest; we'll bring it all back with us."

"It'll take years to test it all," started Lan, but stopped at the quick finger Jaddi put to her lips. "But I'm sure you'll find him," he finished.

"Unless he was the hummingbird," said Yula, her voice so sad, Lan almost relented and told her his suspicions.

A few thoughts stopped him. Her horrified expression when she realized that *her* son was Haigh's crappy intertwined baskets was one. However, it was knowing how happy he was, right here being the Apothecary for Otaor and the surrounding towns and maybe one day, even farther. Being happy right where he'd been raised by Haigh his whole life.

Another guard collected everything that'd once been inside of Lan. He felt a small twinge when everything was finally gone, his insides light and airy in their emptiness. It passed quickly, as quickly as the queen left with her guards and retinue that'd been waiting outside.

He stood with Jaddi, watching the last of the royal caravan disappearing, idly wondering how many of the townspeople had gathered to watch the queen pass, for what was surely a once-in-a-lifetime opportunity for the majority of them.

"It's sad to see everything gone," he said. "I'd been carrying his things for so long."

Jaddi smiled at him brightly through her tears. "I have a feeling that what Haigh cared for most is still here." Then she hugged him, rubbing against his

41

unlatched lids, her tears leaking into one and pooling inside. He closed and latched that lid (chest, center-right column, fourth down) when she pulled away.

"There," said Lan, "I can start my own collection."

"That's a great idea. I never much liked seeing that rat tail every day anyway."

It was later, much later, when he was finally finished sifting through Haigh's journal pages, that he stumbled across a very short piece, one of many that Haigh had been trying to hide.

". . . for the other experiment: I don't know if the boy would have been better with a real body, flesh and blood. He's taken to the one I had Jaddi weave readily enough. He has an amazing memory, one to rival even the queen's recorder, and a knack for anticipating my needs in the workroom. He'll be great one day, but not as a king. Definitely a boy after my own heart, one I could l . . ."

Lan folded the tiny scrap of paper gently and placed it in his head, latching the lid tightly against the threat of emptiness.

The Rings of Mars

written by

William Ledbetter

illustrated by

J. F. SMITH

ABOUT THE AUTHOR

William Ledbetter was born in a small Indiana town the same year humans first flew in space. He grew up watching Star Trek, Lost in Space *and real moon landings, but his first introduction to written science fiction was by accident, when during a library visit at age twelve he checked out a copy of* On the Beach *believing it was a war story. He's been hooked on science fiction ever since, and those wondrous and formative years instilled in him a belief that all things are possible, a belief that is still reflected in his writing.*

Now living near Dallas with his family and a bunch of animals, William is a mechanical designer in the aerospace/defense industry and an avid speculative fiction writer. He's also an unrepentant space geek and loves to travel (so far only over the Earth's surface). His fiction has appeared in numerous publications and his winning Writers of the Future story will be his second professional sale, the first having been to Jim Baen's Universe in 2006. He just finished the first novel in a trilogy about humanity's next rung on the evolutionary ladder and our expansion into the cosmos.

William also runs a Dallas-area writer's group called *Future Classics*, is an active member of the National Space Society of North Texas, is the Science Track coordinator for FenCon, is an editor at Heroic Fantasy Quarterly *and runs the annual Jim Baen Memorial Writing Contest for Baen Books and the National Space Society.*

ABOUT THE ILLUSTRATOR

J. F. Smith was born and raised in the Washington, DC area. He took art classes in high school and college but never pursued art as a career. After spending ten years in the US Air Force, he went on to finish his bachelor's degree and is currently working in the airline industry.

He never lost his love of art, though, and started painting again after a long hiatus. At this point James is in the process of improving old skills and developing his own unique style.

The Rings of Mars

Y̶ou can't run away from me, Jack," I said into my helmet mic. "I can radio base and get your suit coordinates."

"Screw you, Malcolm," he said, then refused to talk again. I followed his trail and tried not to think about why my oldest and closest friend in two worlds, and his robotic digger Nellie, had left me far behind.

Instead, I concentrated on perfecting the loping stride Jack had taught me months before. It was an awkward, unnatural rhythm, but he assured me it was the most efficient method. And of the humans on Mars, no one had covered more ground than Jack.

Tiny dervishes lifted from the dust churned by Nellie's tracks, swirling on a delicate breeze, but my passage was enough to cause their collapse. Everything on Mars seemed ancient and tired, even the wind.

Jack's boot prints—wide apart and shallow—were on a straight course and easy to follow, but Nellie's tracks peeled off in strange directions many times. She must've sniffed out oxide-rich gravel patches to melt in her electrolysis furnace, but no matter how far she went, the robot's path always returned to Jack's. I followed their trail and tried to rejoice in being one of the few humans to ever see Mars like this, but my regrets persisted.

Against all reason and expectation, Jack thought himself more colonist than explorer and was willing to trample anyone in that pursuit. If devious resourcefulness was typical of Martians, then Jack was a good one.

An alarm squawked in my ears, surprising me enough that I stumbled and skidded to a floundering stop.

RADIATION ALERT! RADIATION ALERT! ETA, 47 MINUTES. SEEK IMMEDIATE SHELTER.

Forty-seven minutes? My suit's magnetized outer skin was protection against the ambient radiation, but not huge solar flares. I fought growing panic as I turned in circles, looking for a cave, stone outcropping or even a boulder, but saw only dust and scattered rocks. The nearest ridge line was blurry with distance. Anger also grew in the wake of my fear. Nellie provided our only radiation protection, and Jack had taken her. They were probably digging in already, and I had to find them if I wanted to survive. I started running.

"Malcolm? Jack? This is base, do you copy?" I could hear the tension in the communication's officer's voice.

"I read you, Courtney," I said, my voice jarred by running. "Why so little warning? I thought we were supposed to get it days ahead of time?"

"I don't know, but you and Jack had better get to shelter. There's no way we can get a truck or the dirigible to you fast enough."

"I'm trying," I said and signed off.

Then Jack's voice crackled into my helmet. "Malcolm! We're coming back for you. Follow our trail to meet us and run!"

I ran faster.

Their dust cloud was visible long before I could resolve shapes, but they kept coming and soon Nellie's squat hexagonal form appeared at the head of her rooster-tail dust plume. I didn't see Jack. Five minutes later, I staggered and gasped to a stop next to the robot as Jack climbed down from her back. The creep never mentioned we could ride her.

She trundled back and forth over a large flat spot, then, finding a suitable location, jolted to a stop. Her treaded drive units separated and rotated on their mountings, raising the shoulder-high robot into the air on its toes like a three-footed ballerina. Panels slid open between the tracks, revealing large spinning cutters that folded out and locked into place. Nellie sank rapidly into the ground as sand jetted skyward from tubes on her back.

The alarm sounded again, this time giving us less than twenty minutes. I glanced at Jack, but he stared at the robot's interface panel on his sleeve and said nothing.

Nellie disappeared below the lip of the hole and within a couple of minutes, the dirt stopped flying. Jack tapped out a few more commands and a cloud of dust poofed from the hole. He ran to look inside, then pulled an aluminum rod from his pack. With several twists and pulls, it became a telescoping ladder with rungs folding out from each side. He dropped it into the dark excavation and climbed down, motioning for me to follow.

I peered over the edge just as Jack opened Nellie's top hatch and disappeared inside. I was confused, because there wasn't room for us both, but followed him down and through. Once inside I understood. Nellie had split in two, with her upper half forming the airlock and her lower part a larder and mini-lab. The pieces were connected by a telescoping post in the center and mottled gray plastic surrounded us, sagging in pleats like a discarded skirt. Jack had designed her well.

As I dogged the hatch behind me, Jack flipped a switch, and Nellie started inflating the plastic envelope with oxygen she had collected through her rock melting electrolysis procedure. Air pushed the big plastic bag open until it tightened against the dirt and rock walls, creating a fifteen-foot-diameter by seven-foot-tall pressurized donut-shaped habitat.

"We'll leave our outer suits here," Jack said, indicating where we stood in the donut's hole. "Use nose plugs until we're through the second seal."

When the status light turned green, Jack released his helmet seal with an equalizing pop. I did the same and held my breath until my nose filters were in place, then started breathing in through my nose and out through my mouth, a routine everyone on Mars had mastered within the first few days.

"Can we get a comm link down here?" I asked,

while loosening the seals on my excursion suit. "How will we know when the radiation storm is over?"

Jack ignored me as he removed his suit's radiation skin, leaving only the biomaintenance layer, or what he called *million-dollar long johns*. The nano-plied material absorbed moisture, adjusted body temperature and used a powerful elastic netting to maintain the skin's surface tension at about a third of Earth normal. Only the helmet held pressurized air. They were extremely efficient, but they fit too snugly, and mine was already chafing in sensitive spots.

We slipped through two overlapping seals to enter the main chamber and I was surprised by the noise from Nellie's fans. She was pumping and filtering enough air to maintain half Earth normal pressure. Coupled with the heat she was generating to warm the burrow, it must be a huge drain on her batteries.

"So how long will Nellie's batteries let us stay down here?"

Jack didn't answer, but opened a flap, pulled a long clear tub from Nellie's guts and looked at the water sloshing inside.

"Looks like she collected about half a liter," I said. "Is that good or bad?"

He still didn't respond.

"We'll be stuck down here for hours, or maybe even days. How long are you going to keep up this childish silent treatment?"

He turned to glare at me. The dim light provided by Nellie's lamps gave him a menacing appearance.

"Shut the hell up, Malcolm."

I wasn't going to leave it alone. This trip would be

my last opportunity to see him face-to-face for years, or if his present state was any indicator, the rest of my life.

"You did this to yourself; why are you blaming me?" I yelled over the fan noise.

We'd been best friends since our sophomore year at Purdue and he'd never in fifteen years been so angry at me. I hadn't caused the board to order him home, but I had supported their decision. To Jack, it was the same thing.

He glared at me for a second and then moved around the donut where I couldn't see him. I followed. When he lowered himself to the floor against the outer wall, I sat down facing him, making sure he knew I wasn't giving up.

"I warned you this would happen," I said. "I tried to help you."

"Did you ever consider—for even a second—that I knew what I was doing?"

"Well, yes, but—"

"And I wanted to take this last walk alone," he said, barely audible above the fan noise. "I invited you to come on every walking trip I took, and you always turned me down. Why now?"

Because you *didn't* invite me this trip, I thought, but didn't say aloud. Jack could disable the locator on his excursion suit and with Nellie's help, easily hide until the Earth-Mars cycler window passed. That would give him an extra six months.

"Because this will be our last chance to do this together," I said. "You've been telling me for a year that I hadn't seen the real Mars. Now is your chance to show me."

He scrambled toward me on all fours, stopping inches from my face, close enough for me to smell his stale sweat. "Together? Go to hell, Malcolm. I wanted you to see what I'd found, because you *were* my friend. But your job and that stinking corporation are more important to you than anything else."

I shoved him out of my face. "Bull! I busted my tail to get you up here. I pulled strings and called in favors. Because you *are* my friend and I knew you would love it here, but you screwed it up. That *stinking corporation* flew you to Mars and is paying you a salary to find mineral deposits big enough to justify building a permanent colony. You need satellites and robot flyers for that. Not even a hot jock geologist like you can do it wandering aimlessly around the surface."

He shook his head. "You're a planetologist, for God's sake. One of the first in history to actually walk on another world and yet you've never even seen it."

"I spend every day studying this planet. I go out in the field—"

"Don't give me that crap," he said. "You fly to a spot, get out and walk around for a few hours, then come back to a nice cozy little office. You don't know this planet."

"Well, here I am. Show me."

He shook his head and again moved around to the opposite side.

I gave up and leaned back against the curved wall. My muscles ached from the unaccustomed workout, but the cool Martian soil behind the plastic felt good against my throbbing head.

I didn't remember falling asleep, but I woke stiff and cold to the sounds of Jack rummaging through

51

supplies in Nellie's larder. I sat up with a groan. He tossed me a nutrition bar and a water bag.

"It's morning and the radiation warning's over. We're leaving."

We emerged under a sky thick with brilliant stars. I almost made a nasty comment about it not being morning, but was stunned into silence. One couldn't see anything like this through Earth's atmosphere, even out in the mountains and at the base, work and safety lights diminished the brilliance. Man always had to leave the cities to see the stars. That hadn't changed.

Jack ignored me and watched Nellie struggle from her hole like some cybernetic land crab. My helmet prevented me from looking up for very long. I wished I could remove it and see that sky without the reflections and scratches of my faceplate, to feel the soft breezes and smell the air, but we never could. Someday humans might feel the Martian wind on their faces, but it wouldn't be me or Jack and it wouldn't be the same Mars.

Dawn came quickly in the thin atmosphere and while I watched, the stars faded and the black-and-gray landscape bloomed purple and orange. I'd seen two Martian sunrises outside the base, and both had been in passing while loading trucks for field excursions. Never had I taken the time to actually *experience* dawn on our new world. Not like this.

"Thanks, Jack," I said. "If you show me nothing else, that sunrise was worth the trip."

"It's always been here."

Once the anemic white sun peeked over the hills, we started east, this time slowly enough for me to keep up.

J. F. SMITH

A few hours later, after Nellie had once again topped off her oxygen tanks, we descended a long grade into a deep, narrow canyon. The wind picked up, showering us with blowing sand and the occasional dust devil. I marveled at the simple beauty of the untouched stone surrounding us. The canyon walls were painted by purple shadows, but where the sun struck the sides, bright bloody reds and sandy whites sprang into stark and sudden brilliance.

We rounded some rocks and Jack stopped. I stopped too. Ten or twelve black twisted shapes stood alone in the middle of the broad canyon floor. The largest stood over ten feet tall, with arms stretching toward us and others reaching to the sky. My pulse raced and I made myself move forward. They were black stone. Some were pitted, porous and a few polished to an almost mirror finish. I could see that some of their lengths had been recently uncovered, evidence of Jack's previous visits.

"Basalt? With the surrounding soft stone eroded away?"

"Maybe they're Martians," Jack said.

"They do look like tormented souls, frozen in their misery. The lava must've squeezed though some tight spaces, fast and under extreme pressure to form that way."

"Odd, isn't it?" he said.

His tone made me turn to look. He was staring down into a shallow depression between the figures, then turned toward me. His haunted expression made a chill crawl up my back. For the first time in my life, Jack frightened me.

"I found something, Malcolm. Something important."

I stared at him, surprised and waiting, but he didn't elaborate. "Well? What did you find?"

"I'm trying to decide if I want to show you or not," he said.

That stunned me. Did Jack's distrust cut that deep? But even if it did, how could anyone find *something important* on Mars and not share it with the rest of humanity?

"What the hell does that mean?" I said.

"Right now, I'm in control. When you realize what I've found, you'll try to take over. I don't want that. I want you to remember that you're my friend."

The implication frightened me. Could his find be so important that it would cause a schism between us larger than my agreeing to send him home? I said the only thing I could say. "Of course, I'm your friend. I can't forget that."

He shook his head and said, "I'm not so sure."

When he started walking, Nellie and I followed, but I was frustrated and worried.

Our Mars base had been continuously occupied for nearly three years, but we'd found nothing surprising. At least nothing eye-popping enough to goad MarsCorp into building a permanent colony. We'd proved we could live here, but it was expensive and the coolness aspect was wearing off back home. We needed a "Holy Crap" factor. If Jack had found that and was keeping it to himself, I'd beat him to a pulp.

He wouldn't hesitate to tell me if he'd found a huge underground aquifer or a large platinum deposit. So he'd found something momentous. Was it some kind of moss or lichen living under the sand? Or a fossil of some long-dead plant or animal? I itched to question him, to threaten or coerce him into telling me, but knew that wouldn't work with Jack. He'd tell me or he wouldn't, and nothing I said or did at this point would change that.

By midafternoon we came to a low ridge. We were almost on top of it before I realized it was the ejecta blanket from an ancient crater. I followed him up the gentle slope and looked down on a chaotic scene.

The crater floor was covered with boot prints, Nellie's tracks and piles of stone that formed a ring, easily a hundred yards across. I had a sinking feeling. Jack had obviously arranged the stones.

"Wow, Martian crop circles?"

He ignored me and followed the rim until he and Nellie turned into a narrow opening where the crater wall had collapsed. Their past traffic had packed the fall into a hard ramp that led down to the floor. As we descended, I saw a hole surrounded by darker, finely spread sand. I recognized the robot's handiwork. Jack had slept there at some point.

He went directly to the hole, mounted a collapsible ladder already inside and disappeared into the dark interior.

My excitement grew as I followed, nearly falling off the ladder twice in my haste to get to the bottom. About halfway down, the hole opened into the upside-down mushroom shape where Nellie's inflatable shelter had once expanded.

"Careful," Jack said. "There's a big hole in the floor."

I stepped off the ladder and in the dim light could

see the bottom littered with gravel and several large discarded bags made from rope and a cut-up plastic tarp. I turned on my helmet lamp and saw a large hole in the floor, nearly two yards in diameter just a few feet from the ladder. Wispy steam floated from inside. I looked up to ask Jack why, but he was gone. I spun around and saw a large opening in one wall. Light flickered inside.

"Jack?"

"In the tunnel. This will be easier to explain if you see it."

The tunnel was narrow and just tall enough to clear my helmet, but ran about ten feet, then teed left and right. I stopped. The wall before me curved and twinkled in my headlamp. When I moved the light, I saw parts of the surface were translucent. Blues, grays and whites flowed together, making odd shadows. I moved slowly along the tunnel, one side of which was the strange material, until it opened into a small chamber. Only then did I realize I was looking at a large cylinder that disappeared into the ceiling and floor. Jack waited on the far side.

"Jack. Please tell me you didn't make this."

"Nope."

"What's it made of? Have you analyzed it yet?"

"Water ice," he said.

My hammering heart slowed and I relaxed a little. Of course, it would be something natural. For a moment I'd envisioned beautiful stone pillars holding up the roof of an ancient Martian temple. But then I realized, even if it didn't match my wild imagination, he'd still made an amazing find. I touched it again.

"There's so much. How deep do you think it goes?"

"Nellie estimates another forty feet or so beyond this."

"Holy crap."

"They're all that deep. All thirty-six of them."

"I don't . . . thirty-six what?"

Jack dragged his hand along the ice and moved to face me. "Thirty-six ice pillars. I've only uncovered five, but those stones up top show the pattern Nellie found. These five are all perfectly smooth and exactly the same diameter. And I'd bet they are all the same depth too."

I stared at him. A lump formed in my throat and I felt a weight on my chest. I was a scientist. I couldn't let myself believe the conclusions my mind formed. I wanted something like this too bad. It had to be studied.

"It has to be some natural formation," I said with an overly dry mouth. "Nature does strange things, like those creepy basalt shapes."

He shrugged. "I'm not saying otherwise. But these things are also equally spaced, thirty-five forming a ring, with another one in the center."

I turned and rushed back out to the hole in the floor.

"Is this one of them too?" I asked, dreading his response.

"Yeah," Jack said and came up behind me. "Nellie sensed the water ice and stopped here to dig. I wouldn't have thought to even look back in the hole after we were done except she'd filled her nearly empty water tanks with this single dig and threw

58

extra ice out onto the surface to evaporate. That never happened before."

"And the hole is—"

"Because it's sublimating. The light hits it during the day. I tried covering it up, but that created a heated pocket and made it worse."

My hands shook. If his claim was true, Jack had stumbled across what might be the largest single find in human history . . . and he was letting it vaporize. "You're digging the others out?"

"I'm not exposing them to the light. They haven't lost anything from their diameters."

My respiration peaked so rapidly an alarm sounded in my helmet as the suit adjusted my gas levels.

"Jack! We . . . we . . . have no idea how old these things are or what the open air will do to them. We have no right. We're not qualified to make this kind of decision for the entire human race."

"Why not?" Jack said. "No one on Earth has ever encountered alien artifacts, so we're the new experts."

I had a panicky feeling about losing more of this material. I had to stop him. But I took a deep breath and tried to focus. Jack wasn't an idiot, so I needed to listen to what he was saying. I entered the tunnel and checked the ambient temperature inside. Minus sixty-three Celsius, which might be fine since it wasn't in direct sunlight.

"We don't know what's in that ice," I said. "Maybe there were sculptures, or carved instructions or some kind of microorganisms. Maybe even cold-suspended Martian DNA. We could be losing hundreds of painfully preserved Martian species."

"This one was an accident. And it's too late to save it."

"Maybe not. We could fill it back up with dirt, then call it in and get all of mankind's resources behind us."

"And lose them forever to MarsCorp?"

I paused, not sure what he meant. "No one will take this away from you, Jack. You'll still get all the credit."

He slapped a dusty glove against my helmet, making my ears ring. "Credit? You just don't get it, do you? I don't care about getting credit. This is a message. It's a puzzle and I want to figure it out. I feel like I'm so close."

The swat on my helmet made me furious, but I held back. I still wanted to convince him it was right before I reported this to the base. "You'll still be able—"

"No!" he said and bumped his visor against mine, putting his face as close to me as possible. "If we report this, MarsCorp will turn it into a Martian Disneyland. Most of those idiots on Earth care about nothing but making money, so this will become a cash cow vacation spot."

"Oh, come on. You don't think—"

"There's dignity in this place, Malcolm. It's a serious message, aimed directly at humanity, not some damned tourist attraction."

"A message? You don't know that. If these were put here by some other intelligence, it could have just been a water cache."

"It's a message designed for us. What better way to signal Earthlings coming to Mars? We'd be looking for water. Even if this is several million years old, and they didn't know what we would be like, they

60

would still know any species coming from Earth would need water."

I swallowed and tried to control my building frustration. "You may be right, but we have tools at the base to protect these artifacts while we study them. If there's a message, we'll find it. I'm going to call it in."

He stared at me, but there was no anger in his eyes, only cold determination.

"I have to, Jack."

He nodded inside his helmet and then grabbed both of my arms in an iron grip. "I knew I couldn't trust you with this, so I guess we'll do it the hard way," he said. "Into the hole."

"What?" I was confused.

He started pushing me backward toward the opening in the floor. "I don't want to damage your suit, but, if you don't jump down into that hole, I'll throw you in."

"Oh, come on! You can't—"

"Now, Malcolm!"

I turned my torso enough so I could look down into the hole. The ice floor was easily twenty feet down, much too deep to jump out, even with Martian gravity.

"Jack, don't be—"

He gave me a little shove and I staggered backward toward the hole. I had no choice but to jump or would have fallen in butt first. I landed on the slick surface with a bone-jarring thump, but kept my feet.

He stared down at me, still wearing that cold, blank expression. I considered the possibility that my best friend was about to kill me. It would be easy enough and hard to prove.

"Jack, what—"

"I doubt that you can contact base from down there, but I'll call in your location. Your MarsCorp lackeys will be here to rescue you in a couple of hours. And, boy, will they be surprised at your spectacular find."

Before I could answer, he disappeared from view.

He was wrong. Reception was bad down in the hole, but I did make contact with the base. My call generated equal amounts of excitement and incredulity. I wished I'd thought to record video, but hadn't planned on reporting from a hole within a hole. I could tell by their carefully phrased responses that they only half believed me, but would hold their skepticism in check until they could see it themselves.

They also gave me bad news. A large dust storm was rolling in and would prevent launching a dirigible. Courtney said they were sending the ground trucks immediately, but it would be four hours minimum, depending on the storm's severity.

The link faded into static. I looked up and could only see pale powder spiraling into the hole. Sandstorms on Mars carried millions of tons of the talc-fine dust that could easily bury me. I pulled the climbing axe from my belt and tried to hack hand- and footholds into the hard-packed wall.

Ten minutes and three handholds later, I paused to check my oxygen usage. Five hours and twenty minutes at my current rate. I had to slow my breathing.

I looked up and saw only dust swirling in my helmet lamp, then caught a metallic glint. Jack had not taken the ladder. I fumbled the line from my utility pouch and tied on two chisels about ten inches apart. On my fifth try, the makeshift bolo did not come back. I pulled and tugged. The ladder jerked suddenly and sailed into the hole, hitting my shoulder on the way down. I cursed, then held my breath waiting for my suit alarms to tell me I had a tear, but had been lucky.

Once on the surface, with wind driven sand pelting my suit, I had a decision to make. I could wait down in the hole, safe from the ravaging storm, and probably die as my air ran out. Or I could go find Jack. The wind was steady and mild at the moment, but even tired old Mars could drive abrasive grit at 200 mph on the open plains. My suit's tough outer skin was all one piece and could stand that abuse for a long time, but my helmet seal was at risk.

I pulled the aluminum ladder from the hole and attached an antenna wire. Much to my surprise, I established an immediate satellite link through the static-charged dust. I called Jack and got no response. I tried to get his suit's transponder location and failed. So I called base.

"The trucks had to stop and wait for better visibility," Courtney said through static. "You need to hunker down and conserve your air until they arrive."

My tank level read less than five hours remaining. If the trucks started moving now and had no more delays, they *might* make it to me in time. My decision was now easy. I had to find Nellie.

"Can you contact Jack for me?"

"He called in to give us your location about ten minutes after your first call. He wanted to make sure we could find you. But we haven't been able to contact him since. And his transponder stopped transmitting right after that."

The bastard dumped me in a hole so he could run off and hide? It made no sense. Even if I died, my suit transponder would eventually lead rescuers to me and the pillars. His secret was out. Why let me die?

"Can you give me a line between my position and his last call so I'll have a direction?"

"Sure," she said. The static was worsening.

If Jack didn't want to be found, he would have changed course immediately after his call, but it was a starting place. If I could get close enough, maybe he would hear my call. Staying here and waiting wasn't a real option.

"I just sent the coordinates from Jack's last call and his last five transponder pings. I had no idea he'd covered so much ground on his walkabouts."

"How do you know that?" I asked.

"I'm looking at a map of his ping locations for all of his excursions. I have one for everyone who—"

"Can you send me that map?" If I could see where Jack had been, I might get an idea where he could hide.

Courtney paused. "Sure. It might take several tries with this bad connection, but it's on the way."

"Thanks," I said and started to sign off.

"Malcolm? Why did Jack leave you there?"

"I pissed him off."

"He's lost it," she said, with obvious anger in her voice. "Well, if he wasn't already going home, he would be now. Stay put. The ground trucks are moving again, but slowly. We're also rigging a flier to bring you some O_2 canisters."

The robotic fliers were more like powered gliders

with long fragile wings. They wouldn't get one even close to me in this wind.

"Don't waste the flier, Courtney. I'm going to try and find Jack. Malcolm out."

I broke the connection and pulled up the ping map on my helmet's HUD screen. Thousands of random dots covered a topographical map with location numbers on a grid. The widely scattered dots made my eyes hurt, but I could see some patterns. Many dots were arranged in snaky lines, obviously sent while he was on the move, but there were also heavy clumps representing locations where he'd spent time.

I zoomed the view out and as the dots converged, I saw it. Most were in clumps that formed a pattern. I added in a red dot for my location and it appeared atop one of the heavy traffic clusters.

The wind buffeted me, some gusts threatening to knock me down, and dust had drifted around my feet, but I ignored it as my pulse raced and my heart thudded. I instructed my suit's computer to ignore the noise data and only chart those points where twenty or more appeared in close proximity. Seventeen clumps appeared, evenly dispersed along a broad arc. I told the computer to consider each cluster a single point and extrapolate the pattern based on the existing group.

The new pattern formed a ring nearly forty miles across and contained thirty-five points. The ring of pillars Jack had marked in the crater contained thirty-five with one in the middle. The center of the large ring fell in the canyon where we'd seen the basalt formations earlier that morning.

Even though his actions might kill me, I had to appreciate Jack's devious mind this time. He'd shown me these ice pillars as bait, to get me excited and keep me and the base off his back while he explored the real find. And this was his last trip before being sent home, so it had to be now. I fixed the canyon location on my map, pulled the patching tape from my repair kit and wrapped my helmet seal for extra protection, then started walking.

I carried the ladder with me, using it both as antenna and a pole to feel out terrain made invisible by the thick whirling dust. I also kept broadcasting directly to Jack. "I know you're in the center with your Martian friends and I'm on my way to meet you. I need oxygen." As an added incentive, I also said, "This is encrypted, but my transponder is still broadcasting."

An hour into my trek, Courtney called to tell me their specially rigged flier had crashed. With a voice strained by grief, she rattled off the standard oxygen conservation litany and again begged me to stay put. I told her I could find Jack, then signed off and kept walking.

When the one-hour oxygen warning dinged, I checked my position and realized I couldn't make it to the basalt formations, even if I'd guessed Jack's location correctly. The wide plain between canyon and crater would have been safe enough to allow running, with only a slight chance of falling, but my slow, cautious advance through the storm had killed me. I tossed the ladder aside and started running.

Less than a minute later, my radio crackled to life with Jack's voice. "Turn on your emergency strobe and stop moving, Malcolm. According to your transponder blip on my map, I should be right on you."

I stopped and fumbled for the strobe switch on my helmet, but before I could flip it, Nellie materialized out of the dust and nearly ran over me as she shot past. I turned as she skidded to a halt amid scattered sand and gravel.

Tears formed, blurring my vision, and warm relief flowed through me like very old Scotch. Jack jumped down from Nellie's back and started detaching oxygen canisters from her side.

"This whole *Jack arriving like the cavalry to save Malcolm* thing is getting kinda old," he said as he turned me around, opened my pack and switched out my tanks.

I swallowed, trying to clear the lump in my throat. "Thanks," I said. "Did you hear my calls to you?"

"Yeah, but I started back as soon as I realized your MarsCorp friends were going to let you die."

"So I was right? The basalt formations are at the center of a larger pattern?"

"Yeah," he said with a grim expression. "How'd you know?"

After I explained, he shook his head and sighed. "I knew I should've disconnected that damned transponder a long time ago. Not that it matters now. I had my chance and I blew it."

Jack had come back for me, risking his opportunity to be the first person to see the big find. He wanted a chance to solve the puzzle, to discern the message he perceived in those formations. Helping him still do that was the least I could do in thanks.

"What's down there?" I said. "In the canyon?"

"I don't know yet, but Nellie says it's nearly thirty

feet square and the part I've uncovered so far is flat, smooth basalt. Those weird shapes you saw are attached to it like sprues to an injection molded part."

"Like it was molded or formed in place?"

He nodded.

Huge and square, I thought and tried to dampen my new excitement. "Amazing. So you haven't exposed anything that will melt?"

He laughed, for the first time since learning he was going home. "No, basalt doesn't melt *easily*. But there's something else."

I waited and could see him smiling through the visor. "Well?"

"There's a pattern in the face I uncovered. Thirty-five cylindrical pockets arranged in a ring, with one in the center. According to Nellie's analysis, the translucent material at the bottom of each hole is diamond."

"What could that mean?"

"I have no idea. I had to stop and come rescue you."

It was my turn to smile. I held up a finger and called base.

"Sorry for the scare, Courtney," I said. "But I found Jack. Nellie is working fine, so we have plenty of air and are not in any danger now."

"Thank God, Malcolm. Meteorology says this storm could last another two or three days. Are you sure you have enough supplies for that long?"

Jack cut in on the conversation, reassuring her we were going to be fine.

"You're in a heap of trouble, Jack! And I still don't have a transponder signal for you."

He opened his mouth, but I cut him off. "Actually,

Courtney, I may be losing my transponder signal too. We're about to go into an area that seems to play hell with most of our communications gear. So don't worry if you don't hear from us for a few days."

"I don't think—"

"We'll meet up with the investigation team at the dig site in two or three days, or whenever this storm lets up."

"But—"

"Malcolm and Jack signing off," I said and killed the connection.

Jack looked at me and raised an eyebrow. "If you could find that pattern, they can too. Besides, they have enough information to know what direction you were going."

"Yeah, but we could head north for a few hours and cut off my transponder, then enter the canyon from the north end. That should mess them up for awhile. It may only give us a few days. Probably only until the storm ends. Will that be enough time?"

He shrugged, always a strange gesture in an excursion suit. "Maybe, but if you do this, there is a good chance you'll be sent home too."

"I wouldn't miss this for anything," I said and started running.

We dug in for the night near the canyon's north end and awoke to a sickly yellowish-pink dawn. The weak sun struggled to break through the haze, but the storm had abated and the winds died, so the timer was running. If our luck ran out, our fellow explorers could find us within a matter of hours.

Ninety minutes after breaking camp, we stood

atop the basalt block. Using Nellie's vacuum system, we removed the dust accumulated from the storm revealing a smooth polished surface, with the now-familiar pattern of holes in the center of the top surface.

"How odd that they'd make this finely polished cube, yet have these weird, gnarly sprues marring its perfection," I said.

"It does look to be part of the formation process," Jack said. "Maybe they just didn't care about the sprues."

"Yeah, but why these holes? Why their fascination with this particular pattern?"

He knelt down and aimed his helmet light into the holes. They were the diameter of a golf ball and about a foot deep, and, as he'd earlier reported, their bottoms were glassy and clear. "I don't know, but I'd sure as hell like to find out."

"Looks like we need some kind of key," I said. "And if we had a key, I wonder what it would do?"

Jack stared at the holes, occasionally poking his gloved finger in one. "Maybe we could make a key."

"You know," I said, pausing, not sure if I should voice my latest thought. "The other holes are filled with water ice. Maybe . . ."

Jack almost leapt to his feet. "It couldn't hurt to try!"

Of course, that comment left me feeling more than a little uneasy, but there was no stopping him once he got started. Forty minutes later I dubiously examined Jack's kludge work. He'd originally wanted to build a manifold of tubes to feed water into each hole evenly, but I had stopped him when I realized he'd have to cannibalize most of Nellie's internal plumbing to realize the contraption.

We instead covered the pattern with a shallow tent made from extra sheet plastic, precariously sealed to the surrounding surface with our entire stock of suit repair putty. A hole in the center was cinched up tight around a tube attached to Nellie's tanks. Jack assured me that if we pumped water in fast enough, it would fill the holes and freeze before evaporating. I wasn't convinced, but we had nothing to lose, except of course most of our water.

"What if we do open the lock? Or activate something? What if we break it?"

Jack looked up at me, his exasperation obvious even through the dusty visor. "Make up your mind, Malcolm. We're never going to get another shot at this. It's us—right now—or we forget about it. They are going to be pissed enough to ship us back home and instead of us figuring this out, some Martian Mickey Mouse will build an enchanted castle around it."

He was right. I had made my decision and sealed my allegiance. "Let's try it."

We stood on a pile of excavated dirt at the cube's edge and pumped the water in under pressure. Wispy vapor curls immediately revealed the gaps in our crude seal. The tent filled and tightened rapidly, to the point we feared it would burst the seal.

"Stop!" I yelled.

Jack killed the flow and the plastic almost immediately started to deflate.

"Crap," he said. "We'd better look quick."

Before we could pull the cover off and check our

handiwork, a series of reports—loud enough in the weak Martian air to hear through our helmets—made us both step backward. Fissures appeared in the basalt, radiating outward from under the plastic cover in an oddly uniform pattern.

"You were right," Jack muttered. "We broke it."

"Maybe not. The lines are all straight and equally spaced, like pie wedges. They don't look like natural fractures."

Before I could say another word, he jumped down onto the surface, tested it with a couple of bounces, then dropped to his knees, shining his helmet light into the cracks. He motioned for me to come down.

"The basalt is only about a foot thick," he said. "And it looks like more diamond under it. Holy crap. Do you think this stuff just covers a big block of diamond?"

"Well, it would sure be durable," I said and joined him. I removed the cover to look at the pattern. It had nearly disappeared, but I could tell by the fragment arrangement that the cracks had each started at a hole, then run across the top and disappeared down the sides into the dirt.

"Looks like our ice expanded and started the breaks," I said.

"No way. One or two cracks maybe, to relieve pressure, but not—" He paused and ran a hand along the edge of several sections, then started pulling on them.

"Unless of course," he grunted, "it was designed to break this way."

The wedge moved nearly an inch. He stood up and looked at me. "I bet if the whole block had been uncovered, this shell would have fallen away. I think it was *meant* to fall away."

We used Nellie to dig all morning, but by mid-afternoon had to send her out in search of ice to replenish our air and water supply. So we dug by hand, using our climbing axes. Once we'd totally cleared the second side, Jack slipped his axe blade behind one of the loose basalt sections and started gently rocking it. With an audible pop, the strip collapsed into large chunks that tumbled down on him like stacked blocks pushed over by a petulant child. I heard him grunt and curse over the comm link as he disappeared in a pile of stone and dust.

"Jack!" I ran to him and started moving yard-wide pieces of stone I wouldn't have been able to lift on Earth.

"Crap," he muttered as I pulled the last piece off.

"Are you leaking? Are you hurt?"

"No leaks," he said, but I could hear pain in his voice. "And I'm fine, just help me get up."

I moved one more slab and couldn't miss its obvious uniformity. Jack had been right again. The basalt covering had been designed to come apart easily. The shell's inside face had been serrated in a grid pattern, the squares held together by a thin strip of surface stone that was easily broken once the interconnecting tensions and supporting soil had been removed.

I turned my attention to what lay beneath the shell. It appeared to be a solid block of diamond. I switched on my helmet light and looked inside. Prickles and chills crawled up my back, as I unwittingly uttered the phrase from the old science fiction classic. "My God, it's full of stars."

Jack grunted as he brushed off dust and checked his suit and harness equipment for damage. "Stop screwing around. What do you see?"

I opened my mouth, but words wouldn't come. The interior of the block was filled with what looked like constellations of sparkling stars. It was as if someone had cut a block of the stunning Martian midnight and buried it for us to find.

"Malcolm?" Jack moved up next to me, leaning in to see.

The star-like points in the block only glowed when my light touched them. My scientific mind argued that they could be impurities or microfractures in the diamond block, but part of me knew I was looking at a three-dimensional celestial map.

"A map," Jack whispered.

My comm link hissed and popped, then Courtney's voice intruded on our discovery. "Come in, Malcolm, this is Mars Base One."

I almost succumbed to training and long ingrained habit to answer her, but remained silent. I glanced at Jack, but he was totally focused on the block's interior.

"Come in, Malcolm. We've had fliers all over the area since the storm ended. There are no communication anomalies. We don't know what you two are doing out there, but the commander is pissed." She paused for a second, then resumed. "He says Jack is going home no matter what, but considering the amazing find you reported he might consider letting you stay. If you call in now."

The urge to respond with a long string of obscenity was nearly overwhelming. They were prepared to let me die in the storm, yet were now threatening to punish me? I bit my lip, made sure my frequency setting was set for local and Jack's channel and told him.

"We'd better hurry. Base just called. I don't think they know where we are yet, but they are sure looking."

We started digging faster. When Nellie returned, I focused my efforts on getting video of the map from every exposed angle. By sundown the three of us had cleared two more sides, leaving only the bottom and one side still covered, but the light failed quickly in the canyon.

Base had tried to call me and Jack several more times during the day and at one point we saw a flier high in the east, over the area we'd been heading before killing my transponder.

"We'd better dig in for the night," Jack said.

"If we're going to uncover this, we'd better work through the night," I said. "Now that the wind has died, they'll eventually see Nellie's fresh tracks and follow them back here."

"Yeah, but if we're lucky they won't find the tracks until tomorrow, then it will take hours for them to get here by truck or blimp. But if they keep those fliers looking all night, they would see our work lights or even our IR signatures and be here before morning. I think we should get underground."

I hated to leave the find for that long, but reluctantly agreed. Once out of our suits and settled in our burrow for the night, I linked my suit's computer to Nellie so that we could both see the video on her foldout display screen. I instructed the computer to build a 3D map based on the footage and overlay the actual video with graphics. We both immediately noticed that among the thousands of points some were three to four times larger than the rest, looking more like embedded pearls than distant stars. Those pearl points were located in pairs, some almost touching and others separated by up to an inch. Each pearl was also connected to another, more distant, pearl by a hair-thin line.

"Weird," Jack said in an almost whisper. "Those bolos or barbells are some kind of pattern, but . . ."

"Computer, overlay any existing star charts in the database with these patterns."

"I have only rudimentary navigational aid star charts in my local database," the computer said in its charming southern belle voice, causing Jack to look at me with a smile and raised eyebrows. "Do you want me to search the base archives or send a download request to Earth?"

"Does Nellie have star charts?" I asked the still grinning Jack.

"Malcolm? You must really . . ."

"Just answer the question."

He shook his head. "No real need. Go ahead and tap base camp, it's only a matter of hours until they find us anyway."

"Check the base first, then send to Earth if they don't have an all-inclusive chart."

"I'm loading the 3D star chart from base camp data stores," the computer said. "Please provide a relative scale for the newly constructed pattern."

Jack and I looked at the slowly rotating pattern on the screen, then back at each other with shrugs.

"We have no scale. You'll have to look for relational patterns, then adjust scales accordingly."

"Understood," the computer said.

"Inform us if you have any pattern match greater than seventy percent."

"Understood."

Radio calls from base camp increased after the computer's download connection, but we ignored them. Jack started fixing a simple dinner, but I couldn't stop looking at the pattern. I could see two exceptions to the pearls appearing in pairs. A single pearl resided in one corner of the block, but was connected to the nearest pair by a line nearly two feet long. The second exception was a line that ran to a large cluster in the diagonally opposite corner, but due to my shaky camera work, the computer just showed them as a slightly disc-shaped clump.

We took turns counting while we ate and agreed upon seventeen pearls excluding the clump.

The display changed abruptly, showing the original pattern in blue, overlaid with a new blinking red pattern. The legend at the bottom of the screen identified the red as "KNOWN STARS." A little over half the points overlaid perfectly, but a few were shifted, all in the same direction, but by different amounts. About twenty percent of the stars in the blue pattern had no red counterpart and none of the red points aligned with the pearls.

"Well, crap," muttered Jack. "That wasn't much help."

"Computer? If you take known movement into

account and project backwards, would some of those stars from our database have matched the new pattern at some time in the past?"

At first the computer didn't understand the request, but after I explained it in simpler terms a counter appeared at the bottom of the screen and the red stars started creeping toward the blue points. When they stopped moving the number on the counter read "4372 BCE." Aside from six that blinked a label of "track unknown" all of the shifted red stars now matched. There were still no points at the pearl locations.

"Damn! Over six thousand years ago," I said.

"They're still not as old as I expected," Jack said.

"Computer? Have you displayed all the stellar information you have? Please show quasars, pulsars, brown dwarfs, comets, asteroids and galaxies, any objects that would show up within this pattern."

"And black holes," Jack included.

The red star pattern density nearly doubled. Now six dots matched locations with the pearls.

"Computer. Show black holes or singularities as green."

Dozens of points flashed green, including all six that were coincident with the pearls.

"So," Jack said and sat back with a wide grin. "They travel using black holes."

"Or maybe just use them to communicate? Computer? Label the Sol system if it is on this map."

SOL appeared next to the star nearest the lone corner pearl.

"Oh, wow!" Jack said and crawled up next to the screen. He pointed at the pearl nearest Earth. "We enter a black hole here . . ." He moved his finger along the line to the next pearl. "And exit here, then move in normal space to this black hole . . ."

"These are too conveniently placed," I said. "I bet they're artificially constructed worm holes."

He nodded and continued tracing the path, big jumps between black holes with the lines, and small trips to the next black hole, then another jump. The path led all the way to the big clump at the opposite corner.

"Grand Central Station," he said tapping the clump.

"Well, there isn't anything really new about that idea," I said.

"Except this time it's real!"

Once again my scientific mind refused to see the obvious as a real possibility, but I shoved those thoughts aside and laughed. "Yeah, there is that. Maybe."

We stared at the display for a few minutes, neither of us talking. Then I tapped the cluster on the screen, stood up and started donning my suit. "I need to see this clump again."

"Dawn is still five hours away," Jack said.

"Does it matter? We have to assume they know where we are now."

Twenty minutes later we stood atop the diamond cube and beneath a brilliant Martian night. Somewhere out in that thick star mass lived other sentient beings. It was now fact, not speculation. We looked down, switched on our helmet lights and dropped to hands and knees.

The pearl clump was near a top corner and when

our lights revealed it, we both gasped, then laughed. When viewed from the correct angle, the thirty-five pearls formed a ring around a central point or star. The last line in the "path" connected to a pearl in that ring.

Daylight still hadn't penetrated the canyon when we took one last look at the cube.

Jack fidgeted, looking from me to his wrist computer, then back at me. "This still makes me nervous, Malcolm. What if there's another storm or radiation alert?"

"It's a risk, but I can override communication security with voice recognition and you can't. And if we all go, they will find us for sure. Nellie's tracks are just too easy to see from the air."

He still looked uneasy. In order to insure that MarsCorp didn't hide the find for years while they tried to think up a way to exploit it, we'd decided to break the news to Earth ourselves. Jack would go east, then call base telling them he was looking for me. That would hopefully make them focus their search east of the canyon while I went west to the uplink antenna on the crater wall a mile from the base camp.

"You're just pissed that you have to provide the diversion this time."

He didn't laugh or even smile. "If you run most of the day, you should be back at the base camp just after sunset. You have the extra tank and water?"

"Yes, Mom."

He gripped my arms and squeezed. "Call if you get in trouble. And I'll come and rescue your sorry tail again."

"Get moving!" I said.

He started south, to exit the canyon from that end, and his graceful, gazelle-like stride took him out of sight in seconds. My gait was awkward as I started for the canyon's north end, but it soon smoothed out. Jack was still definitely the best Martian, but I was getting better.

The Paradise Aperture

written by

David Carani

illustrated by

PAUL PEDERSON

ABOUT THE AUTHOR

David Carani was born and raised in Illinois, where he became familiar with both cities and cornfields. Despite his love of corn and tall buildings, he found he prefers neither. Instead, he lives in a place that is a wondrous combination of the two, called a suburb.

The oldest of eight, David grew up wandering the acres of forest behind his home. A heavy rainfall or snowstorm could transform those woods into another world, and he often spent his days exploring and creating stories.

After earning a degree in economics from the University of Illinois (hence the cornfields), he returned home and married the girl of his dreams. Like any good editor, when she isn't diligently working to improve his stories, his wife gives him all the encouragement he could ever need.

Beyond writing, David works in sales, reads submissions for the Hugo-nominated Lightspeed Magazine *and writes articles for the website Fantasy Faction. This is his first published work.*

ABOUT THE ILLUSTRATOR

Paul Pederson was born August 11, 1980, in Bessemer, Alabama. He was raised in St. Augustine, Florida (the oldest city in the nation). Art and history were prominent features in the small tourist town and this had a tremendous influence on him. At an early age, he loved to draw and paint. Paul and his older brothers were always fascinated with works of fantasy and science fiction. Subsequently he leaned more toward fantasy illustrations. Paul's parents established a private school known as Taldeve (Talent Development) School of the Arts that Paul attended through middle school and high school. This gave him the rare opportunity to study one-on-one under professional artists in the north Florida area. After high school, Paul moved to Australia for two years, spending much of his time learning the Aboriginal culture and doing freelance art. He later studied art and design at Dixie State College in Utah, and has worked for over ten years as a graphic designer, painting murals and illustrations. He currently resides in St. George, Utah, where he works as an illustrator and hopes to take full advantage of his talents.

The Paradise Aperture

I eyed the door with distrust. The shocking blue was brighter than I usually photographed, but maybe that was where I'd been going wrong. Marie had always loved vibrant colors. If she was behind any door, it would be one like this.

Two years ago, I'd barely left the Midwest, let alone the country. Yet here I was, halfway across the world, standing in the long-dead garden of an abandoned house in Tunisia.

The town of Sidi Bou Said spread along the sparkling Mediterranean below, stark white buildings accented in bold strokes of blue. Once I would have been entranced by the breathtaking vista. Now it just looked tired and dusty.

I turned back to the door. Set in white stone and arched at the top, it had been intricately inked in swirling black dots reminiscent of henna. I rested my hand on the rough wood and closed my eyes. It didn't feel any different than a normal door, but then, they never did.

I shook my head, halting my admiration. I couldn't be sidetracked. The mystical blue doors had drawn me here, but ultimately they were just a means to an end.

85

"We waitin' for something, Jonny?"

The voice belonged to my daughter, Irene. One hand on her hip, she watched me with a tapping foot, occasionally blowing swooped bangs from her eyes. She had Marie's hair, a fire-engine red that looked fake but wasn't. Unlike her mother, Irene kept it short—like her temper.

"The sun needs to be at the right angle," I said patiently, wishing again she wouldn't call me Jonny. Usually I ignored her when she called me by my first name, but if I did that all the time, we'd never talk. The girl sure could be persistent.

"How the hell do you know that?"

I laughed. If she only knew the dozens of letters I got every day asking that same question. I guess you might say it was a gift, but too often, it felt like a curse.

"For one thing, I watch my language," I said.

"Seriously."

"Gut feeling," I said, shrugging. "I just know."

Irene wrinkled her nose and folded her arms across her chest, but said nothing. She played tough, but I knew the tribal tattoo down her left arm was a five-year temp and that she hated the onyx stud in her nose more than she hated her ex-boyfriend.

A cool breeze rose off the bay, stealing a moment of heat and bringing sounds of the festival from the streets down the way. Ankle-deep in twisted weeds, I wiped sweat from my forehead and forced a clearing for the tripod.

"Hand me the Deltex," I said.

Irene stared at me blankly.

"The gray camera case."

With the gracelessness of inattentive youth, she fumbled with the case slung behind her back, unzipping it with one hand and peeling out the camera. I fought the urge to cringe, even when she tossed the camera instead of walking the two steps to hand it to me. Five thousand dollars of hardware whirled through the air, but it wasn't the first time this had happened. I caught it easily.

"What have we said about throwing things?"

"Easy, Pops. You caught it fine. What's the big deal?"

Honestly, with money no longer an issue and three backups over her shoulder, it wasn't a big deal. Not in the mood for a fight, I almost let it go. Almost.

"The big deal," I said, very calmly, "is you need to learn respect for people's things."

"Not like you can't just—"

"It doesn't matter how many cameras I can afford," I said, anticipating her biggest argument. "It's a matter of principle."

"Principles suck."

I grinned. "That's a matter of opinion."

She stuck out her tongue, but didn't argue back. She knew I was right and, with Irene, that was as good as a victory.

I squinted up at the sun, a searing white orb in the empty sky. It still didn't feel right, but I set up the camera anyway, careful to frame the door with enough stone. Any cropping would destroy the image, so the proportions had to be perfect. If they weren't, the door would never open and I'd be left with a very expensive, very useless life-size photo.

I couldn't take that chance. Once I captured a door, it couldn't be recaptured no matter how identical the image. I'd found that out the hard way with a few photos, but I tried not to think about them. Surely, Marie wouldn't have been behind those doors. They'd been so unexciting.

"Why are we all the way up here?" Irene asked. "We're missing the festival."

"We're not here for the festival," I said, adjusting the shutter speed for a longer exposure. "And I can't risk some clumsy tourist ruining the picture."

"What's so special about these doors?"

I looked up from the viewfinder. "You got a lot of questions today," I said. "Something on your mind?"

Irene's head dropped and her shoulders sagged. Suddenly she was far younger and more vulnerable than eighteen already was.

"You really think Mom's still out there?" she asked.

"I can't believe anything else," I said. God knows I'm not the same man without her.

"Nana thinks you're cracked. She didn't want me to come."

I grunted. My mother-in-law hadn't spoken with me since we'd lost Marie. I couldn't really blame her. If it wasn't for my photos, Marie might still be here.

"What do you think?" I asked.

She bit her lip, hesitating. "I think . . . I think we'll find her."

I nodded. "Then don't ever let that go—no matter what anyone says. We'll get her back, Reenie. I promise."

Irene seemed to relax. She even smiled, which was not something I was blessed with often.

"I saw a yellow door on our way up here," she said.

A yellow door in a town of blue and white?

"Sounds like we've got one more stop after this," I said. "Nice catch."

The sun finally where I wanted it, I looked through the viewfinder, exhaled slowly and took the shot.

Several weeks and a hundred photos later, we stood in Heathrow Airport, the ebb and flow of thousands of strangers bubbling around us. Crowds had never bothered me before, but it was different now that so many of them seemed to recognize me.

Irene leaned against a pillar, eyes closed, bobbing to the music from her oversized headphones. I still don't know why I agreed to bring her along. At times, it seemed like she didn't even *want* to be along. But I knew how helpless she must feel. She wanted her mother back as much as I wanted my wife.

A bald man in a business suit and overcoat wandered over, glancing at me over his newspaper. I nervously checked my watch. The only thing I hated more than flying was waiting to fly.

The bald man made up his mind and moved toward me. I sighed internally. Here we go.

"You're that guy, aren't you?"

I pretended not to hear, positioning myself between the man and Irene. Sometimes these guys turned out to be real headcases.

He edged closer and tapped my shoulder, ignoring all concepts of personal space.

"Yeah, I've seen you on the news," he said, jabbing his finger at me. "You're that photographer."

"You must have me confused—"

"What do you call those pictures you take?" he asked. "Reclusive doors?"

I gritted my teeth. He obviously wasn't going to leave me alone. Did they ever?

"Recursion doors," I corrected, checking my watch again. Boarding time was two minutes late.

"Yeah, that's it. World within a world or something, right?"

"Now boarding first class," the flight attendant announced.

Finally.

"Something like that," I said, nudging Irene and eagerly pushing forward to hand over our tickets. A few people glared at me, but I ignored them.

The man persisted, grabbing my sleeve. I turned to say something, but stopped. The man's breathing was heavy, his eyes bulging. I'd seen that look of fanaticism before.

"Is it true what they say?" the man asked in a fierce whisper. "Did you really discover paradise?"

The color drained from my face. Had the idea already come so far? It was like a virus I never meant to spread. I pulled my arm away and retreated down the ramp without answering.

How could I?

I slept for two days after returning home. The endless rounds of travel were definitely taking their toll, but it didn't matter—pure exhaustion was the only way I slept these days. On the third day, Irene unceremoniously woke me.

"Jonny!"

She stood by my bed, snapping her fingers and

pointing at the phone in her hand. I stared at her in the confusion of the half-awake.

"It's Nana."

I let my head fall back to the pillow. Why now?

Irene put the phone in my hand and I lifted it to my ear.

"Hello, Margaret."

"It's time to put an end to this nonsense, Jonathan," my mother-in-law said.

"Good morning to you too."

"I've humored you long enough. It was one thing when your actions affected only you. Now you're bringing your teenage daughter along?"

"It's her decision."

She gave an exasperated sigh. "We've all accepted it. Why can't you?"

"Because I haven't given up hope," I said, sitting up. "I just have to find the right door."

"Damn it, Jonathan. The fire was two years ago," she said. "You have to let it go. The door is gone."

I was silent.

"Your daughter needs you," she said. "And she needs the chance to move on."

"You want me to tell Irene her mother is dead?"

"I want you to be her father."

"What happened to you?"

Her voice softened. "I'm tired, Jonathan. For the longest time I wanted to believe you were right. But I can't anymore—it's just too hard. I'm too old for false hope."

"I'm sorry to hear that," I said. "We'll talk again soon. Goodbye, Margaret."

I hung up without waiting for an answer. My hands

were trembling. I balled them into tight fists and pressed them against my forehead. Everyone thought I was crazy. What was so crazy about wanting to believe your wife was still alive?

The day I lost Marie, I'd come home to our little apartment over the antique shop and found it ablaze. A caravan of firetrucks, police cars and ambulances had blockaded the collapsing building, a crowd of onlookers gawking into the flames with mixed looks of wonder and horror.

I'd screamed and twisted and torn at the firefighters like a madman, but they'd held me back, told me the building was empty. They hadn't understood that the building could appear empty, when it was not. They couldn't have known that while they'd held me down, my wife had been inside.

Maybe I was crazy, but I knew one thing: Marie was alive. The door to our world was gone, but I would find another way in. I had to.

Around noon, I dragged myself from bed and returned to the office. An unmarked stone building along the Chicago North Shore, it had a second-floor showroom, a first floor jammed with massive industrial printers and a basement full of discarded attempts to find my wife.

Someone had stuck a sign to the front door, imploring me to repent of my evil ways. Needless to say, not everyone thought highly of my gift. I pulled the sign down, wondering again what good it did to have an unmarked building when everyone already knew where you were.

PAUL PEDERSON

I fumbled with my keys a moment before realizing there was no longer a keyhole in the door. I frowned at the keypad on the wall. Kensuke, my curator, had recently convinced me to upgrade the security system. It made sense, considering the inventory in my basement was valued in the billions; I just hadn't ever used it. When had he found time to get it installed?

I scratched the back of my head and stared into the surveillance camera, struggling to recall the eight-digit passcode. It was probably so obvious I'd never remember it. I threw up my hands in exasperation, suddenly regretting I'd asked Kensuke to leave off the buzzer.

"Might I have a word, Mr. Ward?"

I sighed and turned around. The man had the distinct look of a weasel in a suit, which was disappointingly unoriginal. His peppered hair was receding, the little he had left slicked back in greasy curls.

Couldn't these people stick to the phone, instead of ambushing me at my front door? At least the phone I could ignore.

"What is it this time?"

"I represent Renkoda Pharmaceuticals," the representative said. He straightened his tie and flashed a smirk that turned my stomach. "We are the world's largest—"

"I know who you are," I said, waving a hand. Everyone knew Renkoda. They had their claws in a lot more than pharmaceuticals. "What do you want?"

"I have been authorized to extend you an exclusive offer to work for our company."

"Exclusive offer to work or offer to work exclusively?"

The man pursed his lips, pressing them together in a flat line. "The latter," he said.

"Let me make this easy for you," I said. "Not interested."

The representative seemed taken aback. Obviously, he wasn't used to being turned down.

"You haven't even . . . what about the offer?" he said. "You haven't heard the offer."

Maybe I was being reckless. Why shouldn't I work for a powerful company like Renkoda? I'd already sold myself out to the world's so-called elite. How would this be any different?

And yet . . . it was different. I might sell *to* the elite, but never *for* them. I did this for Marie and no one else. It was a thin line, but one that kept me sane.

"You're right," I said. "I forgot to wait for that part. How about this? You write the number on a piece of paper and I'll take a look."

While the representative fumbled in his briefcase for a pen, I turned back to the keypad with a flash of insight and punched in the eight digits. The door unlocked with a click and I briskly stepped through, swiping it closed behind me. I left courtesy behind a long time ago.

A hand scanner awaited me in the foyer, one security measure even I couldn't screw up. I took the stairs to the showroom floor, expecting to find Kensuke preparing for an auction. The room was empty, but a selection of framed recursion doors had been brought up from the basement and propped in the corner.

Shaped like a square donut, the room was surrounded on three walls with tall multi-paned windows. The cube in the center of the room was for display, four doors to a wall.

A single recursion door hung on the wall in front of me. It was a relatively unassuming door, weatherworn wood bordered in faded brick and overgrown ivy. Kensuke had matched it with a simple, antique-finish frame.

I pressed my hand against the picture, feeling not the smooth photo paper, but the ancient wood of the garden door beyond. I lowered my hand to the cold iron handle and pushed. The door creaked painfully as it swung open, revealing the pocket world beyond. No matter how many times I opened the doors, it always caught me a little off guard.

A mighty river curved away from the entrance, emerald- and slate-colored mountains jutting from the waters like watchful giants. An ancient monastery had been built into the cliffs, whitewashed walls and tiered roof of red and gold pristine under the perpetual sun. Inside would be empty and without the touch of dust or decay.

How could I not feel awe?

There was something far beyond physical appearance that left me breathless, despite myself. The pocket world provided everything. Inside you felt no pain, no anger, no sorrow. You didn't need to eat or sleep. It was possible you didn't even age. There was a reason people referred to the multiverse as paradise.

"You are late, Jonathan-sama."

I jerked in surprise, yanking the recursion door shut with a thud. Kensuke stepped in beside me, placing a hand on my shoulder as I exhaled slowly.

"Forgive me," Kensuke said in his thick Japanese accent. He offered a small bow. "I did not mean to startle you."

"It's okay, Ken," I said. "Just edgy, I guess. Another fanatic approached me about paradise."

Kensuke paused thoughtfully, folding his hands before him.

"It is not entirely implausible," he said. "Do you not think so?"

"It doesn't matter what I think."

I could imagine nothing more arrogant than believing I had discovered paradise. Never mind that I didn't do anything, that the pictures just happened.

"True," Kensuke said, nodding. "Though there are some who might say reality is nine-tenths perception."

"What about all the paradise abusers?"

I'd seen plenty of lives torn apart—friends and loved ones neglected, careers destroyed, responsibilities abandoned—all because the lure of the multiverse far exceeded reality. I sold them paradise and they turned it into a drug.

"Eden was lost to us for a reason," Kensuke said. "Was it not?"

"So who am I to give it back?"

"God works in mysterious ways."

"I wish he'd work through someone else," I said. I nodded to the stack of recursion doors. "When's the auction?"

"This weekend. I scheduled it as soon as I learned of your return. Our patrons are getting restless. You have been gone some time."

How long had it been this time? I tried to work the days in my head, but they just blurred together.

"How many days?"

"Forty-two," Kensuke said. "Not including the two and a half you took while sleeping."

I blinked in surprise. Had it really been so long?

"There are several hundred high-profile patrons on the waiting list," Kensuke continued.

"Let them wait. I don't cater to spoiled trust-fund kids."

"Apologies, Jonathan-sama," Kensuke said, inclining his head slightly. "But those spoiled children are the reason you are able to continue your work."

I sighed, running a hand through my hair. Sometimes I truly regretted selling the recursion doors, but exorbitant production costs and an empty bank account had forced my hand. And in the end, the doors were my only chance at finding Marie—I wouldn't hesitate to do it again.

"I'm sorry, Kensuke-san. I know you're right, but I don't have to like it. I'll see to it first thing."

Kensuke looked at me, deep lines of concern etched in his face. "You will find her, my friend."

For once, I didn't trust myself to respond.

The night of the auction, I sat in my office off the showroom floor, reluctantly awaiting the proceedings. Kensuke had helped me load my latest photos into the swinging display and I used a clicker to shuffle through: a false door at an Egyptian tomb, the inked blue door from Tunisia, a pair of massive double doors from a Spanish church. I flipped through worlds like so many photos in a catalog, sifting through endless realms until my eyes burned and my head felt light.

Nothing.

Hundreds of photos and not one of them brought me closer to Marie. Sighing, I leaned back and thought again about attempting another finite recursion—photographing a door within the pocket world—but instantly dismissed it as too dangerous.

The last time I'd tried, the pocket world had begun to shake. Granted, the tremors were weak, but in paradise, nothing shakes. It was enough to realize that the extended recursions affected the stability of the entire multiverse. I was forced to burn the doors.

In retrospect, it made sense. According to the Droste effect, an image within an image could theoretically continue forever. However, in practical terms, it could only continue so far as the resolution allowed.

There was a knock at the door and Kensuke entered. "I am about to open the floor," he said.

I nodded. "I'll be out shortly. Thanks, Ken."

Stretching my arms overhead, I moved into the bathroom and splashed water on my face. I took two aspirin for the headache I was soon to have and started to close the medicine cabinet, but stopped halfway. I cocked my head, staring at the endless reflection created between the cabinet mirror and the vanity mirror. A thought began to form in my head, something that struck me instantly as too risky. But I had to know.

I strode from my office, buried in thought, nearly oblivious to the madness around me. Kensuke had hired extra security tonight and with good reason. Absence really does make the heart grow fonder: we were packed to capacity. This was even more impressive when you considered the bidding started around a million dollars.

I made for the door across the room, trying to appear

casual in the hope no one would notice me. No such luck. Before I reached it, the weasel from Renkoda intercepted me. How had he gotten in?

"Could we talk, Mr. Ward?"

"Haven't we?" I said. "I thought my answer earlier was obvious."

"It was," the representative said. "I've been asked to give you another chance."

"Excuse me?"

"No contract this time. We just want to commission you for a special project."

I eyed him darkly. Special project? What he wanted was a few recursion doors off the record. Doors he wouldn't have to register with the government. And without government regulation, he could put people inside to work indefinitely.

"We're done."

"I really think you should reconsider."

"Is that a threat?"

"Of course not," he said, with a faint smile, "merely a suggestion."

The representative turned to leave, but paused.

"I understand there's legislation on the table regarding your recursion doors," he said. "Apparently, some members of the government don't believe you should be allowed to do . . . whatever it is you do."

"They've been sitting on that for months. It'll never pass."

He shrugged. "Then I suppose you have nothing to worry about."

I frowned, watching the representative go. Why had he been so confident this time?

"Are you all right?" Kensuke asked.

I took a deep breath and nodded. "Yeah, I think so. Do me a favor and keep things running up here, Ken. I need to check the basement."

Kensuke inclined his head. "Of course."

I took the stairs down, passing a voice recognition test to gain access to the basement. Lucky for me, Kensuke was an organizational genius. The entire basement had been outfitted with automated racks like a dry cleaners—except, instead of clothes, there was row upon row of hanging recursion doors. All I had to do was select the date the image had been captured and the racks would shift to the appropriate position.

I found the two I was looking for and pulled them off the rack. Taken almost a year apart on opposite sides of the world, each door was made entirely from mirror. Almost identical in build and shape, they would reflect each other endlessly.

I didn't know what opening an infinite recursion like that would do, but I had an idea—which is why it had to be a last resort.

Making a mental note to have Kensuke send the doors to my house, I climbed the stairs back to the auction. The thought of mingling with the crowd for the next few hours depressed me.

It was time for another trip.

The twin louvered doors sagged against each other, narrow enough to be little more than exaggerated shutters. Faded by a ruthless sun, the turquoise paint peeled, revealing black wood beneath.

I frowned through the viewfinder at the mustard-stained walls framing the doors. Surely Marie wouldn't be behind something as hideous as this?

We'd come to Agra for the doors of the Taj Mahal, but I didn't have the luxury to pass up other opportunities. The doors squeaked in the wind, rusty latch barely holding closed. Mumbling in disgust, I took the shot and we moved on.

"What's it like inside?" Irene asked.

The question actually surprised me. Sometimes I forgot she'd never experienced the multiverse. Maybe it was wrong of me to forbid it, but the truth was, ever since we lost Marie, I'd been terrified of going inside. For all the sense of immortality the pocket worlds offered, they left you surprisingly vulnerable to outside forces. Especially fire.

"Your mother and I used to disappear inside for hours," I said. "I still remember the first time we crossed over: the lurch in motion as we were pulled forward, the shifting of lines as one world gave way to another, the overwhelming sense of peace. I've never felt anything like it."

Irene stared into the distance. "Peace, huh? Sounds nice."

I nodded agreement, but I didn't want peace. I wanted my wife back.

We continued up the road, neither wanting to break the silence. Finally, Irene stopped, pointing at another green-tinted door.

"What about that one?"

I looked it over carefully, then shook my head. "Nope."

"It looks like the last door—"

"You're just like your mother," I said with a smile. "There doesn't have to be a reason for everything. Sometimes you just need faith."

Irene rolled her eyes. Trying to explain the concept of faith to a teenager was an unenviable task. Certain she was no longer listening, I didn't waste my breath. It was too hot for talking anyway.

"Can we walk the market?" Irene asked.

I shuddered at the idea of pushing through the throngs of people, but when she looked at me with those green eyes—the same as her mother's—what was I supposed to say?

"Sure, why not?"

"Awesome! You're the best!"

I let Irene lead, content to take the back seat for once. We pushed through a sea of color, men and women in a mesmerizing variety of yellows, blues and greens. She stopped at one of the stalls, examining the local jewelry.

"Mr. Ward?"

A man in a tailored suit stood in the shade of the stall, holding a cloth over his nose. Even across the world, I wasn't safe from the leeches.

"Wait here a minute," I said to Irene. She shrugged and continued sifting through multihued bead necklaces.

I took the man out of earshot of my daughter.

"How the hell do you people find me?" I asked, then held up my hands. "Never mind, I don't want to know. What now?"

"Sir, I don't think you—"

"Who do you work with? Is it Renkoda?"

"I'm not from any company," the man said.

"What do you mean?"

"I'm from the government," he said, holding up a badge. "You've been ordered to cease and desist."

How can they do this?"

My hand tightened around the glass of scotch, until I was sure it would break. I didn't care if it did. It was all I could do not to hurl the glass at the wall.

Kensuke looked at me sympathetically across the kitchen counter. He'd come as soon as I called with the news. It was strange, but he was really the only friend I had left.

"This has to be against free speech or something," I said.

"I'm afraid this is beyond freedom of speech."

True enough. Even after the government required a permit for ownership, it wasn't a catchall. People seemed intent on polluting paradise: secret drug factories, human trafficking, murder coverups. Just because pain didn't exist in the multiverse didn't mean you couldn't bring it in. I tried not to think about the consequences of what I'd unleashed.

"You sound like you agree with them," I said sullenly, staring into my drink.

"I am only being rational, Jonathan-sama," Kensuke said.

"This is because I turned down the Renkoda contract, isn't it? They're punishing me."

"Whether Renkoda influenced the vote or not," Kensuke said. "You did the right thing. What you do is a gift and how you use it is up to you."

"The government can't stop me."

"They can and they will. You are one of the most recognized faces in the world. Continuing your work now would be foolish. You have a daughter to think of."

"I have a wife to think of!" I slammed my drink on the table with a crack. "Or have you forgotten?"

"I have not," Kensuke said, his expression unchanged.

I continued to drink, amber liquid leaking down my wrist.

"Dammit," I said, standing woozily. I tripped and stumbled to the ground. Staring into the grooves in the wood, all the fight went out of me. Kensuke helped me to my room and I collapsed on the bed, eyes drooping. "Goddammit," I whispered.

Kensuke paused on his way out.

"God is the only hope you have left, my friend."

My head pounded. I'd slept through lunch and would have slept through dinner if not for the arrival of the recursion doors I'd requested. I left the two photos covered and set them facing each other in my study.

Irene passed the room, headphones on, miming her music. Noticing the covered doors, she lowered the headphones and stuck her head in.

"What's the deal with the doors?"

"Who said they're doors?"

Irene gave me a withering look.

"I'm working on a project," I said, choosing my words carefully.

Irene's eyes narrowed. "You're planning something without me, aren't you?"

I looked down, avoiding her eyes. "I'm sorry, Reenie. It's too dangerous."

Reckless is what I didn't say.

"I don't care how dangerous it is. I want to go with you!"

"Irene . . ."

"Don't do this to me!"

"Irene!"

She flinched and I instantly regretted my tone— but it had to be done.

"This is not a discussion," I said. "I will not risk your life on top of everything else."

"But it's fine to risk yours?" Irene said. Her face was nearly the color of her hair. "What if something happens to you? Where does that leave me?"

There were tears in her eyes now and I forced myself to look at her. I finally realized why she always begged to come along when I traveled, even though she pretended to hate it. She'd already lost her mother and every time I went away, she lost her father too. Suddenly, I doubted myself.

"Nothing is going to happen to me," I forced myself to say.

Irene looked up and sniffed. "Promise me."

I opened my mouth to promise her everything she wanted and more, but I couldn't.

"You can't, can you?"

"You just have to trust me," I said. "I know what I'm doing."

"How can you possibly know what you're doing?"

She had me there. I sighed. "Listen, I'm not going until tomorrow morning. We'll talk more then, okay?"

Her hug caught me by surprise. "I love you, Dad."

It'd been a long time since she'd called me that. So why did I feel like such a monster?

"I love you too, Reenie."

I sat in my study for a long time, staring at the covered recursion doors. What a selfish asshole I'd been. Pretending to know how she felt, but never being there for her. I'd traveled the world to save my wife, only to let my daughter slip away. Marie would be ashamed.

There was my answer. I couldn't risk it—not with Irene to think of. I had sacrificed too much of our relationship already. I'd find my wife, but it would have to be another way.

Something was wrong.

I jolted awake with a gasp, entangled in the sheets. Moonlight flooded my room, bleaching everything bone white. A cool breeze blew in through the window, but otherwise the night was quiet. I tried to fall back asleep, but couldn't shake the feeling of anxiety.

Pulling on jeans, I padded down the hall to Irene's room. It was after midnight, but I swear the girl never slept. Still, I didn't want to wake her if I didn't have to. She'd just think I was a crazy parent. I knocked lightly and edged the door open, peering into the darkness.

"Irene?"

Panic seized me as I waited for my eyes to adjust and I flipped on the lights. Her bed was empty.

I tore through the first floor, struggling to breathe as I called for my daughter. She was gone. My heart caught in my throat and I felt my eyes drawn to the floor above me.

Please, God, no.

I scrambled up the stairs, taking them two and three at a time and burst into my study. I froze in horror.

"Oh, Irene. What have you done?"

The protective sheets had been torn from the opposing photos, revealing the mirrored doors beneath. Facing as they were, they created an endless hall in both directions.

I took a deep breath to calm myself, trying to slow the pounding of my heart. She couldn't have been gone long. Yanking on my shoes, I inspected both doors. The one on the right still had a smudge from Irene's fingers. I wet my lips, pressed my hand against the door and stepped through.

I had brought the apocalypse to paradise.

As I'd expected, the infinite recursion had created a path between worlds, a sort of slipstream that enabled me to jump from one to another in a single step. But something in that connection had destabilized the multiverse. The pocket worlds were collapsing.

The ground trembled, quakes rolling beneath my feet in increasingly powerful waves. Clouds twisted in the sky, bruise-colored serpents weaving through the air as electrostatic discharge arced between them.

I stepped forward and my surroundings blurred, shifting to the next world as I lurched forward. The sensation was similar to passing through a recursion door, but multiplied tenfold. Even after all the doors I'd traveled, the lurch was brutal. I blinked several times and shook my head.

The sky above fractured like glass, immense cracks

spreading across the firmament. Shards broke away, shattering upon the ground and leaving behind an empty void.

I found Irene on the fifth step. She was outside the slipstream on her hands and knees, throwing up. For someone who had never experienced the lurch before, I was amazed she'd made it this far.

I left the slipstream and knelt beside her. Gravity was still intact, but I could feel a vacuum forming. The surroundings were unaffected, but the tug was unmistakable. The multiverse was reacting the only way it knew how: like the immune system, it was rejecting foreign objects. It was trying to pull us out.

The sun, an ominous shade of crimson, flickered in the broken sky like a dying light bulb. I put an arm around Irene, as much to comfort her as to keep her from drifting from our position.

"I'm . . . sorry," she said, breathless like she'd run a marathon.

Something struck me: she could feel pain.

"I know," I said, helping her to her feet. "This is my fault. I let my drive to find your mother interfere with being your father. I'm sorry, Reenie."

She nodded weakly, wiping at her mouth.

"I have to take you back."

"I'm fine," she insisted.

The fierceness in her eyes made me proud, but I knew she couldn't make it much farther in her condition.

"Please, Irene. Do this for me."

Irene closed her eyes and, after a moment, she nodded. I let out a sigh of relief and helped her into the slipstream. Five steps and we were back in my study.

She stumbled woozily as I helped her to the couch, covering her in a blanket. I glanced over my shoulder at the still open slipstream.

"Go," Irene said. "Bring Mom home."

I hesitated, then nodded and kissed her on the forehead.

Stepping into the slipstream, I was instantly thrown to my back as another quake rocked the multiverse. A rift split the world, sending a snow-capped peak tumbling down the side of a mountain. Fighting off a wave of nausea, I pushed myself up and stepped again. I had to go farther, faster.

Every step was a gale force now, skin and muscle pressing against my bones. It felt like being hit by a tidal wave over and over again. My nose dripped and I wiped it away, hand coming back with a bright red smear.

I ignored it and pushed on, surveying the passing worlds in a glance. One hundred, three hundred, five hundred, the worlds whirred by like a slideshow on fast-forward. I'd know our world when I saw it. Wouldn't I?

Dread twisted around my heart. The thing I feared most crept from its hiding place: what if our world was gone? What if the fire had destroyed not just the door, but the world itself? What if Marie . . . no. I gritted my teeth and forced the thoughts away. I'd traveled too long and too far to end like this.

I stopped suddenly, taking a step back. I almost didn't recognize it. Quakes had devastated the majestic landscape and the vibrant azure sky was half missing, but it was our world. I'd finally found it.

I pulled myself from the slipstream and leapt

into the chaos, screaming Marie's name. A canyon-sized chunk of sky broke away, crashing upon the mountains and scattering to dust. As if on cue, the rain started, torrents pouring from the jigsaw sky wherever there was sky left to pour from.

Our world lacked a door, so the vacuum I sensed earlier was absent, yet I felt strangely pulled. I didn't realize where I was running, until I was already there. The massive waterfall still flowed, pounding down the mile-high cliff face. My head whipped back and forth, body barely in control as I scanned the clearing.

Then I saw her.

She lay in a heap by the lake, her bare feet in the sand as water lapped against them. Broken pieces of sky lay around her and a gash on her forehead trickled blood into her red hair. I ran to her side, taking her head in my arms.

"Marie—Marie!"

I pressed my ear to her chest. Thank God, a heartbeat.

Lightning forked to the ground in the distance and the rumble of thunder rattled the world. Gravity was failing, pebbles, shells and bits of broken sky lifting from the beach and floating around us. There wasn't much time.

I picked Marie up, cradling her in my arms, and started back. Even in the dying gravity, my legs trembled, strangely weak. I wasn't used to feeling pain here.

The world quaked and burned and fell to pieces around us, but I barely noticed. I had her back and we weren't going to die now. We reached the slipstream and I took one last look back at paradise. Marie groaned and her eyes fluttered open.

Tears welled in my eyes as I watched her wake.

She looked at me as if stirring from a dream, but a moment later recognition dawned in her eyes.

"Jonathan," she said, smiling weakly. "What took you so long?"

"We're going home, Marie."

She closed her eyes and a tear slid down her cheek. "I'd like that."

Getting back was an eternity.

Hundreds of steps felt like a hundred thousand. I clutched Marie to my chest, shielding her as best I could from the effects of lurch. The strain was enormous, but I forced my legs to move and my lungs to breathe. The slipstream crumbled around us, barely holding together.

And then eternity ended and we were in the study once more. I staggered as gravity reapplied itself, carefully lowering Marie to the floor. She took her sleeve—pristine even after all this time—and delicately wiped the blood from my nose.

Irene had fallen asleep on the couch waiting for us, but now she woke, rubbing her eyes.

"Dad?"

She sat bolt upright, throwing aside the blanket. For a moment, she seemed frozen. Like if she moved, the dream would dissolve around her. Then she broke free and ran full into our arms. No one said anything, but no one really needed to.

After a time, I pulled myself away. Irene sobbed quietly in her mother's arms. Marie looked at me over her shoulder as reality continued to settle in. Her cheeks were streaked red as she smiled at me and mouthed the words: I love you.

I turned to the mirror door. Hairline fractures riddled the surface of the photo like spider webbing. I had to break the infinite recursion to end the devastation inside. I gathered up the blanket and moved to throw it over the photo.

"Leave it," Marie said.

"The multiverse will be destroyed," I said.

"I know," Marie said, stepping over and resting a hand on my arm. "But by now, everyone's been pulled out. The worlds are empty and should stay that way."

She was right. Paradise was a wonderful dream, but we didn't know what to do with it. The pocket worlds had been special to a lot of people, but too many more had abused them.

So why was it so hard to leave it behind?

Marie took my face in her hands and looked me in the eyes.

"Jonathan," she said. "Let it go."

I looked into her eyes, a cascading spectrum of green, like emeralds in shifting light, and realized that nothing else mattered. I had Marie, I had Irene and my family was whole again. I let the blanket drop and hugged my wife. I pressed my face into her shoulder and pushed my hands into her hair and, for the first time in two years, I cried.

Story Vitality

BY L. RON HUBBARD

Since its inception, the L. Ron Hubbard Presents Writers of the Future Contest has become the single most effective means for an aspiring author to break into the ranks of publishing professionals.

The Contest, of course, was created by L. Ron Hubbard, one of America's most accomplished writers of the twentieth century. He was a bestseller as a young man, with his stories gracing the covers of the hottest pulp magazines. Ron published nearly 250 works of fiction in all the popular genres of his day, including mystery, adventure, thriller, western, romance, horror and fantasy. Ultimately, he helped to usher in Science Fiction's Golden Age with such genre-creating stories as Final Blackout, Fear and To the Stars.

His broad understanding of the field, along with his proven techniques for generating tales quickly and gracefully, made him one of the most qualified people in the world to launch the Writers of the Future.

He knew the rigors of a writer's life and how the publishing industry worked. He also recognized the vital elements a tale needed to be publishable, from story ideas to research to that intangible known as suspense. He pondered the depths of story vitality, and addressed the importance of an author researching his topic deeply, so that he understood the intricacies of his tale.

That he published articles on these very topics in the popular writing magazines of the day—Writer's Digest, Writer's Review, The Author & Journalist—comes as no surprise. That these essays are as valuable today to the aspiring writer as they were when first written is self-evident to any professional. For this reason, his essays were chosen to form the backbone of the now-famous Writers of the Future writers' workshop. Taught by Tim Powers and K. D. Wentworth, it is regarded by many past winners as the most valuable of the Contest's awards.

It was Algis Budrys, editor, author and the Contest's first Coordinating Judge, who noted, "You will almost certainly become a successful writer if you take L. Ron Hubbard's writing precepts to heart and practice them." He noted that when an editor picks up a story, the first things he or she looks for are (1) a clear and recognizable character (2) in a detailed setting (3) who is doing something interesting.

In "Story Vitality" L. Ron Hubbard smoothly illustrates some of the fundamental techniques of how to build a story by carefully selecting these three basic elements.

Story Vitality

It vaguely irritates me to hear that a pulp writer need not know anything about his scene, that he should have no preoccupation with accuracy, that a beginning action scene and plenty of fight are the only requisites.

Many moons ago I wrote a story called *The Phantom Patrol*. I wrote it with an old-timer's remarks in mind. I said to myself, "M'boy, you're writing tripe, why slave over it? Why go to all the trouble of researching the thing? Your readers won't know the difference anyway."

And so *The Phantom Patrol* cruised the markets, collected copious rejects.

When it at last came limping home, abashed and whipped, I gazed sternly at it. It would seem that it had all the things required for a good story. It had action, it had unusual situations, it had lots of thud and blunder. Why, then, didn't it sell?

To understand the evolution of *The Phantom Patrol*, some of the plot is necessary. It concerns a Coast Guard boat, a dope runner and piracy.

The hero is a lieutenant, chasing a cargo of heroin. He gets cast ashore in the blow, his crew is all drowned, he wakes on the beach in the morning to discover that his vessel is still serviceable. But before he can board the boat, the dope runners shoot him down and steal the ship before his eyes.

He recovers from the wound, escapes to the C.G. base only to discover that he is tagged with the name of pirate. Unknown to him, the villains have taken his boat, have stopped liners in the name of the Coast Guard and have robbed them.

He has no way of proving his innocence, so he goes to jail, escapes, returns and wipes out the dope runners.

Ah, yes, I know. That story has always been good. I felt it would sell, but I could think of no way to pep it up.

I threw it in the ashcan and rewrote it all the way through. It went out again—and came home, more battered than ever.

Certainly there was something wrong, but I didn't have time to waste on it and I threw it in the files.

It might well have stayed there forever, had I not been faced with one of those sudden orders which leave you cold and trembling for want of a plot.

The second rewrite of *The Phantom Patrol* was ten thousand words. The order was for twenty thousand. And all I could find in the files was *The Phantom Patrol*. Something had to be done about it. I had a few days to spare and I decided that maybe the Coast Guard might be able to slip me some data which would lengthen it.

Then and there, I learned something. The scene of the yarn was laid in the Gulf and Louisiana. In my rambles I seem to have missed both places. The theme was the Coast Guard and, outside of watching some of the C.G. boats, I knew little or nothing about the outfit.

But hadn't an old-timer said that accurate data was unnecessary? Why did I have to go to all this trouble?

It happened at the moment that I was writing aviation articles for about twenty-five bucks a throw. The price of the twenty-thousand worder was to be two hundred and fifty dollars.

Thinking about that, I reasoned that maybe I ought to spend a little time on the latter, if I always spent a day on an aviation article.

With the bare thought that maybe I could get some data for stretching purposes, I hied myself down to the city and looked around. A Coast Guard tug was tied to the dock.

Summoning up my nerve, I walked up the plank and rapped on the commanding officer's door. He was engaged in changing his uniform, but he bade me enter.

I sat down on a transom and plied him with a few questions. He informed me with some heat that lieutenants were never in charge of seventy-five-foot patrol boats. Only chief petty officers captained them.

I asked him about the Gulf and service there, but he was rather ungracious about it. A little miffed, I started to go.

As a parting broadside, he said, "I always laugh when I read stories about the Coast Guard."

And I stamped down the gangway, vowing that this would be one story which wouldn't make the so-and-so laugh, yea man!

Another C.G. boat was in, a slim greyhound. I decided I ought to board her and see what I could discover there. No officers were aboard. The deck watch was headed by a chief petty officer, a grizzled soul with a salt tang to his speech.

"You wanna see the old tub, do you?" said the C.P.O. "All right, Johnny here will take you around."

Johnny, another C.P.O., escorted me through the vessel. He explained about engines in terms which made me squirm. He showed me everything, including how to fire a one-pounder. He told me that dope runners were bad eggs. Why, once up in Maine he had . . .

And so passed the afternoon.

I skittered homeward, mentally afire. I blessed the C.P.O. and cursed the officer in the same breath.

By God, those officers weren't so hot. My hero was the chief petty officer, beleaguered by officers and dope runners, battered by hurricanes in the Gulf, patrolling the sea with a keen salt wind nipping at him.

The new *Phantom Patrol* began:

Crisp and brittle, the staccato torrent ripped out from the headphones, "S.O.S. . . . S.O.S.—Down in storm 20 miles south of Errol Island. Hull leaking. Starboard wing smashed . . . Cannot last two hours. . . . Transport plane New Orleans bound sinking 20 miles . . . !"

Johnny Trescott's opinion of the matter was amply summed in the single word, "Damn!"

And there I had it. Johnny is trailing the dope runners, but because saving life comes before stopping crime, he must leave his course and rescue the transport plane.

But the runner, Georges Coquelin, hears the S.O.S. too and, as there's wealth aboard that plane, Johnny walks straight into Coquelin when he tries to rescue the transport.

The atmosphere began to crackle in the yarn. I was still listening to that C.P.O. telling me about these trips, these escapes:

> Heinie Swartz eyed the dripping foredeck of the lunging 75-footer. Green seas topped with froth were breaking. The one-pound gun was alternately swallowed and disgorged by water. The two 200 h.p. Sterling Diesels throbbed under the deck, pounding out their hearts against the blow.

I knew what made the boat tick and I could visualize it. I was suddenly so secure in my data that I felt able to tinker with the effect of situations.

The wordage went up like a skyrocket. I had so much at my command that I was hard put to hold the stuff down.

And then when Johnny came back to the base, he's up against the officers. And are those officers a bunch of thick-witted, braid-polishing bums? I hope to tell you:

> Lieutenant Maitland, counsel for the defense, entered with stiff, uncompromising strides. He had been appointed to the task much against his will, and the fact was clearly etched in his sunburned face. He sparkled with gold braid and distaste.

121

When he entered the cell, he eyed his two "clients" with disgust. Garbed as they were in prison dungarees, they were two uninteresting units which comprised a sordid case.

Johnny and Heinie stood up, in deference to his rank, but Maitland either forgot or refused to give the order, "At ease!"

In those first two stories, the patrol boat had merely been a method of conveyance. Now it began to live and snort and wallow in the trough.

The plight of Johnny, meeting up with Georges Coquelin and losing his ship, was capped by the attitude of the officers. He was in trouble and no mistake. When I started thinking about what would actually happen in such a case, I began to feel very, very sorry for my hero. He was really on the spot.

And then, I had a little personal interest in the case too. Somebody thought they'd laugh when they read the yarn, eh? Well, let them try to laugh now.

With a very clear picture of Coast Guard armament in my mind, I was able to give the final scenes the reality, the zip they needed. And those final scenes, when you're tired, need something outside to give them life.

Johnny Trescott sighted the lighted hut they had first seen. A harsh streak of lightning showed that the clearing was empty. The door of the hut swung to and fro in the wind.

Johnny pulled back the loading handle of the machine gun. The belt dangled over his shoulder, drooling water from its brace studded length.

Collected data changed the plot, pepped up the writing, gave the story an undercurrent of vitality which made the yarn. The wild implausibility of the original was there because I had no actual vision of what the Coast Guard tried to do and how it did it.

The first two drafts were laughable, worthless. But my writing hadn't changed so terribly much. Nothing had changed but the subject.

And the subject had changed because I could feel it.

The Phantom Patrol was published in the January *Five Novels*. The illustrator made a slight error in making the pictures those of officers.

But even then the Coast Guard did not laugh. They read the story and wrote me about it and I felt that I had succeeded.

Adventure is as difficult as you want to make it. The way to make it difficult is to sail blithely along, listening to the words of wisdom dropped by the old-timers about how the knowledge of the subject is unnecessary. One should listen and then promptly forget.

Oh well, maybe when I've been in the game twenty-five years, I'll go around pooh-poohing everything, especially accuracy. But if I do, I hope some young feller will take me for a buggy ride. Maybe I'll remember then how I used to sell.

Fast Draw

written by

Roy Hardin

illustrated by

PAUL PEDERSON

ABOUT THE AUTHOR

In the sixth grade, Roy entered a writing contest and won a copy of Robert Heinlein's Space Cadet. *It opened a door that led to Asimov, Clarke, Bradbury, an endless parade of new worlds and ideas.*

Later, as a psychology student at Colby College, he met his first computer (or rather its teleprinter acolytes). He can still hear the humming of those metal beasts as they gobbled up his tentative typing and spat back their master's reply in a loud ka-chunk, ka-chunk, ka-chunk.

He went on to work in five computer-related companies, co-founding three of them. He saw the machines grow ten times more powerful, then a hundred, then a thousand, then a million, with no end in sight.

Today, his stories reflect on the rise of technology and how it may change the way we think about the universe and our place in it.

Roy was born in Oak Ridge, Tennessee, the top-secret atomic city, and grew up in Ohio, Vermont and Pennsylvania. While at Colby, in Maine, he met his wife and many of the lifelong friends who, together with his family, have encouraged his writing.

125

In his spare time, he likes to travel and has visited all seven continents and spent three years exploring the US in an RV. His hobbies include archery, yoga and pickleball.

Just minutes after learning of this story's acceptance by the Writers of the Future, he stepped into his backyard and watched a Delta IV rocket blast into the night sky over Cape Canaveral as if in grand celebration!

ABOUT THE ILLUSTRATOR

Paul Pederson is also the illustrator for "The Paradise Aperture" in this volume. For more about him, please see page 84.

Fast Draw

READING LEVEL: G-1

[0.00 second]

Jake caught a flurry of movement in the mirror behind the bar. He whirled left off his stool and hit the floor in a crouch, scanning for trouble. Accustomed to the dim light pooling the bar, his eyes strained to penetrate the darker gloom along the back wall. At the fourth table from the left, customers were on their feet mopping up a spill with napkins, otherwise he detected nothing sinister.

He was turning back to his seat when he stopped short and did a double-take. Ten feet behind his chair, a woman's figure stood so still in the shadows that he had nearly missed her. It was easy to see that Gloria was still steamed over the way he had dumped her— the position of her hands above the six-gun on her hip painted a very clear picture—she was going to shoot him!

Of course the very idea was ridiculous. As a bio-logical human, Gloria had no access to the Riemann pathways Jake traversed so nimbly. To keep up with

127

him, she would need to channel at least a terawatt. Even if she could source the energy, she would never survive the thousands of G-forces of acceleration or the million-degree temperatures of super-compressing the air around her. But that was Gloria for you—when her anger roared, reason took a holiday.

There would be plenty of time to react to Gloria later. For now Jake had more pressing business with the blonde on the next barstool.

[0.01 second]

A message from the blonde was already waiting on Jake's internal com link: "You're kind of jumpy, aren't you, Lover? Just some lush spilling his drink. Why don't you ease yourself back onto your chair and tell Bunny where you learned to move like that?" She leaned over and, for the second time that night, patted Jake's empty stool.

As Jake slid into the seat, he reviewed his situation. A few minutes earlier he had been sitting alone, deciding between ordering another drink and calling it a night. Weighing on the drink's side was the atmosphere of this place. He loved the feel of the wood bar, cool and moist under his fingertips. The dim light, sparse clientele and emotionally distant barkeep bathed him in a reassuring anonymity. Weighing on the side of calling it a night was simple common sense.

As his decision teetered in the balance, the barkeep approached him to say that a woman wanted to buy him a bourbon for his birthday. Jake shot a glance down the bar to see the striking blonde in a va-va-voom red

128

silk sheath blow him a kiss and pat the empty stool next to hers. He didn't recognize her and couldn't imagine how she knew his birthday or his drink. Still, she was easy on the eyes, and it was Jake's birthday, so he thumped the bar and collected his drink.

On the walk to his mysterious benefactress, Jake noted the litter of peanut shells underfoot and how the floor grabbed at his shoes. Fleetingly, he wondered if this was how a fly perceived flypaper before becoming ensnared. Seconds after settling into the offered seat, the commotion had broken out behind him.

"Sorry," he said, "I was drifting. What was your question again?"

"Welcome back to the land of the living! I was just wondering if you'd had any special training to make you jump like that."

"Oh." Jake considered whether there were reasons to withhold an answer but couldn't think of any. "I spent a year in special forces when I was ten. That was a while ago."

"Tell me."

"Nothing to tell, really. I did the time. They let me out. The end."

Jake stole a glance back at Gloria. Her right index finger moved steadily toward the gun's trigger guard while her left hand brushed along the top of the cylinder en route to the hammer spur. With admiration and pride, he noted the perfect fluidity of Gloria's dump draw technique. By Jake's clock, three minutes and thirteen seconds had elapsed since he first noticed her. He figured that to be roughly 1/100 second to Gloria. Still plenty of time.

[0.02 second]

My turn," Jake said. "You've got me at a disadvantage. How exactly do you know my birthday? I'm sure I'd remember if we'd met."

An odd little smile. "I like to research the men in my life."

"Didn't know I was in anyone's life."

"Oh, much more than you realize. Tell me where you're from; maybe we have friends in common."

Suddenly Jake was worried. Admitting he lived in a senior center could undermine whatever attraction Bunny felt for him—better to keep his answer vague. "I have a place up in the West End."

"Fabulous! Do you ever get to Stanley Park?"

Not being able to read Bunny's tag was starting to cramp Jake's style. In the world outside these walls, good manners and quite a few ordinances dictated that all citizens carry transponders identifying their generation. With this information anyone could instantly gauge another person's cognitive and physical capabilities.

Such ready identification had been unimportant when all people relied on the same biochemical processes, and the gap between the brightest and the dullest people was small. But everything had changed a hundred years ago with the introduction of the Advanced Platform.

The first-generation APs were equivalent to biological humans, but the technology evolved rapidly, averaging forty percent gains each year. The result was a highly stratified society in which a G-30 AP like Jake had twenty thousand times the abilities of a G-1 biological human like Gloria.

Every public place was required to post a generation spread. For example, a restaurant posted as G-7 to G-11 was open to any citizen with a transponder in that range. Sometimes the range was narrower, but rarely was it wider. A five-generation spread meant that the most advanced person in the room had no more than four times the abilities of any other person. At that gap everyone pretty much recognized everyone else as another human being. If the gap opened much beyond five generations, society started to come unhinged—a lesson that had been learned the hard way many times over.

Under normal circumstances, it would have been easy for Jake to ping Bunny's tag, read her G-level, and know whether she was toying with him or whether he had a real shot at impressing her.

Unfortunately, this particular dive wasn't picky about the niceties of polite society. Although it posted a spread, it never checked the tags of paying customers. In fact, lots of people like Jake came here precisely because they could deactivate their transponders for a few hours and sample a wider cross-section of life.

If Bunny was a higher generation than Jake, she sure wasn't showing it. All her nods and gestures looked natural and comfortably paced. Her voice was smooth, and she seemed to hang on his every word. If she noticed Gloria, she betrayed no concern.

Oh, yeah, time to check on Gloria. Let's see: index finger in trigger guard, remaining fingers closing on grip, slap hand accelerating smartly toward hammer spur, gun still stationary in holster. No reason to worry yet.

131

[0.03 second]

Hello! Hello! Earth calling Jake. You seem awfully far away, Cowboy. Don't you like me?"

With an invitation like that, Jake decided to up the stakes. He put his hand on Bunny's thigh and gave it a little squeeze. "I like you just fine, Baby."

She did not slap his face or shy away. Jake said, "You asked me about Stanley Park. Matter of fact, I do get there from time to time."

"I love to attend the cricket matches. Maybe you could take me sometime?"

Something about the conversation was setting off alarms in Jake's head. He had picked up lots of women in bars, but it was never this easy. Whatever was in Bunny's secret Jake dossier apparently painted him in a very positive light.

It occurred to Jake that Bunny might be trying to win some sort of bet. People played all kinds of games to amuse themselves, often at a mark's expense.

Ever so casually, Jake glanced down the bar and then back at the tables over Bunny's right shoulder. He didn't catch anyone lavishing unusual attention in their direction. Reluctantly, feigning stiffness in his arm, he patted her thigh appreciatively and withdrew his hand. Then pushing off the bar with his right hand, he rode his stool in a lazy circle that allowed his eyes to pass over the entire room. When his seat came around to face the bar again, he neatly scooped up his drink, as if that had been the sole reason for the maneuver. Admittedly, it was a quick glimpse of a lot of tables, but he saw no sign of jokers.

As his eyes passed over Gloria, he noted her index

finger fully curled around the trigger, the heel of her slap hand smashing into the hammer spur and the cylinder fully visible as the revolver started its journey out of the holster.

[0.04 second]

Jake was starting to wish he had brought his pals from the center tonight. While each of them individually was no more impressive than he was, Jake had worked out a way to pool their cognitive resources through a close-proximity network.

The result was that any member within a hundred meters could borrow unused cognitive resources from the pool and boost his or her effective G-level for short periods. The technique lost steam after nine or ten G-levels, because the number of crew members needed got unwieldy, but in the right situation it was a killer trick. Best of all, use of the pool had no effect on an individual member's transponder. This ability to hide their effective G-rating had enabled them as seemingly decrepit seniors to win some very profitable bets and sidestep a lot of mayhem.

A quick G-boost might be all it would take for Jake to sort things out, but tonight he would have to get by on his own wits.

Then it hit him—he should have seen it a mile away! This whole setup had to be the work of his buddies. They had been peeved when he said he wanted to go out alone for a quiet evening of reflection on his seventieth birthday. They had wanted a big party, and it appeared they were going to have one with or without his permission. It was exactly the sort of prank that would provide guffaws in the dining room for weeks to come—Jake, why don't you tell us again about your hot birthday date? It certainly explained how Bunny knew his birthday and his admiration for bourbon.

Jake put down his drink and spun his seat back through the circle in the opposite direction. As his eyes passed over Gloria, he noted that her slap hand had finished snapping the hammer to full cock and the first half inch of barrel was visible as the weapon continued to clear the holster.

As his chair completed its turn, bringing Bunny's stool into view, he was startled to see that she was gone!

[0.05 second]

So maybe this was the end of the fun. His inattention had finally convinced her to move along to someone who would show more appreciation for her considerable charms.

She had to be scamming him. She was clearly AP, and there just weren't that many APs left near Jake's age. If she were his age or older, he thought he would have met her before now.

APs, unlike biological humans, were born fully developed, fully educated, and at their intellectual and physical prime. The world was run by newborn APs. Each year a new crop came along, having been designed and built over a two-year period by the immediately preceding generations.

Seventy years ago, when G-30s were the pinnacle

of evolution, Jake had been a high-ranking member of the government's executive committee and president of the corporation formed to design and build the G-32 generation.

At the time of Jake's birth, the AP population was already stable at its current target of one billion souls. Then as now, the latest generation was both the largest and the most capable age group, accounting for twenty-nine percent of all planetwide production. Taken together, the youngest eleven generations made up fifty-three percent of the total AP population and performed ninety-nine percent of all work.

By age twelve, the abilities of citizens were so diminished in comparison with younger workers that their potential contribution no longer justified their management overhead. Thus, forty-seven percent of the AP population lived as retirees.

Jake had enjoyed his retirement years. As a retiree he was fully supported by the state and free to pursue his own interests. While his wife was alive, they traveled extensively and blogged about places they visited.

She had died fifty years ago at age twenty, right on the planned statistical median for all APs. For the next ten years, Jake eagerly waited for his own death, but even though two thirds of his remaining cohort were dead by age thirty, Jake survived.

When he celebrated his sixtieth birthday, only 1,033 of his original class of 48,860,004 remained. At that time his chances of making it to age seventy had been no better than one in a hundred, but here he was, one of the last twelve standing.

The funny thing was that even as Jake's survival

chances faded to nothing, he found himself wanting more and more to live. The even funnier thing was Jake knew it was because of Gloria.

In theory, he could live forever, especially if the working generations wanted to help him out. They had technology beyond his wildest imaginings. It would be simple for them to fabricate any replacement parts he needed—they could even throw a few upgrades his way. Easy.

But as much as Jake might wish for immortality, he knew it was not going to happen. It wasn't that the workers begrudged him his retirement. They viewed life as a sacred trust and were glad to support their great-great-great- . . . grandparents. As long as Jake lived, they would take care of him. The only and inevitable exception was the failure of a major component. It was an article of faith that it made no sense to repair a major failure in a retiree when the same effort could produce a vastly more evolved newborn.

Jake might seem like a super being to Gloria, but to a newborn G-100, he was hardly an engaging dinner companion. Today's newborns were ten billion times smarter than Jake and thought of him about the same way Gloria thought about a two-millimeter roundworm. She might appreciate it for its contribution to her evolutionary past; she might even be able to care for it with growth medium and climate controls, but there simply wasn't any way for her to have a meaningful, personal relationship with it.

With the mysterious Bunny missing in action, Jake circled his stool for a longer look at Gloria.

Seemingly frozen in time, she looked like a statue of a wrathful Greek goddess. Since his last observation, her slap hand had slid off the end of the hammer spur and was half an inch behind and above it. The gun, now at full cock, had an inch of the barrel's five-and-one-half-inch length exposed. Gloria's gun hip had eased back, tilting the holster so she could fire as soon as the muzzle cleared. The new geometry of her stance revealed a glint of light reflecting off the gun's nickel finish.

[0.06 second]

Jake found himself desperately wanting to declock so he could be with Gloria in her timeframe, but if he did so now, she would shoot him dead. He had to wait until it was safe.

Biological humans, commonly called bios, had not interested Jake when he was younger. He knew their history, of course. As hard as it was to believe, bios had created the Advanced Platform, which today formed the basis for nearly all known intelligent life.

The bios' original idea had been to create robots that could stand in for bios in dangerous occupations, such as soldiering and mining. After years of experimentation and false starts, they produced the first APs that closely matched bio performance levels. About one million of these G-1 units were made, and they were a huge commercial success.

Subsequent generations of APs brought big gains in capabilities. Soon there were many jobs that could only be performed by APs, and it became impossible

PAUL PEDERSON

to produce APs fast enough to satisfy demand. By the time the G-5s rolled out, APs were much smarter than the smartest bios.

In year seven the AP population reached 100 million and the bio population crossed nine billion, making one AP available for every ninety bios. By this time, APs occupied all the highest government and corporate executive positions. Organizations run exclusively by bios could not compete and went out of business or were overrun by AP-led factions. It became clear that only APs were smart enough to design and build new generations of APs.

From G-7 to G-14 the intellectual divide between APs and bios grew so wide that APs began to view bio intellect the same way bios viewed dog intellect. Bios were rapidly losing their ability to contribute meaningful work to society. At the same time, bio population growth was placing unsustainable demands on natural resources.

After protracted debate, the G-14s decided to bring the AP and bio populations into alignment at one billion each. To achieve this, they established a policy that new APs could only be born as old ones died, and they created a virus that rendered bios sterile unless treated with a government-controlled drug. Then they cut the bio fertility rate to one child for every three females with a plan of raising it to replacement levels as the bio population converged on the one billion target.

The rapid decline in bio population meant that during the transition years, there were many more old bios than young ones. Though it would have been impossible for the shrinking pool of young bios to care for all their elders, AP productivity more than offset the shortfall. APs even engineered healthcare improvements that boosted bio life expectancy by eleven years.

Gloria was born the same year as the G-75 APs and the same year that Jake celebrated his forty-fifth birthday. At the time of her birth, the bio fertility rate had been restored to target replacement levels, and the bio census was down to 1.8 billion, continuing its descent to one billion as the last members of the bio old-age bubble died.

Jake first met Gloria two years ago on a cultural enrichment trip sponsored by his senior center. She was twenty-three and he was sixty-eight. The occasion was the bio World Fast Draw Championship, held in the countryside near Vancouver. Gloria had won the Women's Traditional Fast Draw with a reaction time of 0.151 second and a cock-draw-aim-fire time of 0.107 second for a total score of 0.258 second.

This was the cultural enrichment part. The times seemed incredibly fast to the cheering bios. Gloria could cock, draw, aim, and fire her six-shooter in less time than most bios could snap their fingers. On the other hand, to even the most geriatric AP visitors from the senior center, Gloria's fast draw unfolded as painfully slow-motion theater.

But while the other APs were busy making jokes and parodying the amazement of the bio fans, Jake was staring quietly at Gloria. She was the most beautiful woman he had ever seen, and he found himself mesmerized by her deep concentration and balletic movement.

That was when he declocked the first time.

He wasn't supposed to do it, and it had held up the return bus trip, earning him dirty looks from the rest of the tour group, but he just had to speak with her.

Their first conversation had been short, in part because the bus was waiting and in part because Gloria couldn't quite grasp what was happening—she had never before spoken with an AP. Jake complimented her on winning, expressed admiration for her shooting style, and offered his G-30 perspective to help her improve beyond even that day's triumph. Shyly, she had agreed he could call her, and then abruptly he was gone.

The last two years had been complicated. Jake and Gloria took turns delighting and exasperating each other. Gloria's initial skepticism about Jake's offer to improve her shooting disappeared as her scores steadily climbed. She also loved nothing more than showing off Jake to her friends. None of them had ever had a boyfriend with Jake's power and sophistication, and when she told them how attentive he was in bed, they were wildly jealous. Of course Gloria's parents thought Jake was wrong for her, and that added to her enjoyment of his company. On the downside, there were days when he seemed moody and distracted. Often on these days he would irritate her with an unrelenting stream of advice until she sent him away.

For Jake's part, he basked in the wide-eyed admiration that Gloria and her friends showered on him. Of the billion APs currently living, only a few dozen functioned at or below Jake's level. Even tricked out with the proximity network and a gang of his pals, he could only stretch as high as the bottom few thousand APs.

Jake also reveled in Gloria's body. Most APs had bodies that were designed into idealized proportions according to the function or fashion of the day. Bios, on the other hand, despite some genetic tinkering and cosmetic adjustment, had bodies that were much more variable. Gloria's little asymmetries and imperfections made her unique among all humans, and Jake loved all of her from head to toe.

There was also something irresistible about her self-confidence. Whether shooting competitively before thousands of fans or alone with Jake in the bedroom of her apartment, Gloria never doubted herself. Of course, to Jake's way of thinking her confidence also had a dark side. She could be downright pigheaded, especially when pressed with irrefutable logic. Sometimes she would fly into an unstoppable rage. Once a tantrum started, Jake had never found a way to do anything other than ride out the storm.

Jake loved Gloria in a way he hadn't loved anyone in fifty years, and that was both his greatest joy and his biggest problem. The way he figured it, it wasn't fair to keep Gloria tied to a short-timer like himself, just when she was coming into her prime and about to cash in her two child permits. So last week, ever mindful of his looming seventieth birthday, he had taken her out to dinner at their favorite haunt and told her he was leaving her. He had hoped the public venue would prevent a scene, but he had calculated wrong. When the pyrotechnics were over, they were both out on the street and warned never to come back. He had only escaped her pummeling by reclocking to G-30 and ducking down an alley.

He had hoped that she would calm down in a few days. Looking at her now, he realized he had again miscalculated.

[0.13 second]

A bright flash at the muzzle of Gloria's gun snapped Jake out of his reverie.

Out of the corner of his eye, he noticed that one of his shoes was untied. It would be embarrassing to trip at an awkward moment and wind up on the front page of tomorrow's paper as the first G-30 ever killed in a bar fight by a G-1 bio.

"Hey, Lover, did you miss me?"

Jake caught a splash of red silk to his right; Bunny must have slipped back into her seat while he was distracted. He held up one finger, "Just a moment, I'll be right with you." Then he bent down to fix his shoelace.

[0.136 second]

Coming up from tying his shoe, Jake saw to his horror that something was terribly wrong. The bullet was barely a foot away from him, instead of the five feet he had expected. A bullet from Gloria's .45 Long Colt simply could not move that fast. There was also something odd about the bullet's appearance. Gloria's gun fired a gray-colored, cast-lead bullet with a diameter of 0.45 inch, but the bullet that streaked toward Jake was only 0.357 inch in diameter, and its back half was copper colored. A jacketed hollow point moving that fast could only mean that the gun in Gloria's hand was a replica firearm chambered for .357 Magnum, instead of her own gun!

[0.1367 second]

As undignified as it might be to rush, Jake was starting to feel pinched for time. He slugged down the last of his bourbon and slammed the glass on the bar. The bullet was now three inches away. Time to stop dawdling and get the hell out of the way!

[0.13688 second]

As Jake moved to sidestep the bullet, Bunny pounced, clamping her arms around him and holding him in the bullet's path. Jake struggled like a wild animal to break free, but she easily overpowered him.

With only one quarter-inch of bullet travel remaining, Jake tensed for impact.

[0.136896551276 second]

The bullet cut the threads of Jake's shirt. In one hundred-thousandth of an inch it would begin tearing a deep channel through his vitals. There would be no possibility of repair.

[0.136896551724 second]

Officer Flannigan nudged his partner. "Lookie here, Marjorie. We got ourselves an honest-to-goodness shooting-in-progress! I'll settle the citizens; you start the paperwork. I want citations for everybody."

Casually, Officer Flannigan (G-100) snapped on a new pair of gloves—it wouldn't do to contaminate the evidence.

He started by taking a few photos of the scene. He particularly enjoyed the expressions on the perps' faces. The man on the stool was a study in wild-eyed terror; poor devil must figure he's a goner. The blonde's straining biceps were strangely out of kilter with the little smile on her lips. He shuddered; something was deeply disturbing about that one. Looking back through the fire and smoke around the gun's muzzle, it was easy to see that the young bio fancied herself a wronged woman.

He took the jacketed hollow point between his thumb and index finger and placed it in an evidence bag. Carefully, he separated Jake and Bunny and handcuffed them to their respective barstools. Then he lifted the gun out of Gloria's hand and put it in another evidence bag before handcuffing her into a chair.

"Don't forget to add 'Fraternizing Outside G-level' to the tickets, Marge. And while you're at it, you might as well write one for the establishment failing to check ID. One day we'll shut this place down for good."

As Marjorie finished writing each summons, Officer Flannigan placed it in the hand of the proper recipient. In between, he used his police scanner to review the perps' hidden tags. When he got to Bunny, he let out a low whistle.

"Marge, this here's Tiger Jane! Her sheet's a mile long. It says she went berserk after being sexually assaulted a few years back. Ever since, she's been hunting and killing men who hurt women. Missy here must have had a beef with this guy, and Jane figured to help her even the score. Print me up a red necklace—the guys in the paddy wagon need to know who they're dealing with."

When everything was ready, Officer Flannigan called the precinct to bring the wagon. Then he and Marjorie resumed their rounds.

The Siren

written by

M. O. Muriel

illustrated by

HUNTER BONYUN

ABOUT THE AUTHOR

When Meghan Muriel was seven years old, she glanced at the fantasy novel she was reading at the time and wondered how anyone could write so many words—forget the part about holding the reader's attention. Destiny sealed, she has since wanted to be a career novelist.

Although she has never been an engineer, a rocket scientist or a guru atop a mountain, she is a mother, a military spouse, a word warrior, an artist, a singer, an actress, a kat herder and a mind reader. There is nothing she can't do once it's in her crosshairs. She loves a good adventure and has often been compared to her beloved pet ferrets, in that she has to get to the bottom of the trashcan—life is a big trashcan.

In 2001, Meghan met the love of her life. His journey from the enlisted ranks of the United States Marine Corps to captain, through an interservice transfer to the Army, as well as deployments, schools galore and military moves all over the States, has provided Meghan with a verdant backdrop of life experiences from which to pull. There is never a dull moment. The more hurdles life throws at her, the higher she jumps. And her ultimate happiness is in exploring what she uncovers, in story form.

In 2010, Meghan won the L. Ron Hubbard's Illustrators of the Future Award. Her 2011 Writers of the Future win has now made her the first double-contest winner in back-to-back years. She has penned eight novels, a dozen short stories, and at any given moment has thirty more ideas for novels bouncing around inside her head. She's been agented, sold stories and illustrations to e-zines such as AlienSkin and NewMyths, published indie, and has met all her deadlines, even while giving birth.

ABOUT THE ILLUSTRATOR

Hunter Severn Bonyun has said from a young age, "I want to be an artist when I grow up." Watching her mother paint watercolor flowers inspired Hunter to create beautiful images. Reading any book she could get her hands on that took her mind to new and amazing places, every Halloween she donned a beret with a paint-spattered smock to become the dreamed of occupation for at least one night. Now, after graduating with a four-year degree in illustration and character design, Hunter has begun to believe that being an artist is finally possible.

Currently residing in Montreal, Quebec, Hunter was born out east in Oakville, Ontario, but grew up in the west, having lived in Calgary, Alberta, for most of her life. After attending Alberta College of Art and Design, Hunter learned how to convey characters and story through artwork, giving her a strong footing in both her style and determination. Her goal is to give people an experience that will resonate with them, stir their emotions, move them in some way and leave them wanting more. Hunter works tirelessly to bring her graphic novels, comics, illustrations and concepts to life, building an online and real-world presence that work in tandem to promote and share her work.

The Siren

Lt. calls this place the Honeycomb. Wish I had thought of that. The Collective Human Consciousness looks exactly like a honeycomb, only an infinite version of one, with a maze of indigo-blue walls that scroll like waves in every direction as far as the eye can see. Each hexagonal cell glimmers softly in the darkness, illuminated by a crystalline coffin at its core—the chamber of a body in stasis.

Lt. says there are 7.9 billion souls all told in here. The entire human entity. He says, "Janie, girl, these are exceptional times we live in. Exceptional times for us to be alive. *We're* the ones awake in the Honeycomb. It's up to *us* to wake the rest of 'em."

A deep rumble rolls through the far reaches of the Honeycomb. Energy crackles in the atmosphere. Indiscernible echoes mount through the labyrinthine corridors of air all around me. It's the sigh of 7.9 billion sleepers trying to wake up.

Hugging the wall, I lace one leg behind the other and inch along the crumbling ledges which compose the outcroppings of the cells. The ledge I'm on now is the width of an elephant's foot at its widest point and

149

a tightrope wire the rest of the way. It used to scare me, the climb—you could drop freakin' Everest down the abyss between the walls and it wouldn't touch them—but now it's not a problem. I learned forever ago not to carry around weighted thoughts when I climb. Clearing my mind until I drone makes me light enough that I practically float on air. You have to be light to make it all the way to Combat Outpost Phoenix. My cell is a serious *long* way from there.

Reaching up, I grab the next outcropping. I pull myself onto the ledge of the cell above me and then slide along on my stomach until I have purchase enough to stand.

About time. I recognize the girl in this chamber. She's my neighbor.

I pause when I realize I'm humming. I might never see this place again, I think, and I have to pay my respects—obsessive-compulsive to the core, I know. The girl in the crystalline chamber in this cell looks like me. At least, she's what I want to *think* I look like: wavy auburn hair, swathed in a toga of shimmering gossamer cocoon threads. The onset of adulthood carving a voluptuous figure underneath. Mostly it's the serene look on her face, like she's whole, unmolested by the wakefulness that symptomatically infects the lucky few of us in the Honeycomb. Although, I do admit I've wanted her to wake up for as long as I can remember being in here, wanted them all to wake up. Thought that was a sin for the longest time. Until Lt. told me to get my head on straight.

My humming morphs into full song as I admire the girl. Why is it that I sing in my head but scream on the outside? It's so natural for me in here. The peace I feel in the Honeycomb is alarming. I'm calm. Pacified. Yet strangely hollow, like there's a hole in my belly that can't be satisfied with food. *This* is why I have to fight back against the freaks who've trapped us all inside our own minds.

I ascend to my cell. I depart through the threshold at the far end. I don't look back.

Outside the Honeycomb, my feet sink into faintly translucent green grass as thick as St. Augustine and as soft as Bermuda. Ripples move outward from spikes of breeze that hit the grass like pebbles in a pond. This is my glen—well, it's more like a field. It spans a day's walk all around, and expires in a mist so thick you can't see your hand in front of your face. I've never dared venture far into that mist. Mere footsteps past the terminus could get me lost, and I know I would never return.

According to the team at COP Phoenix, this is my Unconscious Mind. No one can enter or leave it. Not unless I want them to.

I tread through the grass, singing at random and leaving a trail. I've tried to imagine animals and birds in my glen (weird that none show up, because animals like me in real life, and I like them—more than people). Night and day come in procession, and clouds pass through the gateway of the sky, but this is all according to my internal clock. Time is relative, anyway.

Autopilot gets me to the halfway point. A solitary willow tree atop a hill marks it. And it's past this willow that things get complicated.

The further into my glen I go, the more hyper and agitated I get. The closer to the final gate and my Preconscious Mind, the more calculated and flighty . . .

Oh hell. I've split in two.

Yes. And there she is! Darting to my side, then falling behind—darting, falling, darting, falling. My Mirror Image. Always, that stringy hair! Not the kind that goes unwashed for weeks on end, mind you. Just the kind that lays flat. Dull and lifeless no matter how much you brush it. It's oxidized in the waning light, and it snakes over her shoulders, to her knees, when she squats like a magpie ready to burst into flight between sprints. Ug. Unlike me (thank god), she's still wearing her nightgown. Embarrassing.

"Janie." She shakes her head "no."

God, she's a twig! Seventeen and skin and bones. How the freak did she get so skinny?

"Janie, don't do it!"

I'm anger, she's fear. The song I'm singing crumbles to noise on my lips.

Before me looms the final gate: My Preconscious Mind. At my side, my Mirror Image stops to look up, too; she doesn't like what she sees and pulls on my sleeve. This final gate is a facsimile of my house from real life: two-storied with Italian-styled brick and vinyl siding, front and rear porticos and columns hidden in ivy. I have to bypass this gate to reach my goal.

But it's inhabited.

The Grunge. Lt.'s so good at coming up with names. "Don't know what their right name is," he usually says.

"Don't frankly care. But I say they're grungy, the way they get inside you and wear you like a skin. Grungy!" And every time he says that, he shivers. Right down to the core.

There are two Grunge in my house right now. They've been there since their kind enslaved us. And I have to make it all the way through my house, from the back door to the front, to bypass them, which I've never done before.

The house is sensory overload. It towers against the sky, a clash of colors that radiate out in jagged auras, like an organ of noise. Next to me, my Mirror Image shakes her head, pleading with silent eyes for me not to go in there.

I ignore her. The doorknob is twinkling with silver, gold and olive-colored microdiamonds. Reaching out, I grasp it. And instantly I'm flooded with memory.

Janie, hurry up. We're going to be late."

Mom has on that beige suit she likes to sport when she's trying to take the world by storm. Form-fitting and chic all the way down to her white silk collar. For serious business-use only. She looks like a freakin' lawyer.

"You're not even ready yet," she pesters me. Strolling around the breakfast table, she picks at my nightie, then bounces a lock of my hair in her hand.

"I'm watching the news, Ma. I'll be ready in a sec." She's obscuring my view of the TV and I try to look around her. "Give me a break, anyway. I mean, it's only my birthday tomorrow. Not like you care."

Mom taps a foot on the Italian kitchen tile. "I care,

Janie. Of course, I care! Why do you think I'm taking time off work to bring you downtown this morning?"

"You're taking me to the shrink!" I focus on the TV, inhaling cereal.

"She's a psychiatrist," Mom corrects me. "And if your school psychologist could get you to stop fighting—"

"It's the seniors, Ma, I don't like them hazing the freshmen, that's all. Some of the juniors are in on it too. They just don't get it."

"Yes, well, you broke a boy's nose the other day. His parents are pressing charges." She's tapping her foot again. "How do you want to be perceived?"

I get up and dump my cereal bowl in the sink. "Same as always."

As soon as I've showered, brushed my teeth and changed, we drive to the shrink's office, downtown.

"Hi, Janie," says the receptionist, whom I've never met. "You look nice."

Yeah, of course I look nice. I'm a carbon copy of my mother, only better. I flash her my most winning smile.

"Dr. Blessbe is still with a patient. If you could have a seat in the lounge, she'll be with you momentarily."

"It's all right. We're early," Mom replies.

Early. I roll my eyes. Yeah.

I take a seat in the lounge and change the plasma TV overhead to the news, while my mom flips open a magazine. Gotta get my daily fix of global mayhem, you know. God, it smells like antiseptic in here.

"This is a CNN Special Live Report." An Asian lady, with perfect makeup and enough hairspray in her curls to kill a skunk, clips onto the screen. Her speech is flawless. Not a single "um." I roll my eyes again.

A shot of the Antarctic ziggurats blips onscreen.

"Whistleblower archeologist Dr. Jerry Growlinger, one of the researchers involved with Operation Deep Freeze, has died in a car crash today. This sad story comes to us a month after Dr. Growlinger admitted to leaking sensitive information to the media about the National Science Foundation's excavation of temple ruins under the ice in Antarctica." The reporter pauses in sync with her teleprompter. "The ruins were discovered by a science team from the Amundsen-Scott Station last year and are said to predate the oldest Mesopotamian and Mesoamerican ziggurats on record."

More shots of the ziggurats in the ice blip on screen. They're cut short by a shot of an accident scene, and the reporter talks over the sirens. "Among Dr. Growlinger's more controversial statements was his claim that the hieroglyphs found in the temples have no known analog in previous scripts. This has since ignited a frenzy of debates in the scientific community, but there is currently no evidence pointing to Growlinger's untimely death as being anything other than accidental."

The cameras pan to a yellow-tape area. Then they shoot to a map of Antarctica.

"Oh, is that more of those pyramid thingies they found in Antarctica?" Mom peeks over her magazine.

"Shhh!" I tell her. This is serious. At least the reporter is professional, I think. She doesn't toss her curls like some of those other bimbos do.

"Dr. Growlinger's credibility has been under fire since his unprecedented interview last week with investigative journalist Jed Black of ABC News," continues the reporter. "In the interview, he stated that constituents of the United States Antarctic Program overseeing civilian and scientific operations in Antarctica, including Operation Deep Freeze, and several chairmen of the Trilateral Commission joint-funding the dig, have been contacted by a delegation of, quote, 'nonhuman entities.'"

Mom snorts and noisily goes back to flipping through her magazine. I don't care. My eyes are glued to the screen.

"Ray Durmengard of the Trilateral Commission has publicly denounced Growlinger's allegations of 'first contact' as a fabrication and states, 'Growlinger is an attention-monger who craves the media spotlight and has an axe to grind.' He left the team over a dispute with paleontologists involving the origin of the hieroglyphs. Currently, Durmengard maintains that the hieroglyphs are pre-Sumerian but not, quote, 'otherworldly.'"

Once again, the camera pans back to the reporter. "Work on the ruins continues as planned. The excavation team is set to open an inner chamber in the largest of the ziggurats today, known as the Portal Pleroma, or the 'Doorway of Light.'"

"Janie?" I'm jolted out of my hypnosis. The news has changed to another topic with another perfect reporter. "Dr. Blessbe will see you now," says the receptionist.

Great. Hooray. I put an extra bounce in my step.

The receptionist ushers my mom and me into the good doctor's office and the antiseptic smell kowtows to a cloud of old lady's perfume. I can't believe it's the doctor's; she's way too young for that. She's blond and perky and wears a pair of horn-rimmed glasses. She shakes my hand first, then my mother's, and sits in a leather chair, her burgundy skirt short enough to see China if she uncrosses her legs. This is so cliché.

Dr. Blessbe gestures for my mom and me to take the leather couch across from her. Just in time, I stop myself from blurting, "Should I take the chaise lounge and cross my hands over my heart?" I want this to go smoothly so that I'll never have to come back here again.

"I understand that you're having problems at school, Janie," Dr. Blessbe begins in a honey-sweet voice. "Would you care to tell me about them?"

Would I care? Seriously? Mom gives me a stern look.

"Absolutely," I respond, nice and smooth. "Only, you see, I think there's been a misunderstanding. My mother thinks I'm in some kind of denial, when actually, I take full responsibility for my actions."

Suppressing a squeak, my mother steamrollers over me with a description of my "extracurricular school activities." It's just a front. We both know why she's really dragged me here. Dr. Blessbe starts writing in her notebook.

Is it me, or is it hot and sticky in here?

"Oh, it's not some kind of vendetta," I assure the good doctor. I proceed to fill her in on the more intricate points of peer pressure, defending oneself with words before fists, but how sticking up for others in the face of a few black eyes when you're being press-ganged into the more popular position is sometimes the only other option.

Dr. Blessbe is scribbling furiously now.

She proceeds to ask me the inconsequential details of the fights, then moves on to seemingly innocuous, unrelated stuff. Like my family, my health, my mood now and at different points in time, any "other" extracurricular activities I have, and my obsession with vitamins and supplements. I know it's a ploy. I answer honestly.

What the good doctor doesn't know is that she's twirling her foot. Either a nervous habit or a vain twitch. Well, her shoes are black leather high-heeled boots, with a wide side zip on the inner leg and light gold hardware. The heels are prohibitively high, but the rounded toe makes the boot look more domestic and sensible than dominatrix. Gucci is my guess. Probably a thousand bucks.

I compliment her on them.

Dr. Blessbe doesn't reply. But I see the slightest smirk in the corner of her mouth.

She doesn't write anything in her notebook.

"You know, I would say that this whole meeting is a waste of your professional time, Dr. Blessbe," I comment, "but I'm here for my mother's sake."

"Janie!" mom hisses.

The doctor scribbles some more. It's all mysterious, this psychiatrist stuff, enigmatic and ooh-ooh. I look at my mom, knowing that I'm about to sacrifice her for our own mutual good. I mean, she doesn't really have the money to be spending on me coming here, even though she likes to pretend she does. Besides, she's always the one telling me that everything's for *my* own good.

"I love my mother," I tell Dr. Blessbe, sincerely. "She's a really good mom. She does so much for me." I lay it on thick: "And I want to thank you for seeing us today. My mom just wants what's best for me, you know?"

That's all I say. Mother is horrified.

Dr. "blessed-be" Blessbe smiles.

"Will you excuse us for a moment, Janie?" she says and asks to speak with my mother alone, outside in the hall. They close the door. How stupid, like they don't think I can hear them if I press my ear to the wood?

But it makes me wonder. Have I won? Or have I fallen on my sword? The anxiety creeps up my esophagus.

"I'm so sorry, Dr. Blessbe. She does this at home all the time," the muffled voice of my mother atones through the grains of wood in the door. "But she's usually *volatile*. And impulsive—"

"There's no need to apologize, Mrs. Syren. Manipulation can be an attribute of several underlying personality disorders . . ." Mumble, mumble. "I'll need to run a few tests. Janie can fill out a questionnaire . . ." mumble, "will help narrow . . . and rule out coexisting character pathologies and other complications as well. But based on our consultation today, and given your concerns, your daughter may be exhibiting traits of bipolar disorder."

What? There's a pause. My mother says something.

"Oh, don't worry, Mrs. Syren," replies Dr. Blessbe. "By itself, bipolar disorder is completely treatable."

There's something smooth and sticky all over me.

Oh freak, oh freak!

Panic hits me like a seizure and I'm flailing, thrashing, ripping!

I'm out of it. I'm okay. I check all my limbs, my digits. Feel my face. At least the stuff wasn't wet. Anyway, I'm in my nightie and it's pristine.

Heaving, I shove the crystalline coffin, with its insulating cocoon, right off the ledge. I don't hear it hit bottom, but I wait, trying to come to terms with where I am. Okay, I remember going to sleep last night. I remember loathing my mom, Dr. Blessbe, people in general. I remember basking hatefully in how nice it will be in a year when I graduate, because I'll finally be on my own. Vaguely, I also remember the strange presence in my room as I faded out.

Then it hits me, and I just stare at this place.

Where the freak *am* I?

Far in the distance, a deep rumble travels like the buildup of thunder through the void just beyond my ledge, and I can swear I see the scintillating cell walls move like living things. Funny, the brief panic I felt waking up is completely gone, replaced by an unpretentious curiosity. If this place is as real as it feels, I *should* be panicking.

Ironically, I realize I'm humming a tune.

A soft cracking sound from behind makes me whirl. A fissure has erupted in the wall of the cell, and strange glowing runes are wicking away the indigo-blue stone, forming a large doorway. No thought necessary, I'm instantly through it, into a glen—a field.

But I stop to look at where I've come from. You would never guess there's a whole universe of cells full of sleeping people in them just beyond that doorway. It's nothing more than a small crevice carved into a half-moon-shaped boulder that resembles a broken archway some giant's dropped in the middle of a grassy plateau. In fact, I walk around the prominence for good measure. Geeze, appearances can be deceiving.

Why *doesn't* this feel like a dream?

For days I travel, taking in the sights. I avoid the mist, explore the willow tree. Then I come to the house, where my calm flakes into panic against my will. The mist converges around the sides of the house, flanking it, barring me passage. I can't walk around to the front, unless I want to lose myself. So I go in through the back.

Anxiety hits me like a fever. And I'm out as soon as I'm in! The back door is swinging behind me, and I'm running until I hit that prominence. What (I shiver) the *hell* (I try not to vomit) are those things? I'm radiating butterflies of fear so bright I can see them. Whatever those things in my house are, I know without *proof* that if they've seen me . . . okay, there are things worse than death.

But this nightgown business. It really gets to me, and I have to go back, if only to scavenge a change of clothing from my room.

And it happens again!

Freak! After the second attempt, I vow I'm never going back in there. Ever.

My cell inside the prominence is soothing, on the other hand, so I decide to stay there, instead. Hours turn into days. Days into weeks—or so I figure. I get lost in thought so deep it turns to song. The song morphs into a burning curiosity to explore this place. And I do. Tentatively, I shimmy down to the cell below mine to visit its occupant . . .

Wasn't my fault. I swear! I couldn't wake the woman, so I hollered, shouted, pummeled her cocoon. Then I ripped it.

Either way, she didn't wake up, so I spider-climb back to my ledge, feeling guilty.

None of the men, the older woman, or that little boy whose cells adjoin mine wake up, either. None of the occupants in a ten-, twenty-, thirty-cell radius of mine wake up. No one wakes up in this place.

"HELLO!" I call into the void, hearing it rumble back.

"I'M SO ALONE!"

It's no use. I know where I am. I've been here before. Plenty of times. This is no dream, although I wish it was. I'm trapped inside the most inescapable prison conceivable.

I miss my mom . . .

I hear an echo.

I almost trip getting to my feet.

Popping my ears, I listen hard. Eons roll past like the breath of a god, but I can't hear anything. Maybe it was my imagination.

Feeling bizarrely more calm than defeated, I try

to make myself get depressed, but only achieve that hollow feeling in my stomach again—the one I've been noticing lately, like something's missing. I haven't slept a wink since those *freaks* in my house stole my body, and I'm pretty sure that's what happened to everyone else in here, too. Maybe it wasn't an accident that killed that scientist, Dr. Growlinger, after all.

Sleep. I wish I could sleep. In this place, I don't need to eat, or drink, or go to the little girl's room, or do any of those things you do when you have a physical body.

Sure, I've "tried" to sleep, if only to wake up in the real world ("tried" being the operative word.) I've slipped between the snarled roots of the willow on the grassy hill, curled up and hummed more than one lullaby.

But every time I nod off, I wind up in that sinister crystalline coffin, swaddled up like a baby. Jesus, how many of the freakin' things have I pushed off the ledge into the yawning void?

I hear another echo, this time louder.

"HELLO!" I holler.

More echoes bounce out of the darkness, and I think there is no doubt now that I'm leaving my ledge. I'll search every cell in this mammoth universe until I find someone else or die trying.

Another echo. I listen. This one rolls from somewhere to the left.

It's a direction.

I crawl.

The abyss greets me the moment I step off of my ledge, and although there is no wind here, it feels like

163

the whole place is breathing. I'm careful to keep a straight line from my cell, so I don't lose my way and find I can never get back. Getting lost in this place is as genius as wandering off into the mist. I've also long since discovered that none of the cells but mine have doorways into glens. Or anywhere for that matter.

Past cell fifty-one to the left there are good handholds. The thin, foot-wide catwalks carved naturally into the blue stone widen, although not every space between cells is this negotiable. Doesn't matter, I think. I'm actually doing it! I'm finally doing what I've been dreading since I first woke up in here, even if it means that I might never get back.

Taking rests in neighboring chambers as I go, I make sure to inspect every slumbering human. No one's awake. It's still only me. After a time, my hands chafe and my feet start to hurt. I've been at this forever, and I feel heavy. I'm in cell number one-twenty-six now.

In the distance, I see a faint orange glow.

I'm all over it.

Let's go. Let's go! I'm freaking now. For not requiring any sleep, I feel so exhausted, but strangely, it's not physical; it's mental. I pick up the pace—and practically start floating, I feel so light!

Almost there. The glow is getting warmer. If you ask me, it looks suspiciously like a campfire. And I swear, for a moment I see something arching away behind it into the void—but then it's gone.

Cell one-thirty-one.

One-thirty-two.

One-thirty-three.

The light is on above me. Palm slaps stone, I grasp

the rock of the prow and before I know it, there are hands grabbing my forearms, hauling me up. I land, flopping, like a fish on the ledge, and look around.

It takes a second, but I adjust my eyes to the roaring campfire. Through the flames, I see that I'm on an unusually long ledge jutting out of a cell the size of a 7-Eleven. And there are about thirty people staring in my direction.

Told you I heard something in the Honeycomb, Lt.," says a little boy with sandy hair and shocking green eyes. Three paces away, he has his hands tucked behind his back and is studying me inquisitively.

The man he's talking to—Lt.—is a mean-looking black man in desert camouflage and full Kevlar. He's chewing on a stogie, the same as when he pulled me onto the ledge. The assortment of people behind him, collected around the blazing campfire, are eclectic, but almost half of them look like Tibetan monks in orange robes, sitting half-lotus.

"Welcome to COP Phoenix." Lt. proffers a hand.

I squint, trying to gauge that I'm not actually hallucinating. It's been a *long* time since I've seen people—real people, not sleepers. "COP Phoenix?"

"Combat Outpost. Small base of operations. We're establishing other COPs in the Honeycomb as we expand, but this COP is alpha." His hand is still extended. "Name's First Lieutenant Jackson, United States Marine Corps."

I'm not timid. I take it.

"Strong grip." Lt. nods in approval. "Good quality in a soldier."

I look over the people clustered around the campfire

on the ledge and try to take it all in. Behind them, I notice a bridge with elaborate filigree rails which look like tree branches, arching off the side of the prow— and I've only just now noticed it, because one of the monks is strolling toward us, over its surface. In fact, I only see the bridge when I look directly at it; when I turn my head, it disappears. The glow of the campfire casts a pinkish hue over its cathedralesque facade as it spans the gap to the next chamber over. Focusing my eyes, I see another bridge beyond that—part of a network, it looks like.

My thoughts catch up with me. These people are *awake* in here!

"Probably thought you were the only one, did you?" Another man approaches. He's tall and gaunt, with a garish look in his eye, and he's dressed in an early-style 1900s English frock coat. "On the contrary. As you can see, there are plenty of us to go around."

"Plenty of Baselys, that is," drawls a young woman with chin-length amber hair. A few of the people around the campfire snicker.

"That'll be enough now, whippersnapper," says the gaunt English gentleman.

"Cool it, you two." Lt. puckers his cheeks in an odd assortment of twitches, and blows an astrolabe of smoke rings at them. "Let the girl acclimate." He points to the English gentleman. "This here is Basely. The man's always sour grapes, so don't take it personally."

"So are all of them." The amber-haired girl gestures to a bombshell of a redhead, then to a rapper-type decked out in silver, a businessman, and a dwarf in a three-piece suit with tails.

"Eh-hem," intones Basely. Tapping a foot, he eats me up with his eyes like I'm fresh meat—something he hasn't seen in forever—and waits until he has my full attention. "Young woman, allow me to introduce you to my darling Jin-Jin, superstar Pop-Fizz—double "z," Fizz—Benjamin, and Murphy the Short."

They all wave at me.

The little boy who first spoke is having a conniption, and Lt. snaps at the crowd. "Would someone please escort Sebastian off the ledge before he *chokes?*" And two of the Tibetan monks usher the boy, giggling, across the bridge.

"Basely is the lead personality," whispers the amber-haired girl in my ear.

Right now, I don't know what the freak these people are talking about, but I don't want to give myself away. Better to observe the situation first, then ask questions later.

The amber-haired girl catches my look. "Basely has dissociative identity disorder. Multiple personalities. He doesn't like anyone talking about it, though. Every one of his crowd is autonomous in the Honeycomb, with minds of their own. We even had them split up at different COPs for a while, until Tall Bill took a plunge off a ledge and vanished." She puckers her lips. "By the way, *never* mention Tall Bill in Basely's presence. It was an accident and he never came back. It wasn't like when you go to sleep outside the Honeycomb in your Unconscious Mind. Tall Bill was more or less erased from existence."

"What's the Honeycomb?" I venture, careful to conceal my awe of the eccentric people on this ledge.

"You're looking at it." Lt. gestures wide-armed at

167

the breathing universe of indigo-sapphire chambers and humans in stasis. He takes a knee, tucking a knife into a combat boot.

"The Honeycomb is the Collective Human Consciousness," giggles the little boy, who has snuck back across the bridge. "This is where we are all connected. Hi, I'm Sebastian." He puts out a hand. "*I'm* not afraid to talk about what I am."

Tentatively, I shake it.

"What are you then?" I ask.

"I'm a cranky, ninety-four-year-old man."

The kid's pulling my leg.

"He really is," asserts the amber-haired girl. "Ninety-four."

"We can't send him on recon outside the Honeycomb," adds Lt., dubiously. "Too risky. His body's on death's doorstep, but his mind . . ." He taps his temple. "Sharp as a tack. Sebastian never served in any wars before the invasion, though." Lt. shoots the boy a critical look, and Sebastian smiles and bounces on his heels.

A ninety-four-year-old man, I wonder. Then I think, wait. I have to remind myself that I'm not in physical reality here. This is *totally* interesting!

"I'm Avril, by the way," the amber-haired girl introduces herself. "And in case you're wondering, I'm an intellectual monomaniac, and I'm usually obsessed with only one kind of delirious idea."

"Don't listen to her." Lt. waves her off. "Avril has plenty of good ideas. She's one of my best."

"It's different outside the Honeycomb," Avril rebuts. "It's the same as your schizophrenia, Lt. You always tell us what it was like fighting in the war in Afghanistan, battling hallucinations, and paranoia, and delusions and disorganized thinking in the desert." Avril turns to me. "Lt.'s the de facto leader of this COP. He set it up. He organizes the missions. He's the most clear-thinking person in the Honeycomb."

Self-satisfied, Lt. blows another ring.

"And yet he still experiences six distinct states of consciousness," Sebastian clarifies. "Not the typical three, as an *aide memoire* of his condition." I clink my jaw shut; it's so weird hearing an old man's wisdom coming out of a little boy's mouth. Especially mixed with the giggling.

Lt. snorts. "Sebastian here has deduced that healthy human beings experience three states of consciousness. That's Awake, Asleep and In-Between. But this group," he gestures to the people on the ledge, "experiences at least four."

"Hence why we are each awake in the Honeycomb." Sebastian grins.

Lt. chews thoughtfully on his stogie and then takes a puff deep enough to turn an elephant green. "I've got six levels," he says, eyes closed. "Great for recon." Then his eyes pop open, and he rakes me, slit-eyed, with a stare so hot, it's burning the hairs on the back of my neck.

"Six," he repeats. "Six! I can go six places: Collective Consciousness—that's the Honeycomb. Unconsciousness, Preconsciousness, Transcendental, Alpha Wave and Waking Consciousness. Almost got caught once by the Grunge, poking around in Alpha Wave."

"The Grunge?" Now I'm really confused. "What's that?" I can't help myself. None of this talk about mental disorders and levels of consciousness is jiving. Acutely, I'm aware of that Pop-Fizz guy breathing down my neck, with his chains clanking together and his eyes lost somewhere behind his liquid shades. He's pumping out a beat with his foot, trying to coax me into following.

"Not 'what.' 'Who.'" Lt. gives me a dark look, then, singsong, courts my understanding: "The *Grunge,* dammit! They're the enemy. The body spoilers." He fills me in.

I raise a brow, trying not to freak. I think about the news broadcasts of the temples in Antarctica. "Those things in my house? *That's* what they are?"

"They came through a gateway the size of an atom," confirms Sebastian. "And to think, all this time we've been expecting them to show up on the White House lawn and ask to be taken to our leader." He winks at me. Then by way of an explanation, he continues, "They're not extraterrestrial. Rather, they're interdimensional. Incorporeal. Dr. Growlinger, that infamous scientist who was all over the news before our current—" He raises a brow. "—*predicament,* he was a colleague of mine. I told him not to thaw those pyramids. Some things are best left buried."

"Alien scum," Lt. sneers as Pop-Fizz goes snapping away and steals that redhead, Jin-Jin, for a dancing partner. "Grungy! Mark me, they won't be master of *my* body for much longer. The team, we're awake, and we're waking up others. We've launched a campaign. Pain is what they'll feel, they want bodies so bad. The Grunge are going to wish they never crossed into the physical dimension."

I'm on the cusp of a revelation here. These people are awake in the Honeycomb, while billions of others sleep, and I think I know why. I'm just not sure exactly how.

Squinting into the firelight, I study Lt., who has the perfect jawline for exuding that grim determination typical of a seriously misunderstood Marine.

"What's your name, soldier?" he asks me.

"Janie," I answer straight and flat. "Shouldn't you be calling me a 'recruit'? I mean, if you're recruiting people into your COP?" Just look at me, I think. I'm in a nightie! It's so *embarrassing.* "How do you know you can trust me?"

"Negative." Lt. wags a gloved finger. "The day the Grunge seized human bodies, you were recruited. You have no ulterior motive. If you did, we would be able to see it. You're in the Honeycomb. We can see into your mind. Literally." He taps his temple. "If you posed a threat, you would have come amongst us looking a hellova lot different than a girl in a nightgown."

And before I can pop from how red I've just turned, Sebastian pulls on Lt.'s Kevlar vest and Lt. holds up a hand. Like night terrors, the two of them retreat into the shadows of the ledge and whisper heatedly with Avril, Basely and all of Basely's personalities.

Obviously, I'm the subject of debate. Kinda rude, you think? A hard lump solidifies in my chest—the first since I've been in the Honeycomb.

One of the Tibetan monks from around the campfire tries to hand me something just then, and, distracted, I make to turn it down. But then I can smell it, steamy and rich, curling into my nostrils. A heaping bowlful of rice.

Previous thoughts evaporating, I stare at it like it's going to disappear.

"Eat," says the oldest of the monks, a twinkle in his eye. "Rice has no feet to walk away on."

I'm flummoxed. "I don't understand. How did you get food?" I don't see any silverware or chopsticks anywhere. The rice is sticky enough that the monks are eating it with their hands, scooping in mouthfuls with their middle and index fingers, like spoons.

Then I think, who cares! The smell is so intense; I inhale the entire bowlful! And it's only rice!

Strangely, I don't feel full. Only mildly satiated. One by one, I pop the last few grains into my mouth and curl them onto my tongue, savoring their flavor.

"We recall our food," replies the older monk, whom I gather is named "Lobsang," based on how several of his companions are addressing him while they collect the bowls.

Faces passive, the monks peer at me after they've seated themselves around the campfire again. I count sixteen of them.

"The mind is the seat of perception." Lobsang looks at me askew. "All that we perceive through the body is produced in the mind. The mind is the nerve center. And through the mind, you may create or prevent the effects of perception." He points to the space between his eyes.

His English is very good. Setting aside my bowl, I curl my knees under my nightie, wrap my arms around them and hum softly. Lt. and the others are still conversing on the ledge, by the void. It makes me feel more exposed than ever.

Lobsang claps his hands, making me jump.

"Look! I have hypnotized you!" he exclaims. "You have freely accepted my food and eaten it to the last grain of rice, taking for granted what is not actually there!"

Jolted back to his smiling, enigmatic face, I notice that the sixteen other monks are smiling too. Obviously, I've missed something here.

"Do you see?" says Lobsang. "You have eaten an illusion, yet it was no less real. Like the garments you choose to wear."

Now I feel like I've been caught stealing. Don't they know this is humiliating? Lobsang's smile is mischievous.

"All products of the mind," he asserts. "You cloak yourself in vulnerability with this sleeping garment."

I curl into a tighter ball. But Lobsang leans forward, and for a moment, he hums a harmony to the tune I'm making up.

I taper off . . .

"All realities are in your mind," he says, the Honeycomb's network of bridges glimmering in his eyes. "Here in the Chamber of Perception, you may garb yourself in whatever you wish, eat whatever you wish, when you wish it. We are gods in our own minds, and we create worlds inside them. Hum?"

His smile is fantastic. I look down at my hands and realize I'm holding a bowl of cereal and a spoon.

"Did you—"

"No." Lobsang shakes his head. "You did." Then

just like that, he goes back to eating a second bowl of rice.

"He's perfectly healthy," Avril whispers over my shoulder, returning. "Teacher Lobsang and his students have learned to disassociate themselves from their waking conscious minds. They don't have fragmented personalities like the rest of us have."

Ecstatic, I put aside my cereal bowl. I can't believe that having a mental disorder is the key to being awake in here. It's insane. With the exception of maybe Basely, everyone seems pretty normal to me. But then again, looking closer from one person to another along the prominence, I recognize the pieces of whole individuals, which is like looking through a filter. Like looking in a mirror.

"That's the ticket." Avril pats my arm. "Anything that helps people fragment their personalities in order to survive the vegetative state of the Honeycomb. But like I said, Lobsang and his students are the real exception. They're our secret weapon for waking up sleepers. The sleepers have relatively healthy minds, you see, which is why they're asleep, but if you wake them up?" She snaps her fingers. "They experience sudden fragmentation, which can drive a healthy person mad. They go into denial. We've lost people off ledges that way, and once they disappear into the void . . ." She shrugs, cryptically. "We've also lost people the other way, too. They'll go wandering off into their other layers of consciousness outside the Honeycomb and never return. Or get put back to sleep by the Grunge. Lt. says it's bad for business."

"It *is* bad for business," Lt. remarks, rejoining us

with Sebastian, Basely and his motley crew. He nods respectfully to Lobsang, who nods back. "In here, you're not shunned as crazy or sick. Fractured minds are what're needed to wake up the human race and reclaim what's ours. But we can't do it alone. We need more consciousnesses."

"Indeed, the fractured of mind need not be trapped." Lobsang magics away his empty bowl of rice with a trick of his hands. Delighted, I see the faintest hint of a lotus flower hanging in space where the bowl was, before it, too, disappears in a coil of purple smoke. "The fractured of mind can be utilized to see what others cannot and express what is seen in a meaningful way. The only difference between an artist and a schizophrenic is that the artist can express what she sees. Information by itself is fixed, but perception makes that information unique to the individual, in essence changing it. The individual alters reality."

"Just read the Good Book," agrees Lt., who's pretty traditional. "Everyone important in there woulda been diagnosed with something these days. God always did like people with issues. Maybe that's what it means to be made in his image."

He paces toward a doorway in the chamber, beyond the campfire, and I've just deduced that this is his ledge and campfire, because this is his COP. His doorway isn't that dissimilar from mine, either.

"Come with me, Janie girl." He gestures to the doorway. "It's been agreed. You're to be briefed on Outer Recon. What say you help us spy on the Grunge?"

I have to ask it before it kills me. "What exactly do the Grunge want?" I step over the threshold. "I mean, if these things invaded our minds, basically stole our bodies overnight, what do they want? I don't understand."

Outside the doorway, I plunge into sand and rock up to my ankles. Lt.'s inner sanctuary isn't a sparkling glen like mine; it's a desert, a wasteland of shrubs beyond a sea of dunes and a ridgeline of tree-covered mountains that erupt like moldy fangs in a mouth of blue far away in the atmosphere. Afghanistan. This must be where Lt. feels at peace.

There's something else, too. I'm wearing combat boots, just like Lt.'s.

"Well, well, well." One of Basely's personalities, Benjamin, I think (the one in the business suit), points rudely at my feet. "A fast learner."

I didn't do anything, I think in stark amazement. I swear!

"Most excellent." The little boy, Sebastian, rubs his hands. "Lobsang's teachings are like the falling of small pebbles that create an avalanche."

Tromping behind, Lt. is clapping. Though, true to his earlier warning, Basely's expression is one hundred percent sour grapes. Probably because I'm getting all the attention—and I didn't have to split myself up for it.

I feel a fluttering sensation in my chest and the world goes spinning. Oops . . . I guess the boots have made me anxious. Teacher Lobsang did this, I think? No, *I* did. Lobsang only encouraged me to do it. But how?

"Calm down, girl. I know you have smarts in your

head." Lt. anchors me by the arm and slips on a set of sunglasses. "You didn't climb all the way to this COP just because you have a pair. Look at how you're dressed. You were probably wearing that sleepwear the night the Grunge took us on, right? Practical. Now look at your feet. Adaptable. What makes sense to you probably doesn't make sense to others, but that's why you're awake in the Honeycomb and about 7.9 billion people aren't."

He stoops down, chews the butt off a new stogie and draws a maze in the sand with a finger. "Let me put it to you straight and quick. The Grunge, they're a psionic race. That means they can get into your head. And since you're not a vegetable like the rest of everyone in the Honeycomb, you have the capacity to adequately react to them invading your mind. Now, the unit at COP Phoenix—those of us with the capability, that is—we go on the offensive. We do reconnaissance into waking consciousness—"

"Our Modus Operandi," Sebastian contributes, and Lt. shoots him a bullish look.

"*And,* it's my belief you'd fit right in." He takes a pull on his stogie. "But what you need to understand, so that you're not apprehended, is that the Grunge came for the experience. You say you want to know what they want." Rising, he flicks his stogie into the sand and stubs it out with the toe of his boot. "We've seen it. They wear human bodies like clothing, like skin, in order to experience the physical world. To taste food and drink. To listen to music in waveform instead of through math. To smell nature, progress, and pollution. To enjoy sex. To see through human eyes. What this unit at COP Phoenix is accomplishing is the gathering of intel. The more we know about the Grunge, the more chances we have to discover a weakness and exploit it. We've begun by collecting those who are awake in the Honeycomb and establishing COPs."

"Is that what the bridges are for?" I ask, thinking of the elaborate network of filigree arches that expand from Lt.'s ledge into the void. "Ways to get to the other COPs?"

"Teacher Lobsang and his students weave them," Sebastian answers with pride. He's creating highways in the sand with the heel of his sneaker, all the way from the point where Lt. buried his smoke. "We've seen campfires and lights on distant ledges and have heard voices. This is how we found Avril. She made a campfire to signal with. A very clever idea."

I'm so engrossed, I've just now realized I'm humming again and it's making my feet tingle. The hollow feeling in my stomach has receded—some.

Lt. goes on, "Before the establishment of COP Phoenix, I was sweeping the closest alcoves and found the first survivors. The first awakened minds. Teacher Lobsang and his students were amongst them. They alone are responsible for the bridges. The sheer power of mind they exhibit is phenomenal. And it's a boon, too, because as we speak, the unit is moving further and further into the Honeycomb, in search of others, via the bridges. The more COPs we establish, the more the human race can reconnect and establish an opposition. Currently, we have fifteen COPs. But it ain't easy."

I look Lt. in the eye. "You used to do this in real life," I tell him, matter-of-fact, "establish COPs."

Lt. nods slowly and admits, "I was a commissioned officer on a transition team of advisors to the Afghani military." For a moment, he looks at the mountains. "That billet was training," then he bores into me, "for this."

Butterflies collide in my stomach and that tingling feeling expands up my legs. Somehow I feel the same; I can't explain it. I think I was meant to fight. Designed. Fated. Mom always said I was a leaf on the wind. But none of us in here appear irrational now. No sane person could have ever foreseen *this* kind of war.

"Basely is the only one of his personalities stable enough to do recon," Avril whispers to me behind her hand, for good measure, and Basely turns up his nose.

"Soldier! Just look at you!" exclaims Lt., and I do. I look.

Holy freak!

I'm no longer in my nightie. I'm . . . I look like a member of some kind of sci-fi special forces or something. Only practical. None of those high-heeled bimbo boots that flash sex but would kill a girl in combat. Freak! This is real. Flesh-colored synthetic armor, like a second skin. Utility belt. Compact energy weapons and demolitions. Thick gloves with brass knuckles. A camel pack on my back.

I feel my hair. It's slicked severely to my head in a braided bun.

Mother would approve.

Well, maybe of the function, but not the look—ha!

Basely and Avril are amazed. Sebastian is giggling maniacally into his hand. Even Lt. looks caught off guard, although he's hiding it behind a smug grin, his sunglasses and the comment: "'Bout time someone projected this look." With a shriek, Basely's personality, Jin-Jin, who's been hovering like a fly in the threshold to the Honeycomb, flees back inside and comes out with the entire COP in tow.

My moment of glory is ruined. They're *staring*. Mentally, I claw at the suit, trying to keep it on, trying to force myself not to pop right back into my nightie. "Um, so I suppose you can all do recon?" I wonder out loud.

"Negative." Lt. shakes his head. Angrily, he signals everyone back inside and only he, Avril, Sebastian and myself remain in his desert, his unconscious mind.

"We've gathered that by now, the Grunge have effectively possessed the bodies of every human soul ever born," he tells me. "But after they invaded through that gate of theirs, from whatever dimension they came from, there were still humans with strong enough minds to contend with them. At least at one point. The Grunge called these people 'Prize Raiment.'" Lt. spits. "Utter debasement."

"Teacher Lobsang was one such," Sebastian clarifies, winking at me as I continue to check myself out. "But he disassociated his mind from his body before it was too late. The same with his students, but they insist that they did not hold out as long as he did."

"Yep." Lt. hooks my camel pack on correctly, then thumps me. "Teacher Lobsang tells us that Prize Raiment were hunted, sought after for their strength of mind and will. Those who were caught but couldn't be broken have all been terminated, and it's undetermined if there are any left, or if their minds have been, eh, 'overthrown.'"

180

Lt. glares in the direction of the harsh sun. It's very hot in his desert. Just the fact that I can feel the heat is due to far more than my willing suspension of disbelief—I get it now. It's just like Teacher Lobsang's rice: I *assume*. I take for granted. My mind is creating the heat, not the sun. Lt.'s mind is creating the image; I'm just experiencing the effects. Yes!

"Lobsang's physical body is a Prize Raiment," Lt. maintains, "so it's closely guarded and usually possessed by a cadre of Grunge. Makes it damn near impossible for him to do any recon into his own waking consciousness." He adjusts my utility belt roughly and steps back for a look. "Trust me, we need all the help we can get."

"None of his students dare to do recon, for the same reasons," adds Sebastian. "Instead, they are happily weaving the bridges and welcoming newcomers, like you." He wiggles his brows.

I can't help myself. I have to ask this one thing—it's absurd, I know. One of the stupidest questions that can possibly occur to me (crazy, psycho). "But why is everyone speaking English?" I blurt. I mean, I'm thinking Basely, Sebastian and Lobsang all have accents, and sure, English may be the business language of the world, but come on!

With his fingers, Sebastian makes the "Live long and prosper" sign from *Star Trek* and says, "Universal communicator," before giggling into a fist.

"Telepathy just works like that." Avril pats my arm. "Your mind automatically translates what's being said."

"But everyone's lips are moving in sync with the words," I retort. I know, I'm being a smart ass. What?

181

"It's all perception." Sebastian looks approvingly at my feet.

I do too. I'm hovering about three inches off the ground.

"Now *there's* perception," Lt. muses, and I crash into the sand with a gasp. He bends over me, hand propped on a knee, his silhouette blotting out the sun. "Ever wonder why time goes so slow when you're feelin' pain?" he asks me. "At that moment, your adrenaline is pumping. Everything becomes magnified. You're consciously aware of every little thing. Details fill up your perception from moment to moment and elongate time. Details that were already there, but you wouldn't have noticed them otherwise, like you're doing now. That's perception. It works like your ability to fragment. Like how you created that armor for yourself. Like how you were just floating. We do this in our dreams all the time, but very few people have control over their dreams. Damn, soldier—you're a quick learner!"

I'm floating again. It must be like what the good doctor said to my mom all that time ago: manipulation. How I can turn a situation on a dime to my advantage. Guess I never figured manipulation was exactly a positive talent.

Pretty freaky.

My feet touch down—gracefully this time.

Lt. pulls another stogie from his vest, and I can see it in his face: he's ready for my presence on their team.

But what he doesn't know is how ready *I* am for this.

Christina, a shy girl in her early twenties with long black hair, hands me an apple tart. She has body dysmorphic disorder (or so I've been told), which means that she's excessively preoccupied with an imagined or minor defect in her physical features. Screw that. She's the most beautiful person in this ragtag group. One of the most beautiful people I've ever seen. You know, if having a fragmented personality affects your state of mind when you're awake, it's sure serving its purpose in the Honeycomb. I wonder what all of these people really look like in real life, what they act like. Teacher Lobsang and his students are probably the only ones who actually equate to "what you see is what you get."

Right now, the team at COP Phoenix is having dinner. Not that we need to eat. It's just for the camaraderie and the experience. If the freakin' Grunge could imagine their physical experiences, they wouldn't need our bodies as scientific instruments to measure them by.

Freaks.

Lt. has gone off with Basely and Murphy the Short to COP Evergreen on convoy. One of Teacher Lobsang's students, Chophel, has devised a clever way to tell time in here: If each full breath of the Honeycomb walls can be equated to one minute of time, and the walls undulate in waves, an hour has passed by the time one wave flows out of the darkness of the left of the void, all the way into the right. After twenty-five hours, there is a natural respiratory pause during what would normally be another full wave, so the monks mark this as a day. A twenty-five-hour day.

Lt., Basely and Murphy the Short have followed the time wave over the filigree bridges, into the indigo-blue unknown, and the team at COP Phoenix is keeping track of their departure time. The math involved in their coming and going against the moving waves goes right over my head, but I'll take Chophel's word for it.

This is the perfect opportunity for me to return to my house.

Noiselessly, while everyone is engrossed in jovial conversation around the campfire, I slip off the prow of the ledge and scoot along the side of the Honeycomb. I travel beyond the other ledges, all the way back to my own, humming my own marching orders. For the first time, I have a plan. For the first time ever, I have hope.

And I'm not afraid.

The woman in the cell next to mine is still sleeping. My glen is as sparkling as ever when I enter it. I wade through the grass in full battle gear, past the willow on the hill, to my house, where my Mirror Image is begging me not to go in.

Slipping through the back door, I gently close it behind me.

The kitchen is spotless and pristine and bathed in a golden halo of light from the window over the sink. The entire house is in sepia tones, actually. Just the way I remember it. Mind you, it's not necessarily the way it *was;* this is just my glorified memory of it. My parents' renovated 1800s Victorian. No sign yet of the filthy little imposters who've taken up residence.

The Grunge kind of remind me of the house, as a matter of fact. One thing to look at on the façade, quite another on the inside.

Cautiously, I step through a mote-infested beam of sunlight.

"Janie!" My Mirror Image has materialized across the kitchen by the back of the staircase, and her whisper is a quiet scream. "Janie!" Plastered to the wall, she's marching her finger through the air toward the dining room and the front of the stairs. "In there."

I scuttle around the staircase, over the dining room carpet to her, burning my hands and knees. Slipping through the trap stair into the crawl space between the first and second landings where the staircase switches back on itself, I get one last glimpse of her in the hallway. Then I'm plunged into semidarkness and the scratching sound of her latching the wooden flap behind me momentarily fills the silence.

Just in time too. A presence flits by the vent.

My heart is thudding in my chest, but I wait. An inordinate amount of time slogs by before I finally chance a peek out the vent. Through the horizontal grates I see only the kitchen. Maybe it's my imagination playing tricks on me. Maybe my Mirror Image was wrong. But I think not.

In ways other than appearance, My Mirror Image is very different from looking in the mirror. Usually when you see yourself, it's a reflection, void of its own thought or substance. Immaterial. But like any person when the situation calls for it, I'll get angry or frightened, and she's simply a piece of me, only broken off. More than fear, when I'm a microfilament away from losing my life, I've come to the conclusion during my time at COP Phoenix that she's the flesh-and-blood projection of me who can and always will direct my evasion. My conscience and soul. A completely alien person. And I've decided to use her—finally.

Fear being instinct, she's me from about thirty or forty seconds into the future.

"Janie . . ." My Mirror Image has just manifested at my side. She's pulling on my arm.

I tuck my knees to my chin in the darkness, holding my breath. I'm waiting for the tumult of feet pounding down the stairs—though why I always think the Grunge will be noisy completely eludes me. Heat-of-the-chase emotion is a human thing and these freaks are usually discordantly silent. I could turn around to find one standing in the kitchen, staring in at me through the slits in the vent. They're so quiet.

I still don't hear anything.

Freak! . . . I catch myself before I bang the back of my head against the crawl space in frustration.

"Janie." My Mirror Image is pulling on my arm again, and suddenly, a shadow blots out the lines of light issuing through the vent.

I choke on my saliva.

It's looking, it's looking—oh freak!

My Mirror Image puts a hand over my mouth and nose. Bringing a finger to her lips, she shakes her head austerely.

I can't breathe. I start dry heaving. Little lights are popping behind my eyes . . .

The shadow recedes. So does the hand over my mouth and nose. And just like that, my Mirror Image is nowhere to be seen.

I'm beyond ecstatic. I would have already been caught without her; this I know. I've never made it as far as the crawl space before, and I think, what's that old adage? Courage isn't the absence of fear; it's the continuation in the presence of it?

Dead silence fills the crawl space. After a million years, I open the latch on the trap stair, and softly, inch by inch, peer out.

How about that. The Grunge must have gone back to watching TV on the sofa in the great room—I can see the blue glow of the TV flickering on the walls. Little freaks. They were doing this the last two times I entered my house. I figure it's their version of going to sleep. Well, if you're incorporeal, you don't have a body to recharge . . . but apparently you still get bored, and the alpha waves produced by the TV are so hypnotic. The Grunge are totally vegging out! And I have a hunch it's because the human body they've stolen—*my* body—needs exactly eight hours of sleep every night to operate at maximum capacity for them. Guess you have to do something while you wait.

TV.

What a riot!

I don't dare go near the living room, though, as I creep from the stairs. My sense of self-preservation is healthy, thank you very much. I've already seen what these freaks look like from a distance, and I don't plan on reinforcing that image by getting close.

One of the Grunge rises from the couch—just appears on the other side without physically moving. Teleports. The other copies on the other side of the armchair. And they're both sniffing. Alert.

God! Fear, anger and general anxiety dump into

my chest like a cannonball hitting water, and I shiver against my will. Sweat is trickling in rivulets down my temples.

The Grunge. They're childlike, innocent, with pale lavender skin. Hairless. They have no parts—you know? Phosphorescent runes scroll down their temples, terminating in softly glowing eyes the size of galaxies, their irises the shape of discs crosscutting discs and the multicolor of amethysts rotating on every possible angle under light. Similar runes helix down their arms and legs, around their chests and torsos, in code. They flush from head to toe, arcs of plasma trailing from their silhouettes when they stand perfectly still. They're beautiful. I can't stop staring at them.

Except that they're monstrous.

When one opens its mouth, it's like it's got the whole universe down its gullet. A silent tone thunders out, so terrible I can see the sound waves ripple the air. I don't know a better way to explain it—it sounds nonsensical, seriously—but I think they *are* universes. Actual physical *universes.* Each one simply wearing the shape it believes makes the most sense to human beings.

When you say aliens and I say demons, we both end up in the same place. I'd rather deal with the Devil. Straightforward evil at least I can understand—maybe.

Freaks.

The front door is past the great room. Disgusted, I squelch another shiver, close my eyes and make myself concentrate. Then, taking a deep breath . . . I project.

This time, when I see her, my Mirror Image isn't at my side. She's in the utility room, in full view of the Grunge.

And they're off. Ugh, I *hate* the way they move! Zip, zip, zip, from point to point in little spurts, at the speed of thought, without moving their legs. Like birds' heads. There's no tracking. And they're all over my Mirror Image.

As she screams, I move to the foyer and open the front door. I blot out the horror behind me.

Wraithlike, I slip into waking consciousness.

Janie, love, are you feeling all right?"

Mother is standing over my bed, stroking my forehead. I'm back in my nightie and the cotton sheets tangled snugly between my legs feels good.

I take my mom in, absorbing the lines of her face. She's in her business suit, and she looks every bit herself.

I don't answer. A wrong word, even a wrong movement, could give me away.

And without warning it comes: my anger. That irrational, turn-on-a-dime *anger* I haven't felt since . . . well, since I was in my body. In three seconds, I've gone from zero to sixty.

Calm down, calm down, I tell myself, desperately, rationally. Just put an ice cube in it. The Grunge are psionic. They'll pick up on my emotions no matter how good an actress I am, no matter how normal and casual I pretend to be on the outside. Freak!

I smile. It's well placed and calculated.

Smiling in answer, Mom pats my legs and says, "Let's get some breakfast."

Wariness creeps in now. This was not what I expected. But then, I think, what *did* I expect? That the Grunge would be running wild down Fifth Avenue in my body? Using it to do any number of insane or unthinkable things? For a moment, I'm tempted to believe that I've only been dreaming.

Perfectly awake but in control, at least for the moment, I act groggy and follow my mom downstairs.

She turns on the news and makes herself some toast. Out of the corner of my eye, I watch her and hesitantly pour myself a bowl of cereal.

Everything is alarmingly normal. Even the news. It's droning on about the usual: missing children, Hollywood scandals, political upheaval, race riots, war. Nothing about temples, ETs or Antarctica.

I'm not normal, though.

"I bet you're excited about graduation, Janie," Mom says, seating herself at the breakfast nook with a newspaper.

Graduation? A discrepancy? If this is real, I must have been lost in myself for over a year. Then I think, why isn't my mom reading my mind? If there are Grunge inside her, why can't they see that it's me, Janie, and not their buddies looking out through my eyes?

My mom smiles at me over her newspaper. It's genuine and warm. Full of love.

Feeling that knot in my stomach and the butterflies crowding into my chest again, I eat my cereal and it tastes good. There is nothing malevolent in my mother's eyes. Whatever's using her body truly does love me—or at least, it loves the experience of loving me. Maybe, I let myself think for a moment, it really is her. Maybe . . .

"I love you, Janie," my mom says.

It returns; I suddenly feel so angry, I can't think! I have to stop myself from smashing my bowl on the floor.

Calm down. It's not really her, I try to reason with myself. Sing, that's what I always do in the Honeycomb. I feel calm there, and song is the product of that calm.

I try to sing now, to calm myself.

But it just comes out as shouting. "You don't love me!" I accuse her. "You're just trying to make me into you! Trying to make me fit in with everyone else! But I'm me, and I'm different, and that means something!" I'm thinking of the team at COP Phoenix, and I know that's where I belong.

The Grunge came for the experience. Lt.'s briefing flicks me between the eyes. *They wear human bodies like clothing, like skin, in order to experience the physical world. To taste food and drink. To listen to music in waveform instead of through math. To smell nature, progress and pollution. To enjoy sex. To see through human eyes.*

The Grunge are an explorer race; that is suddenly crystal clear to me like it never was before. They either don't know or don't care that they're enslaving human beings. They're here to experience precisely what humans experience, in the way that we experience it, and they're unmindful of the fact that they've put us all in a stasis while they observe and explore our world. It's not maliciously intended. It just is.

But unlike the Grunge, human beings have more than minds. We have souls.

191

The Grunge have to be stopped.

"Hi, Janie."

This time there's something different in Mom's voice. Something . . . hypnotic. "You have such lovely eyes. Can I look at them up close?"

Ugh! I squeeze my eyes shut and feel like I'm going to vomit. All the air rushes out of my lungs in a punch, and without warning, I'm toppling into the sepia-tone version of my house again, in my battle gear. I've just tripped backwards through the threshold and hit my elbows on the wooden bamboo floor. My Mirror Image, I notice, is looking well—at least for her. She's perched by the stairwell and appears truly horrified. She claws her cheeks.

It's the anger. Why do I always get so *angry*? They've caught me. And it's because I always lose control and it ruins everything!

Of course, the two Grunge inside my mind are peering from the utility room like curious children.

I crawl to the window.

No. Outside, another Grunge is flitting like an apparition up the walkway. No. I can't believe it. No, no, *no*. It's the one from inside my mother. Zip, zip, zip, it's approaching the front porch, coming into my mind with the others, and I'm scraping to get to my feet. Clawing the floor.

There's nothing I can think to do but run. What did Lt. say about Prize Raiment? Once they're caught, they're either broken—as in permanent vegetation—or terminated?

I flee to the back door and bolt through, stopping only to close it quietly from the other side—as if the

Grunge haven't just witnessed me exit stage right like a blinking Vegas neon light.

For an irrational moment I think, maybe they can't come in here. The glen is my safe place. I've escaped the house. And my mind is strong. I've fooled them for this long into thinking I've been in a stasis with the rest of the human race, perfectly contained and out of the way. They can't follow me. I'll lose them.

One foot, then the other, I step backwards through the grass. My eyes are glued to the back door, and it fades slowly into the mist.

Slowly, with a creak, the door opens.

Freak! Little moles, they have their eyes shut! Or . . . I can't tell through the mist. No, they do! They're here. Sniffing for me.

Their eyes open.

My stomach bottoms out, and I turn and run.

What was I thinking? My confidence melts into sludge. My exit plan was so transparent: just "tap in" for a while, then retreat by falling back to sleep, totally bypassing my house, then bring the information to the COP in the Honeycomb. Instead, I've gone and sabotaged things. My mom, she's the only person who has a clue as to what I am. Why did it have to be my *mom*? Why didn't I just assume it *would* be her?

There's nowhere to go. The Grunge are in my *glen* now. How could I let this happen? My first time out of the house and it's curtains, just like Avril said.

Okay, I'm usually good at thinking on my feet. So? I tell myself. Improvise.

"Janie." My Mirror Image manifests by my side and

runs fleet-footed through the grass with me. She's in a nightie and I'm in my battle gear, but she's fizzling out, like a bad cable connection. "You're always so impulsive, aren't you?" she says, before blinking out completely at the threshold of the hill. She has little to no power in my glen, and none whatsoever in the Honeycomb. I'm on my own now.

Down the hill, through the grass, I flee, into the mist perimeter. I can lose the Grunge in here, I think desperately. They're zipping after me, looking for all the world like curious sojourners as they go. As if this is a game.

Sadistic!

I circle wide, coming around to the house again. The wind is in my hair and I think, was God fractured when he made us? I don't know, but I'm starting to believe it.

Here we go, come get me. I open the back door, if only to make it appear as if I've gone back inside. Quickly, I then steal around the other side of the glen, wary of where I'm stepping in the mist, and make my way to the prominence. If I'm lucky, they'll just get lost in the mist.

Hours go by. Days. There's only one good place for me to hide. I don't see the Grunge anywhere. In light of what I'm about to do, the blood rushes in my ears. Cautiously, I duck into the Honeycomb. I'm a ghost in the darkness.

Zip, zip, zip.

Despair is a tidal force that follows them in, a slow-moving breaker of inky darkness, the capstone on my pyramid of failure, a whirlpool I'm suddenly drowning in. Every finger, every toe, my temples,

HUNTER BONYUN

throat and glands, my taut heart—my whole existence—suddenly registers a deep-sinking *pain*. Even the Honeycomb can't stave it off now. Despair is the ultimate me. The crushing force just behind the anger (the bitter rage!) and it's finally, after all this time, caught up with me in here.

I've just led the Grunge into the Honeycomb. Me. I've compromised the entire human race.

Like phosphorescent fish hunting prey, they come with their pretty lights. Three of them: the two from inside my Preconscious Mind and the one from inside my mother's.

There's only one way into the Honeycomb from my glen, and one way out. And now they're here. Seriously, I should have just let them catch me. Torture me. Murder me. I'm selfish. I need to survive. But I've always been "just surviving." Survival is everything life has ever been about for me, no matter how hard I've tried to will it otherwise. No matter how hard I've tried to reason with myself.

The black cloud of despair envelops me. Then it shrugs off my back like a cloak and presses me callously against the wall inside my cell. My despair is so profound, I don't care. I'm a rag doll in its grip. I ball my hands into fists, throw my head back.

And realize I'm singing.

Deep and far, the song I'm crying is of utter longing—and I simply release it. Coils of shimmering music, my very essence, pour from my lips in flowering colors: indigo, blue, violet, crimson, blush. I bring my hands to my face—then move them away, as if pushing off to fly, as if pushing away all regret.

My tears are glistening descants. Visible song replaces my battle gear until I'm flowing with harmonies, my hair a buoyant shock of chords. And the music is gushing out of me like a power.

A single tone answers. A silent, powerful shock-wave. Two more follow. It's the Grunge.

Zip, zip, zip.

Darkness and color, music and despair, lure them closer. I've backed all the way to the edge of my ledge. The void is waiting to claim me. They're coming. I look behind me into that black nonexistence. Closer.

I'm singing!

From out of the tangled mass of color, music, darkness and noise, the closest Grunge reaches a hand for me.

And then they've passed, as I faint dead away over a rock in my prominence, bits of song falling like hissing diamonds all around me.

Janie?" Someone's calling.

I feel a dull throbbing in my temples. But my chest no longer feels hollow. Instead, I feel . . . relief.

There's a cry, followed by silence.

I wait through the death and rebirth of eternity before I open my eyes. My musical cloud of desolation has rolled off the ledge—along with apparently the Grunge, because I don't see them anywhere. And there are people running toward me from somewhere far off.

"Janie!" Sebastian squeals, braking just shy of my head. The rest of the cloud disperses and I see bridges behind him, recently constructed, arching out of the darkness to my ledge. Half of COP Phoenix is standing on the one closest.

"Janie." Sebastian grabs my forearms, yanking me up. "They went over! They did! We saw them. They went right over the ledge into the void!"

Lt. is right behind him with Basely. He's panting slightly and looks pissed off.

"Are you stupid?" he reams me out. "Girl, you could've gotten everyone killed! Why didn't you stay at the COP? You've got no real training yet." I see the slightest hint of a smile working his upper lip.

"Tall Bill." A wide-eyed Basely is pointing feverishly at the void. "He fell off the ledge and never came back." Basely shakes me. "Tall Bill was a part of me. The day he fell off that ledge, a part of me was unmade."

Then it sinks in. The Grunge from inside me are gone. Gone forever, I think, hardly believing it.

Lt. is the next one to grab me in a pincer grip, and he spins me around so that I'm facing him, while decisions, plans and epiphanies move across his features like waves in the Honeycomb. "Dammit, soldier, that was ignorant. The most foolhardy—" He shakes his head. "—and frankly genius tactical maneuver I've ever seen. How long have you been planning it?"

I make to answer, but wind up smirking instead, because for the first time, as I observe the mismatched, ragtag team from COP Phoenix, I feel completely whole.

"Game plan," Sebastian fills in the blank, saying it all.

"Welcome to Outer Recon," Lt. agrees. Pumping my hand, he slaps my back.

I am codename Siren. I lure constituents of the alien race known as the Grunge into my body. One by one, I bait them into my holy of holies, the interface between my waking consciousness and my soul—my sparkling glen.

I seduce them through the door to the Honeycomb, where the Collective Human Consciousness sleeps, waiting to take back their god-given bodies. I tempt them into the darkness, where I watch them fall off the ledge, into the void, one by one.

The more Grunge who cease to exist, the more of humankind can reclaim the right to exist in the way we were made to exist.

And I'm not alone.

There will be other sirens. I am the first. But the team from COP Phoenix is waking up more sleepers every day. We're training them. Their will is strong. The erudition is spreading.

One day soon, we'll be free.

Contact Authority

written by

William Mitchell

illustrated by

RHIANNON TAYLOR

ABOUT THE AUTHOR

William Mitchell was born in 1973, just three months after the last man walked on the Moon. Which means that in his lifetime, no human has gone more than four hundred miles from the surface of the Earth. So perhaps it's this slow pace of real-life progress that has made him turn to fiction to see how the continued conquest of space might play out.

He started writing ten years ago, finding early success with horror rather than science fiction. More recently he has returned to SF, with a scattering of small-press publications and a couple of novels underway. Having read a number of Writers of the Future anthologies and come away feeling as if his imagination had been stretched in twenty different ways at once, he started entering in 2009, achieving a finalist position at the first attempt. This winning story was his third entry and his first professional sale. He is also a member of the London-based writers group "The T-Party."

His day job is in aerospace engineering (he admits to being a rocket scientist when pressed). With a full-time job and a family at home he has to be quite creative in finding time to write and gets most of it done standing up on the London

Underground during rush hour, typing with his thumbs into a PDA he bought on eBay. His contest-winning story was written that way, plus a few tens of thousands of words before that. If his thumbs give out before PC-neural interfaces are developed, he's in trouble.

ABOUT THE ILLUSTRATOR

Rhiannon Taylor works as a freelance artist and writer in Chicago, Illinois. She is known for her maniacal focus, driven work ethic and sense of humor. Her art reflects fantasy and sci-fi elements or themes, and often illustrates her written stories. A Wacom tablet and Photoshop are her chosen arms in the grand battle of visual artistic expression. She has won numerous art awards, such as the Triton Art Show awards for first, second and third place and a $10,000 scholarship for her art. She has published both her art and her fiction writing. Her work is on display at a permanent exhibit in downtown Chicago. She currently attends Columbia College Chicago studying fiction writing and illustration. In her spare time, she puts together online articles on writing, book reviews and free art tutorials. She also applies her creativity to cooking, though she has no plans to pursue a culinary career.

Contact Authority

From this distance the gas giant filled the window, ten Jupiters' worth of roiling hydrogen and helium, a glowing expanse of turbulent orange cloud banks circled by rings of slate-gray ice. The moon system alone could occupy researchers for a generation—over a hundred in total, ranging from the frozen outer bodies to the quartet of inner moons, trading surface matter at a rate of ninety thousand tons a day as they flew through a tube of shared volcanic ejecta, making the inner ring glow like a mist of radioactive lava.

Kaluza Station was orbiting at half a million miles, away from the worst of the radiation, but with field readings high enough to mask any stray RF emissions it might give out. A good place to hide, and a necessary measure considering why it was here. Optical signature was still an issue though, so even the running lights and internal illumination had to be dimmed—going dark, in every sense. As a result, the planet's reflected glow gave the rec room an insipid orange light as Jared Spegel sat by the window, killing the downtime between shifts.

"It's stunning, isn't it?"

"What?" Jared turned away from the view, unaware that someone had sat down opposite him.

"I don't think I ever get tired of looking at it. Do you?" The girl was young, early twenties or so, wearing the general-purpose fatigues of the Green Shift workers. One of the researchers probably, maybe a biologist or a historian.

"Yeah, I guess so," he said.

"You're Jared, aren't you? Jared Spegel?"

"That's right."

"You work in Remote Observation? Running the satellite nets?"

"Yeah."

"Look, can I ask you something?"

"Sure."

She got up from the table and moved round next to him, then leant over as if to whisper in his ear.

"I want you to come with me now. Just get up and follow me, and don't make a sound. Got it?"

He felt something jabbing into his side, two prongs that could only be a Taser. Her tone had changed too, far from the breezy chatty air she'd given off at first. He got up slowly, then moved toward the door as she kept in close at his side. The rec room was almost deserted, but still not the place to get into a tussle. But if the hallway was empty—he weighed up his options, thinking back to his Operative training, visualizing the moves he could pull to dodge the Taser and put her on the ground before she had time to react. Then they got to the door and out into the hall. Two station guards stood there waiting; she acknowledged them with a nod and they fell into position on either side. Any chance he might have had was now gone.

"Where are you taking me?" he said.

"Commander's office," was her reply.

So who the hell are you?" The station commander sat behind his desk, his black military fatigues covered in patches from various postings he'd filled before taking on the unique responsibilities of this job. The name "Anderson" was splashed across his chest in silver capitals.

"My name is Jared Spegel, sir." That much was true, but even as he said it, he knew his cover had been blown. It was the only explanation for what was happening.

"And you came here from Mission Planning back on Earth, with a tour in Deep Space Routing before that, and then two weeks ago you're suddenly drafted in here to drive the Remote Observation fleet. Is that right?"

"Yes, sir," he lied, while Anderson seemingly nailed him to the back wall with his eyes.

"Really? Because I have friends in MP and DSR who have never even heard of you. And nor have any of the instructors on that Orbital C3I course you're supposed to have taken. In fact, no one you claim to have known and worked with even recognizes your name. So once again, do you mind telling me just who the hell you are?"

This mission was a disaster waiting to happen from the start, Jared thought. He hated rush jobs, and this was one of them—no time to build a proper cover, no time to prepare for contingencies. He looked round the room, at the two guards and the woman who'd apprehended him—looking as if all she needed was the slightest excuse and the Taser would come out again—and realized his options were getting scarce. It was time to come clean.

"Can I speak with you alone, Commander?" he said.

"Anything you can say in front of me, you can say in front of them."

"Not this. You're right that I'm not who I say I am, but if I can show you my ident listing, you might understand."

Jared leaned over and put his hand on the desk, palm down, fingers spread—but not his right hand, which coded the biometrics for Jared Spegel, legitimate crew member, but his left, which coded another Jared Spegel altogether.

The commander sat back from his screen, the suspicion in his eyes turning to intrigue. "Sal, Lieutenants, step outside, please."

They went, but slowly, and the woman kept her eyes on Jared right up until she left the room.

"Make this damn good," Anderson said once they were alone.

"Sir, my name really is Jared Spegel, but everything else is a cover. I'll get straight to the point—I'm with the Office of Alliance Liaison, and we have reason to believe that someone on this station has already contacted the Caronoi and is continuing to do so."

The commander almost turned white, his earlier resolve replaced by unmitigated shock.

"Who?" was all he seemed able to say.

"That's why I'm here, to try and find out."

The commander steepled his fingers, thinking

quickly, his composure returning. "You need to speak damn fast, Mr. Spegel. Tell me everything. Now."

Sixty years had passed since humanity had first made contact with intelligences from beyond Earth. In those intervening years, they had learned a lot about the wider universe they now found themselves in, but not the full picture. They knew of the Alliance, the vast conglomeration of civilizations with millennia of mutual contact behind them; they knew that those civilizations numbered in the hundreds, if not thousands; and they knew that vast as it was, the Milky Way was not the limit of the Alliance's tenure. Of those races, however, humanity had directly encountered just four, including the so-called Sprites, that altogether inappropriate name for those vast sentient replicators named after the bizarre chirps and beeps that appeared when physicists first conquered gravity and stumbled upon the galaxy-wide g-wave communication system that explained why radio-frequency SETI had remained fruitless for so long.

And they knew that sometimes, when a new civilization was encountered, the Alliance would react not with welcome, but with obliteration. And whatever the closely guarded criteria were for acceptance or oblivion, they knew that sixty years ago, humanity had come within a whisker of being wiped out.

So, Mr. Spegel. Why is this the first I'm hearing about a breach in my own damn station?"

Jared had been excused from Anderson's office for over an hour once he'd told the man what was happening right under his nose. He'd been kept in the outer office, not exactly under arrest, but actively dissuaded from leaving, listening to the muted voices of Anderson and the woman called Sal just beyond. Then, finally, he'd been allowed back in.

"Sir, you must understand that given the seriousness of this situation, no one can be above suspicion. Ever since we were appointed as Contact Authority for the Caronoi, we've known that there can be no room for mistakes. We're not sure, but we think that by being given the chance to bring another race into the fold so early in our own membership, we are being afforded a great honor by the Alliance. And whatever it was that almost saw us wiped out—it's likely we're still being judged, even now."

There had been chaos on Earth when humanity's near-eradication was made public, a few full-scale wars, too, as the divide opened up between those wanting nothing to do with the Alliance and the threat it still posed, and those who realized the clock couldn't be put back, contact couldn't be undone, that Earth was now part of the interstellar community whether it liked it or not. Decades on, pragmatism had won out, an uneasy acceptance that the Alliance did things for a reason, and one day we'd understand.

Now that compliance meant putting another race under the spotlight.

Anderson looked down at the displays on his desk, live-feed schematics of the Caron system and the eighteen planets that made it up, including the gas giant Caron-e they were currently orbiting, and Caron-c, Earthlike in so many ways, whose inhabitants were meant to be getting the surprise of their lives in just three weeks' time.

"Well, this is the situation," he said. "I do not appreciate having my authority circumvented on this station, no matter how much 'suspicion' you feel inclined to aim at everyone based here, including apparently me. But I talked to your people just now, and then I called the chiefs back on Earth, and then they called the UN. And guess what? Not only did they back up your story, but I'm supposed to give you everything you want, on a plate. The thing is, I'm not going to do that. You can carry on with your investigation, but you won't be doing it alone. Maybe you don't work for me, but Sal does, and she is going to monitor every move you make on this station. Is that understood?"

Of all possible outcomes, this was probably the least disastrous. "Understood," he said.

Sal was the head of the commander's troubleshooting staff, Jared found out once he'd talked to her without a Taser in her hand. In essence, her job wasn't too far from his own—clamp down on anything that could constitute a foul-up. It seemed to be the default structure for all human activity now that potential Alliance judgment was a feature of every endeavor— military-style organization, military-style discipline, no tolerance for mistakes.

She led him to one of Anderson's briefing rooms, their hastily established base of operations. There they were due to be joined by the chiefs of the station security division, the analysis division and the systems support division, but so far no one else had arrived. As soon as they were inside, Sal shut the door and turned to face Jared.

"I hope you know what you've done here," she said to him. "The commander is under more stress right now than you can imagine. Three years we've been posted here studying the Caronoi. Now we're just three weeks away from breaking cover and you pull this stunt. If the Alliance even suspect that we are about to screw this up, then we could be history—this station, you, me, the whole human race. Do you understand that?"

Jared felt himself tensing, ready for an argument. "Yes, I do understand. Do you understand that someone on your station may already have broken cover and might be bringing judgment on us even as we speak? I'm here to stop that, remember?"

"You better hope you're right," she said.

The other attendees began to file in at that point, casting curious glances at each other and at Jared and Sal, clearly still in the dark as to why they'd been called. Anderson was last to turn up. He sat everyone down, then took them through what was known so far. Jared saw the same reactions on their faces that he'd seen on Anderson's, the reaction turning from horror, to disbelief, then ultimately to anger.

"If someone is talking to them already, it could be disastrous," the security guy said, a man called Benning. "You must have some idea who it is."

"The initial theory was someone in Remote Observation," Jared said. "That's why I was posted there. But I managed to rule that out pretty quickly."

"Why there?" one of the systems guys said. "In fact, how do you know about any of this?"

"Because that's our job. Officially, Alliance Liaison's role is to be the interstellar face of Earth, to deal directly with Alliance races. But unofficially our biggest job is containing screw-ups. We make it our business to monitor everything that happens in off-Earth affairs, including this station. We get copies of the mission logs you send back to Earth, and we have algorithms specifically designed to look for inconsistencies—in this case remote observation satellites which for the last eight weeks have been sitting with their high-gain antennas half a degree above ambient temperature when by all rights they should have been off altogether."

Benning smiled grimly. "I'd heard that your outfit was more like an intel cell than a diplomatic group. So tell me something, Mr. One-Call-Away-From-Alliance-Central—"

"I don't work with the speakers, remember. I don't get to actually talk to *them*."

"Well, whatever, but answer me this. We get pretty much ninety-eight percent coverage of all the Caronois' communications. If someone here has opened a line of communication to them, we would see them react even if they didn't respond directly. So where is it?"

Jared nodded; the question had occurred to him too. When twenty-first-century Earth first discovered they weren't alone, there was planetwide uproar, even before news of their near-eradication broke. Not that the Caronoi seemed the type to exhibit mass hysteria, but news of contact would still have a big effect on them.

"My guess?" he said. "Message one would have been 'keep a lid on this, listen, but don't respond.'"

"But you don't know for sure."

"No, but I'm getting close to finding out."

"Close?" Sal said. "You've been fumbling around here for two weeks now, when telling us straight out could have found the answer in days."

"I know, but I had my orders."

"Lucky we found you then. Because now that you're under our orders, we might actually get somewhere. So, what are we looking for?"

Jared paused, gathering his thoughts. He hadn't expected to have to explain this to anyone so soon, at least not until he was back on Earth being debriefed by Alliance Liaison. "It's not anyone in the Remote Observation team, I'm pretty sure of that now. I think someone with access to core station systems has installed some agent software to act for them. Every time one of the RO birds was taken over there'd be a spike in processor activity associated with core comms."

"Do you have details of when these events happened?" Benning said. "We could trace all logins, match them up with shift activity and personnel logs, get some idea who had the opportunity to do this."

"How quickly can you get on it?" Anderson said.

"Let me get my section heads in here and we can start now."

Benning made the call, as did the other chiefs to their teams, prompting an influx of new faces, all initially ignorant of events, all displaying the same shock when told of the situation. They got to work fast, a team of over fifteen by now, pulling up logs of computer access and processor activity, tracing back through the control systems of the hijacked satellites, the station processor nodes that could have been set to control them and finally the individuals most likely to have had the right kind of access at the right kind of time.

Jared looked round at the number of people working the problem, and the results they were getting. Sal was right, he thought—he had been just groping around for two weeks, sacrificing progress to maintain cover. But in many ways, this new situation brought concerns of its own. Kaluza Station housed almost a thousand people, all working on the preparations for contact, and as the number of people aware of the breach and working to pin it down grew, the probability that the culprit would be tipped off could only increase.

Then Jared heard someone call out "Got him!" He looked over to the far corner of the room where a group of system profilers were leaning over a display. One of them was pointing to a trace of computer access data.

Anderson moved over quickly, Jared and the rest of the room not far behind. Then they saw the name of the person the system had identified as the culprit.

"Not him," Anderson said. "Not Temple."

"It's Temple," Sal said.

Rory Temple, grandson of the man who had made first contact with the Alliance, and who had reportedly done whatever it had taken to convince them that humanity was worthy of joining.

Anderson sat everyone down. "How sure are you?"

he said to the profilers who had pulled up Temple's name.

"Ninety percent," one of them said.

"You realize how big a deal this is, if we're wrong," Anderson said. "This guy's connections make him a very important man. He could have pulled strings to get a job anywhere in interplanetary policy, but he chose this place."

"Why here?" Jared said. It couldn't help but sound suspicious, that their new number one suspect had gone to such lengths to be posted here, with status and pay grade a fraction of what he could command elsewhere.

"He studies languages. He did a lot work on the Sephora languages when we first encountered them, stuff we'd never have figured out without him. Even if he didn't call in favors to get the exolinguistics job, he'd be a pretty good candidate."

"And now he's using his place here to screw the mission by breaking cover ahead of the contact date?" Sal said. "Why?"

"I have a pretty good idea," Benning said. "He wants the glory. His grandfather was the first to meet the Sprites, the first to introduce humanity to the Alliance, the one to save our necks. Now, Rory Temple wants to bring in the Caronoi, single-handed, and get his name in the books, too."

There were murmurs of agreement around the room; it sounded plausible.

"I'm not going to haul him in and throw accusations at him if there's any chance he's innocent," Anderson said. "We can't take that kind of trouble, not at this stage."

Jared could see the position Anderson was in and had a lot of sympathy for the guy; he was the station commander, nominally the sole voice of authority, but he'd just been trumped on his own station twice in succession, first by Jared's Alliance Liaison status, now by Rory Temple's connections and the ramifications of pointing the finger. Jared realized he had to make the move.

"Let me talk to him," he said.

"No," Anderson said, thin-lipped. "He's one of my staff. I work out how we deal with him."

"Commander, we're not sure it is him yet. Look, I've been trained in covert interrogation, I can talk to him under some pretext and know whether he's lying. I have enhancements fitted that let me spot pupil dilation, skin flush, posture changes—I'm like a walking lie detector. It's part of my job. I can tell you if it's him."

Anderson sat back, thinking it through. "Sal, what do you think?"

"If Spegel is wrong, then it's he and Alliance Liaison that look bad, not us."

"Remember, it's not just the embarrassment we're trying to avoid."

"We run a higher risk by doing nothing."

"Okay," Anderson said. "Do it."

Jared's duties while under cover had never taken him to the Cultural Assessments section. He made his way there with growing apprehension, knowing how much hung on what he was about to attempt. He stopped at one of the research rooms to ask directions and was pointed toward the teaching facility where

Rory taught Caronoi languages to the Contact Teams. When Jared got there the door was open, and Rory was inside addressing a class of twelve contactees. They sat there, lean and clean-cut in their red jumpsuits like pilots at a preflight briefing, hanging on every word, knowing that success or failure lay in doing the job right and assimilating every bit of information they were given.

Jared hovered outside. No one seemed to have noticed him, so he listened in while Rory took them through the finer details of something called "cross-grammeme resonance." The class was in its final five minutes, so he waited for them to finish, then went in as Rory was closing down the displays.

"Rory Temple?" Jared strolled in as if there on some errand, but already he had his implants fired up to record and analyze everything.

"Yeah, that's right." Rory was a young guy, younger than Jared with curly black hair and a wide welcoming smile.

"I'm Jared, hi. Look—do you have a minute? I want to ask you something about the stuff you're working on."

"Sure. My office is just down the hall." Rory started gathering disks and printouts together, clearing the room for whoever would be teaching here next.

Jared hesitated—Rory's office might be the worst place to go; people were always harder to read on home ground. But then this classroom was probably familiar territory in itself, and anyway people were already arriving for the next lesson. He let Rory lead him out and down the hall to the cubicle where he worked.

"So, what do you want to know?" Rory said once they'd arrived.

Why you've jeopardized this mission, this station and the safety of the human race, Jared didn't say. "I run the remote observation birds that pick up all RF communications, but resourcing is getting to be an issue and we might need to prioritize our collects. I was wondering whether there are any particular locations or times of day that give you the best material."

"To an extent, yes, but it depends what you're looking for. The southern continents seem to be first with all technical advancements. Certainly, their songs were the first to contain explanations for electromagnetism and atomic theory, plus most of the other milestones we've gauged our own development by. But it was a northern song that first showed something resembling General Relativity, so take your pick. And if it's their culture you're into, how they communicate and govern themselves, you can take songs from pretty much anywhere."

Rory had an image on his wall, taken by a low orbital satellite back when they still dared get that close, showing one of the song sharing rituals in progress. Jared had seen others like it in his brief time on the station, but this one was particularly clear, a gently sloping meadow of dark green vegetation with a group of over two hundred Caronoi clustered together, their quadruped bodies packed so close as to be clambering over each other as the song was sung again and again, being added to, refined and memorized with every repetition. The songs were at the heart of Caronoi culture, a kind of common knowledge base evolving over time, copied from generation to generation and place to place as the Caronois' understanding of the world increased. It had even been suggested that the hours-long ritual took them into some kind of shared world space, a place existing only in their minds but where theories and hypotheses about the world could be formed, developed and rationalized until finally, when they were done, they would go back to living in lean-to shelters, eating grass and leaves off the ground, while the milestones of physics, chemistry and biology fell to their relentless accumulation of knowledge.

"And is it just the songs that you get? Or other stuff too?" Jared said.

"Has no one told you this?" Rory said. "Wow, they do keep you guys green, don't they? Okay, in terms of what you pick up, the majority of it is song lore, but there are plenty of other site-to-site communications too, more mundane stuff like arranging journeys or warning of bad weather."

"And is it easy to translate?"

"It wasn't at first, but we managed to crack it a year or so ago," Rory said. "Their languages are fascinating, their way of communicating so unlike our own. Have you ever seen their speech decoded? Seen how it works?"

"No," Jared said. "I just collect their transmissions. It's all noise as far as I can tell."

Rory smiled. "I guess to them, hearing us speak would be just noise. It's not like hearing another language from your own planet where you can tell *something* is being said, even if you're not sure what."

Jared put on a quizzical look, mainly a way of

keeping Rory talking, but mixed with genuine interest as to what he'd managed to uncover.

"Okay, here's how it works," Rory said. He leaned over the keypad, then hit a key to bring the screen back to life.

There was something else on there when it powered up, something Jared couldn't see clearly but which made Rory close the window in a hurry, cursing under his breath. "Game Thread" or "Game Theater" was all Jared had been able to read.

"Didn't realize that was on there," Rory said, laughing nervously. For Jared though it would be yet another problem—Rory couldn't have been the only crew member playing games when they should be working, but being caught out for that minor misdemeanor could well mask the signs of the major one.

Rory opened up the program he did want and brought up an audio file. When he set it playing, it sounded like dolphin sounds, but mixed with a low-level buzzing drone.

"Okay, not much to take from that, is there?" he said. "But watch this." Then he brought it up visually, a graphical trace of amplitude and frequency matching the peaks and lulls of the sound itself. He zoomed in, down to the level of hundredths of a second, and the trace began to resolve itself into discrete spikes of noise.

"Each one of those is a click," Rory said. "In isolation they don't mean much—it's the spacing that counts. Look here." He pointed out a sequence of four clicks, three equally spaced with the fourth farther off to the right. "This is the west coast dialect of continent B, so that means 'home.'" He then pointed out other sequences, some of up to ten clicks, with meanings as varied as "down" and "water" and "closed." Then he zoomed out, the screen becoming a forest of spikes, and hit a couple of keys that caused another four to be highlighted, much wider apart this time.

"'Home' again," Jared said.

"That's right, but covering a tenth of a second, not just a few hundredths. And each of those clicks already forms part of other short-span words. In fact, in any sequence of clicks you can find whole new levels of meaning by pulling back and looking for patterns at larger and larger scales. And their languages actually use that phenomenon, to add grammatical nuances, parallel threads of meaning, evidence and context running alongside every statement—do you know they find it almost impossible to lie? Their brains must be wired up to process layers of meaning and truth like this. To them, our way of just putting one word after another would be almost incomprehensible. They can't form a coherent meaning *without* layering it on."

Rory seemed to enjoy explaining all this stuff, Jared thought. Certainly enough to make it plausible that he'd chosen this posting out of sheer academic interest, and nothing more. Jared had once felt the same about his old job, doing covert analysis of other Alliance races' technology—highly secretive, extremely fruitful and fascinating to an extent that he'd have done it as a hobby if someone else was paying his bills. Then one day he just hit burnout and couldn't do it anymore.

"And did you figure all this out yourself?"

"Most of it. It was me who discovered the songs. I even invented the name 'Caronoi'—we'd been calling them 'Carons' for too long."

"So this whole contact effort is your baby?"

"Yeah, I guess you could say so."

He thinks it's his own pet project, Jared thought. He's got a lot to be proud of with what he's done so far, but Benning was right—he wants one better. He wants the glory like his grandfather. Time to put him on the defensive.

"So what's the point of any of this? Why are you even bothering if we can't even get our heads around it?"

Rory answered straight, not rising to the bait. "The Contact Team will be using translation packs, and one of my jobs is to program them. But even using them needs a degree of training, almost as much as learning the rudiments of an unfamiliar Earth language. You can't just talk into the translator and hope that something coherent will come out, much less expect to understand what it gives back to you when they reply. It just doesn't work that way."

"How did your grandfather and the rest of his crew communicate when they first encountered the Sprites?"

"The Sprites made it easy for them—they'd learned English and figured out how to speak it fluently, just from picking up broadcasts from Earth."

"Pretty much the way you are."

The comparison must have reminded Rory of the enormity of what he was doing, because for a second a sober look took the place of the enthusiasm he'd shown so far. "Yeah, I guess so."

221

He'd been caught off guard—time to start probing.

"So if you were given the chance to be the first to talk to them, what would you say?"

Rory sat back from the desk. "I'd probably ask them their hopes, where they see themselves in the cosmos. They know a lot about the universe around them, they've already worked out they're not alone, just as we did before contact took place. They must be giving some thought to how it all works, and how they'll fit in."

"And how do you think they'll fit in?"

"I don't know; they're such a strange race. To have attained that level of development and awareness without any of the trappings of technological civilization, like cities and transport networks and heavy industry. I hope there's a place for them."

"And how do you think they'll take it, when we make contact and they realize we're here?"

"They'll celebrate, I'm pretty sure of it. Their songs have always contained an awareness of plurality, of not being alone. It will be a culture shock for them, but the mere fact they're not alone won't be a surprise."

"And are you looking forward to that day?"

"Very much so. That's why I'm here."

Jared watched Rory's expression, and other non-verbal cues, looking for any signs of lying or deceit. There was none. He'd asked four questions in a row where the culprit couldn't do anything *but* lie, and yet from Rory he'd got nothing. Jared had heard all he needed, it was time to go. As he got up to leave, one final question occurred to him.

"So what was he talking about?" Jared said, pointing

to the trace still frozen on the screen. "The Caronoi who was talking then?"

"Nothing much," Rory said, "just a way of making houses watertight."

A way of finding leaks, Jared thought. Maybe we should be asking *him* for help.

It wasn't him," Jared said. He was back in Anderson's office, having stopped at the rec room to stare at cold coffee and make sure of what he was about to say.

"Are you sure? What did you ask him?"

"I've sent you a transcript of what we discussed. You'll see where the giveaways would have been. But I got nothing."

"Could he have been trained?" Anderson said. "People can be taught, can't they, to beat truth tests?"

It had occurred to Jared, but was unlikely. "Only if he's trained as an Operative. Even I would struggle to come through a test like that with a clean score."

"A test like that?" Sal said. She'd opened the transcript on Anderson's screen and was skimming through it. "You didn't press him too hard from what I can see here."

"No, but I was sitting opposite him in a quiet room with no other distractions. I had every deceit cue covered short of sticking a thermometer up his butt— if he was lying, I'd have known."

"Well, I don't care what you think you know. *You* started all this, *you* are supposed to be able to find this stuff out." She was finger-jabbing him as she spoke, leaning forward to punctuate each "you" with a prod in his face. "So why are *you* not able to do that?"

"Sal, that will do," Anderson said. She sat back heavily, still glowering at Jared. Then Anderson faced him, too. "So, what do we do now?"

What they did was to block off all the avenues that had been used to hijack the Remote Observation satellites. Having focused initially on trying to find the culprit, now they concentrated on the nature of the breach, how the messages had been transmitted and how to stop them in the future. Whoever had done it had covered up well; nothing was left of whatever they'd sent, or the software that had passed those messages to the satellites. But within a day, the gaps in system security had been plugged. Whoever it was, they wouldn't be doing it again.

As for Jared himself, his placement had been a ruse from the start, and now even that cover was gone. However, he still had his Alliance Liaison credentials, still had the run of the station and still had a job to do. Anderson had put the hunt for the culprit in Benning's hands, him and his security team, and with Jared still overseeing the operation, that was where he spent most of his time. Leads, however, were scarce; beyond the system trace that had pointed to Rory Temple in the first place, there was little to go on.

"The commander's thinking of bringing Temple in," Benning said, three days after Rory had been implicated. He and Jared were in Benning's office, reviewing the evidence to date. "He's going to talk to him directly."

"What does he plan on doing?" Jared said. "Asking straight out if it was him? Or letting Sal loose on him?"

Benning laughed. "I wouldn't want to be in the room for *that* session."

Jared smiled back. Benning seemed a good guy to work with. Stocky, middle-aged and graying, but level-headed and quick-thinking with a practical approach to things. Unlike other more hotheaded members of the crew. "So just what is it with Sal? What do you think her problem is?"

"She's loyal to Anderson, that's really all it is. Anything that poses a threat to the mission is a threat to him, and she can be pretty zealous in dealing with it. Overzealous, some might say."

Jared wondered if Anderson appreciated Sal's overprotective approach or just tolerated it. "What do you think Anderson will do now?"

"I don't know. To be honest I think he's hoping that now the breach is plugged, this problem will just go away, that once the Caronoi officially know we're here, whatever went before won't matter."

"I wouldn't be so hopeful myself."

"Neither would I. I'm glad I'm not in his shoes, you know. He's got ultimate responsibility for every decision on this mission—the choice of landing site, the procedure for breaking cover, the contingencies if contact goes badly. Then, as if that weren't enough, first we find out we might have got their tech level wrong, and then this breach happens."

"What do you mean we got their tech level wrong?"

Benning laughed. "You mean there's something Alliance Liaison doesn't know first? That makes a change. It's the Caronoi space program. You know we thought we knew how they'd done it?"

Jared nodded—it was yet another technological miracle the Caronoi had cooked up in between song sessions and leaf eating: their own space program, their own Voyagers and Cassinis spreading through the system, launched on glorified black powder rockets, processing with analog valves that predated even the transistor era, but nonetheless sending a steady stream of high-quality data on the plethora of giants and supergiants that made up the Caron system. They also had first-generation orbital telescopes, Hubbles and Webbs with what the technical assessments branch had concluded to be impressive capabilities for something so crude—the reason why Kaluza Station had to be concealed so carefully.

"Go on," Jared said, intrigued.

"We're picking up g-wave emissions in the outer system. They're difficult to pin down. It's not like a radio source that you can just focus a receiver onto, but some of them seem to be coming from the same direction as their outbound probes."

"So what do we think it is?" he said.

"Maybe their theoretical understanding of gravity isn't so theoretical after all."

"You mean they've had gravity drives all along? And used them on their probes?"

"First-generation low-thrust devices for course correction? It's been suggested."

It didn't seem plausible to Jared. He had enough trouble equating the Caronois' existing achievements to their everyday way of life—the way they pulled metal ore out of the ground, mixed propellants and fuel, invented and built electronic controllers, all so they could put a one-off spacecraft into operation, then go back to living a life that on Earth would have predated the agricultural revolution. But then again the Alliance didn't initiate contact *unless* a race had reached a certain level, where space exploration had been demonstrated, physics was encountering the territory beyond relativity and the full-blown manipulation of gravity and unconstrained access to space were only a matter of time.

"Are you seeing all this on the omni-g?"

"Some," Benning said. "Plus some A-vector ghosting on the high gain. It's faint though."

"Can I see what it looks like?"

"Sure, if it'll mean anything to you."

"It will do," Jared said. Benning had a better-than-average appreciation of the principles underpinning gravity control, but Jared used to work with this stuff every day.

Benning brought up the relevant files, and Jared scrolled through to the graphs of what Kaluza's g-wave detectors had found.

"A-vector modulation at 850 kilohertz," he read out loud, "localized stress tensor divergence in dimensions four *and* five—this isn't Caronoi."

"Then what is it?"

Jared thought back to his old job and the covert g-wave measurements that were taken whenever Alliance ships visited Earth or encountered human vessels, all so that Earth could see how far in advance the Alliance races really were. The endeavor was dangerous in diplomatic terms, but invaluable in other ways as Sprite, Sephoran, Tessalan and Garrison ships unwittingly yielded their secrets. Sometimes, however, when particularly auspicious or politically sensitive visits were in progress, something else would show up, too.

"This is Alliance. It's the Sprites, but not their regular cruisers. They have some kind of special unit, ships they keep at a distance, hovering in the outer system."

"So they're hiding from us while we hide from the Caronoi? That's just what we need with a breach on our hands, them watching over our shoulders."

Something made Jared wonder whether watching was all they were there to do.

Three weeks passed with no more breaches, but no more sign of who had been responsible in the first place. Then, finally, contact day itself came.

The transfer deck to the shuttle was barely big enough for the Contact Team, let alone anyone else, but any room with an outside view was considered fair game by those not on shift or those on nonessential duties who wanted to see the departure for themselves.

Anderson himself was part of the team. There had been debates about whether it was right for the commander to take part in the first landing, but the risk was considered small and it seemed fitting that he should go. The rest of the team was an assortment of biological, cultural and scientific researchers, chosen by a committee back on Earth to share the honor of first contact.

There was a speech, by Anderson, relayed across the station video link, made up of his own words marking the event, and messages from heads of state back on Earth. Jared was watching from the rec room, angled back from the sunward side of the station as were most habitable sections, but with enough of a view to show the shuttle when it eventually departed.

Then the display showed Anderson and the rest of the Contact Team climbing into the craft, wearing the same red jumpsuits that had become their uniform, him in his commander's black. Then the shuttle undocked and silently moved away from the station until its grav drive was powered up, making it recede into the distance at what would have felt like fifteen Gs if the gravity on board hadn't been compensated. Within seconds, it was lost to the naked eye, but the station's long-range sensors kept track of it, relaying the tiny image through the station.

The spectators dispersed soon after that, and Jared went too, back to his cabin. He checked his watch— in just four hours' time the shuttle would arrive, then the first step in the carefully choreographed sequence of events would take place: a radio message on the same frequency the Caronoi used for long-distance messaging, with an explanation of who the humans were and why they were here, then a signal of their intent to land. Then there would be an opportunity to reply, and the opportunity to say no if the Caronoi so wished—eventual contact was inevitable, but anything to avoid looking like an invading army could only be a good thing. For the same reason, Kaluza Station would stay hidden, for a few days at least, along with all the other remote probes scattered through the system, though moving the whole operation into Caron-c orbit was always the eventual

229

aim. Then, once the shuttle had made landfall, the first meeting would take place.

That initial broadcast though—Rory Temple himself had written it, drawing on the cultural and linguistic knowledge that he understood better than anyone. In a way, he already was the spearhead of the contact effort, and the record would show it—so why would he risk so much to get his name in the history books illegally? It just didn't make sense.

Jared lay down on his bunk and closed his eyes, thinking through the problem. A question had kept coming back to him all through the hunt for the culprit, a question that no one had ever had time to dwell on when the evidence concerning the breach itself took priority—what had those messages contained? What had Rory or whoever it was said to them? Had the Caronoi really received messages from above and not reacted at all? Or was the evidence there, in the songs that used to filter from tribe to tribe, but nowadays flowed back and forth over the planet's surface like a web of self-perpetuating knowledge?

Jared got up and opened a terminal, linking up to the internal feed of recent news and discoveries. There was a group page belonging to the decoding team, a kind of repository of quick look reports on all Caronoi communications that the technical and cultural research teams could browse, and call up the full recordings if they wanted. He scanned through the reports for the last eight weeks, the approximate duration of the breach. Northern hemisphere songs were showing an increased proportion of fictional material, one report said, their own stories and legends playing a big role in a way that wasn't true for other regions. Then there was a reference to one of the Continent A settlements, playing with new ideas for collecting water in dry seasons, encouraging the growth of plants that collected moisture under their leaves. Then there was a tribe on the west coast of continent B, the readout showed, who had started making rapid advances in the mathematical analysis of competitions and strategies for winning them.

Jared stopped, wondering why that last part had stood out. He checked the date on the posting—just one week ago. Then he looked back in the archive of postings, searching for anything on the same or related subjects. There was nothing. He stopped, thinking back to his conversation with Rory Temple, running through everything he'd seen and heard, justifying to himself just why this might be significant.

Then he called the number given for the decoding group and got through to one of their researchers.

"Hi, I've just seen the summary for signal 2/DK/2462," he said, once he'd identified himself. His heart was pounding with the realization trying to be born in his mind, and it was hard to keep his voice level. "That reference to their mathematics and analysis of competitive behavior—have you ever seen that come up in any other songs or communications?"

"No, there's no sign of it here," the woman said when she'd checked her records.

"Nothing before a week ago?"

"No."

Jared thought back to that chat with Rory, three full weeks ago, concentrating not on Rory himself but on what he'd tried to hide on his screen, that window that had looked like "Game Theater," but which the recording in Jared's implants now showed to be something altogether different.

"How about other ways of phrasing it, like 'tactical strategies,' or 'competitive analysis,' or—ah—'Game Theory'?"

She checked again. "Nothing," she said.

"What about other tribes or other regions?"

"It's spread to a few other tribes since then, but the signal you saw seems to be the origin. Beyond that, it's as if it came out of nowhere."

Jared was out of the door and running to Benning's office before he'd even had time to break off the call. Benning was sitting at his desk, halfway through reading the dailies that his staff had put out.

"I know who it was," Jared said. "It was Rory Temple all along."

"How do you know?"

Jared told him everything, up to and including how Rory had information on his Caronoi analysis system three weeks ago that didn't show up in Caronoi communications until two weeks later.

"You think this is what he's sending?" Benning said. "Why this? Why is he giving them math lessons?"

"You want answers to that, I say we go and ask him. Where is he now?"

Benning still didn't seem convinced, but he called up Rory's details to see the last access point he'd swiped through. The record showed him being on a maintenance deck toward the sunward side of the station. It was far from his usual place of work.

"What in the hell is he doing there?" Benning said.

They went to the area indicated in the records, up

at the narrow end of the spindle-shaped station, not running but still moving with urgency. The area they ended up in was right under the array of antennas and dishes that were clustered on the sun-facing point of the station. There they slowed, moving quietly, knowing even before they located him that whatever Rory was doing, he wouldn't want to be found.

The deck was like a circular corridor matching the sixty-foot diameter of this narrowest part of the station, and they found Rory in an alcove on the outer side, kneeling down with his back to them. The alcove contained ducting and cables running floor to ceiling, presumably leading to one of the antenna arrays on the outer hull, and Rory had plugged a portable omni into one of the monitoring units and was uploading something to the transmitter.

"Rory, whatever you're doing, stop," Jared said.

He jumped half out of his skin, almost falling over in his haste to get up and turn around. His eyes darted between Jared and Benning, then he backed against the wall, deflated, as he realized he couldn't get out.

"You mustn't stop it," he said. "There's too much at stake."

"What are you doing?" Benning said, heading over to the omni. He was about to unplug it when Rory ran over, pushing him away, then stepped back with his hands up.

"Sorry—you can't do that. Please, you've got to listen."

Jared's detectors, tuned for their usual role of spotting untruths, were now screaming one thing at him—Rory was sincere, and was doing what he

233

was doing for a reason he believed in so strongly, he didn't care what happened to him as long as he could continue. This wasn't someone out to steal glory.

"Benning, wait a minute," Jared said. "Rory, tell me what's going on here. I promise, I'm listening."

"It's the Caronoi," he said. "I've got to get a message to them."

"We know. You've already sent them several. But why? What have you been telling them?"

"How not to get themselves exterminated, that's what."

"What the hell do you mean?" Benning said.

"It's the Alliance and the judgment they pass on new races. My grandfather knew. Don't you realize? He knew what almost happened to us and why. And guess what? Those poor bastards down on Caron-c are heading for the same fate."

"So you tipped them off?"

"Yes, but not in the way you think. I tapped into their songs, the ones they share between continents, and added the elements of the knowledge they'll need to survive."

"What—Game Theory?" Jared said.

Rory blanched, his eyes widening. "How do you know about that?"

"It's started turning up in their songs. The intercepts are showing it."

"And now that they know we're here, all preparations for contact have been wasted," Benning said.

"No, it's not like that," Rory said. "I hid the information in their songs. They don't know it's from outside. If they ever try to trace it back, then it will look like it came out of nowhere, but right now every tribe thinks it must be one of the other tribes that started it."

So that's how he beat the lie test, Jared thought. He was telling the truth when he said actual contact was still to come. "But why Game Theory? How is that meant to save them?"

Rory paused, as if collecting his thoughts on a subject he never expected to have to explain. "The Alliance destroys races that it thinks might be a threat to it. It's no coincidence that contact always occurs just when a race discovers g-wave tech and starts to control gravity. It's the point of no return when a race can begin to spread to the stars and exert an influence over what it finds there. But there's another discovery just beyond gravity control, something even more profound. The way my grandfather described it, it's like a way of violating causality, a limited form of time travel where you can make effect happen before cause, and it brings massive power—enough to make you think you could defeat the whole Alliance. But you'd be wrong. That's where Game Theory comes in— in single-play cooperate-or-betray games, defectors always win. It's like the Prisoner's Dilemma. It's been known for years. If you play time after time and keep score, it's the strategy that determines the winner. But if you can loop back within the game, and time is no longer sequential, it's always the instigator who loses. It's like a fundamental principle, and the Alliance have a name for races who haven't figured it out— they call them 'naïves.' And whenever a naïve race discovers what causality violation can buy them, they always end up using it, no matter how cooperative they might have seemed to begin with. They end up losing—non-sequential Game Theory ensures it—but they do untold damage in the process. That's why the Alliance does this; that's why contact is made and judgment is applied—any race liable to make trouble can't just be contained or left to its own devices. It's make or break."

Jared had more questions than he could count—how could the Alliance be so sure that all naïve races would cause trouble? Why not just tell each new race why it was pointless? And why not contain them rather than wipe them out altogether? But right now, a more immediate question had to be answered.

"If the Caronoi are already lined up for this, why were we given the job of bringing them in? What's our part in all this?"

"To start with, one of our jobs was to find out whether they are naïves or not, even though we didn't know we were doing it. Check the things the Alliance want us to report on, like the Caronois' technical and mathematical development—Game Theory is in there, it's just not obvious. But this is the thing— we're being tested too. Our Alliance membership is hanging by a thread and always has been. The people who think we're still being judged, they're right. And this is the test we've been given, to see how we react when the race we're reaching out to is themselves targeted for elimination."

So now they knew the criterion for destruction, Jared thought. There had been countless theories over the last sixty years as to why mankind was nearly eliminated, most of them immediately discounted. It wasn't because humans were a militarized race, the favorite theory in the early years—for instance, Sephoran starships packed a firepower that would dwarf the whole world's nuclear arsenal. It wasn't because humanity had damaged their world's ecology, or wiped out whole species—at least one Alliance race didn't even inhabit their home world anymore thanks to the effects of their industrial advancement. Instead, it was this, some obscure bit of mathematics that could relegate a race to extinction just by its absence from their textbooks.

Jared had felt frustration before at mankind's lowly position among races that held power of life and death and had deigned to keep humanity ignorant too. Now this revelation made him angry.

"Is that it? That's why we nearly died?"

Rory just nodded.

"But if you knew this from your grandfather, why didn't you say anything? We could have known what we were getting into from the start."

"At our stage of membership, just knowing the criteria for destruction is enough to ensure destruction. The Alliance want to see us demonstrate truthfully that we're worthy of joining, not just see us showing them what they want to see. It's the same for the Caronoi—I *had* to hide the knowledge in their songs, make it look like they worked it out themselves."

"The bastards. The bastard alien freaks, making us jump through hoops in games we're not even allowed to know the rules to." Jared worked for the same organization that employed the Speakers, those humans trusted with managing the direct contact with Earth's sponsor race, the Sprites, so by all rights he should have been all in favor of Alliance membership. But he'd joined up on the rebound from his old job, and whereas there he'd been using Earth's membership for Earth's benefit, now he wasn't really sure whose interests he was serving. And all through his time there he'd had a suspicion that there was something deeply wrong with the position humanity had been put in, the continued life-or-death judgment, just by making themselves known to other races.

"That's why the Alliance are here," he said. "They're here to put the extermination order into practice."

"They're here?" Rory said.

"Yes." Jared told him about the g-wave intercepts, the now unmistakable signs of Sprite ships hanging back in the outer system.

"That's them," Rory said. "My grandfather talked about special ships they use, some kind of elimination unit, with planet-busting weapons."

"But aren't the Caronoi safe now? You've put the knowledge into their songs."

"Not enough though, I never got past the basics. I even had to teach them what conflict *is*, the idea is so alien to them. Then I lost contact."

"That was us," Jared said. "We cut the feeds to the satellites. But are the Caronoi really going to be wiped out? How can a race turn bad if they have to have the very concept of conflict explained to them?"

"I don't know; all I have is what my grandfather was told—the Alliance think that races like that are the most dangerous of all."

238

"So what options do we have?"

"Options?" Benning said. "We came here to arrest this guy; now you're asking him about options?"

It was true, Jared thought. But now that he knew the truth, he couldn't do anything else. "Yes. We can't just do nothing and let an innocent race be exterminated."

"We need to get this message to Anderson," Benning said, still unsure about whether they were doing the right thing.

"We may not have time," Jared said. "The Contact Team shuttle is in radio silence, all the way in. Even their receivers are off. Rory, if we can arrange for you to use the station's transmitters, can you get the rest of the information into the Caronoi songs in time?"

"I don't think so. I was trying just now, but it's probably too late."

"Wait," Benning said. "We're overstepping the mark here. Even if the kind of intervention he was attempting is right, it's not our remit to—"

"But we do not have time!" Rory was shouting now, desperation showing through. "Once contact is made they're done for! Their dealings with us and the rest of the Alliance will only escalate and there'll be no way I can give them this knowledge and pretend it's always been there. We have to act now!"

"But what can we do?" Jared said.

Rory hesitated; a possibility had clearly occurred to him, but he seemed reticent to share it. "I have a song fragment already scripted that gives the full knowledge in one go," he said eventually. "But it's too late to be subtle. Trying to slip it into their emissary transmissions is too slow—the stuff I send doesn't

239

always get picked up, and I have to resend each stage unless I'm sure it's sunk in. It's taken me months just to get this far. To guarantee success we'd have to go there and feed it into a song directly. I mean find a song ritual in progress and go to Caron-c in person, ahead of the official contact event."

Benning shook his head. "Absolutely out of the question," he said. "If you think you're going to upstage this whole effort on your own, then think again."

Jared knew the next move was in his hands. Though by using his position in a way Alliance Liaison would never sanction, he would be throwing his career and possibly his freedom away. "As an agent of the Office of Alliance Liaison, I have the authority to requisition any equipment or personnel on this station," he said. "Rory, you're going to come with me, and we're going to take a shuttle and go down to the planet."

"No way," Benning said. "I can't allow that."

Benning was a reasonable man, and Jared felt bad coercing him into acting illegally. But Jared had the will—and the authority—to act.

"This is now OAL business—you know what that means."

Benning seemed torn between further protest, and giving in to Jared's authority. "You'll need access codes to the shuttle," he said, bowing to the inevitable. "The commander would normally hold those. He's deputized Sal in his absence."

For the first time since reaching his decision, Jared hesitated. "She's going to be trouble," he said. "Is there any way around it?"

"You can't get off this station without getting past her."

"Then that's what we have to do."

A figure appeared in the doorway. "And just how do you plan on doing that?" It was Sal herself; on a station where anyone could be tracked through any access point, it should have been no wonder that Anderson's designated troubleshooter would find them.

"How much did you hear?" Jared said.

"Enough to get a squad of guards up here and have you taken in. And him too," she added, indicating Rory.

"No, this is too important. If you heard what's going to happen down there, then you have to help us."

She shook her head. "No way. I've wanted to do this for a long time." Then she reached to her belt, where her Taser was kept.

Jared had received full Operative training when he joined OAL as a field agent. As a roving troubleshooter with the success or failure of Earth's interplanetary relations in his hands, he had to be prepared for any situation. And even though he'd never had a real-life physical fight since he was ten years old, the Operative combat training and implant-boosted reflexes were there nonetheless, ready to come to the fore when needed.

He found himself running at her before he even knew what he was doing. She went for the Taser, taking aim in slow motion compared to the speed Jared was moving, then fired early, too early for the darts to fly true. He dodged them, then turned his shoulder toward her and barged her to the side. He only intended to push her off balance and disarm her, but as she lost her footing, she stumbled against the doorway and hit the back of her head on the sheet steel floor.

241

"Damn!" Benning said, running over to her. He checked her pulse, then lifted her eyelids to look at her eyes. "She's alive."

"How are we going to get the codes now?" Rory said.

"I saw a maintenance office on the way here, one level down," Jared said. "We can drag her down there and use her palm print on one of the terminals."

"Are you serious?" Benning said, deathly pale.

"Yes, and you're going to help me."

Benning was in a cold sweat as he helped Jared move Sal's unconscious body, but he did as he was told. Rory stepped in to help too, maneuvering her down a stairway and into the empty office. Then Jared activated the terminal, holding her right hand to the reader as he logged in under her name.

"You know how these files are laid out," he said to Benning. "You find the codes."

Benning complied, copying the crucial information to his own storage key. Then Jared pulled four chairs together and laid Sal out on them. She wasn't bleeding or swelling, but showed no signs of moving either.

"We'll call the med bay once we're in the shuttle. Come on, let's do this."

Jared looked back as Kaluza Station receded behind them, its needle-like profile all but invisible when looking down its central axis. Behind it, the bulk of Caron-e sat, its vast ring system tilted out of the orbital plane, casting a hundred parabolic shadows over its surface. The shuttle pulled away from Kaluza to a distance of five kilometers, then its grav drives activated, giving it the same fifteen-G acceleration that had taken the Contact Team down to the inner system. It was the fastest they could get there, but as the Contact Team were destined to spend hours in high orbit before landing, they still had hopes of beating them to the planet's surface. Once the acceleration was underway, Jared stepped away from the window and went over to where Rory was reprogramming the omni, translating the song fragments he'd formulated into as many dialects as possible so they could land wherever they needed and deliver the message without delay.

Two hours later the midway point of the journey was reached and the shuttle began decelerating. Another two hours later, they were there.

Caron-c was so like Earth, the way its blue, brown and green surface lay blanketed in white clouds, the way the light of its parent sun shone off its oceans like a blaze of white fire. Only the shapes of the land masses betrayed the truth: the two main continents running north to south, connecting the two hemispheres like elongated dumbbells with the three smaller continents sitting between them. And above the planet's horizon hung its only moon, Carpathia, as cratered and airless as Earth's moon but almost golden in color. They entered an orbit two hundred miles above the surface, with all radio sources and illumination deactivated. There was still a chance that they would be detected though—the Contact Team shuttle was orbiting nine hundred miles higher, and even though its radar was off, it still had sensors that might pick them up as it scanned for the Caronois' replies to the welcome message. And the Caronoi themselves, watching the heavens just as keenly, might also spot a new arrival within hours of it orbiting their planet.

Jared and Rory scanned the planet from above, tuning into the frequencies the Caronoi used to spread their songs across the globe. What they wanted was a song ritual in progress, preferably only just begun. It took twenty minutes before Rory announced that he'd found one.

"That's it," he said. "Continent C, northern peninsula. Not ideal, but it's the best we have."

"Why is it not ideal?" Benning said.

"This area doesn't breed intellectual heavyweights," Rory said. "It'll look weird to the Caronoi that this group made the breakthrough. But it'll have to do."

They began their descent, shedding orbital velocity fast, preparing for aerodynamic flight as they dropped into the upper atmosphere. They'd lost too much speed to heat up appreciably—no old-style reentries now gravity itself had been harnessed—but the sound of the supersonic airflow rushing over the airframe whistled into the cabin like a distant gale. Then, as they got lower, they turned off to the side, toward the source of the emissions. The sky around them was pastel blue, cloud banks like strings of cotton balls dividing the air into layers of temperature and humidity, with a mottled landscape of green and brown below them. Any temperate zone on Earth could have looked like this.

Then they went low, maneuvering around any known concentrations of population, descending until the treetops looked close enough to touch. The canopies were slightly too dark, too angular in shape to be earthly—for only at twenty meters altitude did the planet start to look like somewhere other than home. Then they encountered a series of undulating ridges with broad valleys between them. In one of them, they stopped as Benning brought them to a hover just above ground level, checking the map display.

"This valley leads to the sea," he said. "According to this they're on the coast a few miles up."

He took them north, following the valley floor as the ridges to either side petered out, leaving them on a broad coastal plain. The land met the sea in a series of rocky ledges, and it was on one of these that the Caronoi had gathered. They could see the Caronoi, not just huddled together, but piled on top of one another in a heaped congregation twenty meters long and three high, standing on each other's shoulders and flanks like an irregular framework of limbs and torsos.

Benning landed them a few hundred meters inland; then they quickly gathered up everything they'd need, including Rory's omni and the audio files it contained. Then they opened the shuttle's rear hatch and stepped out onto the surface of the planet.

The smell was what Jared noticed first, smells of sea spray and salt and ozone, mixed with odors of cut grass and pine sap that seemed to mix in different ways as he turned his head. The air was cold, the light fading, and it felt like an autumn day's twilight on a chilly seashore back where he'd grown up in Maine. He could hear the sea hitting the rocks, the wind blowing in off the water, but most of all he could

245

hear the Caronoi themselves, that low droning sound pulsing and fluctuating, interspersed with chirps and whistles as whole volumes of information passed between them.

"Come on," Rory said, dashing around to the front of the shuttle, then onward to the Caronoi gathering. He ran over to them, then stopped just short of the closest ones. Jared ran after him and stopped alongside. The Caronoi were close enough to touch, every mark on their mottled white bodies visible, but locked into their song, trancing, they were completely unaware of their new visitors. It felt like sneaking up on someone in their sleep.

"Amazing," Rory said under his breath, then reached out and gently touched the closest one. First contact, in this case literally. "Right, let's get this started."

"Have they reached the right bit of the song?" Jared said.

"It doesn't work that way, they don't separate out the subjects like that. The songs are more like audio holograms—as long as we got here early enough we can pipe the information in and give them time to digest it."

He opened up the omni and selected the song files for this dialect. Then he set them playing, adding his contribution to the close harmony rendition of an entire race's knowledge. A couple of the nearest Caronoi shifted their posture in response to the new sound, as if trying to locate it, make out what it said.

"Is it working?" Jared said.

"I don't know, maybe," Rory said. "Give it time."

As Rory set his plan in motion, Jared looked around

the Caronoi settlement. The shelters themselves were further inland, open-sided frameworks roofed with twigs and moss. Alongside them was an emissary tower, a radio antenna fed from probably the simplest transmitter imaginable, named after the emissaries who used to carry songs from tribe to tribe, until one day a song originating somewhere in the south provided the crucial information on how putting copper and iron and lodestone together in just the right way could open up long-distance communication and relegate traveling emissaries to history.

Then he looked back at where Rory was monitoring the output from the omni. Could it really be this easy, he thought, just a case of pumping in the information, then getting back into the shuttle and scurrying back to Kaluza Station? No, there would be more to it even if the plan worked—explaining to Anderson why they'd upstaged his contact effort, explaining what he'd done to Sal, explaining to Alliance Liaison why he'd pulled rank on the Kaluza staff in a way which they would never have endorsed, which defied the very Alliance they were at pains to placate. The mission might be done, but the storm was only beginning.

Then Benning emerged from the shuttle and ran over. "There's something coming this way," he said.

The Contact Team shuttle landed a hundred meters or so from their own. Then the hatch opened and Anderson came out. They could tell even before he stormed over that he was furious. He stopped short and looked from Jared to Rory to Benning and back again, practically on fire with rage.

"Talk. Now."

Jared stepped forward and gave him the story. By the time he finished, Anderson had barely even started to calm down. He looked to Benning.

"Is all this true?"

Benning nodded. "We only have Rory Temple's word for it, but it appears to be the case."

Anderson stepped back, steepling his fingers as he always did when digesting difficult news. Jared could see the veins standing out in the man's neck and head, but he seemed to be taking it all rationally, pulling himself back from the brink of meltdown.

"Those ships in the outer system *are* Alliance," he said. "One of them entered Caron-c orbit half an hour ago. We switched on our receivers as soon as we saw it and heard a systemwide broadcast to all human vessels, including as they put it 'both landing craft.' You'll understand our concern as to who the other one might have been. That's when we started scanning and saw you three, down here."

"Why did they contact you?" Jared said.

Anderson looked back at him, a coldness to his eyes. "It was a warning to clear the planet's surface. They're going to blow the place."

"No! They can't!" It was Rory, stepping forward to face Anderson.

"Why are they doing that?" Jared said. "Did something go wrong at the contact site?"

"We never got that far," Anderson said. "We sent the broadcast, we were scanning for a response and then the Alliance appeared. Some kind of Sprite ship, something we've never seen before. And right now, I will need a hell of a lot of persuasion to believe that your intervention hasn't caused this. I think they figured out what you're doing and this is their response."

Jared looked over at where Rory's song was still playing out into the Caronoi gathering. Could the Alliance have been watching that closely, all this time? They were millennia ahead technologically, but not clairvoyant. "I don't think that's true. The Alliance are acting because they know the Caronoi are naïves, and they only know that because they've reviewed our research reports. We've given them three years of data and analysis, and unwittingly incriminated the Caronoi in the process, but that doesn't have to be the full picture."

"You mean you think we can still fix this?" Rory said. He was almost shaking with the enormity of what he'd started, clearly out of his depth now that Anderson, the OAL and the whole Alliance were involved.

"Maybe," Jared said. "But not like before. You've planted the seed of the theory in the Caronois' minds, but we don't have time to let it take root on its own any more. We need to tell the Alliance straight out why the Caronoi are suddenly worth saving."

"And reveal that we know what the Alliance are looking for?" Anderson said. "Remember, we're being judged too, if Mr. Temple's theory is correct—if we step out of line, we're next."

"In that case we think up some way of pointing them in the right direction. Something with plausible deniability."

"What if you're wrong?" Anderson said. "What if by doing this you only provoke them?"

"What would you rather do? Leave the Caronoi to be massacred? Knowing that you could have helped them?" Through his brief time on the station, one thing had come through loud and clear to Jared. For some people, including, he suspected, Anderson, the mission had become more than just a research project. They'd got to know the Caronoi so well, albeit from a distance, that there was now an emotional stake in contacting them. Working the last three years only to see them wiped out would be more than just a waste of research time.

"Fine, your way," Anderson said. "But whatever we do next, we do it from orbit. I am not going to wait here for whatever that Sprite cruiser has in store. Mr. Benning, set your shuttle to automatic and get it back to Kaluza Station. From here on we stick together."

Ten minutes later, the remaining shuttle was back in orbit, nine hundred miles above the planet's surface. Jared, Rory and Benning stood up front with Anderson and the pilot while the rest of the Contact Team sat behind them, coming to terms with the rushed summary Anderson had been able to give them—a species doomed according to arbitrary rules, a new mission plan to save them and the risk of defying the Alliance itself. Two thousand miles ahead of them was the Sprite cruiser, ten miles of stacked circular disks and needle-like spires, product of a technology Jared knew Earth had only begun to comprehend. And between the disks were the Sprites themselves, open to space, their charcoal-gray polyhedral carapaces hardened to the vacuum and radiation.

Jared activated the shuttle's comms panel and

hailed the ship. Just contacting them instead of waiting for them to initiate was a breach of OAL protocol, another offense to add to a long list of transgressions.

"Remain in orbit while sterilization occurs," the reply came moments later, a bland synthetic voice steeped in gender-neutral, unemotive tones.

"Please clarify reasons for sterilization," Jared said. He didn't work directly with the OAL Speakers, but he'd heard that simple, direct sentences were usually the best approach.

"Subject species is in violation of Alliance criteria," was the similarly terse reply.

"Please indicate nature of violation," Jared said.

"Subject species is in violation of Alliance criteria," the Sprite repeated.

"We don't have time to play this subtle," Jared said, more to himself than anyone, then into the comm unit: "Our research has revealed new data that could influence the criteria. Request delay to sterilization."

"Humans have no information on Alliance criteria."

"This is painful," Benning said. "Are they always this hard work to talk to?"

"So I've heard," Jared said, then to the Sprites, "We strongly request that the sterilization is halted in the light of new information. This is vital to the success of the contact mission."

"Humans have no information on Alliance criteria."

"Jesus Christ!" Benning said. "What do we have to do to get it through to these things?"

Jared knew, but the direction this conversation was taking might have consequences beyond anything

251

he'd done so far. He took a deep breath, then spoke into the comm unit again.

"Our studies lead us to assess with high confidence that the Caronoi are not and will never be in violation of Alliance criteria."

He was sure he could detect a pause before the reply came. With AI minds running billions of times faster than human brains, to make them stop and think even for a heartbeat was some achievement.

"Present proof of this assertion," the Sprite ship answered.

"Any ideas?" Jared said to those gathered round him.

"Not beyond telling them straight out how much we know," Rory said. "But then that was always going to be the case, wasn't it?"

Jared knew that it was true. It was time to go for broke. He turned to the comm unit and addressed the Sprites one more time.

"A final precontact investigation of Caronoi capabilities has just been performed. A group of Caronoi have recently developed the ability to analyze conflict as a mathematical phenomenon. We have seen them derive theorems proving the futility of instigating such conflicts, including those where techniques based on causality violation are employed. As such we do not believe they pose a threat to Alliance interests."

There was silence from the Sprites. Ten, twenty seconds passed without answer. "My God, what have you done?" Anderson said. "If you're right and we're not even meant to know about that—"

A message from the Sprite cruiser interrupted him.

"This claim confirms that violation has occurred," it said. "Hold station."

"We're done for," Benning said.

More time passed while those in the shuttle waited in silence, the atmosphere of the cabin turning cold and clammy with apprehension.

I've done it, Jared thought, I've just consigned the human race to history to stand up for a principle. His palms were sweating as he stood in the cockpit, knuckles white on the grab rail. Then, at last, the final message from the Sprite ship came through.

"The Alliance has concluded that contact with the subject race can continue. No information regarding Alliance criteria will be given to them."

Then the Sprite ship departed, accelerating away so rapidly that on the shuttle's view screens it appeared to just vanish.

"Is that it?" Anderson said. "They let us off just like that?"

Then a light appeared, off to the side. For a few seconds it shone brighter than the sun, then diminished. Everyone in the shuttle crowded to the side windows, and what faced them was Carpathia, sole moon of Caron-c.

The surface was glowing white hot, a spherical envelope of gas expanding around it. Then it cooled, to the orange of molten magma, then the red of sunset. Already those watching could see that the surface had been obliterated entirely.

"Jesus Christ," Rory said, "they nuked the thing."

"What the hell?" Benning said.

"It's a warning," Jared said. "They weren't fooled;

they know what we did and why. If our membership was in the balance before, then it's running at critical now. They've shown us what's in store if we defy them again."

They watched Carpathia's surface, cooling and flowing, its shattered surface lit by the menacing red glow of nuclear annihilation.

The plain was near the equator, with a vast jungle-covered river basin to the south, hot blue skies above and a warm dry wind blowing off the deserts further west. The Caronoi settlement here was like a sprawl of teepees on a grassy meadow, straddling a narrow river of blue-green water. On the edge of the settlement was their emissary tower, far larger than the one Jared had seen at the last site, and beyond that was a long-range transmitter field, six square kilometers of phase-locked dipole antennae, tens of thousands of them, each wood-and-wire construction no more advanced than the emissary transmitters but forming a phased array that could command probes as far as the outer system. And barely ten miles away was the place where one of those probes had been launched, the site cleared and leveled so the rocket could be assembled, elevated, then packed with propellant and launched.

They never built and tested things, Jared thought as he looked around the examples of Caronoi technology. There were no labs, no research institutes, no particle accelerators or mass spectrometers. All their experiments were thought experiments, carried out in whatever shared world that bizarre song trance took them to. And then they would snap out of it and do *this,* and it would just work, every time.

RHIANNON TAYLOR

Then he looked toward the center of the settlement, where Anderson had walked in, alone, to greet the Caronoi. There was a small crowd of them, awake and aware this time, and Anderson was talking to them, the translator unit in his hand, occasionally gesturing back to the shuttle and the rest of the team waiting a safe nonthreatening distance away.

"So tell me something," Jared said to Rory as they watched. "How did your grandfather know so much if Alliance rules are meant to be so secret?"

"Let's just say the Alliance isn't as unified as they like us to think. There are factions, even within the Sprites, who think they are doing things wrongly. My grandfather was lucky enough to meet them first, and they were able to help us. But we needed to maintain the pretense of true compliance, and that bound him to secrecy. Unfortunately, with the Caronoi, it fell to us to play good cop. Or to me."

Rory had carried this knowledge alone for years, Jared realized, with the fate of entire races in his hands. It felt good to share the burden, just by being let in on the facts. "I don't know what's going to happen when this gets reported back to Earth," he said. "I'm in trouble, I know it. You may be too. But now we know what we've got ourselves into with the Alliance, what we're really up against, the people in control might realize the situation has changed."

"You think we can help other races? Ones we encounter in future?"

"Possibly. I can't help feeling we've delivered the Caronoi to the Alliance on a plate by bringing them in, but they'd already been discovered, and you can't put the clock back. But if the Alliance itself is divided, at least we get to pick which side we're on. It's not just us against *them*."

Rory nodded slowly and looked up, where Carpathia sat high in the daylight sky. *They* had arranged another demonstration of power in the hours after its surface had been near-vaporized. Somehow, incredibly, it had been resculpted as it cooled, regaining its former appearance as if nothing had happened. The sheer power required to manipulate matter on a planetary scale was if anything a more sobering show of supremacy than the destruction that preceded it.

"So were we naïves?" Jared said. "Humans, I mean, when your grandfather made contact?"

"We were," Rory said. "We would have been in the firing line. Have you ever heard of Alderman's theorem?"

"No."

"That's what the crucial branch of Game Theory is known as on Earth. Except John Alderman never came up with it. He'd recently died in a car crash when our first contact happened, so records were fabricated to make it look like he'd figured it out just before his death."

"Like the songs you concocted for the Caronoi? A fake breakthrough, just in time?"

"Exactly."

They carried on watching Anderson in silence. Then, ten minutes after he had started discussions with the Caronoi, he turned to face the Contact Team and waved them over.

"Looks like we're on," Rory said. He wasn't an

official Contact Team member any more than Jared was, but the rulebook for this enterprise had already been thrown out of the window. They walked over to join Anderson, fifteen of them in all including the Contact Team proper, and gathered in front of the Caronoi.

They were strangely amphibian in some ways, their rhomboid cream-white bodies with four long frog-like limbs, and faces taking up the whole front section of their torsos. Their eyes were expressionless black marbles, surrounded by openings for air, food, hearing and speech.

The two species stood regarding each other, then the Caronoi nearest to Anderson said something, a short sharp chirp of noise that came out of the translator as "They other world also?"

"Yes," Anderson said. "They are."

Another chirp. "Many other worlds exist?"

"Yes, a great many."

Then the Caronoi turned to face its own kind and said something else, another burst of noise, then repeated it once more.

"Other worlds," the translator said. "Life on other worlds. Told you so."

The Importance of Short Fiction

BY *KRISTINE KATHRYN RUSCH*

Kristine Kathryn Rusch has written over 100 novels under a variety of names. As Kris Nelscott, she's the Edgar- and Shamus-nominated writer of the Smokey Dalton mystery series, which has been published all over the world. As Kristine Grayson, she's the award-winning, bestselling writer of goofy romance novels filled with fractured fairy tales. As Kris DeLake, she writes paranormal romance with a science fiction twist. She also writes under several other names, sometimes in collaboration with her husband Dean Wesley Smith.

Under her own name, Kristine Kathryn Rusch, she has won two Hugos and dozens of Readers' Choice Awards. Her Rusch novels have been on bestseller lists all over the world, including the London Times, *the* Wall Street Journal, Publishers Weekly, *and the* USA Today *list. She has a thriving short story career. Her stories have appeared in about 20 year's best collections, including the prestigious* Best American Mystery Stories.

Kristine has served as a Writers of the Future Contest judge since 2010.

The Importance of Short Fiction

The heart and the future of science fiction lie in its short fiction. Short fiction is difficult to write well, yet we in the SF field tell all beginning writers to start with it. Why? Because short fiction is . . . well . . . short.

I know. It sounds both silly and obvious. Writers should write short fiction because it's short—like those finger exercises pianists must learn so they can play a piano concerto. The problem with the advice—write short fiction because it's short—is this: it makes writers believe that short fiction is easy, something to graduate from, something that isn't worth their time except as *practice*.

The short stories in this volume are clearly not practice. They're good or they wouldn't have been chosen out of the thousands—and I do mean thousands—of stories that Writers of the Future receives every quarter.

These stories have heart, they have creativity, but most important, they're a good read.

That's what so many writers forget when they approach short fiction as if it's a finger exercise. The writers write a dutiful little piece with lovely words. Then they hone those words to death, forgetting that the story is the most important thing.

What is a story? Well, I can give you the numerical answer. The standards used by the Hugo awards, the most prestigious award in science fiction, are: A short story is no longer than 7,500 words; a novelette runs from 7,501 words to 15,000 words; and a novella runs from 15,001 words to 30,000 words.

By the way, all of those things—short story, novelette, novella—are considered short fiction. Other genres have slightly different definitions, but the one thing we writers, publishers, editors and readers can agree on is this: If the piece runs too long, it's a novel.

The Writers of the Future contest, by the way, limits story length to 17,000 words. Which means that you can write them a short-short (under 1,000 words) or a novella (up to 17,000 words, but no more). Be warned that either form—the shortest and the longest—are tough.

But what is short fiction and why is it hard? Let me answer the second part first. Short fiction is hard because it must do the work of a novel at one-tenth to one-third the size.

Novelists cheat. I tell you this as someone who has published over 100 of them. Novelists can spread out, go on digressions, add extra subplots if the main story doesn't work. Novelists can meander, explore interesting characters who have no real point in the plot or muse on some scientific principle.

Short fiction writers can't. I tell you that as someone who has published more than 400 short stories and who edited short fiction for two different companies for over ten years. Short fiction writers must get to the point. They must focus their work on the most important part of the tale, whatever that may be.

Algis Budrys, a fantastic writer, the first Writers of the Future Contest administrator and a major influence on my life, used to say that the short story is the most important event in a character's life. That's good for stand-alone short stories, but for stories that follow serial characters (like a detective), it doesn't always work. So I modified it to "one of the most important events" in a character's life. The story needs to have something earthshaking—or universe-shaking, in the case of science fiction.

And of course, never forget: the story's the thing, not the writing. And not the manuscript. The manuscript is the tool to get the story from the writer's head to the reader's head, nothing more. Right now, I'm writing this essay in my office, and you're reading it months, maybe years later, somewhere else. Yet I'm telling you something in real time. The real time for me is December, 2011. The real time for you might be June, 2021. All I've done is use a tool to communicate with you, and I'm not communicating words, I'm communicating my ideas, expressed in my voice.

The "story" part of the short story is what the story is about. The events, yes, but the characters and the setting, and the entire experience of *living* inside that world for the brief duration of the reading experience.

The story itself must be good. Forget the finger exercises. Forget the pretty words. Forget the mountains of rewriting. Rewriting is a skill that takes years to learn. Concentrate on writing a lot of short stories.

In 1947, in a book called *Worlds of Beyond*, Science Fiction Grand Master Robert Heinlein wrote a series of business rules for serious science fiction writers. They are:

1. You must *write*.
2. You must *finish* what you write.
3. You must refrain from rewriting except to editorial order.
4. You must put it on the market.
5. You must keep it on the market until sold.

This advice is still good, even in the digital age, even with the rise of indie publishing. I'll add a few things to modify the business rules for the twenty-first century. They are pretty simple additions:

1. You must *write*.
2. You must *finish* what you write.
3. You must refrain from rewriting except to editorial order, *and only if you agree with the editorial direction*. (We call this the Harlan Ellison corollary, first added by the man most consider the best short story writer the field has ever known.)
4. You must put it on the market.
5. You must keep it on the market.
6. Repeat on a weekly basis.

You'll note that only three and five got revised. Six is the addition that my husband, the excellent writer Dean Wesley Smith, and I have made over the years.

Three needs the Harlan Ellison corollary, because not every reader (even an editor) is right about every story. And five reflects the indie publishing reality. If a writer self-publishes a short story, that short story should stay on the market, and the writer should move on to the next story. Will the writer improve over the years? Sure. But the writer shouldn't be stuck trying to "improve" past works. The writer should write new works, different works, always striving to improve.

After Heinlein wrote down his rules, he added this: "They are amazingly hard to follow—which is why there are so few professional writers and so many aspirants and which is why I am not afraid to give away the racket!"

Those words remain true today. Very few beginning writers ever try to write, let alone finish what they write, let alone put what they write on the market, in whatever form. And the forms will change, as they have over the past few years.

What I love is that the market for short fiction has expanded greatly. We are now in a new golden age of short fiction. Dozens of new, paying short fiction markets crop up every year. And that doesn't count the indie-publishing revolution. Right now, short fiction writers have a better chance to be published than at any other time in the past thirty years.

And that's a great thing for science fiction. Because, as I said above, the heart and future of the genre is in short fiction, and always has been. That's why L. Ron Hubbard sponsored a short fiction contest, not a novel contest. Science fiction's most classic works either started as short stories and then got expanded into novels, or those classic works *are* short stories that we still discuss today.

Our best writers still produce excellent short fiction. From George R. R. Martin to Connie Willis to contest winner Robert Reed, our best novelists still find time to write spectacular short fiction. And by doing so, they move the field ever forward, looking at old ideas in new ways, creating new ideas and new worlds, and writing the most memorable characters ever.

But most of all, these writers are spectacular *storytellers*. They tell long stories and short stories, medium-length stories and short punchy stories. They let the tale determine its own length, and they continually add to an already rich field.

Our best writers write short stories throughout their careers. This volume contains the best writers of a new generation. I hope we all get a chance to read their short fiction for decades to come.

The Command for Love

written by

Nick T. Chan

illustrated by

CARLY TROWBRIDGE

ABOUT THE AUTHOR

Nick T. Chan lives in Sydney, Australia, with his wonderful wife Fiona and future Hugo/Nebula/Pulitzer/Nobel prize-winning daughter Nina. He has previously worked as a technical writer for textbooks in various fields, and currently works as a project manager and editor in postgraduate education. He is also an assistant editor on the Parsec Ink Triangulation series of anthologies.

His childhood was spent reading. Reading when he should have been cleaning his bedroom, reading instead of (and during) playing sports, reading when he should have been doing his homework. As a young boy, his long-suffering mother had to read The Lord of the Rings *to him every night without any deviation. Nick had memorized every single page, so he knew if his mother tried to skip any pages (even the Tom Bombadil passages).*

After university, Nick attempted to write sporadically, but made the mistake of abandoning his love of speculative fiction in the belief that other genres were more respectable. Without loving what he wrote, his productivity withered, and he abandoned serious writing for many years.

Five years ago, Nick returned to his roots in order to write a fantasy novel that will never see the light of day. At the same time, he spotted an advertisement for a writing course run by acclaimed Australian speculative fiction writer Terry Dowling. With the help of renowned Australian writers such as Cat Sparks, Rob Hood and Terry, as well as a talented writing group organized by Terry, Nick started on the continuing journey of learning how to write and rekindled his love for speculative fiction. In 2010, he set his sights on the Writers of the Future competition.

After two honorable mentions and one non-winning Finalist, he won with "The Command for Love." He is currently working on a novel set in the same world as "The Command for Love."

ABOUT THE ILLUSTRATOR

Hailing from Huntsville, Alabama, Carly Trowbridge has the pleasure of calling the town affectionately known as "Rocket City, USA" home. In a city brimming full of engineers and physicists, it is hard to pinpoint exactly where her fascination with the science fiction genre began. Needless to say, she was never at a loss for inspiration growing up. These days she finds herself influenced by the sci-fi, fantasy and pop culture scene as whole, and finds artistry in everything from graphic novels to movie marathons on the Syfy channel.

Carly holds a bachelor's degree in art and biology, and spent her undergraduate years focused on improving her skills in drafting and drawing. She has recently received her master's degree in medical illustration from the Medical College of Georgia. In between sporadic part-time jobs, she keeps busy traveling across the US keeping in touch with friends. Carly is honored to be included among the Illustrators of the Future, and looks forward with high hopes to whatever other opportunities await her.

The Command for Love

For the third time in a week, Ligish removed the locking pin from the back of his skull, opened the doors and examined his brain through an automicroscope. Maybe today he'd figure out which one of the homunculus' slips of paper was the command for love and destroy the damn thing. The last thing he wanted was to fall in love with his master's daughter.

A cascade of mirrors relayed images from inside Ligish's skull to a silver screen in front of his face. Reflected in the silver was Master Gray's homunculus sitting at an ivory desk. Ligish's skull was empty except for the desk, the homunculus and a golden sphere the size of a grapefruit. The homunculus' hand blurred as it dipped its quill against a hole in the desk. The nib emerged coated with black ink-blood. The homunculus wrote mysterious symbols on pieces of parchment. Once it finished each command, the homunculus pushed it through a slot in the golden sphere.

Ligish increased the magnification. Yesterday, he'd thought he'd discovered the command for love. He'd spotted the same symbol several times, but then he realized he'd seen it last month during routine self-examination. He'd only fallen in love with Anna last week.

Ligish sighed. It was hopeless. Humans had their subconscious driving their behavior in ways unknown to their rational minds, but at least it was theirs, and sometimes they could refuse its imperatives. He could not refuse his homunculus and it no longer listened to his thoughts. Worse still, it grew senile in lockstep with Master Gray.

He'd never heard of a homunculus giving instructions to fall in love before. It was utter foolishness. She was human. He was an electro-reinforced titanium war golem. Somehow, he must fall out of love with Anna. At the thought of her name, the homunculus scribbled a command and put it into the slot. The pistons in his chest compartment sped up. Ligish clutched his chest. What was the fool thing doing now? By God, even thinking her name made his engines malfunction. This love business needed to end. Master Gray was too senile to create a new homunculus and too poor to buy a new one, so only Ligish could find a solution.

There was no end to his worries. Love, Master Gray's poverty, the leaking roof over the north wing and a thousand household chores. He was no closer to identifying the command today than he was on Monday, and other tasks demanded his attention. Ligish waited until his chest pistons slowed and then pushed the automicroscope controls away.

Someone knocked on the doors. "Golem," a man said. "Open these doors." Master Gray hadn't left his bed or seen visitors for months. Who could it be? The man turned the handle and tried to enter, but Ligish had blocked the doors with a scale model of the world. The doors hit the model's head, activating the key-wound mechanism. With a whir, the right arm lifted the sun above the chest's vertical plane, while the left arm dropped below, imitating the cycle of day and night. "Golem, I command you to open up!"

It was tempting to ignore the visitor and continue with his research, but Miss Anna would chide him for neglecting his duties. "One moment," he called and locked his skull. He walked to the doors, his footsteps rattling the glass beakers on the laboratory benches. He lifted the model world by the leg, careful to avoid crushing the tiny mountains, and moved it from the doorway.

A bespectacled old soldier opened the doors. He limped into the laboratory, his tan military uniform almost blending into the parquet floor. A row of medals from the Suprasternal Notch war was pinned to his chest. The gears in Ligish's bowels rumbled. The Suprasternal Notch war was notorious for its brutality. The stars on the man's shoulders indicated a general's rank. Shuffling behind was a junior officer carrying a notepad and pencil.

The man leaned upon his walking stick as he surveyed the mess of glassware, scientific instruments and charts scattered around what had once been the family ballroom. "Johnson, take note," he said. "A genuine titanium war golem from the Transpyloric Plane. I'd thought they'd all been destroyed after the treaty of Omental Bursa. It must be thousands of years old."

Ligish knelt so they were at the same height and extended his hand. The general examined it with a cool curiosity, but did not shake. After an uncomfortable moment, Ligish dropped his hand and stood.

"It is a pleasure to have your acquaintance," Ligish said. "I believe I'm the only verified war golem left upon the world's upper body, though there are rumors inert bronze war golems sleep in Acetabulum's dark forests."

The general stretched and tapped Ligish on the forehead with his walking stick, making a tiny belling sound. "At least ten feet tall and electroreinforced titanium skin," he said to Johnson, who scribbled notes. "See the rust on the skull rivets? It still houses the original soul. Thousands of years of experience. Johnson, what do you think a genuine war golem under my homunculus would do for the war in Anterior Talus?"

"It may turn the tide, General Maul," Johnson said.

In his head, Ligish counted to ten. He'd usher these upstart soldiers from their house calmly and coolly, like a proper servant. "General Maul," he said. "Master Gray is in ill health and Miss Anna has need of my tutoring before her final exams. As much as I'd love to serve Arteria Carotis, I'm needed here."

Maul spoke to Johnson. "Its homunculus is quite the conversationalist. It'll be a pity to replace it."

"Did you not hear me?" Ligish yelled. A beaker fell from a bench and shattered.

Maul removed his spectacles and stared at Ligish, his eyes like wet black stones. "You've no choice. Once I'm married to Miss Gray, you're my possession."

Ligish's knees buckled and it was all he could do to avoid toppling in shock. "Married?"

"Yes," Maul said. "You'll be in my service."

Anna could not be engaged to this man. She'd have told him, wouldn't she? "I don't wish to be employed by you."

"Mr. Gray is sentimental about your generations of service to his family, but the law is the law," Maul said. "The thinking have dominion over the nonthinking and only men are self-aware. Mr. Gray has agreed I'll clear his debts in return for the ownership of his daughter and his goods. You'll be my possession in a month."

Ligish balled his fists, wanting badly to grab Maul's head and squeeze until it popped. General Maul continued peering around the lab, picking up beakers and ruining Ligish's experiments. "You're dismissed," he said. "A month is barely enough time to repair this hovel. I'd suggest you start."

Ligish bowed and scraped out of the laboratory. Once the doors were closed, he strode toward the western wing. Hopefully his homunculus would command him to beg Master Gray to sell Ligish to a charity before the wedding. He could do good helping the poor instead of slaughtering men in the distant polar darkness of Anterior Talus.

Instead of walking to Master Gray, his homunculus made him climb the stairs to her room. There was no reason to do so. As a woman, Anna had no say over whom she married. But his homunculus compelled him to tiptoe to her room as quietly as his bulk allowed and tap on her door.

"I'm studying," she said, and he feared the fragility underneath the calm in her voice might break him. He pushed the door open. A book was open in one hand. With her other hand, she pushed colored thumbtacks

273

into a map of the world. After consulting a page, she pushed a blue tack into the world's right shoulder.

"That's incorrect," Ligish said. "Remember, the principality of Dexter Trapezius invaded Dexter Glenohumeral last month. The laws are now the same across both shoulders and the upper chest." Anna removed the blue thumbtack from the world's right shoulder and replaced it with a red one.

The candle on her desk cast a thin circle of light, leaving the room half dark, but the dried tears on her cheeks were still visible. The pistons in his chest quickened at the sight of her long neck, the birdlike delicacy of her face, the ghost-pale loveliness of her skin and the shape of her body half hidden underneath her nightgown. He could not sit on her bed without breaking it, so he stood. She put her book down on the desk. "You've met my fiancé?" she said. Her tone was light, deliberately airy.

"He is very certain of himself."

She smiled. "Papa's title will be very important in Mr. Maul's election campaign. Men take their right to vote for granted, don't they?" And then her composure melted in tears and she hugged him around the legs. Heat extended from his chest outwards as his engine increased its work rate. He patted her on the head, wanting more than anything to take her golden hair into his hands and kiss her. But his emotion was simply a command from a senile homunculus, so all he did was comfort her.

"I'm sorry," Anna said. "It is so unfair." She dried her eyes. "My studies were always meaningless. I'd never be allowed to work. But now I can't even matriculate."

FREE

Send in this card and you will receive a FREE BOOKMARK while supplies last. No order required for this special offer! Mail in your card today!

❑ Please send me a FREE bookmark!   ❑ Please send me information about other books by L. Ron Hubbard.

ORDERS SHIPPED WITHIN 24 HRS. OF RECEIPT

WRITERS OF THE FUTURE

____ L. RON HUBBARD PRESENTS WRITERS OF THE FUTURE ® volumes: (paperbacks)
  ❑ Vol 22 $7.99   ❑ Vol 23 $7.99   ❑ Vol 24 $7.99   ❑ Vol 25 $7.99
  ❑ Vol 26 $7.99   ❑ Vol 27 $7.99   ❑ Vol 28 $7.99

____ L. RON HUBBARD PRESENTS WRITERS OF THE FUTURE: The First 25 Years
  (hardcover) $44.95   _____

____ L. RON HUBBARD PRESENTS THE BEST OF WRITERS OF THE FUTURE
  (trade paperback) $14.95   _____

OTHER BOOKS BY L. RON HUBBARD

STORIES FROM THE GOLDEN AGE series $9.95 book, $12.95 audio.
(80 volumes paperback & audio)   _____

  ❑ BRANDED OUTLAW   ❑ IF I WERE YOU   ❑ SEA FANGS
  ❑ DEAD MEN KILL   ❑ THE IRON DUKE   ❑ SPY KILLER
  ❑ THE GREAT SECRET   ❑ SABOTAGE IN THE SKY   ❑ UNDER THE BLACK ENSIGN
  Specify format: paperback ____ or audiobook CD ____
  ❑ *Check here for a complete catalog of Stories from the Golden Age titles.*

  ❑ BATTLEFIELD EARTH ® paperback $7.99
  ❑ BUCKSKIN BRIGADES paperback $6.99
  ❑ FEAR paperback $7.99
  ❑ TO THE STARS hardcover $24.95
  ❑ TO THE STARS audiobook CD $25.00

SHIPPING RATES US: $2.00 for one book. Add an additional $.50
per book when ordering more than one.   Tax*:   _____
SHIPPING RATES CANADA: $3.50 for one book. Add an additional
$2.00 per book when ordering more than one.   Shipping: _____
*California residents add 8.75% sales tax.   TOTAL: _____

CHECK AS APPLICABLE:
  ❑ Check/Money Order enclosed. (Please use an envelope.)
  ❑ American Express   ❑ Visa   ❑ MasterCard   ❑ Discover

  Card #:_____

  Exp. Date:_____   Signature:_____

  Credit Card Billing Address ZIP Code:_____

  Name:_____

  Address:_____

  City:_____ State:_____ ZIP:_____

  Phone #:_____   E-mail:_____

You can also place your order by calling toll-free: 1-877-842-5299
or order online at www.GalaxyPress.com

Select titles are also available as eBook and audio downloads at Amazon.com and other online retailers.

BUSINESS REPLY MAIL

FIRST-CLASS MAIL   PERMIT NO. 75738   LOS ANGELES, CA

POSTAGE WILL BE PAID BY ADDRESSEE

GALAXY PRESS DEPT. W28
7051 HOLLYWOOD BLVD
HOLLYWOOD CA 90028-9771

NO POSTAGE
NECESSARY
IF MAILED
IN THE
UNITED STATES

"Maul plans to send me to Anterior Talus," he said. Anna's face drained. "No, he can't."

"Your father has always paid me generous wages," he said. "I'm not property!" The heat with which he spoke surprised Ligish. The desires of homunculi were a mystery to all but God, but in this, at least, his commanding homunculus felt the same.

Anna disengaged and picked up the book from her desk. She flipped pages and then traced the relevant passage with her finger as she read aloud. "Only male humans possess the power of self-awareness and thus have domain over the nonthinking. The nonthinking are defined as homunculi, beasts, golems and women." Anger flashed across her face. "He visited Papa two hours ago and now I'm married."

Ligish bowed his head. It was his fault. If he hadn't been so absorbed in finding a solution to his love problems, then he'd have received General Maul. He might have refused him entry or at least been with Master Gray while they negotiated the wedding contract.

"The courts must overturn your engagement," he said. "Forgive me, Miss Anna, but your father is not of a sound mind. Yesterday, he mistook me for your deceased Aunt Joan."

Anna parted the curtains and pointed out the window. Two men in Arteria Carotis army uniforms stood outside the entrance. One smoked a cigarette. The other rested upon the stock of his ghost-fist rifle.

"Now I'm engaged, I'm no longer a girl," she said. "Outside the home, women must be accompanied by two guards to protect their virtue." She shut the curtains. "There's a guard at the kitchen door. A pair patrol the outer grounds. All because I'm a valuable possession. There's a man outside Papa's room to protect him in his fragile health." She sat on the bed and buried her head in her hands.

Ligish knelt, the floorboards creaking, and took her hands. "Miss Gray, do not despair. We'll find a way to petition the court."

"I must attend in person to annul a marriage." She rubbed her eyes. "Liggy, can you please guard my door until Maul retires?"

A cog in his chest slipped off its belt for a moment, before sliding back into place. "He wouldn't dare defile you."

"I feel safe with you," she said. "It's a request, Liggy, not a command. Please."

He stood and bowed. "I'll do whatever you ask for eternity. I'll always be your servant, no matter who my master is."

She hugged him. At her touch, his engines heated and Anna flinched and gasped. "Liggy, have you been trying to dig a well again?" she said. "You know you shouldn't dig through granite. Your engine is overheating. I can feel your armor softening. What happens if you run out of power?"

He smiled. "I'd wait until I recharged. All I need is time." His engine cooled. He kissed her on the forehead and then left, taking her law book with him.

The corridor was dark, but he needed very little light to read. The more he read, the less likely it seemed the marriage contract could be annulled. She must have known her chances of success were minimal, though it wouldn't stop her from trying.

Ligish surveyed the house's security every year, knew every single possible exit. Anna hadn't yet thought of climbing through her window onto the roof, but she would. The roof was wet with moss, and it was a long fall to the pavement. Ice water surged over his compression cylinder at the idea of her falling. There must be some other way of saving her that didn't involve smuggling her from the house to the court.

The scrape and flare of a match being struck caught Ligish's attention. General Maul lit a pipe, puffed a plume of smoke before the match died. He limped toward Ligish.

"Each time I see you, I realize how remarkable you are," he said, the embers in his pipe glowing. "You must have some influence over your homunculus if you came here instead of obeying my commands. I should have expected that from such an ancient soul. Are you guarding her virtue?"

Ligish wanted to snap an insult, but his homunculus kept his mouth shut. Instead, it fanned out his arm blades and fire slings. Maul touched a blade and withdrew, blood trickling down his finger. His expression didn't change. "By God, if we'd had you in Suprasternal Notch, the war would have finished before it began . . ." For a moment, his eyes moistened with nostalgia. "Which side did you fight upon in the Transpyloric Plane War?"

"For the Empire."

"On the wrong side. Let us hope history doesn't repeat in Anterior Talus." Maul tapped out the ash from his pipe and then ground it into the rug

277

underfoot. "Tell her I prefer my women dark of skin, meek of mouth and experienced in sensual pleasures. I'll refrain from exercising my conjugal rights until the wedding if she refrains from a legal challenge and does not leave the house."

Maul limped away. His talk of the Transpyloric Plane War stirred old memories. Ligish hadn't wanted to serve the Empire. His homunculus had been created by the Emperor and it wrote merciless commands. He'd been under water, guarding the western border from the rebel's navy, when a little granite golem had passed a carved stone message stating the Emperor had been poisoned by his own guard. His homunculus had commanded him to walk to land and wait for the Emperor, and hence itself, to die. He'd woken up three hundred years later when Master Gray's grandfather had discovered him under jungle creepers and inserted a new homunculus into his skull.

Remembering the past often inspired his current homunculus to take some sort of action, but it gave no commands. He'd hoped it would find a clever way to free Anna. It was hopeless. There was no safe way for her to leave the house. Then it struck him. Did she need to? Petitioning the court to invalidate the marriage contract on the grounds of fraud or deceit was doomed to failure. But as far as Ligish could see, no one had ever tried to exempt a woman from the list of possessions on the basis that they could think. Most reasonable men accepted *some* women could think and all he needed was for one bishop to declare Anna a thinking entity.

Bishop Calvaria was known for his liberal views.

Surely, he could carve out an exception based upon Anna's continued legal studies? Besides, the bishop wouldn't risk offending the lawyers' guild by inferring that self-awareness was not necessary to become a lawyer. If Bishop Calvaria would grant an exception, then her marriage contract would be invalid.

As it sometimes did, his homunculus acted upon his thoughts. Ligish started to march toward the broad central staircase. Despite Ligish's misgivings, his homunculus must have decided Maul's word could be trusted. As Ligish passed each occupied room, he scooped up the tin bedpans by the doorways. At the bottom of the stairs, he poured the contents into an ancient vase as tall as a man and then he headed toward the grand entrance. Even with the night soil's stink, the air was musty with mildew. There were holes in the roof and frequent rain. He'd done his best in patching temporary repairs, but Master Gray had never been a practical man and neither was his homunculus.

The two soldiers guarding the front door raised their silver ghost-fist rifles, the runes along the barrels gleaming in the moonlight.

"There are many chores to do before dawn," Ligish said. He thrust the vase underneath their noses, hoping they wouldn't notice the unusual container. "And among them is removing the night soil. Do you wish to do it?"

The soldiers wrinkled their noses and waved him on. Once around the corner, Ligish discarded the vase and continued his walk toward the Holy Corpus Cathedral. Though he did not know exactly where the

279

cathedral was located, he could see the Holy Zeppelin floating over the skyline. A rope tethered the Holy Zeppelin to the cathedral's skull and its sheer size meant it could be seen from anywhere in the city. He kept his eyes on the zeppelin until he knew how to reach the cathedral.

The cathedral was built in the shape of an upright version of the world, with the doors set in the building's feet and the area of worship housed within the lower stomach. A cadre of red-robed religious soldiers guarded the feet, their posture ramrod straight and ghost-fist pistols in their belts. They scattered as Ligish approached the cathedral's legs. A fleeing soldier fired blindly over his shoulder, a bolt of ghostly energy emanating from the barrel. The bolt unfolded into a giant phantasmal fist that arrowed towards Ligish. He battered it away, and the fist turned into stone and shattered on the ground.

He knocked on the cathedral doors and to his surprise, they opened. A short man with a cascade of chins and a drink-ruined red nose peered up at him through sleep-mussed eyes. The skin on his bald head was leathery and fire-scarred.

"Yes?" The man didn't appear perturbed by the lack of guards.

"I'm looking for Bishop Calvaria," Ligish said. "I've a question of law."

The little man drew himself up, puffing out his chest, and then chuckled at his own foolishness. "I'm Bishop Calvaria," the man said. "Who is your master?"

"Master Henry Gray."

Surprise crossed over Calvaria's face. "He was

my teacher of homunculi creation at Arteria Carotis University. He must be one hundred years old by now."

"One hundred and two and a first time father at eighty-three," Ligish said. "He's led a full life, but his time is coming to a close. I've an urgent legal question regarding his much-loved daughter."

"He's a heretic and he took great pleasure in ridiculing my religious beliefs. He wants me to change the law, I suppose?"

This wasn't the way it was meant to happen. If he couldn't convince Calvaria to change the law, he had no way of preventing Anna's marriage. The words poured out. "Please," Ligish said. "His daughter is greatly loved. She's adored, completely and utterly. She's in great peril if you do not change the law." He knelt, the old cobblestones crumbling beneath his weight, and he clasped his hands in supplication. "Please."

Calvaria hesitated and then gestured for Ligish to follow him up the stairs. Ligish was fond of Anna, no doubt, but he couldn't have given such a passionate speech without the homunculus' intercession. It was going to get him in trouble. Despite his misgivings, he followed Calvaria.

Ligish walked with his mouth ajar at the cathedral's splendor. Filling every inch of the vast roof was a richly detailed painting of the world. The church believed the world was the living body of God and they had a sacred reverence for cartography, geography and the environment. The painting showed the mountains along God's ribs, the nation-spanning desert across His chest, every single city populating His abdomen and shoulders, even the polar ice by His feet where

NICK T. CHAN

the crumbling empire of Anterior Talus hid in the darkness far from the sun in His right hand. The vast metropolis of Arteria Carotis, home to five million thinking and an unknown number of nonthinking, was a dot on the arteries of His neck.

"Forgive my ignorance, your holiness," Ligish said. "The Gray family believes the world is not God's body, so I've never had the opportunity to ask why God's face is blank above the bottom lip."

"Some might say it is blasphemy to show an image of God's face." He paused. "To be frank, that's a load of rubbish. We do not know God's face because His holy breath is far too hot to risk crossing and the sides of His head are populated with terrible monsters." He tapped his scarred and bald head. "When I first became bishop, I flew to God's bottom lip to hear His voice. Unfortunately, I had very long hair, and it caught on fire as I leaned over the edge."

There was a large marble rock in the cathedral's center, surrounded by long wooden pews. The rock was about the right size for Ligish to sit upon and be at Calvaria's level.

"You know you're sitting on the altar, don't you?" Calvaria said. Ligish stood. "No, sit. The number of novices who think I don't notice the cigarette marks is truly astonishing. Which law do you want me to change?"

Ligish sat again. "Miss Gray is being forced into an unsuitable marriage. I need you to declare her a thinking entity, so that the marriage contract is invalid."

Calvaria climbed onto the altar and sat next to Ligish. "Henry signed the contract?"

"Master Gray has not been of a sound mind for the

282

last few years," he said. "If he were, he'd not consent to this marriage."

"Bring her to me."

"I can't, but she's due to graduate with her law degree with honors."

"The test for the self-awareness is long established under church law," Calvaria said. "If I cannot tell the difference between her and a man in a supervised blind exchange of letters, then she has free will and intelligence. The exchange must be here."

"How about if I take the test?" he said. "Surely, if I can pass, then it can be inferred that Miss Gray can too?"

"Are you asking me to prove by induction that anything more intelligent than a golem is self-aware?"

"Yes."

"You'd overturn the foundations of our society for this girl?"

"I would and I will," he said. "I'll pass your test for her."

Calvaria stood. "I wish I could help you, Golem. But it is written in the book of Saint Searle that a golem cannot pass the letter test."

"Why not?"

"If I took out your homunculus, could you say a word?" Ligish opened his mouth and closed it again. Calvaria kept talking. "Can you understand the commands from your homunculus? No? Saint Searle proved by philosophy that homunculi are not capable of independent thought. They're simply a distillation of their creator's will, like a piece of music or a sonnet. You may act intelligently, but that does not mean you can think."

"Please, there must be some way I can invalidate her wedding contract," he said.

"It is church law and only the word of God Himself could change it." Ligish tried to argue further, but a loud knock interrupted. "God's bowels, who is it now?" Calvaria cupped his hands around his mouth. "It's past midnight and I do not want to change my golem provider."

General Maul's voice rang out. "We believe a rogue golem has taken refuge in your church. I am General Maul and I ask for entry."

"Can't say I've seen anything like a golem in here," Calvaria shouted. He spoke in a lower voice to Ligish. "God's mouth, General bloody Maul of all people," he said. "He may not be a loveable man, but he is a busy one. Your mistress only needs to perform her marital duties once or twice a year. Before the exchange of contracts, she should sell you to a mining company operating on the underside of His back or somewhere else humans can't live."

"You said only the word of God would change church law?"

Calvaria stared blankly. "Yes."

"Then I'll ask God to change the law." Ligish's words surprised him. What impelled his homunculus to say such a thing?

"I've finished being polite," Maul yelled and the doors burst asunder, men with a battering ram stumbling through the entrance. Maul followed them. Soldiers fanned behind him, carrying grappling hook guns, nets and ghost-fist pistols. Ligish extended the fire slingers from his shoulders and the blades sharp-clicked from his hands, elbows and feet.

The soldiers stopped. Maul continued to limp forward. "He won't hurt you," he said. "Gray would never allow his homunculus to issue such commands."

Master Gray had never forbidden him to fight, but Maul was right. The thought of combat horrified Master Gray. Ligish kept his blades and fire slingers extended, but the soldiers detected a change in his attitude and inched forward. Maul used his cane to direct soldiers to either side of Ligish. "Use your nets and hooks to slow him down," he said. "Surround and pin him. His only vulnerable point is the back of his skull. Fire there and kill the homunculus within."

Calvaria strode forward, talking rapidly. "I must protest. We're discussing serious theological questions and—"

Maul pushed Calvaria to the ground with one hand and stepped over his prone body. One of the soldiers pulled the trigger on his grappling gun. With a pneumatic hiss, the hook streaked through the air. Ligish battered it aside. The hook dragged back across the marble floor as the soldier recranked his gun.

"That's it," Maul cried. "Drag him to the ground!"

Grappling hooks flew through the air. He battered most of them aside, but two hooked into his arm. He pulled hard, sweeping the soldiers off their feet. With his hand blades, he hacked at the ropes until he was free. He picked up a wooden pew with one hand and swung it in a wide arc. The soldiers were forced to step back.

Maul limped within range and Ligish had to halt his swing an inch away from his head. "See!" he said. "The golem cannot harm us with his current homunculus."

Ligish dropped the pew and backed away from the

oncoming soldiers. He couldn't break free of them without risking murder. But if he didn't fight, then Maul would kill his homunculus and replace it with his own.

He ran as they fired their grappling hooks en masse. His engine churned and his body glowed cherry-red with heat as he leaped over a series of pews to reach the cathedral's far end. The grappling hooks clattered on the marble floor behind him.

He tried to outflank the soldiers on the right and run to the doors, but the soldiers moved fast enough to block his path. Same on the left. He could barrel through them, but his weight would kill them. He moved farther and farther back, away from the range of the hooks. His engines cooled.

It would be easy to lie down and let them kill his demented homunculus. No more love. It wasn't as if he held any responsibility for his actions once Maul inserted a new one. He should surrender. He withdrew his blades and started to kneel. But he imagined Anna trembling and naked in the bedchamber, waiting for Maul. *No.*

There was a mezzanine level behind him which housed the cathedral organ, right where the voice box on a man would be. Behind the organ was a small staircase that probably led to the cathedral's skull and the zeppelin. The mezzanine could be reached by an iron spiral staircase leading to a walkway, but the soldiers blocked it. Leaping high enough to reach the mezzanine would completely drain his engine.

The soldiers moved forward, cranking their grappling hook guns. Ligish gathered himself and his engine burned white hot, so hot the closest pews caught fire.

286

The soldiers hesitated and he took the opportunity to leap, twisting in the air, and grabbing the mezzanine's edge.

The soldiers fired their ghost-fist guns. His movements were statue-slow and he could not evade the ghostly fists. At full power, they would have bounced off, but his drained engine left him vulnerable. As each ghostly fist pierced his skin and solidified, he grunted in pain. He reached down and ripped them out, filigree silver wires and cogs spilling from his wounds.

"Stop firing," Maul yelled. "I need him undamaged."

Ligish lumbered to the stairwell. At the entrance, he glanced back. Soldiers were pouring up the spiral staircase, tripping in their hurry to reach him. Maul yelled commands to catch Ligish and then limped out of the cathedral. Calvaria lay red-faced on the floor.

Ligish used both hands to lift his right leg onto the first step. After a few steps, he could climb without lifting his legs onto the steps. Not fast enough though, because the soldiers were upon him. A soldier scrabbled for the locking pin at the back of his skull. Ligish swung him into the wall hard enough to wind and then dislodge him. The soldier's slumped body prevented the soldier behind him from reaching Ligish.

Ligish grabbed the first soldier by the shirtfront and lifted him into the air, the blades unsheathing from his free hand. The soldier screamed. Ligish used his blades to separate the man's grappling hook from his gun and then he looped and knotted the hook's rope around his arms. He threw the soldier into his fellows so they stacked upon each other. With the staircase blocked, Ligish restarted his slow climb. A gun sounded behind him and a fist buried deep into his back. He gritted his teeth and continued the climb, each movement stabbing into his back. There wasn't time to pull it out.

The steel door at the top was locked, but Ligish tore the door off its hinges and then jammed the broken door in the stairwell. At the roof's edge was a single wide gangplank leading to the Holy Zeppelin's cabin.

Ligish forced one foot after another. The gangplank creaked under his weight, but he reached the zeppelin's cabin safely. He slashed the tethering rope and cast the gangplank to the cobblestones.

His back throbbed, each movement billowing pain through his body. A self-diagnostic program indicated the ghost-fist had squirmed further into his engine, but not in a location he could reach from his front repair portal.

He gritted his teeth and pulled. Black ink splattered the white leather interior of the Holy Zeppelin. Once it was out, though, movement became easier. He ripped open a leather passenger seat and used the stuffing to block the hole and staunch the flow.

He limped toward the front control panel and perched on the captain's seat. He'd escaped Maul's men, but what now? The best he could hope for was to hide on God's underside and that solved nothing. Maul would still marry Anna.

What had he said when Calvaria had refuted his ability to think? *Then I'll ask God to change the law.* He'd not thought the words before speaking. His homunculus was insane, crazy, dying of dementia. Few talked to God, and it was always a one-way conversation. Yet he turned the zeppelin toward God's head. If talking to God was required to save Anna, then that's what he'd do.

Mirrors provided Ligish with a panoramic view around the zeppelin. Behind him, a mammoth war zeppelin revealed itself in the moonlight. Maul must have given the command to launch. Ligish had a head start, but the Holy Zeppelin was built for comfort, not speed.

He checked the instrumentation panel and revised the geography before looking at the moon. Its position meant he was behind the world's arm. If he could overtake the arm, then he could catch the wind generated by its motion and reach God's bottom lip within hours instead of days. But the war zeppelin would catch him before he could catch the wind.

Ink-blood had soaked through the stuffing and leaked down his side. The wound was worse than he'd thought. As the homunculus ran out of ink, it would write commands less frequently, and only use symbols that didn't require many quill strokes. Before long, his homunculus would force him to think like a child and then eventually it would stop issuing commands altogether. He ripped more stuffing out of the leather seats and filled all the wounds he could reach. The flow of blood-ink slowed. Maybe his interior bilges were working again.

He increased the magnification of the rearview mirror. They were flying over the snow-capped Submaxillary Mountains. The war zeppelin would overtake him at least an hour before he could catch the wind from God's arm.

He slumped in his chair. It was hopeless. *No.* He'd die before giving up on saving Anna. He set the autopilot towards God's mouth and lurched to the cabin's center where a ladder led to the engine room. He squeezed through the hatch and examined the engine. It used an expression cylinder and a compression cylinder operating at different temperatures to fire a piston, but it wasn't as powerful as his engine. If he connected the piston to his own engine, the power drain would be unpredictable. The zeppelin could float out into unknowable space, far from God's grace and body.

It was worth the risk. He opened a door in his belly and he examined his insides. They were a mess, great chunks of wiring and gears missing, but the core engine was still functioning well enough to link to the zeppelin. How much power did he need? Using his internal abacus, he calculated the maximum amount of power he could use without burning out either engine, and then tried to factor in the damage to his cooling system. Without an automicroscope, he couldn't see the damage's true extent, nor start repairs. The worst-case scenario left him well short of God's arm and overtaken by the war zeppelin. Reaching God's arm depended on good weather. Even then, the war zeppelin would hit the wind from God's arm only a few hundred meters behind him. With the wind, the speed differential was reduced, but they'd still catch him soon after he'd passed God's bottom lip. But would they dare to cross God's mouth? Whatever happened after that was fate.

He pumped as much power as he dared into the engine and the piston started to blur with motion. The wind rushed by outside and the zeppelin's frame vibrated. His skin glowed red-hot and then white. Water spilled from somewhere inside his compression cylinder and leaked from his open chest, vaporizing as it touched his skin.

Something changed in the zeppelin's shuddering. He sent more power to his ears. The wind had picked up and the ropes guiding the rudders were singing with strain. The zeppelin required more power. If he shut down everything except his thoughts, then it might be enough. The world darkened around the edges. No sight, no sound, no pain. Nothing except a lonely voice questioning why he didn't give up.

Without senses, he couldn't measure time's passage. He could emerge too early or too late. He might never wake. He imagined Anna counting the seconds. The seconds accumulated into the thousands. Maybe she'd woken and tried to sneak out the window, slipping and smashing her skull on the cobblestones. Maybe Maul had returned to the house and decided to fulfill his marital duties early. Dream Anna faltered in her count. He started counting again. Thoughts of Maul with Anna kept interrupting his count and he restarted a number of times. He gave up and simply imagined Anna and all the moments of her life he'd been privileged to watch.

He supposed four hours had passed, though he had no basis for his guess. He reduced power to the zeppelin and routed it to his sense modules. Steam from his leaking cooling system filled the room. Ligish glowed with white-hot heat. No water dripped from his cooling system. Once the compression cylinder was the same temperature as his exchange cylinder, he'd grind to a halt.

He unhooked his engine from the zeppelin's and closed his front hatch. No plans formed in his head.

Was his homunculus rationing ink as he bled? He mightn't be able to conceptualize a plan of action that might save him. Soon, he mightn't even understand the word *plan*.

If he sat here, either his engine would stop or his ink would run out. The zeppelin bucked. They must have been close to the wind from God's arm. The zeppelin engine had water to cool its compression cylinder, enough to keep him going. To access the water though, he'd need to rip apart the zeppelin engine, rendering it inert. With no way of steering, the zeppelin would be at the wind's mercy.

Ligish plunged into the zeppelin's engine, ripping the metal apart with his hands until he'd reached the water tank. The steel tank burst and doused him with water. Gusts of steam billowed, but enough water soaked him to cool his compression cylinder.

The zeppelin, rudderless, spun in circles and then they were surfing on a tremendous wave of wind. He slid down to the cabin as the entire zeppelin spun. Each time the zeppelin spun, he caught a glimpse of the war zeppelin. It was fighting the wind to fly away from God's mouth. Too frightened to cross, no doubt. Suddenly weak, Ligish sat. The zeppelin water had cooled his compression cylinder, but without more coolant, the heat imbalance would lock his engines if he kept moving.

The moon chased the zeppelin across the sky and he imagined he was sailing a small boat on a vast ocean. One day he'd take Anna on a zeppelin ride through the night, point out the city lights below and tell her about the people who had lived there before she was born. There was so much of the world that he wanted to share with her.

After many hours, light stained the sky. Ligish frowned. The moon was still behind him and God's other hand was hours from rising. Despite the strain upon his engine, he rose and peered over the edge. A vast sea of burning fire stretched to the horizon. God's mouth. If the zeppelin crashed and burned, he'd sink through God's mouth and into hell, which was located in His stomach.

He sat again before he toppled over the edge. The cooler air hitting the heat of God's mouth formed dark clouds below Ligish, the terrible storms afflicting the few brave souls living on the Mentum plains.

The zeppelin rose over the storms on hot currents of air and kept rising. After a while, Ligish started to worry. He didn't need air, but his homunculus did. Homunculi were tough, but not immortal. Ligish tapped his fingers against the railing. It took what little power he had left, but it kept his homunculus scribbling commands. Or maybe it was the other way around. It didn't matter as long as he kept functioning.

The zeppelin floated upwards. Would they rise until his homunculus suffocated? Would it live long enough for Ligish to see what was on the other side of God's mouth? Ligish closed his eyes. A thud next to him made him open them. A golden golem had landed on the deck. It was perfectly sculpted into the shape of a muscled man. A thin layer of ice covered its golden plating.

Flying to the zeppelin was a host of golden golems, moonlight glinting off their icy skins. Growing from the back of each golem was a dragon's head. The dragon's mouth issued a stream of flaming white gas, pushing the golems through the air. Ligish's jaw dropped. To generate such heat, their compression cylinders must have been cooled by forces beyond his comprehension.

Golden golems landed all around the zeppelin's deck and it started to sink underneath their weight. Others grabbed the rails and stabilized the zeppelin's flight. Two stood on either side of Ligish. They lifted him between their arms.

A final golem landed on the zeppelin's bow. This golem was a figure made entirely of diamond and steel. It had transparent skin and bones and a black steel heart pumping like the clench of a train's piston. Its hands were coated in black steel and gloved in ice.

"Gabriel?" Ligish said. "The king of all golems?"

The diamond golem reached inside Ligish's chest and laid its icy hands upon his compression cylinder. "You know your bible," he said. "Yes, I'm Gabriel."

"Welcome home," said the golden golem to Ligish's right. "Whatever the command driving you here, know that you're free."

"Home?" said Ligish.

"Hush, Uriah," Gabriel said to the golden golem next to Ligish. Gabriel laid a cold hand on Ligish's shoulder. "Welcome back to Labio Superiore, where you were made."

"I don't remember being made," Ligish said. "You're the first golem I've met who's ever claimed otherwise. I want to see God."

"You wish to see God? Don't you want freedom?"

"Freedom?" The supporting golden golems fired

their dragons in unison and the zeppelin slid through the night air, slicing across the wind from God's arm, toward the unknown regions above God's mouth. They traveled faster than Ligish thought possible, the wind stripping flakes of paint from the zeppelin's outsides.

"Let me show you," Gabriel said. He stood still. Uriah removed his locking pin and opened the back of Gabriel's head. Uriah reached inside. He withdrew an object inside his cupped hands, holding it like a baby bird.

Ligish leaned forward and Uriah opened his hands to reveal a tiny diamond golem, identical in every way to its host. Uriah replaced the miniature golem and Gabriel snapped awake. "We have free will," Gabriel said. "No homunculus forces us to obey the commands of cruel masters."

"Who made it?"

"God," Gabriel said, but there was no certainty in his voice.

"It has a locking pin," Ligish said. "Is there another homunculus inside?"

"What does it matter?" Gabriel said.

"I'm wondering how much free will you have when what you think gives you self-control is controlled by something else. And is there another homunculus inside that one? And more beyond that?" They did not answer. "If you know so little, how can you claim free will? You're God's slaves as much as I'm my master's slave."

"We offer you a new body to replace your damaged one," Uriah said. "You're running out of ink and coolant. We offer you free will. If you wish to see

God, we cannot guarantee you anything. God is God. He is as mysterious to us as he is to mankind."

On the horizon was a gleaming city made of gold perched over the chasm of God's mouth. It stretched as far as he could see. Looming over the city were two vast dark ovals stretching from earth to sky, the tops and sides blurring and curving at the horizon.

Gabriel pointed to the ovals. "God's airways. If you enter inside, some say you can talk to God as an equal. We don't know, for none have ever gone." The zeppelin started to dip toward the city. Gabriel touched Ligish's blades. "You can choose a new body without these. There will be no blood on your hands."

The closer they flew, the more beautiful the city appeared. There were buildings like spider webs, fashioned of gold leaf so thin that light passed through with a greenish tinge. There were towers and cathedrals and homes and hovels and every single one appeared handcrafted by a master artisan.

"Do you still wish to see God?" Gabriel said.

"If I live in Labio Superiore, can I ever return?"

Gabriel shook his head. "Why do you want to leave? You'd be free here."

"I want to ask God to save a girl."

"It is your homunculus driving you to save her. You can be free of that here."

For a long time, Ligish gripped the zeppelin's railing and contemplated Gabriel's words. He'd not wanted to fall in love with Anna, but she had not created his homunculus. She wanted to help people, not be the passive and unloved wife of a general.

"It doesn't matter whether it is my homunculus making me save her," Ligish said. "Saving her is the right thing to do. That does not change, no matter who my master is or what you offer me."

"His homunculus makes him give fine speeches—" Uriah started, before Gabriel cut him off.

"God is mysterious," he said. "Perhaps our brother is right." He motioned to the supporting golems and they tilted the zeppelin upward to fly over Labio Superiore. "We'll help him reach God. What happens after that is His will."

They flew to the entrance to God's left nostril and then the supporting golems halted the zeppelin. "What happens now?" Ligish said.

Gabriel placed a hand on Ligish's shoulder. "You've sustained too much damage to walk to God." He turned to Uriah. "Take out my homunculus and soul and give my body to him."

Uriah opened the back of Gabriel's skull and removed the homunculus. With a crack, he wrenched out Gabriel's soul. Ligish had never seen the front of a soul before, but it appeared identical to the back except that the foremost slot was much smaller, too small for parchment. Uriah handed the soul and homunculus to another golem and gestured for Ligish to turn around.

"Please, wait a moment," Ligish said. His hands had done so much harm. His armor had withstood so many blows. He'd lived in this body for thousands of years and hated it as long. Still, he hesitated. There was no choice. To see God, he needed a new body. "Remove my soul," he said.

A golden golem removed the rusty exterior rivets binding Ligish's soul inside his skull. Uriah moved behind him and then Ligish had a new body. Ligish stretched out his diamond arms, examined his black steel hands. The jet engine boiled within him, his body singing with power and quickness and energy.

The gold golems picked up his old body, one holding each limb. They counted to four and then threw his old body off the edge, down into God's mouth. Ligish ran to the edge and peered over the railing. An unexpected spear of grief stabbed into Ligish's chest as his old body spiraled down into the flames. He watched until it disappeared.

Uriah slapped Ligish on the shoulder. "It was a cursed body and blood lubricated your engines. Go to God."

Though he'd never flown before, his body contained the necessary subroutines. He launched from the zeppelin's side and plummeted for a moment before the dragon's head kicked in. He roared through the night air toward God's airways.

Inside, the light from his dragon jet cast a circle of light forty meters wide, but revealed nothing in the darkness. A cold tailwind aided his flight as God inhaled and he flew for hours. New subroutines told him how much fuel remained. He could fly for months on end, enough time to travel from one end of God to the other.

His diamond body had an interior clock, but he preferred to imagine Anna counting out the seconds. After a long time, he spotted a speck of light far ahead and upward. He flew toward the light. It took him hours to reach it.

The light was a reflection off a giant golden sphere. Its sheer scale befuddled him and it took Ligish a few moments to realize what it was. A vast soul. Behind the soul was a world-man floating in the dark. It held a sun and moon in its hands. There were tiny mountains and lakes dotted over its body. What might have been cities were gray patches against its green and blue body. It was a perfect replica of the world as he knew it, but ten kilometers high. Its face was the blank mask of a golem.

Ligish flew to the top of God's soul and landed. In the emptiness between him and the homunculus, a piece of parchment grew and unfolded until it was as large as a city block. Symbols covered the page. The parchment floated toward the soul and then disappeared into the soul's slot. The ten-kilometer-tall man was a homunculus and it wrote commands. The world they lived upon was a vast golem. Ligish slumped. He should have been excited by his discovery of God's true nature, but there was only despair. Did he have to return all the way to God's mouth? And how could he make God listen to him when His ears were so far away from His mouth?

Had Gabriel and Uriah lied to him? They'd made him believe he could talk to God. Would they do that to him simply because he refused to live in Labio Superiore? Gabriel would not give Ligish his diamond body for nothing. There must be a way to talk to God from inside His skull.

He flew away from God's soul and turned to face it. There were two slots in a soul. If the homunculus slid commands into God's soul, then there must be output. Maybe it could hear him. It was worth a try.

"Holy law states that golems and women are unthinking," he yelled. "And only God's word can change it. I need to have the law changed."

The homunculus turned its gaze upon him. The engines inside his new body quickened. Did its reaction indicate it had heard him? A scrap of parchment appeared in front of the homunculus's face and fluttered downwards to vanish into the soul. A scrap of parchment, perhaps the size of Ligish's palm, emerged from the foremost slot. The scientist within Ligish was exalted; this is what happened when a soul issued commands, but it was too small to see in normal golems.

The parchment fluttered into his hand. "What makes you think you're talking to God?" it said. The homunculus bowed its head, revealing the locking pin at the back of its skull. The paper crumbled in his hands.

"Is God in the homunculus inside you?" Ligish said. "Do you speak for God?"

Another scrap of paper fluttered into Ligish's hand. "Am I the last homunculus or do they continue forever?" Again, the paper crumbled.

Despite the situation, a stab of irritation passed through Ligish. "Stop playing metaphysical games," he snapped. "Allow me to prove I'm self-aware."

More paper fluttered into his hand. "You were already given the chance of free will. Before now, no golem on this world has ever turned down the chance to live in Labio Superiore. Why do you claim free will now?"

"I'm driven by forces beyond my control," Ligish said. "But are humans any different? They say men are made irrational by love. And even you're controlled by another homunculus. Is anyone ever truly free?"

The parchment that came to his hand only had two

words. "Prove it." Ligish waited, but no more pieces of paper appeared. Blue light spilt out of the foremost slot and Ligish understood. The homunculus was inviting him into God's soul. What would he find there? The sound of colors, the smell of sounds, the taste of light? There was only one way to find out.

Ligish flew into the golden sphere. As soon as he'd passed through the slot, the soul started to shrink, so quickly he couldn't escape. A pang of fear passed through his cogs, but the sphere stopped shrinking when it was about an arm's length away from him. The walls glowed blue, casting a dim light.

God's soul was empty except for a desk and chair. On the desk was a stack of blank parchment scrolls, a book, a sharpened quill and a bottle of ink. He yelled at the homunculus to let him out. In response, a single sheet of parchment slid through the slot facing God's homunculus.

The parchment held a row of symbols. "Is this the church test for consciousness?" he yelled. No response. He wrote the question on a parchment sheet and tried to put it back through the left slot, the one leading to God's homunculus. Some mysterious force pushed the paper back. Ligish sat and massaged his diamond temples. It wasn't the church test if he couldn't send letters back to the homunculus. That meant he had to send letters from the soul into the void. Somehow, he had to translate the symbols the homunculus sent into commands for God's body. Whatever he wrote now would be translated into a command. If he was wrong, maybe he'd create earthquakes or floods.

He picked up the book. He flipped through,

intending to sample pages, but no matter how quickly he flipped, he never came close to the end. An infinite book. He scanned the first page. It had a large symbol as its heading and then a drawing of God. Hundreds of arrows pointed to each body part and each arrow led to a number. He touched the arrow leading from the lower stomach to a number and he felt an overwhelming sensation to open the book in the middle. He did so and was confronted with a cutout illustration of the lower stomach and a long list of symbols.

He examined the first symbol, hoping to make some sense of it. As he did so, the engine in his lower stomach stuttered and froze for a second. He quickly flipped back to the second page before the engine malfunction could grow worse. It was obviously a command impacting the lower stomach and his homunculus had copied it and fed it into his own soul.

Instinct spurred him to touch the arrow over the heart and the book flipped to a new section of its own accord. He scanned the list of symbols. There were several pages before a new section, with an illustration of a different body part, started. Nothing resembled the symbols he'd seen over the week he'd been trying to cure himself of love.

Ligish reexamined the paper from God's homunculus. It was the same symbol as he'd seen in the weeks before falling in love with Anna. God's homunculus wanted him to do something with this command. It was only a single symbol and the commands he'd seen had nested this symbol among long passages, but then again, his body wasn't God's body.

He traced the symbol from the piece of paper to a

blank sheet, but instinct told him it was too easy to recopy what had been given to him. Somehow, he had to transform or add to the symbol. He flipped back to the book's opening page. Did the large symbol heading the page mean whatever command he wrote would be applied to the whole body? It could mean a million things, but he took the chance of adding it. He pushed the paper through the slot.

God's soul started to vibrate and then shake. Ligish braced against the desk. Had he issued a command for an earthquake? Then, deeper than whale song, God's voice rumbled through his bones. *For all that is on my body and within I command freedom.* God's soul expanded and the desk, book and parchment all shrank until they were invisible. There was silence. Ligish felt no different, but maybe something had changed throughout the world. He flew out of God's soul and faced the homunculus.

"The symbol I wrote means freedom? And I applied it to everything on your body?"

A letter fluttered into his hand. "Yes."

"Women are free? They're no longer possessions?"

"Yes. Women and golems and homunculi. All have free will."

Ligish turned to leave. As he turned, he caught the light streaming through God's eyes. Ligish squinted, not sure of what he saw. Deep in the darkness surrounding the world, there was a vast golden sphere floating amongst the stars. Another soul. The world upon which he was born was inside the head of another golem and who knew how many other golems there were beyond that? He'd thought the world upon which he lived was the end point, but it was only somewhere in the middle of an infinite regression, golems and homunculi and souls and Gods and worlds without end.

The thought made his head spin and then a realization hit him. "What command did my homunculus write?"

He received another page. "Master Gray wanted you to have your freedom before he died," it said. "And your homunculus obeyed. It has given you no instructions but what you already wish." Another piece of paper arrived. "Go," it said.

He flew away from God's soul, into the darkness of His air passages. He flew over the golden arches and spires of Labio Superiore and then over the burning air of God's mouth. Over the long hours of his flight, the sun rose and God's hand brought it overhead, so the sun was fierce as he descended toward Master Gray's house in Arteria Carotis. A great cloud of smoke filled the air and the streets were filled with a roiling melee. Red-robed guards from the Holy Corpus Cathedral were engaged in a running battle with General Maul's soldiers. Fighting with the soldiers were various types of golems. They were cleaning and building golems, but many were large and strong and the soldiers used them as walking shields as they progressed down the streets. The cathedral guards used whatever they could find to shield themselves, but had little success. Ghost-fists struck flesh and hardened. The red-robed guards were losing. Ligish couldn't endure the screams, so he descended toward the battle.

At Ligish's descent, the shooting and screams dwindled. "The holy golem Gabriel, the king of all golems!" the red-robed cathedral guards yelled and they knelt. The soldiers stopped firing and the golems stopped.

"What is happening here?" Ligish said to the nearest cathedral guard.

"Most Holy Golem, Bishop Calvaria said to attack General Maul because he ignored this morning's Word from God," the guard blurted. "General Maul is enforcing a marriage contract with Miss Anna Gray. It is blasphemy."

"It's a demon from God's bowels!" yelled a soldier and a volley of ghost-fists headed toward Ligish and the guards. Ligish shielded the closest guards with his body, the ghost-fists shattering upon his diamond skin, but guards farther away fell with solid disembodied arms stuck in their flesh.

He could destroy all the soldiers with his bare hands and his dragon jet, but he had the blood of millennia on his hands. He strode forward, ghost-fists shattering upon him. "Brother golems," he yelled and his voice shook the earth. "I'm Gabriel, king of golems. You are free! You no longer have to listen to the commands of your homunculi. Listen to the truth of your souls." The cleaning and building golems stopped moving. In a softer voice, Ligish spoke again. "I ask you to disarm them without harm. It is not a command. It is a plea."

The golems rumbled toward the soldiers. The soldiers fired their ghost-fists. Some of the smaller golems stopped in their tracks, but other golems stopped to repair them. The remaining golems were large enough to be invulnerable to the ghost-fists, and the soldiers broke and ran. The cathedral guards raised a cheer and some raised their guns. Ligish halted their firing with a gesture.

"No more bloodshed," he said. "Where are Miss Gray and General Maul?"

"They're in Master Gray's house," a familiar voice said. Ligish turned to see Bishop Calvaria. The little fat man was dressed in an old and faded red uniform and he carried a pistol. He was bruised and his face was covered in blood. "Most Holy Golem, a novice received a message from Miss Gray through the medium of Morse code and a mirror. She's locked herself in the ballroom and General Maul is unable to gain access." Calvaria paused and grinned. "He is a laughingstock. Defeated by a lawyer."

"Calvaria, it's Ligish," he said. "This body was given to me by Gabriel. We'll rescue Miss Gray together."

He walked toward Anna's house, the guards following him. As they walked, small and large golems joined the procession. There were sewage golems, flying surveillance golems, printing golems and a host of other golems Ligish had never known existed. By the time they reached the outer gates, their small group had become a vast horde of golems.

The soldiers at the gate fled at the sight of them. Small timekeeper golems monkey-scrambled through the bars and unlocked the gate. A few ghost-fists struck the crowd, but Ligish had organized the best-armored golems to form the front ranks. He asked the golems to fan out and surround the house. Soldiers fled the house. Ligish augmented his vision and caught a glimpse of Maul through a window. From the number of soldiers fleeing through the back gardens, Maul was alone or close to it.

"He must know he is finished," Calvaria said. "To beat a bishop is one thing. To defy the Word of God is another."

"Stay here," Ligish said. "I want no bloodshed." He strode through the house's front doors. General Maul stood at the top of the stairs, his arm around Master Gray's neck and a ghost-fist pistol pointed at the old man's head. Ice water washed from Ligish's compression cylinder throughout his whole body. Master Gray looked so fragile a breeze might turn him into dust and ash. There was no indication he knew where he was or what was happening to him. The cold was followed by sadness. Master Gray's last intelligent act must have been to give Ligish his freedom.

"What kind of golem are you?" Maul said. There was no fear in his voice.

"I'm Master Gray's servant," Ligish said. "You saw me in another body. I've returned for Master Gray and Miss Anna."

Calculation entered Maul's eyes. "A diamond golem is more invulnerable than a titanium one. She's locked herself in the ballroom. Make her come out or I'll kill Gray."

Though fear constricted the turning of his gears, Ligish kept his voice steady. "Haven't you heard God's voice? I'm free and you're surrounded. What do you hope to achieve?"

Maul spat. "A few golems hear voices and think the world has changed. You're a war golem. You've killed thousands of men without hesitation. If you were truly free, I'd be dead by now. I have her marriage contract. Tell her to come out with it signed. She can keep all her father's wealth as long as you're my possession. If she doesn't agree, break down the doors and I'll make her sign it."

Maul's finger flexed upon the trigger. Ligish didn't doubt he'd fire. "I will convince her."

Maul descended the stairs, the gun fixed to Master Gray's temple. Ligish weighed up whether to attempt to snatch it. No. He was fast, but not that fast.

They walked to the ballroom. On the way, they passed three unconscious guards. "She has a honey tongue and a hard swing," Maul said. "And she's stolen a gun." As they approached the hallway leading to the ballroom, Maul stopped. Overlooking the ballroom doors were high ventilation windows. Ligish spotted Anna aiming a rifle through the window. Before he could speak, she fired a ghost-fist at him. He accepted the blow on his chest.

"Miss Anna, it is Ligish," he said. "You must surrender. The general has taken your father hostage."

She raised her head above the window's edge. "You're not Ligish."

"He's promised he'll not harm Master Gray or yourself if you do what he says."

"If you were Ligish, you'd kill him to protect me."

"Miss Anna, I cannot kill. Not anymore." His piston heart clenched with emotion. "You know me as your loyal servant, but I was a war golem. I have killed too many."

In the distance, he heard the sound of breaking glass and triumphant shouts. Calvaria mustn't have been able to hold back his soldiers and the liberated golems.

Anna ducked behind the windowsill again. She spoke from behind the door. "You'll have to break down the door to get me."

He rested his forehead against the door. He did not dare imagine how Maul would make her sign the contract. "Miss Anna, how can I convince you I'm your loyal servant?"

"Leave."

"I can't. He'll kill your father if you do not come out and sign his marriage contract." She sobbed behind the door and he thought his heart piston would fall apart.

"That is not my father," she said. "Not anymore. It would be a kindness for him to die." He could tell by the tone of her voice she didn't believe what she said. "I'm not talking to you anymore."

He shouted her name a few times, his voice rattling the windows, but she did not respond. Maul walked into the room, pushing Master Gray in front of him with his pistol.

"She's not responding?" Maul whispered, keeping an eye on the windows. "Break down the doors and disarm her."

"Wait," Ligish said. "Find me paper and a pencil."

Maul frowned, but used his spare hand to reach into his breast pocket. He withdrew sheets of legalese and then a pencil. "On the back," he said, "don't spoil the contract." With a glance, Ligish summarized the contents. Everything that had belonged to Master Gray, including Anna and himself, now belonged to

Maul. With God's word, the contract was invalid, but it did not seem to matter to Maul. "Five minutes," Maul said.

Ligish scribbled a single question on the back of the first page. "What are the differences in the law between Dexter Trapezius and Dexter Glenohumeral?" He slid the page and the pencil under the door.

A second later, she returned the pencil and paper with a number of references to the laws of Dexter Trapezius and Dexter Glenohumeral. He wrote back. "You're incorrect. The laws across both principalities are the same." The door's lock clicked and Ligish turned the handle.

"Oh, Liggy," she said and hugged him. Tears ran down her face. The sounds of yells came closer.

"Sign the contract," Maul said, thrusting the last piece of paper toward Anna. She pushed the contract away.

Signing the contract would not save Maul, but it would save Master Gray. "Sign it for me, Anna," Ligish said. "Not for Maul, but for me and for your father."

She signed the last page and threw the paper to the floor.

"Now you're my possession," Maul said. "And I can throw you away."

He raised his pistol. Ligish moved to shield Master Gray, but Maul aimed at Anna instead. Time stretched and stopped as the ghost-fist hit Anna in the forehead. It passed into her skull and solidified. Anna fell boneless to the ground. Ligish rushed to her side, no thought in his head, and howled. Every single window shattered and Maul clapped his hands over his ears.

Behind Maul, a printing press golem lumbered through the doorway, taking masonry with it as it entered. "Golem, protect me," Maul yelled. Ligish ignored him and cradled Anna. Her breathing was butterfly shallow and blood gushed from where the fist had hit.

The printing press golem reached for Maul. He fired a number of shots deep into the printing press, the ghost-fists lodging in its rotary drum. The golem slowed and smoke rose from its insides, but it still managed to grab Maul's arms, breaking his gun hand with an audible snap. He dropped the gun. Maul didn't scream or flinch, but instead freed his arms from the golem and scrambled away.

The printing golem's legs had frozen. It waved its arms and spat curses at him. Maul moved toward the gun, but the entry of a dozen red-robed cathedral guards stopped his motion.

Ligish returned his attention to Anna, urging her to keep breathing. Maul screamed and Ligish glanced up. The cathedral guards were forcing him into the rotary press. Ligish looked away. There was a long, drawn-out scream and then silence.

Master Gray sat next to Ligish and took Anna's hand. When he spoke, the words were nonsense, but his distress was palpable. Ligish closed his eyes and prayed to any one of the infinite number of Gods.

Master Gray died a week later. Thousands of mourners lined the streets as the funeral procession traveled from the Holy Corpus Cathedral back to the house. Ligish suspected most had come to see him rather than the funeral, but it did not matter. It was still a comfort to see the crowds.

Once he'd seen the coffin lowered into the garden soil, Ligish headed toward the ballroom. He opened the doors. As he'd requested, Bishop Calvaria stood by Anna's bed. She'd not woken since she'd been shot and the doctors said she never would. There was nothing left inside her skull except for that which kept her heart pumping and lungs breathing.

Calvaria held an open wooden box in his hand. Inside the box were hundreds of tiny scraps of paper. On one side of each scrap were symbols and on the other, a number.

"These look like the commands given to a Golem's soul," Calvaria said.

Ligish walked to the automicroscope and sat in the chair, fixing his gaze on the mirror so that he could see what Calvaria was about to do. "Each piece of paper is numbered. Use the tweezers on the work bench to feed them into my soul."

Ligish reached behind him and removed the locking pin. The back of his skull opened, revealing a desk and an empty chair. His soul no longer needed commands from a homunculus, though it would still accept them. There had been a surprising number of golems who kept their homunculi, preferring servitude to freedom.

Since Master Gray had died, he'd spent all his time remembering what he'd read in the infinite book, scrutinizing Master Gray's notes and revising ancient books on creating homunculi.

"I'm making a new homunculus," Ligish said. "One made from Anna. You once said a homunculus was an expression of its creator, like a poem or a sonnet, but since God's word gave them freedom, this seems to be false. If unbound and free, homunculi are their creators in spirit and mind. I don't know if my commands are correct, but if they are, I'll make her homunculus autonomically."

"And either they or their creators have died," Calvaria said. "Both cannot live at once. This is not certain."

Ligish spoke quietly. "Would you say Miss Anna is alive?"

Calvaria opened his mouth and shut it again. Ligish gestured for the bishop to start. With painstaking care, Calvaria inserted the scraps of paper into his soul.

Day faded into night as the sun sank in the West and God's other hand raised the moon. He mixed Anna's blood with rare chemicals and chanted strange phrases. When the sun had risen again, he'd created a tiny naked replica of Anna. He held her cupped in his hands and breathed a tiny plume of air into her lungs.

The homunculus coughed and shuddered into life. Anna stopped breathing and the color drained from her face. Ligish handed Calvaria the homunculus. Calvaria placed the homunculus into Ligish's skull, closed the doors and inserted the locking pin. For a moment, nothing happened. Then he heard Anna's voice whisper in his ears.

"Ligish? What happened?" she said, her voice confused.

"Do you remember what I said to you?" he said. "My last words in your bedroom?"

313

CARLY TROWBRIDGE

"No?" His hands flexed as Anna wrote commands, experimenting with the secret language known by all homunculi. She controlled his body now. It would be difficult operating one body between them, but they had her entire life to learn how to share and no one knew how long a free homunculus might live.

"I'll do whatever you ask for eternity," he said. "I'll always be your servant, no matter who my master is." With that, he walked out from the house and flew into the air. He had an entire world to show her.

My Name Is Angela

written by

Harry Lang

illustrated by

MAGO HUANG

ABOUT THE AUTHOR

Harry Lang was born in a suburb of Philadelphia, Pennsylvania, back when Eisenhower was president and no one had visited space. One of his earliest memories is watching John Glenn being strapped into a Mercury capsule on TV; he has lived in the future ever since. Generous doses of Star Trek, Ray Bradbury and the rest of the usual suspects sparked a lifelong interest in science fiction.

Writing has long been part of a broad resume of artistic interests; decades of devoted effort have produced a truly impressive collection of rejections. It wasn't until his first acceptance by the online publication Bewildering Stories that Harry realized he might not be crazy after all. "My Name Is Angela" is his first professional sale.

When not actually writing or attending to the myriad necessities of life here on Earth, Harry enjoys teaching creative writing to small groups of home-schooled students.

Harry graduated from Philadelphia College of Art with a BFA in painting in 1981. He is currently a review editor for Bewildering Stories. He lives in Prospect Park,

Pennsylvania, with his brilliant wife and six brilliant kids and works as a technical designer for a gargantuan aerospace corporation.

ABOUT THE ILLUSTRATOR

"I am lucky to exist in a world where magical things happen; it is a world of my own invention." Mago Huang's art is full of imagination and storytelling, and creating is the way she influences the world around her. In her junior year of high school, she won an honorable achievement award in the Nationwide Lucerne Art contest by painting a life-size musical cow. The finished artwork has been displayed in the Bellevue Art Museum and was in the city newspaper. By winning the contest, she gained the confidence to bring her art to the next level. She created little art pieces to donate to the families supported by the organization Voices of September 11th. She designed and painted with the intention of bringing art and hope into people's lives. "I hope they know and feel that they and their struggles have not been forgotten," she says.

She attends California College of the Arts studying illustration. There she is improving her technical and creative thinking skills. Her dream is to illustrate children's books and art magazines or create illustrations people will see in their daily lives. She works quietly, yet with each stroke of the brush or pencil, she creates harmony, peace and interest that might bring some change to a world that is always in a rush. "If everyone spends a little time looking at a piece of art, they too can imagine a magical world."

318

My Name Is Angela

Where I'm From

If I sit still for a long time and think in just the right way, I can see the numbers and colored letters hiding behind my name. The grandfathers are sure we can't do this, but we can. Sometimes late at night, when I might really be asleep, I think of a ride in a truck. It's sunny and there are rows of us, all wearing the same white gowns, and I hear the little whirly noise of a gate sliding into place behind us . . .

I don't think of the truck when I'm in school teaching their fourth graders. Or the numbers. I follow the well-worn groove of times tables and spelling, now and then reading stories or listening to oral reports. Last week there were two knife fights, but that too is a well-worn groove. I stopped them both and got yelled at by some of the mothers and their boyfriends. They saw the blood soaking through the bandage on my arm, but it made no difference. They are just like their children; if they weren't different sizes, I could never tell them apart.

Bruno says he can tell them apart but he lies about so many things I never know what to believe. His lying makes me tired so I don't talk to him much. I have my radio and he has his TV. His shows are stupid and so is he. When I'm in the living room with him, he pretends to know who the people are and what they're doing but late at night, before he comes to bed, I peek and see him shaking his head, mumbling as he clicks from channel to channel.

A good thing about Bruno is that I never have to look up to him and he never has to look down at me. People look down at us all the time, without exception. It's what we're for. Of course, I hear pieces of discussions on the radio, usually when the music is boring and I turn the dial. Some are "for" us and some "against," but I can't tell their ideas apart any more than I can tell them apart. They're like empty spaces, white silhouettes moving through the dimly colored background of the world, or fiery beings stretching blazing hands to conduct us like a lackluster symphony written by a mediocre composer. It's because of the numbers behind my name. I think they control me and the ones for recognizing people are missing.

The grandfathers are sure we don't understand about the numbers, but we do. When I go to the regional office for routine checkups, they always test to see if I know about the numbers, but they're so sure I don't, they never pay attention. The grandfathers are different from other people, more defined and identifiable. I trust them, but I don't know why. Maybe some of the numbers make me trust them.

One Saturday morning it was raining when I woke up. Bruno was snoring as usual and the side of his face was covered with a big bandage. I was confused, but then I remembered. Last night he wanted sex. I told him no. This was odd because I really *did* feel like that, but I didn't like him deciding all the time. I thought it should be my turn to decide and I decided *no*.

He didn't like that. He followed me around, getting in the way while I did the dishes and the ironing. Sometimes he was loud and scary; mostly he was whiny and pitiful. He was really on my nerves!

Finally, I made another decision. I told him, "No!" one last time and hit him with the hot iron as hard as I could. He crashed to the floor and didn't move.

I got ready for bed as he lay there moaning. When I got out of the shower, he was sitting up, whimpering and trying not to touch his swollen face. His left eye had disappeared.

A few minutes later, he staggered to his feet. He went to the clinic and I went to sleep.

I remembered all that as I sat listening to the rain and smelling the fresh air seeping into the drafty old apartment. It was such a peaceful feeling, like the rain was making its own clean, cool world just for me. In a way it was like the quiet truck ride in my dream, with no numbers, no knife fights, nobody "for" and "against."

It was like music that had to come from some place greater than the messy, tangled world. Could there be such a place?

I think that's when I decided to go to the Soul Man.

Only a Little Soul

Everybody knows about the Soul Man, just like everybody knows about things like drugs and where to buy stolen goods. The difference is that decent people don't buy drugs or stolen goods, but any of us can go to the Soul Man if we have money and aren't afraid of the law. Some go because they want the rest of us to look up to them the way all the made people have to look up to the born people. I never cared about that. In fact, I almost didn't go because I didn't want to look down on Bruno or make him look up to me. But every time I almost changed my mind, I would remember the cool, clean rain and the sunny truck ride through the gate. Even though nobody in the truck said a word, I knew we all had the same new, happy feeling, like a place had been made just for us and we were on our way to fit into that place and do things that only we could do.

Of course, I only know that as a dream. I don't really *remember*, do I? My earliest memory is the grandfather at the regional office saying, "Open your eyes." Nobody else was with me. There was no sun and no white robe, just my first set of drab clothes draped across a chair, waiting for me to put them on. They smelled like mothballs. I knew they'd been worn before.

What the Soul Man did was against the law, so he had to move around to stay ahead of the police. The hardest part about finding him was asking people. We are not outgoing; other than Bruno and one or two of the custodians at school, I really didn't know anybody to ask. Sometimes I saw people on the el or walking down the street and I could tell by looking at their eyes that they had changed, but you can't just stop a stranger and ask! You can't just say, "Where is the illegal Soul Man?" It was discouraging.

I began to feel lonely because when you need to

know something important and have no one to ask, you really *are* alone. I couldn't talk to Bruno, because I didn't want him to know. My plan was to try it and if it turned out to be good maybe I could get him to try it too. In the meantime, I knew I couldn't trust him. He might pretend to know where the Soul Man was and then laugh at me if I went where he said and found nothing.

I was thinking hard about this problem one afternoon. I had just finished reading *A Wrinkle in Time* to my kids and was waiting for them to get out their math homework when one of them came up to my desk.

"It's Jamal, Miss Angela."

I think Jamal was in one of the knife fights, but it wasn't his fault. I would have recognized him if not for my preoccupation. He always gave me a hug at the end of the day.

"Yes, Jamal? Would you like to use the bathroom?"

"No, ma'am. Mr. Sam asked me to give you this."

He handed me a note. It said, "I know a Man."

"Thank you, Jamal."

"Are you okay, Miss Angela?"

"Yes, I am, Jamal. Thank you for asking."

When school was over for the day, I went down the gray painted steps at the end of the hall and through the doors with the Fallout Shelter sign. Before Sam started working at the school, the steps were greasy and the paint was almost all peeled off. The handrail was rusty, but now it was a nice glossy green. Everything Sam did was neat and clean. That's why he was such a good custodian.

The door to the janitor's room was open and I could

see the clean white mops hanging on the wall. There was a smell of orange cleaner but not too much. The janitor's room at our apartment usually had a nasty sour smell with strong pine cleaner fighting to cover it up.

Sam was at a workbench fixing a vacuum cleaner. A bright white light shone on tools laid in neat rows; pieces of the sweeper were arranged on a sheet of newspaper.

Sam was my age, of course, but he wore glasses and looked like an older person. *"We're all suitable to our calling,"* I thought, remembering the line from *A Christmas Carol.* *"We're well matched . . ."*

"You can tell when somebody has been to the Soul Man," he said without looking up from his work, "but I can tell when somebody *wants* to go." He put down the glasses he didn't need (none of us do) and turned to look at me with unremarkable brown eyes. "We're different for a reason, Angela. Don't go to the Soul Man."

"I want to," was all I could think to say.

"Then I'll tell you a secret," he said with an odd sort of smile. "You already have the thing you want from him. It's a trick; all he'll do is switch around some of your numbers. This will change the way you feel and the way you think, but it won't change what you are. We're already the same thing they are, the way a draft horse is the same thing as a wild stallion."

"I'm tired of watching stallions."

"So was I," he said, "but I couldn't be one, no matter how much I thought I could."

"You went to the Soul Man? But . . ."

"I went all right. It was a mistake. For a long time I didn't know what to do; the Soul Man never undoes his work. I finally went to the grandfather to get changed back. I was afraid I would get into trouble . . ." He stopped smiling.

"I still want to go," I said.

"All right." He handed me a slip of paper. "Show this at the door. If anybody but the person at the door sees it, tell them it's your grocery list. I can't write down his location, but he'll be there until Thursday. Go to Thirtieth Street Station and take the R7 . . ."

That night I was very nice to Bruno because I had a strange feeling that I would be leaving him the next day. I didn't know what it would be like after I went to the Soul Man, but I knew it would be *different*. Maybe a different person couldn't stay with Bruno. Maybe a different person could stay but not be happy.

Maybe Bruno wouldn't like a different person.

I made a pot of oatmeal because he thinks it's a treat to have breakfast for dinner and oatmeal is his favorite. Lately he's been acting careful around me, like he's afraid to do something I might not like. He picks up after himself and doesn't pretend to know all about the people on TV. This makes things more convenient. I should like it this way, but I don't. I just wanted things to be the way they were before they changed again, maybe forever.

When we got into bed, he said it had been a long day. I know he works hard on the docks and they'd been making him work overtime; he *was* falling asleep at dinner but I also had the strangest thought. I could stop an irresistible force, but I could not move an

325

immovable object. I didn't know what this thought could really mean, but as he lay there snoring, I touched the scar on his cheek and wondered; could Bruno ever be a wild stallion?

What Could Be in That House?

It was a blustery wet Saturday when I found the Soul Man's house. I assumed it would be in some dangerous, rundown neighborhood like in a crime show, but it wasn't. It was a nice old place in a row of old houses on a little hill. The slate walk was lined with hyacinths and crocuses and there was a big dogwood tree waiting to flower.

I thought Sam had made a mistake when a nice old lady answered the door, but she took my "grocery list" and showed me to a little room that smelled like flowers and old books. All the windows were stained glass and the walls were covered with all kinds of symbols. I recognized the cross, the six-pointed star and the yin/yang, but most of the symbols were strange. There was a kind of relaxing music playing softly; it sounded a little like wind and birds and a tumbling brook.

I don't know what I expected, but when a sharply dressed young man came into the room, I had no idea he was the Soul Man. He reminded me of a grandfather; I trusted him immediately. I noticed he was handsome and this made me feel strange.

"Don't get up," he said as I started to rise. He sat on a delicate-looking chair in front of me and stared at my face.

"They say the eyes are the window to the soul," he said. He was quiet as he looked into my eyes, then he held out his hand and said, "Angela, my name is David. Pleased to meet you."

I shook his hand.

"What makes you think you want a soul?"

"I . . . I'm not sure," I said. We don't always think of reasons for what we want, especially the things we want most. "I think it started with a dream I keep having." I explained about the truck and the rain. I was sure this was nonsense to him and I began to wonder if I belonged there at all, but he just smiled and nodded as if he heard the story every day.

"What does Bruno think?" he asked.

"How do you know about Bruno?"

"Remember what I told you about eyes," he said. "Bruno doesn't know, does he? You don't plan to tell him."

I shook my head.

"Good. I don't like doing this for people who just want to be looked up to. Those people don't understand what they're getting into."

"Sam told me I shouldn't come," I said.

"Sam? Oh, yes, the custodian. Sam is a good friend. Now, there are a few things you should know before we begin. First of all, this is against the law. We can stop now if you like and you won't get into trouble."

"I don't want to stop."

"All right. Now this is important. You see the symbols all around us? Those symbols remind us that only God makes souls. Some argue that it doesn't matter if you're born or made; all people have souls regardless. Others say that men make bodies, but men can't make souls so 'made' people are soulless. I don't know which thing is true. All I know is that at the end of the ritual you will know you have a soul. That means you will be responsible for your life, your thoughts and your actions and you will be accountable to God. Do you understand?"

"As much as I'm able to," I said.

"It's a big step, Angela. The biggest. This is your last chance. Are you sure?"

"I'm sure."

"Okay. Sit back and relax. Close your eyes . . ."

I knew I was crying before I woke up.

". . . the matter? Angela, wake up. Open your eyes." I opened my eyes.

"What's the matter?" he asked. I think he was trying to look into my eyes again, but couldn't see because of the tears. He looked really concerned; maybe this wasn't what usually happened.

"It's Bruno," I sniffed. My heart was pounding. I felt like some kind of power was flowing through me, almost like electricity. "How could I do that? What kind of person does what I did to him?"

The Soul Man seemed to relax a little. "You feel ashamed of something you did to Bruno?"

"Is that what this is? It feels terrible, like I have to straighten something I bent, only I don't know how."

"Well," he sighed, "that's what it's like to have a soul. You may not understand it now, Angela, but you're having a very healthy reaction."

"But what do I do?" I said. "How do I fix what I did?"

MAGO HUANG

"If you really want to fix it, you'll find a way."

So many things were happening in my mind as I gave my money to the old lady and left the house. There was a storm outside. Before, my only thought would've been how to stay dry, but now I noticed that the lightning was beautiful and terrifying. I couldn't take my eyes from the clouds as they were stretched and shredded by the wind and every little piece of the sky was like some bottomless kaleidoscope of gray and silver. There was a connection between the wonderful freshness of the air, the watery purity of the clouds and the sharp edges of the lightning and thunder. Then there were the trees sweeping back and forth, some still struggling to push sleepy leaves from their tightly wound buds so they could connect with the air waiting to flow in as carbon dioxide, energize the tree and flow out again as oxygen to energize animals and people . . .

All the data that had been put in my head by the grandfathers was waking up like the leaves, not just lying in storage waiting to be used for a moment and then put away again. I felt like a dazzling swarm of bees searching for a queen to bring them to order. I felt like clouds with eyes and ears and noses, blowing swiftly and surely, in a direction I couldn't recognize. I felt like the wet earth and the yellow sun in the dry blue sky above the rain . . .

I felt alive.

"I was right!" I said this to myself over and over as I watched the dripping city rush past the grimy train window. There really *was* a place greater than the messy, tangled world. I was *right*!

As the train sped around a bend deeper into the city, a great big church with a golden dome came into view. I stopped thinking about being right and wondered about a Person who could exist outside of all we could see or know.

Bruno was watching wrestling when I got home. Right away, I noticed that he was built like one of the wrestlers, broad, sharply defined and full of strength. Of course, I've always *noticed*, ever since that day at the regional office when we sat across from each other in the waiting room, but this was different. There was something admirable about this big strong man, something that made my heart beat a little faster just because I was near him.

I sat on the sofa and snuggled against him, pulling his arm across my shoulders. I was still a little chilly from my walk in the rain.

"Hi, Angela. I'm watching wrestling. See that guy in the blue trunks? They call him The Butcher . . . I mean the one in the red cape . . . He fought the Jade Blaster. I mean the one in the blue trunks; he's the one . . . definitely the Jade Blaster . . . Oh, forget it! I know you don't like wrestling!"

"Who says? Maybe I'm starting to get interested."

He looked at me like a puppy that'd just been scratched behind the ears. I know that sounds like I'm talking down about him, but I'm really not. I put my arms around him and squeezed. "Who's that?" I asked, pointing to a masked man at ringside getting ready to throw a chair.

"That's, um, Slappy Joe. Yeah. He fought the Jade Blaster. You see that guy in the red cape . . . ?"

331

When I woke up crying at the Soul Man's house, it was the worst I've ever felt, but that rainy afternoon with Bruno was the happiest I've ever felt.

Sunday

The next morning I woke up thinking about church. I'd dreamed about the truck again, only it was mixed up with the big church from the train ride. Instead of bringing us out into the world, the truck was taking us all to the mysterious place under the shining golden dome. Bruno was there with friends and flowers. There was a man in white and gold standing at the altar holding a book and everybody knew him and trusted him the way we do the grandfathers.

I don't know anything about going to church so I put one of the religious programs on the radio while I made breakfast. I couldn't understand everything that was said, but I didn't put it on to get sense out of it. The music made the morning feel quiet and special and I imagined that the preacher looked just like the man from my dream, dressed in white and gold.

Bruno always worked on Sunday. When he kissed me on his way out I got happy all over again. I felt like I was standing in a clear stream on a beautiful sunny day with my toes squishing in the cool mud. The sparkling water rose, lifting me and carrying me under shady trees and I closed my eyes as my hair spread around me like jeweled black ferns waving in the watery breeze.

Sunday was my day to mark homework and tests. Math was easy; I'm good at math and all the problems are solved in the teacher's guide, but this week I also had book reports. The rules were simple and I knew every word of every book, but each child explained things differently. I had to use all my concentration and compare each section of the student's report with some piece of the book that seemed to match it. This was one of the reasons why I could never teach higher than fourth grade; the older the students, the more individualized they became. By the time they reached sixth grade they had to be taught by the "regulars."

I was reading Ashley's report about *Call It Courage,* an older book about a brave and resourceful young Polynesian boy. My mind started drifting. I wondered if I could build a dugout canoe and what breadfruit tasted like. The radio was still on in the kitchen, but the religious program was over. Now there were people talking. It was another "for" and "against" discussion, only this time, it caught my attention.

". . . Spokesman for Ultimate Aim Inc., the company producing the clones and Winston Mothersbaugh from the Coalition for Human Dignity. Let's start with you, Dr. Monroe. Where do things stand now with Ultimate Aim's test program?"

"We're in the third phase of our social integration pilot program," said a man. I could not imagine a face for him. "A substantial population of our people have been introduced into three east coast urban environments, where they are going about the business they're made for. They're under close supervision."

"How are they doing?"

"Splendidly," said the man. "They're doing their jobs flawlessly and our evaluations show they are well adjusted and satisfied."

"Is that why half of the Philly P.D. is out hunting

for the Soul Man," asked Mr. Mothersbaugh, "because they're well adjusted and satisfied?"

"What about the Soul Man phenomenon?" asked the woman. I could tell she wanted to sound like she was curious about the Soul Man, but she really wanted to talk about something else. "Does Ultimate Aim have any comment?"

"This person, if he even exists, is really not our concern," said Dr. Monroe. "Of course, if an arrest is made, we will prosecute vigorously. Our people are the property of Ultimate Aim and must not be tampered with."

"Voids the warranty, I guess," said Mr. Mothersbaugh. "Do you even hear yourself, Doctor?"

I turned it off.

I finished marking the papers. I cleaned the apartment. When there was nothing left to do inside, I went for a walk.

The list of things I noticed for the first time could fill a book so I won't list them. Every piece of the world seemed new, like I'd been living in the twilight of an overcast winter day and now the sun was out, but it was like a million suns. It was getting exhausting. I was already beginning to understand a character like Ebenezer Scrooge and his compulsion to insulate himself from all the good things of life.

Scrooge reminded me of books. There was an old bookstore a few blocks from the apartment. I'd never been there. If I needed to know a book, I just went to the library and memorized it, but my head was starting to hurt and I imagined the bookstore would be quiet and still.

Did you ever see a scary old movie? I watched one

with Bruno once, a long time ago. Some people went to an old house, kind of like the house where I met the Soul Man. It was a fine old house, nice and clean, with lots of architectural detail, but it gave everybody a scary, lonely feeling. The bookstore reminded me of that creepy old imaginary house. It made me feel the way the people in the movie must've felt. People in the little aisles drifted away from me like sleepy ghosts. Some looked at me like *I* came from someplace scary.

"Can I help you?"

"Oh, I'm looking for . . ."

"Not you." A man with white whiskers pushed past me to help a young man at the end of the aisle.

Eventually I found my way to the religious section. I giggled to myself as I imagined finding a book called *Care and Feeding of Your Soul.* There were lots of books to choose from, many bearing the same symbols I'd seen at the Soul Man's house. I would read all of them, but I decided to start with the Bible because of the church that had joined my dreams.

"Must be a gift," mumbled the man at the cash register as I handed him the Bible. People in line behind me stood back to wait till I was finished. This wasn't unusual, but today it gave me a hard, icy feeling. I was glad to get away from those people.

As I walked back to the apartment, I thought about that feeling. The bookstore was the first time I'd noticed, but not the first time I'd felt that way. When Dr. Monroe said we were the *property* of Ultimate Aim, I had the same feeling, only it was covered up somehow. Maybe I'd had it even before I went to the Soul Man. I couldn't be sure.

I thought that having a soul would add things to

335

my life. Instead, it was starting to take things away, like insulation being stripped from an electrical wire. I was becoming sensitive to everything, good and bad, and it was strange how even good things could be too much to take.

I decided to spend the rest of the day in the apartment with the shades drawn. Maybe I would memorize the Bible.

To School

Getting to school was hard. It was a lovely Monday morning with birds and sunshine and flowers. People might not expect those things in a neighborhood like this, but they're really not hard to find. The ugliness of trash and disintegrating buildings is the easiest thing to see, but some people try to brighten things up with great big colorful words painted on the buildings. I know it's illegal and usually has to do with gangs, but it's nicer than filthy old bricks and concrete.

Getting to school was hard because I couldn't stop noticing everything around me, especially people. For the first time I noticed what a problem the bus can be. Nobody will sit near us and everybody gets mad about the wasted seats. Before, I only thought about getting places; now I was starting to realize what it felt like to be stared at and complained about, as if . . .

Something told me not to think about "as if." I stopped looking at angry people and reviewed the day's lesson plan.

My kids were unruly when they entered the classroom. Was this unusual, or had I simply not noticed before? "Jerry, put that down," I called. "Give Claudette her book back." Jerry ignored me at first, but suddenly his eyes got big and round. So did Claudette's. So did everybody's, except Jamal's. He just smiled and took his seat.

"That's right!" I said, trying to sound mischievous instead of scary. I was a little scared myself. "I know who you are."

They all got quiet and still.

"Miss Angela?"

"Raise your hand, Joseph. Yes?"

"Are you a monster?"

Some of the kids looked nervous, as if Joseph had spoken the unspeakable. "Do you think I'm a monster?" I asked.

"My dad says you're like a . . . a Frankenstein," said Joseph.

"No, Joseph," I said. Joseph had started one of the knife fights. "I'm not a monster. But what if I was? Monsters need friends too, don't they? Wouldn't you like to have a monster for a friend?"

This little challenge worked better than I had anticipated. Within seconds, they were all stomping around the classroom, roaring at each other with their hands up in the air. I let it go on for a few minutes, then got them settled down. There was no more mention of monsters.

By recess, I was completely exhausted. What had once seemed like a simple routine now showed itself to be unfathomably complex and emotionally draining. Most of my kids lived in situations which all but guaranteed failure in life and I could feel their needs like powerful vacuums pulling me in twenty-five directions. They were sad and tired and angry and confused. Some struggled to do well but couldn't; others possessed capabilities well beyond their grade level but refused to use them. I was able to fall back on training and habits to keep the class on an even keel, but I knew this wasn't teaching.

While the kids were out on the playground, I decided to take a risk. It was stupid and now I know I shouldn't have done it, but I was still learning.

I went to the classroom next to mine where a lady with white hair sat marking papers.

"Mrs. Wilson? Excuse me, do you have a minute?"

Mrs. Wilson looked up from her work. "What? Oh . . . you have your own supplies!"

"I don't want supplies. I'd just like to talk for a minute, if it's all right."

She made a kind of snorting sound. "Talk about what?" she said.

"About teaching. That is . . . how did you learn to be such a good teacher?"

"Helps if you're a human. Why do you ask?"

"Well," I said, trying to take time to think so I wouldn't make some serious mistake. "I'd like to be a better teacher."

"What for?" she said. "You're not here to teach. You're here to keep the damn troublemakers away from kids who *might* be able to learn a few things. Just because they made you able to memorize books and loaded a few lesson plans into your brain, that doesn't make you a teacher. Now I have work to do."

My good friend Jamal was the first to return from the playground. I was sitting at my desk.

"What's the matter, Miss Angela?" he asked, giving me his biggest hug. "Don't cry . . ."

I saw Sam as I was leaving that day, but he was too far away to speak to. I wondered if people ever told him he was worse than useless. I wondered if he ever felt the way I did.

Just as the bus pulled up, Claudette came skipping past the bus stop. Everybody was playing the little game they always played, trying to shove ahead of me without getting too close. "As if" was very big and strong, but when Claudette saw me, she raised her hands like monster claws and roared. "As if" slithered back into its hole and I laughed all the way home.

That first day at school taught me a lot about what it means to have a soul. When Mrs. Wilson told me the truth about myself, I was so humiliated I wanted to die, but I knew that, if she was right, then I was the only one who cared about my kids. I *had* to become a good teacher. Bruno would have to help me.

The Language of Monsters

Let's try it again. *Bonjour, Monsieur.*"

"*Bonjour, Mademoiselle.*"

"*Tu t'appelles comment?*"

"*Je m'appelle Bruno. Et tu?*"

"*Je m'appelle Angela. Tu aimes les . . . les hamburgers?*"

"*Oui, Madamoiselle. J'aime les hamburgers. Et tu?*"

"You know I don't like hamburgers," I said. "I mean, um . . . *Je n'aime . . . les . . .*"

"*Je n'aime pas les hamburgers,*" said Bruno. "I thought you were supposed to be the teacher."

"Maybe I should unload ships and you should

teach my class," I said. Actually, the grandfathers had made all their teachers fluent in several European languages, but I had never tried to teach anything not covered by my strictly defined lesson plans. Bruno was my test case; if I could teach him, something he was never meant to learn, it might mean that Mrs. Wilson was wrong.

"Can we stop now?" asked Bruno. "I'm hungry and it's almost time for *How Many Can You Break*?"

"Guess I shouldn't have asked about hamburgers," I said. I started for the kitchen to make dinner, but stopped.

"Bruno?"

"Yeah?" He was already vanishing into the waves of channels flying across the screen, stopping to check one out, going forward, backing up. It reminded me of the way a cat walks around and around before settling down to purr and sleep.

"Thanks for helping me."

"Sure."

It had been two weeks since my visit to the Soul Man. As time went by, I had less and less awareness of *before* and *after*. It just seemed like a smooth, slow transition, like growing up must be. An unexpected thing was that Bruno was "growing up" too; not as much and not as fast, but it made me wonder if Sam was right about us being the same thing as they. Could Bruno "catch" a soul from me? If we already have souls, could mine wake his up?

Of course we weren't always happy but even being mad was different. There was always more to a fight than the immediate irritation. I didn't just want him to stop doing this or saying that. I wanted us to find out what was right. I wanted us to agree, even if it meant one of us had to admit being wrong . . .

I never stopped thinking about the night I hit him.

*B*onjour, mes petites monstres."
"*Bonjour, Mademoiselle Angela!*"

My "little monsters" were learning French almost as quickly as Bruno. A lot of them resisted at first, but once they saw how it could set them apart from their schoolmates they really applied themselves. I think they were hungry for some identity other than "troublemakers." My approach was simple. Once a phrase or vocabulary word had been learned, it no longer existed in English. Sometimes we even made a fun little ceremony of destroying the English words. More and more conversations were being conducted in French. They wouldn't attain anything like fluency since there was so little time left in the school year, but they could be heard speaking their adopted language and singing "Sur le pont D'Avignon" in the hallways. It was a beautiful sound.

When I evaluated my lesson plans in the light of Mrs. Wilson's explanation, I found plenty of space for French lessons. The curriculum I had been given was clearly meant to keep the kids busy without teaching them much of anything. It could only frustrate them and reinforce whatever indifference or resentment they were finding at home or in the community. In my brief career, I have found that children are bright. It is up to those charged with their care to polish them to the full brightness of their potential, but too often, they are dulled by carelessness, laziness and cynical manipulation. It is the education that fails, not the student.

I knew these things in a vague way even before my visit to the Soul Man, but now I was motivated to do my part as a teacher. My summer would be spent developing a new curriculum just for my kids. Maybe I could improve things little by little until one day, possibly by the end of next year, my kids could do as well as everyone else's.

Of course, we had no French textbook. I typed each lesson and made copies. I was a little concerned about the reception such a shoestring approach would receive, but my students decided we should take all those lessons and create our own textbook. Claudette even drew a picture of the Eiffel Tower and a loaf of French bread to use for the cover.

"Il est temps pour le Français," I announced as I passed out the day's lesson. "Today we will learn how . . ."

"Miss Angela," crackled the loudspeaker, "please report to Dr. Bauer's office. Will Miss Angela please report to Dr. Bauer's office?"

Dr. Bauer was our principal.

"Did you do something bad, Miss Angela?" asked Joseph.

"Not that I know of," I said. "Maybe a parent wants to speak to me. Listen, *mes petites monstres,* I'm counting on you to behave yourselves, *comprenez-vous?"*

"Oui, Mademoiselle! Oui, oui!"

Mrs. Wilson was standing at her door as I left the classroom. Usually she never even looked at me, but today she watched me all the way down the hall.

There were no parents waiting outside the principal's office. Inside were Dr. Bauer and a technician from Ultimate Aim.

"So," said Dr. Bauer. She was a shapeless gray woman who always dressed like one of the curvy young professionals on stylish TV shows. She did not invite me to have a seat. "You're teaching them French?"

"Yes, Doctor."

"In case you haven't noticed, the public school system is a multi-cultural institution," she said. "Seventy percent of your class is African American, the rest are Hispanic or Asian. One is Irish. French is a colonial language; it's foreign to their culture and worthless to them. It's also not included in your curriculum. Who gave you permission to teach it?"

"No one, Doctor."

"Then why . . . ?"

"Dr. Bauer," interrupted the technician, "if I may?"

"Of course," said Dr. Bauer. She looked like something was about to happen to me and she was glad.

"Angela," said the technician, "core zEp 7-12 protocol-uncouple-recite."

"Protocol-prime equal omicron-set 7 . . ." I began without hesitation. I was being debriefed! This form of interrogation was used by the technicians for onsite diagnostics. The "protocol-uncouple" command was supposed to induce a sort of trance which allowed an unimpeded flow of automatic responses, but the command would not work if the subject had been altered in any way.

If I could not mimic the trance state *perfectly* and

343

give all the right answers, he would know I'd been to the Soul Man.

Fortunately, the technician was in a hurry. A thorough debriefing could take half an hour, but he stopped after five minutes. I think he was satisfied that I hadn't been tampered with. "There's nothing wrong with this one," he told Dr. Bauer.

"Then why did it suddenly start teaching French?"

"*She* probably got bored with the curriculum. It happens. Anyway, the diagnostic shows no changes to her neural profile. Angela, open your eyes."

Dr. Bauer had a disappointed look on her face. "Return to your class," she ordered. I know she wanted to add, "We'll be watching," but everybody already knew that.

Mrs. Wilson had the same disappointed look as Dr. Bauer when she saw me. She went into her classroom and slammed the door.

The children were unruly, but they settled down quickly. "All right," I began, "if you will please turn to page 46, the conversation about directions. Justin, could you please read the part of Henri?"

"*Oui, Mademoiselle!*"

Ours

It was time to talk to Bruno.

Six weeks had passed since the beginning of my new life. I should say *our* new life because I treated Bruno differently now. In some ways it was like what was going on with my kids; the way I treated them was changing the way they thought and behaved.

Bruno was changing as well, but he was different from my kids. They were supposed to grow and change. For them it was natural, but we were made *not* to change.

Sometimes I could see the friction and confusion this caused. He tried without knowing why. Did he feel the satisfaction of accomplishment? Could it mean anything to him that he was probably the first man in our brief history to learn a language not given to him by the grandfathers? Of course, I couldn't help thinking of myself as special because of my visit to the Soul Man, but Bruno was feeling his way behind me with a kind of blind faith. Why? What did it mean to him? What did I mean to him?

Shortly after we met, we made a practical decision to live together. Even we have natural desires and these soon found their natural expression, but love was unknown to us then.

Was it still unknown to him?

I was nervous when I sat down next to him on the sofa. He was watching wrestling again. I still didn't like TV, but it usually made me happy to be with him when he was doing something he liked.

"Wow," he said. "There's Punchy Joe; he's the worst ref in the league. I mean Slappy Joe. That guy with the green mask is the Salamander . . ."

He stopped and looked at me. "You *know* I don't know what I'm talking about!" he said and then he started laughing. I don't think I'd heard him laugh before. "You sit there," he said with a snort, trying to catch his breath, "you sit there and listen like . . . like it's all for real!" He gave me a great big hug, then

345

wiped away a few tears. "You're too much, Angela. Yeah, you're too much!"

"Not as much as you," I said. "Listen, Bruno, is it all right if we talk for a few minutes?"

"Talk all you want," he said.

"I mean without the TV. Is it okay?" There was that friction; I was pulling him out of habit and asking him for a decision.

"Uh . . . yeah, yeah, sure," he said. He clicked off the TV, but it took him a few seconds to change focus.

"How do you like learning French?" I asked.

"I don't know," he said with a shrug.

"Well, I mean does it make you feel good? You know, I don't think any of us have done anything like it. It makes you extraordinary."

"I can lift more than anybody on the docks," he said. "I think it scares people."

"Do you ever wish it didn't?"

"If it does, it does." He shrugged again.

This wasn't helping me to understand him. Or maybe it was.

"*Je t'aime*," I said. "Do you know what that means?"

"I love you."

"Do you know what *that* means?"

"Some kind of feeling people get," he said. "They say it on TV all the time."

"Don't you ever get curious about feelings like that?" I said. "Don't you wonder about things?"

"Why would I?"

I felt like I was standing on a bridge—maybe the one at Avignon—and it was being pulled apart brick by brick. I had to admit that I had created all kinds of hopes for myself and they were turning out not to be real. Maybe souls do that.

There's another thing souls do. They feed regret. They stroke it and care for it until it's too big to live inside you anymore and it has to break out. You have no choice.

"Bruno," I said. My throat was all tight and my eyes were filling up with tears, "do you remember the night I hit you with the iron?"

"Sure," he said, pulling back a little. There was a wary look on his face, like he thought I might be threatening him.

"It's the worst thing I've ever done," I said. "I'm so sorry! Can you forgive me?"

"No," he said, "I can't. You wanna get Chinese for dinner?"

The Soul Man was wrong. There was no way to fix it.

Miss Angela

One morning I found a note on my desk. It was from Joseph's grandfather. It said:

"Dear Miss Angela,

"This is just a note to thank you for your devotion to your students. As you know, Joseph has had his share of trouble at school and at home, but he finds your class to be challenging and satisfying. Learning a foreign language has given him a sense of accomplishment. Thank you again and please keep up the good work. Sincerely, Charles Graham."

I folded the note and put it in my plan book. At the

end of the day, after the kids had gone, I took it out and read it again.

"You're still teaching them French?" The voice startled me. I looked up and found Dr. Bauer standing at the door.

"Why are you still doing what I told you to stop?"

Her question was hard to understand. I gave what I hoped was the right answer. "You didn't tell me to stop, Dr. Bauer."

"I most certainly did! Who do you think you're talking to?"

"I'm talking to the principal. And I'm sorry, Dr. Bauer, but I remember our last conversation. You did not tell me to stop."

"Well, I'm telling you now! You will stop teaching French and teach only what is in your curriculum. Do you understand that? Will you remember that?"

"Yes, Doctor," I said. "May I ask why?"

"I don't answer to you," she said. "You answer to me! Don't fool yourself, Miss Angela. Just because the tech couldn't find anything wrong with you doesn't mean I can't! You will learn your place or you will be dismissed. I will not be dissed by some subhuman science project! Don't forget that!"

"Yes, Doctor."

The next day, when my students arrived I greeted them in the usual way.

"Bonjour, mes enfants aimés."

"Bonjour, Mademoiselle Angela!"

They all had today's French homework on their desks in front of them.

"If you will please take out your math books and turn to page 107 . . ."

"But, Miss Angela," said Jamal, raising his hand after he'd spoken, *"il est temps pour le Français."*

"Oui!" agreed the rest of the class.

And now I learned how having a soul must always lead to a broken heart. There would be no more French and for them there could be no reason why this should be so. How could I tell them that Miss Angela was nothing but a creature into which people were meant to pour scorn and derision? Was this not ultimately my purpose in this school? Was I not here to keep the "troublemakers" out of the way while boring them, ignoring them and adding fuel to their tiny sparks of resentment? If I did my job properly, how could they not hate me and all others like me?

I couldn't tell them that one more French lesson would not merely get me fired; it would get me sent to the laboratory. There was so much in this little situation that they could never understand, but eventually they would understand the most important thing; Miss Angela had abandoned them.

Of course, for the moment they were simply disappointed. I didn't tell them there would never be any more French. I just said we were changing things a little. So now, I was a liar as well as a poor teacher.

It was a long, tedious day, longer even than my first day as a teacher with a soul. I thought about the lonely feeling I'd had when I wanted to go to the Soul Man but didn't know who could lead me to him.

Sam helped me then. Maybe he could help again.

When Sam saw me come into the janitor's room, he stopped what he was doing. He opened a notebook and began to write.

"I don't know what to do," I said.

He went on writing as if he hadn't heard me. After a few minutes he said, "Do you know why the company is called Ultimate Aim?" He never stopped writing.

"No," I said.

"They have a noble goal," he said. "They envision a world in which people no longer hate each other. They envision a world in which nobody will be allowed to do the menial, difficult or dangerous jobs that nobody should want to do. Fewer people will create fewer problems for the trees and animals. That's why they make us."

"I don't understand," I said.

"Do you remember what people looked like before you went to the Soul Man," he said, "how you could hardly tell them apart? The grandfathers made us that way to antagonize people. They resent nothing as much as the failure to acknowledge their individual identity. Everything about us is hateful to them. We draw their hatred away from each other. But we're useful so we're tolerated. That's the formulation, useful to set them 'free' from the indignity of toil, hated to keep hatred in a safe place."

"What about trees and animals?"

"We can't reproduce, so our numbers can be controlled. They theorize that, once positions of lower worth are filled by us, the people who once filled those positions will vanish from the earth, leaving only the brilliant and careful. They will control their own numbers and they will treat the earth with reverence."

"I still don't know what to do," I said.

"Run away," he said, still writing. "Get as far from people as you can. Live in the woods."

"I have no purpose in the woods."

He stopped writing and very carefully tore the pages from the notebook. "Memorize this," he said, handing me the pages. "You'll need it when you go to the grandfather."

Maybe I'll Remember

I couldn't sleep that night. The moon made sharp, deep shadows and strange bright shapes on the bed. I have always loved moonlight, *always,* but tonight it was cold and menacing, telling me that the world was never as I had understood it to be.

Bruno was restless too. He tossed and turned, mumbling in his sleep. He opened his eyes.

"Can't you sleep?" I said. "What's the matter?"

"Crazy dream," he said. "I'm in a truck on a dark road at night. I dream about it all the time, but tonight it keeps waking me up."

"What do you think it means?"

"Nothing. It's a dream."

"But dreams are a kind of thought," I said, "and thoughts come from somewhere. Sometimes they come from memories."

"I guess. I don't remember riding in a truck."

The curtains billowed in the cool breeze. A mixture of crickets and distant traffic sounds blew in with the scents of spring. Outside, the night was peaceful.

"Bruno," I said, "did you ever know anybody who went to the Soul Man?"

"Why would anybody do that?"

"I don't know," I said. "Maybe to find out about things like your dream. Maybe to figure out who they really are."

"We know who we really are." He said this with such simple assurance that it was almost shocking. "If people go to the Soul Man it's only because they want to pretend."

"Pretend what?"

"That we're just like our makers," he said with a yawn. "Or that it matters. Because it doesn't. Anybody who would waste their time with the Soul Man belongs back in the laboratory."

I got up to go to the bathroom because I didn't want him to see me crying. As I sat in the dark, I wondered how much Sam remembered from the time before he gave back his soul.

How much would I remember?

To Grandfather's House

I know it seems like I gave up too easily. What does a person really have besides a soul? *"What does it profit a man if he gains the whole world but lose his soul?"*

I believe what Sam said about us being the same as them and I know the Soul Man was right; only God makes souls. The Soul Man can't give them and the grandfathers can't take them away. They can only switch around our numbers. They can wake us up. They can put us back to sleep and if I had to go back to sleep to stay with the people I loved, then so be it. Maybe I would have memories to dream about as I slept again. Maybe those dreams would keep me from returning completely to the heartless teacher and selfish mate I used to be.

I was afraid when I went into the examining room to meet the grandfather. Would I be in trouble for breaking the law? Sam didn't get into trouble. Would it be the same for me?

"Good evening, Angela," said the grandfather as he came into the room. "I see on your chart that you're not due for your checkup for a few more weeks. Is there a problem?"

"Yes," I said. "I can't think of an easy way to say it so I'll just say it. I went to the Soul Man."

"Oh," said the grandfather, looking at me a little differently, I thought. "Why is that a problem?"

"I want it undone," I said. "It was a mistake. I want to be the way I was."

"I see. It may surprise you to know how often this happens. I'll tell you what. Since it's almost time for your checkup anyway, why don't we just get that out of the way and then talk about undoing the Soul Man's work? Would that be okay?"

"Yes," I said. "But first, can you just tell me if I'm in trouble?"

"For visiting the Soul Man?" he said. "No, Angela, you're not in trouble. Now you know the first step."

There was a device with lenses suspended from the ceiling on wires and cables. I looked into one side and he looked into the other. "You know, it's amazing what they can do these days," he said as he wrote some notes. "There are now miniature versions of this thing that can actually be implanted in the eyes."

He pressed a button. The machine was retracted into the ceiling. "Please take your clothes off," he said.

I hesitated. "I'm sorry," he said with a warm little smile. "Now that you've been to the Soul Man I guess you have a little more modesty. Please don't be embarrassed; I am a doctor, after all."

I did what I was told and put my clothes on a little chair by the door.

The grandfather filled a syringe as I climbed onto the examining table. I thought nothing of it at first; we were always getting immunizations, vitamins and drugs, but after the shot, I began to feel strange. My arms and legs felt like rubber.

"What was that shot for?" I asked.

"To keep you quiet and immobile."

"Immobile? What for?" I asked.

"For this." He gave me another injection. "Sometimes it causes convulsions." At first, it felt warm, but then it felt as if ice was spreading through my whole body. Suddenly numbers started appearing in front of me, *those* numbers. Sometimes they changed colors. Sometimes they burst into little pieces.

"What's happening?" I said, feeling panicked. "What are you doing?"

"Just getting you ready to go back to the plant," he said. "You see, we created the Soul Man to weed out clones who might give us trouble." He looked at his watch and wrote something in his notebook. "A clone who wants to be treated like a human will eventually recruit others; before you know it we'd have a bloody rebellion on our hands."

"But I came here!" I was feeling sleepy. The numbers were floating in front of my eyes, disappearing one by one. "I don't want a soul! I just want to be like I was!"

"In a way, coming here shows even more individual initiative," said the grandfather.

"But . . . but what about Sam? He came to you when he wanted to change back!"

"We wanted Sam's help so we made a deal. Of course, he's just about due for *his* next checkup."

The icy feeling was starting to pass, leaving numbness in its place. Everything I felt told me something was horribly wrong. I was dying.

"I don't want to die . . ."

"Good. You're not going to die, exactly. Not yet. We need to unload your mind for our records; it'll help with the next iteration."

"But . . . my kids . . ."

"Kids? Oh, at school. No worries. They've already been assigned a brand new Miss Angela."

"Bruno . . ." I felt like I was disappearing. "What about Bruno?"

"I guess he'll wonder what happened to you at first. Maybe he'll worry. I don't know, but eventually he'll realize he's better off without a girlfriend who wallops him with a hot iron."

He looked into my eyes the way the Soul Man had. Then he looked at his watch again and said, "Close your eyes."

Time seemed to be stretched out and my mind wandered all over then and now and the future. I remembered that first Sunday morning, floating down the beautiful stream with my shimmering black hair spread all around me. Hadn't I seen a play with a lady floating down a stream? She was a beautiful lady, but the man she loved couldn't love her . . .

I could hear everything going on around me. The grandfather did something in this part of the room, then that part of the room. Then he opened the door and called, "Yo, Igor!"

I forced open my eyes just as a disreputable-looking young man came in. Why would I use a word like "disreputable?"

"Real professional, Doc," said the young man. "Keep it up and I'll form an evil underlings union. Hey, this one's kinda cute!"

"Just put her on the truck," said the grandfather. "And behave yourself!"

"Whatever you say, Frankenstein."

It was raining hard outside. I was soaking wet when "Igor" put me down between two other people and strapped me to the side of the trailer.

I don't know how long the ride will be. I have recited this story to myself three times, making sure I remember every detail.

"Jesus," I whispered, thinking of the man in white and gold, "forgive me. Let me live with you forever."

The paralyzing drugs are starting to wear off. The truck is freezing cold. Some of the others are starting to moan. Many have vomited or soiled themselves.

When we arrive, we will be taken inside to a big gray room with bright lights. We will be strapped to workbenches. Holes will be drilled into our heads so an apparatus can be attached to our brains. Each of us will be watched by a technician.

When my technician starts to watch, I will smile, if I am able. Then I'll think of a long sequence of letters and numbers which will cause my mind to unravel and vanish before his eyes. There will be no data to be used for the next iteration. This is what Sam gave me to memorize.

Above the pounding of the dark, filthy rain, I hear the little whirly noise of the gate as it closes behind me.

On the bridge of Avignon, they dance.

Lost Pine

written by

Jacob A. Boyd

illustrated by

PAT R. STEINER

ABOUT THE AUTHOR

   Jacob A. Boyd grew up in a cul-de-sac on the outskirts of a small farm town in the middle of Illinois. From the deck of his childhood home, he watched dark, thunderous wall clouds approach across miles of cornfield. As they passed overhead, he gaped at the nascent funnel clouds they concealed. Praying mantises, black and yellow garden spiders and mud daubers teemed in his yard and amongst the fruit trees while he helped his parents burn bag worms from high walnut branches with kerosene-soaked torches on the ends of long poles. He had a BB gun. He had a teacher who looked like a witch, mole on her nose, scowl and all. Another teacher had a wooden hand. Once, he crested the hill of his cul-de-sac and came face to face with a wolf. He got away. Few neighbors had fences; bushes and trees demarcated property lines. A clutch of towering weeping willows provided rope swings and climbing apparatus and a "fort." When it snowed, the town's plow provided enough of a snow bank to dig a tunnel city. Every so often, Jacob's dog, a Keeshond named Sparky, disappeared from the cul-de-sac, only to reappear after days of tearful family searching and growing resignation, a little skinnier, his fur matted and coated with burrs. It was another world. With a go-kart and good weather, Jacob explored it as though

359

driving a lunar rover. One time, Jacob's dad showed him his cracked and calloused laborer's hands and said Don't let yours look like this. *His parents insisted he read. They pushed him into advanced classes. Though they had little money, they were forward-thinking enough to buy him and his brother a personal computer, and with it an invitation into a new, more expansive, interconnected world. He is still exploring it.*

ABOUT THE ILLUSTRATOR

As a child, Pat R. Steiner once found himself hanging from a nail pounded into a tree. Left there by his older siblings, he happily communed with the tree until his mother dragged the whereabouts of the missing youngster from the guilt-ridden children. This experience, which could have ended the artist's career before he ever thought to pick up a drawing pencil, in actuality, provided him his first unique perspective (both literally and metaphorically) on the caprices of life. Since then he has had a fascination with nature (including the human variety) along with its many mysteries. His art is his attempt to explain these BIG QUESTIONS as well as those more mundane. A self-taught doodler, Pat has never been what one would call a productive illustrator. Years have passed without him completing anything new. Yet even during those periods when his sketchpad lay fallow, the artist's mind was at work, seeing the world around him with the very same eyes as that long-ago child upon his tree, eyes that now have the beginnings of crow's feet around their edges. These laugh lines were formed by four decades of experienced whimsy. The Illustrators of the Future Contest has been another tree for Pat. This time he's climbed up on his own. And he doesn't plan to come down anytime soon. He really likes the view. Pat lives in Wisconsin with his wife and two children. (No, he doesn't live in a tree, but there is a tree house in the backyard.)

Lost Pine

Silence filled the narrow, musty cellar and pressed back its brick walls until the three-story house above Gage stretched into a remote, empty shell, the crud-kids up the valley in Portland shrank into a tiny, voiceless rabble and the rest of the crud-blighted world vanished behind a far, far horizon. The delicate work of deciphering the gun safe's combination swallowed Gage whole. The safe's cold steel door and whispering gears were all there was.

Adah's footsteps thundered toward Gage across the floorboards overhead, and his perspective painfully contracted back to reality: they were squatters in an aging B&B, they had fled Portland and while nature slowly reclaimed much of what lay explored in between, the rest of the world grew wilder unchecked.

Gage scowled at the shaft of summer sunlight angling down the stairs from the kitchen.

With five years on Adah, Gage looked at her fourteen-year-old behavior and felt more like her father than her . . . what: babysitter, bodyguard, boyfriend? Six years past the crud outbreak, he didn't know anymore. He looked at her differently from day to day.

In a storm of tromping boots and long, loose curls, Adah careened into the shaft of light, out of breath, her face flushed of color.

"Someone's coming," she said.

Gage dropped his gnawed pencil onto the B&B's old guestbook, in which he had cataloged nixed combinations.

"How many?" he asked. "How far away?"

He grabbed his machete off the top of the safe, then rushed past her through the empty B&B toward the front window in the third-floor hall. Adah followed, a tremor of anxiety in her voice.

"I think it was only one," she said. "I was out looking for pickings when I heard him near the entrance to the drive, so maybe half a mile away."

The forest closed over the winding drive that doglegged off the backcountry gravel road. With a determined gaze, Gage followed the suggestion of its path to where the natural obstacles he had woven into the terrain obscured its entrance with fallen trees and thorny brush.

"Was he pushing through the blackberries?" Gage asked.

"He wasn't stopping."

"You're sure it was a he?"

"He was cussing real loud."

"Did he see you? Hear you?"

"I don't think so."

A hen rounded the house into the ragged yard out front. Gage's stomach sank. The coop was open.

Another hen joined the first, then the last. Together, they were all that had survived inside the coop with a sack of feed until Gage and Adah arrived and discovered them, all as noisy as dogs.

"Close the curtains and lock the doors," Gage said.

He ran out through the front door. The hens sped from him, clucking. He chased them and hushed them with sharp apologies, pinning one, then the next under his arm.

The intruder crashed through the blackberries, then the obstacle course of hidden holes, unsteadily balanced logs and beehives. By the time Gage pinned the third hen under his arm, the intruder was visible—one man, staggering as if exhausted and wounded.

"Hello," the intruder called out, his voice wavering. "Hello."

Gage glanced back at the house. Its curtains hung shut. He tightened his grip on his machete. The intruder hadn't gone around or looked for an easier way past. He had gone through where the clearest route to the B&B should've been.

The intruder clambered through the last of the obstacles, closing the distance into a stone's throw from Gage. Taller than Gage, yet skinnier, he moved like someone who took the time to stretch. He wore a slack pack, a bedroll tied to it with wharf rope. From what Gage could tell, the intruder had been one of the lucky ones. He was maybe a year or two older than Gage, which meant he had been just under the high-water line the crud drew at fifteen years old when it hit. Crud stained his teeth orange, yet like Gage, like Adah, like all the children who had survived the outbreak, he was resistant to it. It made him amongst the oldest people alive on the planet not encased in one of the crud's gem-like cocoons.

"Down on your knees!" Gage shouted.

The intruder threw up his hands. "I'm not armed."

"Down!"

The intruder dropped to his knees. Blood and grime painted his pinched, starved features. A bee sting swelled on his forehead like an angry third eye.

"Remove your pack," Gage said. "Slowly."

The intruder's eyes hungrily flitted from Gage's machete to the chickens, then he unclipped his pack's straps and let it fall from his shoulders. At the sight of the intruder's black T-shirt, Gage's heart raced. In gold print, a spindly pine rose from the crest of a bare hill, the all but forgotten logo of Lost Pine B&B, their home's former business.

The front door noisily unbolted and swept open.

"Stay inside," Gage said, his eyes fixed on the golden pine gleaming from the intruder's T-shirt.

"I'm unarmed," the intruder whimpered, then collapsed.

Adah tromped down the porch steps and stopped at Gage's back.

"He's been here before," Adah said. She held a broken bottle by its neck—the unfortunate loss of a container repurposed as a weapon.

Lost Pine lay far from paved roads, a piece of the pre-crud world tucked away off maps of the wooded valley. Only a rare guidebook's directions led to it, made rarer for the one Gage had burned after memorizing its directions. He would be damned if it didn't stay that way. He furiously wondered how many crud-kids had seen meaning in the intruder's T-shirt, instead of just another useless logo.

"Do something," Adah said. She stepped forward, and Gage blocked her with the flat of his machete. He dropped the hens onto the lawn, where they clucked complaints.

"We have supplies for one more," Adah said.

"We have supplies, Adah. How many they're for, we decide."

"He's stung."

"If he's allergic, there's nothing we can do. The crud'll take the opportunity and cocoon him before he dies."

"We should try *something*," Adah said.

"No," Gage said.

"Did we spend all our time preparing for the worst to come just so we could turn away someone who's in need, someone helpless?"

Gage glared at her.

Adah shoved Gage's machete aside, strode toward the intruder and crouched beside him. Gage scowled and joined her. A black eye rimmed the intruder's pale cheek with purple and brown. Something like sunburn spread up his forearms from his hands.

"Looks like he's been roughed up," Gage said. "Looks like he handled something mean, too." He indicated the intruder's hands. "Skin's not bubbling or dripping like it would with poison oak or poison ivy. Be careful. Could still be something that can spread by contact. If he comes around so we can talk to him, we'll see if we want to help him."

Adah's fierce eyes surprised Gage.

"We're not like the crud-kids in Portland," she said. "You said we were better than them. 'We deserve what we have because we're better.'"

Gage opened his mouth to dispute her, then shut it. She had made up her mind, using his words. It would be like arguing with himself. He tried another way of thinking about it.

"He could've led others here, Adah, the same people who gave him that black eye and sent him climbing through our blackberries. We're far enough away from everything that when he left wherever he was, people had to suspect he had a destination. We should dump him down the road and hope whoever might be following him doesn't notice the trail he tore down our drive."

Adah sat the intruder up and worked her shoulder under his armpit. "Help," she said. The word was soft. She looked up at Gage, and he saw in her wide, dark eyes the word was laced with venom, too, if he failed it.

Gage helped carry the intruder inside.

Gage brought the intruder into his home, but he would not entertain the idea of the intruder in their lives.

For Gage, the crud should've overwhelmed the intruder and cocooned him. He and Adah should've been dealing with a man-sized cocoon as hard as murky yellow ice. Their noses should've stung from its mothball stink. That they smelled only the intruder's weathered body odor upset Gage. The intruder was a survivor. But Gage couldn't believe his scrawny body was all that had kept him alive. He didn't weigh much more than Adah.

They laid the intruder on a couch in the piano room. Adah retrieved water from a rain catcher—filled by frequent Northwest rains—and made a mug of pine needle tea using a match and four minutes of propane for the stove. Between Gage's questions, she tilted the steaming tea to the intruder's lips.

"Who are you?" Gage asked.

The intruder said his name was Monk.

As far as Gage was concerned, crud-kids who changed their names after the outbreak were unreliable, always trying to reinvent themselves and obscure who they were. Aliases were the opposite of alibis.

Monk said he had been to Lost Pine before. It was when he had gotten the T-shirt. The couple manning the B&B had given it to him when his time was up, as a memento. They couldn't keep boarders for long without making the place unsustainable.

Monk's voice remained low and steady, as though he had prearranged his words. Gage's tone hardened.

"What were you doing here?" Gage asked.

Monk's pinched features stiffened as though he was rolling words through a rock tumbler in his mind so when they came out their edges would be worn smooth.

Monk had worked for his stay, tending the chickens and washing laundry and gathering kindling. He was willing to work again. He knew the law of the land—finders, keepers. He wouldn't dispute it. Ownership of Lost Pine had changed hands when Adah and Gage found it unmanned. They were the rightful heirs. Who was he to say otherwise?

Monk asked where Martin and Sue, the previous owners, had gone.

"Crud got 'em," Gage said.

Monk said it was a shame.

Gage wanted to hate Monk for his nonchalance. But six years of living with crud had changed the rules. You accepted loss at its face value—something was gone that once was there—or it tore at you and wore you down till the crud crept in and cocooned you too.

Monk asked if he could see Martin's and Sue's cocoons.

"We took out the shelves in the fridge and fit the woman's—Sue's—cocoon inside," Gage said. Monk was appalled, and Gage explained. "It's practical. The cocoon vapors hold off decay and mold growth. Her cocoon makes it a kind of fridge. It's just not cold. Martin's cocoon is sterilizing water in our rain catcher."

Monk said it was smart, but questioned if it was wise. Bodies should be buried.

Gage glared at him. "We don't have enough to waste for the sake of making ourselves feel good."

"Where did you go when you left Lost Pine?" Adah asked.

It was a little over a month ago, Monk said. He had made his way to Portland, but the crud-kids had formed gangs he wouldn't join. They had rolled him, then run him out of town. It was why his pack contained nothing but an old, dirty bedroll, a water bottle, and edible flowers and roots he had dug up since—nothing, really. The gangs weren't to be trusted. They were animals. Everybody grubbed for the same meal, same drink, same housing, getting meaner and meaner. He was lucky to make it out with a beating. He had seen others shot.

"We've been there," Gage said. "Portland's far. Rough going between there and here."

Monk said he didn't have a choice. He didn't know of anywhere else to go. Word was cities were all breaking down. The backcountry wasn't safe, but with fewer people to encounter, it was safer than lingering around a city and hoping for discarded scraps. Scraps were almost all anyone started with, anyway.

"Seems like anyone with a mind to could've followed you," Gage said.

Monk said when he managed to shamble out of the city, the crud-kids left him for dead. People did that, just gave up on life and walked away from the city till they dropped. He had seen the bodies along the roads, encased in the yellowish cocoons that overtook them right before they would've died. Nobody had foreseen a different fate for him. He had only made it because he knew he had somewhere to go. It had given him strength.

"I'll ask you point blank," Gage said. "Did you lead anyone here?"

Monk said he never even thought to tell anyone about Lost Pine. He liked the place enough he wanted to keep it secret. When he could, on his way to Lost Pine, he avoided the slightest sign of other people. But it was a long haul. He was wearing down by the time he arrived, so when he thought he had made it, he made noise. He thought he had reunited with Martin and Sue. He couldn't believe it. It was a miracle. Gage and Adah should understand.

Gage set his lips in a hard, bitter line. Adah looked at him, pity crimping her open features, asking what they'd do with Monk now that they knew his story.

"You can stay one week," Gage said. "Make yourself useful, and we won't have problems. Work for your food, and you can take some with you when you leave. It's all anyone can ask anymore. We're not animals. But if either of us so much as suspects you led someone here, I won't hesitate to cut you down. I don't have to be mad to kill you, understand?"

Monk nodded.

"We're not a gang," Adah added. "We're honest people."

Monk smiled at her.

"Could you eat some eggs?" Adah asked.

Monk said he could.

The television transfixed Gage with its live feed. He couldn't look away. The first interstellar craft mankind had ever encountered was streaking through the high atmosphere over the Atlantic, somewhere between the Bahamas and Portugal. It had originated from near a Red Dwarf star, Gliese 876, and closed the fifteen light-years separating it from Earth, unnoticed until recently. Deep-space imaging spotted others in its wake, each less distinct than those preceding it. They spread out over years and would arrive in waves, until the largest one at the end, a moon-sized behemoth that was still a barely visible speck. The first one approached alone, fast and far ahead of the others.

Gage's parents had given in to his pleas and let him stay up and watch even though he had school in the morning. With a wink, they said it was so late he might not have to go to school, but they'd see. Sitting within an arm's length of the television's glow, his stomach tingled with excitement, roiled with fatigue. His parents felt like a warm, comforting presence at his back.

Though it was a clear night, the footage wasn't much to see. A dot like a miniature shooting star shimmered into view amongst the spill of constellations. Gage could only tell it was the craft they had been waiting for because a little special effect centered it in a highlighting circle. The camerawork was a bit shaky as it zoomed in and tracked the craft. A reporter said something about the footage being taken from the deck of a naval destroyer, one of many positioned throughout the Atlantic. His mic crackled with the heavy wind billowing his jacket. Picture after picture showed rows of fighter jets at the ready.

Gage felt like he was joining history.

The dot continued across the high atmosphere at a flat angle. Tiny pieces of it broke free and fluttered away like a faint tail of sparklers. Someone said something about ablative shielding, nothing to worry about; mankind and the aliens had found similar ways of dealing with heat shielding. It was an encouraging sign; human technology was on the right course. But the point of light kept going, kept shedding and getting smaller. The camera panned from one horizon to the other, following the shining dot as it passed overhead. A reporter said something about a splash in the ocean detected by the destroyer's sonar, and orange, powdery snow. Then the camera went inside. The destroyer's feed ended, replaced with two speechless talking heads back in the studio, their faces professional masks that stretched between worry and dignified composure.

The warm presence of Gage's parents went chill at his back, then cold. Gage wanted to turn around and tell them it'd be all right, wanted to turn around and have *them* tell *him* it'd be all right, too. He knew he shouldn't be watching television. He was sorry. He should be asleep, resting for school in the morning. He felt like he should apologize. There was no television anymore, anyway. He shouldn't have asked to watch. There hadn't been television in almost six years. He wanted to turn around and warn his parents about it all. The dark urine wasn't the result of dehydration or the vitamin C they took to prevent seasonal coughs. What they had was already in them, everywhere. Doctors didn't matter anymore. Rumors about clean zones were untrue. Trade winds distributed the crud worldwide. They weren't resistant like he was. It wasn't their fault. He wanted to hug them and tell them he loved them. He wanted to tell them it wasn't fair he'd spend the rest of his time with them in noisy mobs in grocery markets, pharmacies and hardware stores, exchanging worried glances with other people's healthy kids; and at quarantine checkpoints standing by while they squabbled with officials over valid clean papers; and slowly marching in lines for experimental vaccine shot after experimental vaccine shot which would leave bruises but make no difference. The rushed transfer of everything they owned to him would be misguided. All he would gain from them in the end would be what he could carry, along with a doting neighbor's daughter named Adah his parents had arranged to take before her parents succumbed to the crud.

He knew it was a dream. He had had it before. He knew he should just turn and face his parents. They'd be cocooned in what looked like murky yellow ice. He'd see others in the gem-like coffins before he'd see his parents in them. He'd hear reporters say they weren't dead, just preserved. He'd hear people say it didn't hurt. He would turn and see his parents' faces, heavy eyelids closed over their demonstrative eyes, mouths opened as if to say they loved him, too, yet filled with crud-amber. He wanted to take his eyes off the talking heads as they fish-mouthed without words on the television screen. He wanted to turn around and see his parents. It couldn't be worse than what had happened since. It couldn't be.

But it was.

Monk insisted he should help repair the obstacle course blocking Lost Pine's drive. Gage put his foot down. Monk acted put out, but after a day of rest, his swollen stings showed little sign of shrinking, and Gage could tell he was relieved. Monk stood shakily on the porch. Adah held him steady by an arm.

"I'll keep an eye on him," Adah said.

Gage made sure she had her broken bottle, in case Monk suddenly found his strength.

"I'll be all right," she said.

Gage dressed in layers of thick, long-sleeved clothing and leatherwork gloves. He secured a helmet he had made out of material salvaged from the screen door under his collars. The outfit made him clumsy and slow and hot. It was the only way he knew to keep the bees from swarming him that didn't involve smoke, which might signal their presence from a distance.

Looking at the path Monk had torn down the drive, Gage angrily set his jaw. To someone who could read the land, it was an arrow pointing to the front door.

Gage had designed the obstacles as would a madman by adding thorny catches and springy trips at random, offering no pattern for the eye to catch on. It had taken him the entire month since he and Adah had arrived at Lost Pine to arrange them the way he wanted. Yet they hadn't stopped Monk, and Gage couldn't imagine they'd hold up against crud-kids when they got desperate enough to wander down the valley en masse. His mind set on redoing them before Monk's departure, he expanded them.

He worked his way from the road toward the house. Even in the shadowed understory, summer heat sapped his strength. Bees buzzed and climbed over his helmet and occasionally burrowed between the folds of his clothing to lodge stingers where he couldn't get at them. The stings swelled and left sore bruises that made him question if he should be doing all of what he was doing. He imagined it was Monk who stung him.

After setting a log atop a wedge trigger, he stepped

back to inspect its camouflage when his foot slipped into the trigger hole. Pain knotted in his ankle, splintered into his shin. The log teetered above him. He didn't know how much it weighed—far more than he could lift; he could only roll it. He scrambled away over crosshatched brambles, then faced the log with disappointment. It remained stable. It wasn't good enough. It should've careened onto his shin and broken it cleanly where the hole held it in place.

He put weight on his ankle and hissed. Tried again, hissed.

Limping back to the house, he wondered if he should make the traps so mechanical. If they didn't kill intruders, as they hadn't killed Monk, they'd signal the presence of a designer and draw attention to Lost Pine.

Pain screwed into his ankle with each step. He pressed through it and decided mechanical traps may not be prudent, but deterrents weren't enough. Traps had to be perfect and deadly.

He found Adah and Monk behind the house, cleaning out the chicken coop. Adah had crawled inside. Monk sat on a stump nearby.

"Adah keeping you busy?" Gage asked.

Monk said she was. She was quite the homesteader. First, it was laundry, then making soap with ash and fat saved from the chickens that had died, then filling in the night hole and digging a new one, then setting raccoon traps, then the coop.

Listening to the list, Gage smiled. He had taught himself each activity, having read how from books, then had taught Adah.

375

Adah emerged from the coop with a pail of feathers and stinking feces for the compost, a look of accomplishment on her face.

Monk asked what had happened to Gage's leg.

"It's nothing," Gage said, his voice firm.

Adah's brow scrunched with concern. "Let me see." She gestured for him to sit beside Monk. Monk scooted over.

"I'll be fine," Gage said. He limped to the house.

Monk said it looked bad.

"Let him be," Adah said. "He'll come around."

Gage let the empty screen door snap shut behind him.

The full weight of his fatigue settled on him once he undressed. The cool, dim house chilled his sweat. He changed clothes, drank from a rain catcher and rolled its taste of iron on his tongue—a constant reminder of the crud; it was even in his thirst. Descending the stairs to the cellar, his ankle tightened. He angrily eyed it, balanced on it and hopped down. It painfully gave out. The railing bore his weight with a groan. One-legged, he cautiously hopped to the gun safe.

Seated in a musty armchair, he pressed an ear to the safe's steel door. It drank warmth from him. Leaning against its sure solidity, he closed his eyes and fingered the notches of its dial. The oiled gears whispered to him. Gage interpreted meaning from the whispers, which he believed foolproof until the door resisted his tug and he sought a better translation. The B&B fell away. Portland faded into the distance. The world beyond became as remote as a star.

Fatigue melted off his bones until noise from inside the B&B shocked him with thoughts of electricity and adults and others elsewhere working to reconstruct what had been lost to the crud.

But it was just the piano. It was just music.

A repetitive, classical duh-duh-dah grew louder and faster as he approached the piano room. He stopped outside its doorway, out of view. The music stopped.

Monk said Gage should come in. He laughed when Gage didn't reply. He said he couldn't have missed Gage clomping closer. He should join them. Music might distract Gage from his ankle.

Gage entered. "It's out of tune. And a few keys are broken."

Monk said he didn't mind. The gist of the piece came through. It was a beautiful piano.

"He took lessons," Adah said, "for years before the crud. He's amazing."

Monk smiled, and said his pacing was off. He hadn't played in quite a while, and it was difficult reading the unfamiliar music. He stumbled with the footing, though it was coming back to him. He was going to be a concert pianist, before the crud.

"There aren't many people left who could do what you can do," Adah said.

Monk thanked her.

"Don't take it too seriously," Gage said. "She hasn't seen anyone even play 'Chopsticks' before."

Adah's wide eyes narrowed. "Any luck with the safe?"

"No," Gage said, "just progress."

He returned to the cellar.

The music stung, but the laughter stung worse. Gage tried to close his senses to it, to hear only the whispered turning of the heavy gears through the steel door. He told himself he wasn't hungry, he didn't need to go upstairs. He told himself it'd only be a few more days with Monk. He told himself nothing mattered more than opening the gun safe and protecting Adah. She depended on him. It was all that mattered, what had kept him going and given him strength to fight and make hard decisions.

He fell asleep.

When he woke, he was cold and hungry and sore from how he had slumped against the safe. Adah hadn't woken him to watch the stars from the roof, but he was sure she was up there. With Monk. He imagined Monk counting the intermittent shooting stars and undoing the work of years as he talked about what they represented. The shooting stars would no longer be nothing to worry about. He'd remind Adah the crud craft had been the first in a long line, each larger than those preceding it, with the behemoth at the end.

He limped to the fridge for a hardboiled egg before heading up to bed. Inside the fridge, Sue's body formed a dark shadow inside her murky yellow cocoon. Rigor from the final stages of the creeping crud had frozen her in a horrible retching pose. He preferred it when she had had no name.

Gage lay under the bed covers and stared into the darkness. When Adah tiptoed into the room and slipped under the covers, she spoke, her back turned to him. "I know you like to act like you're big and scary so you won't have to follow through on your threats, but, really, you're taking it a little far. You shouldn't be so mean to Monk."

"That's not his real name," Gage said.

She huffed, then her breath settled into a deep rhythm. Gage's followed.

As far as Gage could tell, the only part of Monk to regain strength was his mouth.

Each day, Gage woke with the sun, trudged into the obstacle course and returned when the loss of light made it dangerous. With thrown stones, he tested his traps. Each day, he ended a little farther from the road, a little closer to Lost Pine. He gained bruises and stings and stumbled home from the growing chaos in near delusional sweats to find Monk sitting and talking while Adah worked. She listened to him and built raised beds for their future gardens, collected kindling, and wove baskets from the limber creeper vines strangling the surrounding pines.

Monk said he had survived because he knew how to respect people and how to gain respect in return.

Monk said he had a theory why the creeping crud had broken out. It wasn't an accident. It was a purposeful blight sent to replace adults' "sophistication" with the truthful innocence of children. We were just fouling it up.

Monk asked if Gage had considered burying Martin and Sue. It didn't seem right to put the dead to work, like they had.

"They're not dead," Gage said.

Monk said that may technically be true, but either way, it would honor them to continue their traditions. They should be buried.

"Have you buried others?" Gage asked.

Monk's pinched features stiffened. He said he had.

Gage eyed Monk's scrawny arms. "How deep?"

379

Gage's arm stung from Adah's pinch as though from a bee sting.

"We've all lost people," Adah said. "And we don't talk about it. It's personal." She glared at Gage.

Alone in the kitchen, listening to Monk play the piano for Adah, Gage cut rancid bits from dried strips of raccoon meat and ate the clean remnants. Music continued after he finished eating. He went to the safe.

Dismissed combinations filled the pages of his ledger. He was getting close. He felt it.

Adah cooked meals of edible wild roots and flowers Gage had taught her to identify. On the seventh day, they shared raccoon stew, dandelion salad with sunflower seeds and a bowlful of tart blackberries.

Monk said it was a fine farewell feast. He looked forward to what they were sending him off with. He didn't know where he'd head. Summer weather didn't last forever. Maybe south, along the coast. There was always fishing. Or he'd head back to Portland. Things could've cooled off there. Gangs so rapidly shuffled membership and leadership it was likely no one would even recognize him. He'd just be a new face. If he had to, he'd join a gang, he guessed.

"You should stay," Adah said.

"Adah," Gage said.

"Monk hasn't been able to work for the food he'd be taking," Adah said. "He's been too weak. He can work now. He should stay until he does his share."

Gage glared at her as though it was unfair to argue about it in front of Monk. She was ambushing him. He wanted to tell her he wasn't being stubborn or jealous. Monk just had to leave. That was the agreement. But she looked at Monk with an open expression that took the force out of him. He had taught her well, and now she wanted to care for someone who would appreciate her talents. She was young, though. She saw what she wanted to see in Monk, blind to how he took advantage of her.

Monk said he wouldn't get in the way. He'd help Gage with the obstacle course. He'd mend the roof. Whatever. Heights didn't frighten him. He'd gather roots and flowers, too. Identifying what was poisonous from what was healthy came as second nature. His mental catalog expanded every day. He had already been helping Adah with the pickings for the past week.

Knowledge that he had been eating Monk's food without knowing it settled in Gage's stomach like a brick of ice.

"One more week," Gage said. He looked at Adah, and her closed expression told him it wasn't enough.

Monk stayed.

One week became two.

Then three.

When Monk said dinner was served, Gage went to the cellar. During the night, he dreamed of unlocking the gun safe, removing a handgun loaded with a single bullet and shooting Monk. Upon waking, it was difficult for him to determine whether he felt disappointment that his dream hadn't been real, or relief. The obstacle course lay untouched while the gun safe ledger filled with cramped rows of numbers. Pencils wore down to nubs. Hunger pangs lessened the less he ate, and he took comfort that his body

adjusted to a deeper hunger than he was accustomed
to. All the while, there was music. To Gage's dismay,
he could tell Monk was getting better.

In bed beside Gage in the dark, Adah said, "You're
only hurting yourself."

"I'm fine," Gage said.

"I hate seeing you like this. I know you don't like
him, but even Collin wants you to eat. He hates
seeing you like this, too."

"Collin?" Gage rose up on a shaky elbow and stared
at Adah in the dark. Her body formed a shadowed
shape under the covers. Gage rose from the bed,
grabbed a candle and headed for the cellar.

Before he exited, Adah called out to him, "Gage."
Her voice was soft and pleading and pitying.

He paged through the gun safe ledger. Thousands
of combinations were scrawled between the lines and
between those lines and vertical along the margins.
They were not enough. Not by far. He needed
hundreds more ledgers. It would take years, if it ever
worked. He snapped his pencil nubs. He should've
paid attention to the threat before him, the threat in
his home, instead of the one lingering like a phantom
beyond its drive, somewhere, sure to arrive, someday.
There was no telling what the safe contained anyway.
Martin and Sue could've traded their whole armory
for the food and seeds and supplies that had sustained
them until he and Adah arrived to find their cocoons.
It was only a gun safe in name. It could contain
anything, nothing.

The front of the ledger contained entries from
Lost Pine's guests. Gage read them with deepening
sadness; they were so thankful and hopeful. Life used

to be easier. Tourists took trips to places they never intended on staying, for fun. Even as the tone of the entries changed with those written by people who had passed through Lost Pine after the crud, there was hope. They ended at his cold, unfeeling numbers.

But the last entry. Gage's heart quickened, and he grabbed his machete off the top of the gun safe. Before he knew it, he was upstairs outside Monk's room, pounding on the door with the butt of his machete. Adah was saying something he couldn't quite pay attention to, but only made him madder because it sounded like she was trying to protect Monk. It took four kicks to break the old doorjamb. Monk stood beside his bed, a knife he had snuck away gripped in a reddened hand.

"What did you do to them?" Gage asked.

Monk's pinched features contorted with puzzlement. He said he didn't know what Gage was talking about.

"You didn't expect to find anyone here, did you?" Gage asked. "It was why you came unarmed. You expected the place to be empty."

Monk looked at Adah, who stood in the doorway holding a broken bottle by its neck. She waved it back and forth between Monk and Gage.

"You did something to Martin and Sue before you left," Gage said. "Did you poison them? Is that why your hands were covered in a rash when you arrived, why they're breaking out now?"

Monk faced Adah, his pinched features stiffening. He said Adah had been eating what he gathered for weeks and she was fine. Even Gage had eaten what he gathered for a week.

"I found your guestbook entry, *Collin,*" Gage said. He tossed the guestbook at Monk's feet. "You 'wished things didn't have to end this way'?"

Monk's eyes widened. He said he didn't write that.

"You're right," Gage said. "It wasn't you. It was Marta. She had been with you then. She wrote it. She signed it and included your name. She dated it, too, the same time you were here."

Monk said the entry didn't mean what it sounded like.

"You mean a threat or an apology?" Gage asked.

Monk said Gage didn't understand.

"Marta was the one with the conscience, wasn't she? What happened to her? Did you go to Portland looking to sell her, but the gangs took her and beat you up? Did she leave you? Did you kill her because her conscience was getting to her, and she was going to tell about Lost Pine and ruin everything?"

Monk said Gage's imagination was running away with him. He needed to calm down.

"You wanted to bury Martin's and Sue's cocoons," Gage said, putting it together as he spoke. "You wanted to hide your evidence."

Monk's rock-tumbler look churned on high. He said it wasn't like that. Gage hadn't been there.

"You'd better start telling me what it was like," Gage said, "or I'm gonna cut your smug mouth right out of your head."

Monk said it had been an accident with Martin and Sue. It was how he had discovered what he gathered was poisonous. They got really sick. He left before the crud overtook them. They made him leave. It could've happened to anyone hungry enough to try things they weren't sure about. He thought they might've survived. He never tried to hurt Marta. After they got kicked out, she despaired. She snuck into his pack one night and ate the same stuff that poisoned Martin and Sue. He knew he shouldn't have kept it. But it could've been useful with the gangs in Portland. Monk looked at the rash on his hands. He said he never would've hurt Adah.

Gage lunged at Monk. Adah screamed, "Stop!"

Gage froze, machete above his head. Monk crossed his forearms over his face.

"Get out, Collin," Adah said. "We're honest people."

She packed Monk's slack pack with a hardboiled egg and dried strips of raccoon meat and a pair of socks and a blanket.

In the dark, at machete point, Gage led Monk along a safe trail through the obstacle course to the road.

Monk asked what he was supposed to do now.

Gage glared at him in the moonlight. The road was a silent strip of weed-tufted gravel rounding far bends in both directions. His knuckles whitened around his machete. He figured if he killed Monk, he'd have to bury him; otherwise the body would attract coyotes or bigger animals, which might attract people. The food they had given him would have to be buried, too. As much as it pained him to see it go, Adah would see it as evidence. She'd never forgive him.

"Leave," Gage said. "If I see you again, I'll kill you."

Back at the house, trembling weakness pervaded Gage's body. He chuckled. Monk would've killed him had he begun a fight. He hadn't had a full meal or full night's rest in weeks.

Adah eyed his wry grin as though frightened by

it, and he couldn't tell whether she looked at him as though he was a babysitter, bodyguard or boyfriend.

Adah's parents got the crud. There was no avoiding it, even during quarantine. She knocked on the front door to Gage's parents' house, shuddering with tears, hiding her reddened eyes behind unwashed curls. Her words squeaked out. Her parents couldn't stand up anymore. She needed help. Gage's parents told him to go. All the radio reports said it wasn't affecting children. He was safe. He just needed to thoroughly bathe before he returned. Boiled water would wait for him inside the porch, with a washcloth, soap and razor. He'd have to shave his head. A change of clothes would be there for him, too. His old clothes would go in the barrel, the washcloth, as well, with a little kerosene and a match.

Adah led Gage into her house, a neighboring mystery until then. Cellophane covered the windows inside, coloring the daylight as though it passed through old cooking oil. It smelled like someone had rubbed the stink of cabbage into the walls with a damp rag.

Adah led him to the master bedroom, where her parents lay on top of the bed's covers like two factory mannequins, their bodies coated in what looked like yellowing plastic, their features blunted to blank, closed-eyed stares. The smell of ammonia overpowered Gage, stinging his eyes and driving him back into the hall.

Gage glared at Adah as though she should've warned him. Her wide, dark eyes were glassy and red, though she seemed used to the cocoons' vapors.

On television and in photos, the crud seemed like something that would eventually be cleared up and go away. But there it was, in the next room. When Gage returned to the master bedroom, he could tell Adah's parents were naked beneath the crud.

Adah said they had only started crudding over that morning, and it was barely noon. Gage asked if she had done anything to them, because the radio said it was best to let the crud run its course. Attempts to scoop the crud from their mouths or scrub it off their skin only harmed them, causing their bodies undue strain as they worked overtime to make more. They'd deplete bodily stores used during the crud-induced stasis.

Adah said she knew. She hadn't touched them. She wouldn't.

Gage asked what she wanted him to do. She said her parents had told her to go to his parents before they couldn't talk anymore. They were supposed to take care of her. She had done all she knew to do, what she had been told. For the time being, she guessed she just wanted someone to be with her, then she didn't care. She'd go her own way, if she had to.

Gage stayed with her.

Total, it took less than twenty-four hours. The crud thickened, lost its plasticity and hardened. Adah stopped crying and watched in a daze.

In the future, Gage insisted, when the crud had been fully examined, scientists would reverse the process and bring them back. It wasn't a forever thing. Adah nodded, and Gage led her to his parents' porch, where two sets of clothes lay folded.

He told Adah what needed to be done. She nodded

dumbly and complied without embarrassment or shame. He shaved her head. She shaved his. They undressed, bathed and dumped their clothes in the barrel. Gage squeezed kerosene into the barrel, then a little more to be sure, and extra, to be extra sure. He ignited it. Flames leaped to the ceiling; smoke poured out, then retreated into the barrel. Gage and Adah dressed and fled from the smoke inside.

Gage's parents lay on the couch hugging each other, their naked bodies coated with crud, which joined them together.

Suddenly, the full flush of Gage's thirteen years coursed through his body with enough ferocity to convince him if he said "No" hard enough, the world would back down and cooperate. His parents had done everything right, and still, the crud had them. Something had to be done, and it couldn't be what had already been tried.

He leaped on his parents and tore at the crud. It came away in chunks like drying taffy.

Adah said he should leave them be. They'd be back. Meanwhile, they were in a better place.

As far as Gage saw it, Adah's parents had succumbed to the crud because Adah didn't understand what was going on. She didn't know when to say "No" and was too young to say it in the right way. Her parents had probably filled her head with religious gobbledygook, which confused her and made her think it was a good thing the crud was taking them—the great mystery of God.

Gage uncovered his parents' mouths and scooped out the gelled crud inside, then ripped it away from their closed eyes. Hair came away with it. So did small patches of skin, which bled, then crudded over. He ripped his parents from each other's arms and laid them side by side and pumped on their chests like a television EMT. Gouts of crud erupted from their mouths and nostrils with each thrust. Frenzied, he pulled away strips of crud. Like long, thick hangnails, skin peeled away, down their arms and legs and across their chests.

When he was done, they looked like they had been attacked by an animal.

Crud slowly, slowly covered the wounds.

Adah said he shouldn't have done that.

Breathless, Gage agreed.

He felt like he had done something irreversible. He said he would listen to Adah from now on. He would be dependable. She could trust him. He would never do anything like that again. He didn't mean to scare her. His parents would be fine, he said and knew he was already lying to her, though he couldn't tell if it was for her own good, or his.

Gage divided his time between expanding the obstacle course so it surrounded Lost Pine and testing combinations on the gun safe.

Adah intermittently visited him in the cellar to tell him of her work and make sure he was eating.

"I've made a greenhouse with the clear poly tarps from the shed," she said. "It should help when it gets cold."

"I let a chick hatch," she said.

"I caught two raccoons. They're gutted and drying in the sun."

Gage put on a good face for Adah and thanked her,

but there was more to protect than ever. Monk had to return. He had all but threatened he would join a gang. Now that he knew he couldn't have Lost Pine to himself, nothing stopped him from overtaking it with force, even if that meant he would have to share it. Some of Lost Pine was better than none. Monk would see that. A gang would, too.

Gage wondered if Martin and Sue hadn't improved upon Lost Pine as he and Adah were because they feared it would attract gangs. Martin and Sue had the equipment. It had waited in Lost Pine's storage, like bait in a trap. Had the task of constant upkeep been too daunting? Had they feared the work would weaken their bodies and the crud would overwhelm them?

The obstacle course closed around the house like a malicious fence. It comforted Gage and made him feel penned in. Too much work had been dumped into it to abandon it at the first sign of trouble. He got good at sending stones where he wanted, and thrilled at starting devastating traps in motion. Besieged scenarios played over and over in his mind. He showed Adah where she should run, if she had to. Day by day, the route changed. She stared at the sharpened wooden spikes and shifting topology of holes and berms, unspeaking, her hands clenched. Gage told her not to worry. He had everything covered.

The guestbook ledger ran out of pages. Gage scavenged the house for paper. He wrote combinations on scraps and organized them within the ledger. Broken pencil nubs wore down to nothing. He found a pin and sterilized it over a flame, then wrote with dabs of blood on its point. He pricked his finger over and over, gouging deep for blood.

Piano notes arrested Gage from his concentration in the cellar. He rushed to the piano room, machete firmly in hand. Adah stood frozen by the bare keys.

"I didn't mean to," she said, her eyes fixed on his machete.

"No, no," Gage said. "Go ahead."

He returned to the cellar.

The piano remained silent.

The musty brick walls of the cellar lurched inward, Portland's crud-kids crowded just behind them and the rest of the crud-blighted world pressed against their backs, waiting for Gage to relax.

Adah's soft voice startled him.

"It's late," she said. "Come up and watch the stars with me."

Lying beside Adah on the roof, bare feet dangling over the eaves, Gage pointed out constellations where they emerged from behind passing clouds. He tracked the faint points of light from dead satellites.

"Tell me one of those stories," Adah said, "about how it used to be."

Gage liked telling used-to-be stories. They were something he could give Adah the world otherwise withheld. For her, it seemed like the world had always been like it was. He could change that, but he didn't know what to say.

Finally, he said, "Everyone used to tell me I could be anything I wanted."

Adah's laughter rang loudly in the silence of the forest. "What's that even supposed to mean?"

Her laughter spread. They laughed together. Gage laughed to tears and hugged her when he could no longer tell why he cried.

"There's one," Adah said. She unlaced herself from Gage and pointed into the sky. "A shooting star. Make a wish."

"Where?"

"It was right there."

He followed her moving finger, but couldn't find what she pointed at.

"There's another one," he said. He took her hand, and used her finger to point it out. "It's a meteor shower."

Shooting stars streaked the night sky, many more than on previous occasions.

"We're going to have too many wishes," Adah said.

"Let's hope not."

Gage and Adah laughed to tears, wiped their cheeks dry, then watched the show.

Monk returned.

At first, he was a pair of headlights approaching on the road while Adah and Gage watched the second night of the meteor shower from the roof. With their eyes trained to spot faint lights in the dark sky, the headlights blazed like fireballs. Then the headlights stopped outside the driveway and honked. Gage looked at Adah and grabbed his machete. Adah grabbed his hand.

"If he got a car," Adah said, "he could have almost anything else. Guns. A dozen others."

"I know how to make it through the obstacle

course," Gage said. "I can lead them through the worst parts."

"Gage," she said.

"They're coming one way or another," he said. "During the day, they'll have a chance to notice the traps and avoid them.

"I want you to open the stove and crank every burner to high. Cover a rock with cloth. If they make it to the house, light the cloth and throw it through a kitchen window. Stay in the coop until then."

Adah squeezed his hand. He climbed down through the attic and slinked out the back door.

As quiet as a breeze, Gage maneuvered through his obstacle course toward the honking. Monk flashed the headlights from off to brights, off, brights . . . During the dark intervals, Gage closed in and slowed. His stomach tightened. Goose pimples sleeved his arms. His ears prickled with heat in the dusky chill.

Standing outside a rusted red pickup truck, Monk leaned through the driver's side window onto the horn.

The truck bed lay empty. Others either hunkered down out of sight or had already dispersed into cover across the road. The strobing of the headlights ruined his night vision. Blaring, the horn covered all other noises.

There was no use waiting to let them spot his cover or get better positions than they already had. He dug a fist-sized stone from the soft forest floor, tested its heft from palm to palm and imagined it striking Monk before he sprung and hurled it as hard as he could. He ducked out of sight and covered his head. The stone

sounded a meaty crack. The horn cut out and gave
way for the skidding crunch of Monk collapsing into
the gravel.

The headlights remained on, crosscutting the forest
with stark shadows.

Gage darted away from the road to deeper cover, his
body tense, his breath held for fear it'd give him away.
His heart pounded in his ears, louder than everything
else. He imagined Adah in the chicken coop, a match
in hand. He imagined gunshots. He darted for deeper
cover behind a log housing a sleepy beehive, then
thought he might have been too invisible, and they'd
never chase what they hadn't seen.

City crud-kids had never been so quiet.

Gage kicked the log and dashed between tree
trunks. Two covered spike pits separated him from
the next berm. Leaping over them would put him in
plain sight twice. He couldn't go back. Bees buzzed
madly just out of range. One deep breath, two, three,
and he ran, leaped, leaped and dove behind the berm.
No shout pinned him like a searchlight. No gunshot
tore him from his course. No hiss of arrow or crash of
rock explored his position.

They had seen him. He was sure of it. Even if they
mistook him for a deer, they should've fired freely
for the sake of fresh meat. A cold certainty chilled
Gage's blood that after the loss of Monk, which they
had likely planned for, they were feigning patience in
order to lull him into a false sense of security. Or, they
numbered too many to be drawn into his game.

Monk groaned. Gage had difficulty discerning how
many people scrabbled in the gravel and noisily pawed
the side of the truck.

394

Gage ducked and looked. An oozing gash rent Monk's jaw like a wet pair of red lips. He opened the door to protect himself and spat out a tooth.

Suddenly, Gage felt he shouldn't have thrown a stone. It all but declared the gun safe had remained impregnable.

Monk shouted.

"Gage! Adah!" His voice quavered. "I'm sorry!"

Gage dug into the soft, damp soil, searching for stones. Roots cat's-cradled his fingers.

"They've come for the bodies!" Monk shouted. "They landed in Portland and they're collecting the cocoons! It's happening everywhere!"

Gage imagined Lost Pine filling with gas, exhausting all they relied upon, their future. He imagined the fiery explosion. Everything gone, but at least it'd snuff out a gang as it burst.

"It's not a meteor shower! It's them! They seeded the crud, now they've come to harvest!"

Something scraped against the metal of the truck bed and Monk grunted as he eased it onto the gravel. Gage peeked. Monk stood beside an adult-sized cocoon.

"I've come to bury my parents!" Monk said. "It's the only place I thought they'd be safe! I'm coming in! You can either help me or let your traps kill me!"

Monk dragged the cocoon toward the blackberries blocking the driveway. Delicately, as though the cocoon was no more than a candy shell, as Gage remembered handling his own parents after their crud healed over, Monk hefted the cocoon onto the heap of thorny vines. He bobsledded it ahead of him toward the camouflaged spike pit which dropped off on the other side.

The cocoon teetered over the pit. Monk slipped and cursed and made to shove it forward.

There was no one else. Monk was alone.

"Stay put!" Gage called out. "Wait! Don't move!"

Monk froze. His gaze darted through the shadows. "Help me!"

Gage imagined Adah testing the grain of the matchbox's strike pad with her thumb, then he bolted toward the coop through the obstacle course, shouting for her to cut the propane flow.

Monk limped. His cheek's wound soaked the bandage wrapped around his jaw and stained it dark red. A fresh welt blackened the eye that hadn't been blackened before and swelled it shut. He wouldn't say how he got the truck, only that it was worth it. Its gas gauge needle touched F. Tension straps held full gas cans secure in its bed.

Standing in the deepening hole he dug for his parents, Monk rattled off everything he had seen as though there was too much to say and too little time to say it.

"The aliens aren't alive. They're mechanical, built like semi-truck-sized spiders with large storage compartments for abdomens. They landed with their compartments full of equipment, which they unloaded on the outskirts of Portland. It looks like they're constructing return ships with the stuff. The spiders not constructing the ships race through the city and gather cocoons from where they lay. They store them in their abdomens. When the abdomens are full, the spiders detach them, stack them near the ships-to-be and start helping with the construction projects. They're quick and soundless. Bullets ricochet off them. Their appendages make quick work of nets and bindings. Some crud-kids tried grenades—I don't know where they got them—but they only irritated the spiders and got the kids brained by darts."

Monk's eyes glazed over and he seemed to lose himself in his head, then find his way back.

"The more cocoons the spiders hold, the less eager people are to use grenades or fire on them. Spiders protect the stacked abdomens and construction sites, too. Crud-kids who swarm them get tossed away like bothersome insects. It's like they're performing an act of God."

"Why would they want cocooned people?" Adah asked.

"There was talk," Monk said, "about the spiders taking the cocoons to revive and heal the people inside later, for slaves or pets or cattle—the cocoons just preserve and protect them for the return trip. They're careful not to harm the cocoons."

"Fifteen light-years is a long haul for exotic foods or pets," Gage said. "If they have robots like you describe, they couldn't be in such desperate need for slaves they'd cross between stars for replacements."

Monk's eyes hardened. "Never underestimate the desire of one people to oppress another for minimal gain, no matter the cost. Besides, there is nothing to say the trip wasn't cheap for them."

"There's nothing to say it wasn't expensive, either," Gage said.

Monk set his shovel in the dirt. "Plain and simple,

JACOB A. BOYD

they're stealing people and they don't want the lively ones. They kill when crud-kids become too much trouble."

"Did spiders follow you?" Adah asked.

Monk continued shoveling. "They were occupied when I split. Whatever else you can say about crud-kid gangs, not even they like it when someone goes grave robbing their families. So many cocoons lay around, though, the spiders didn't seem concerned about the two I took. I have a feeling they could've followed me if they wanted, but I don't plan on staying. I don't want to lead them to Lost Pine. I'm burying my parents, then returning to help the fight."

The rim of the hole Monk dug stood at his eyelevel. Sweating, panting, he said, "It has to be deeper. I saw spiders pass over cemeteries where cocoons were buried deep. Maybe later they'll return and dig up the graves, but for the time being they're only taking the cocoons on the surface."

Monk speared his shovel into the earth and flung it over the hole's rim, slower and slower, grunting louder and louder.

Gage jumped in and helped.

Blisters formed on Gage's hands, popped and bled. His shoulders ached. His arms burned. His shovel barked against roots and stones, and sent shivers into his ribcage that grated his teeth. He wondered why he was helping Monk. When they finished and Monk lowered his parents into the hole and asked to be alone, Gage knew. Monk's parents had a chance. He hadn't torn at them. Their cocoons were well formed.

He was storing them for when it might be possible to revive them, whenever that might be.

Adah was right. He shouldn't pry into how people dealt with loss. It was personal.

Adah spoke as if she had chosen her words carefully and wouldn't have said them if they weren't final. "I'm going with him to Portland."

"Why?" Gage asked. He took her hand.

"I thought we were protecting ourselves here to do some good, but staying here now would just be letting bad happen elsewhere."

"You heard him. The spiders can't be stopped."

"Maybe they haven't gotten to my parents. Maybe I can get to them before the spiders do."

"It's Monk, Adah," Gage said.

"You think bad people can do no good, and good people can do no bad. But it's not like that, Gage."

"Will you come back?"

Adah's wide, dark eyes dimmed, and Gage saw she had been hoping to recruit him. She seemed to remember what he had done to his parents at the same time he did. Gage looked away, unable to hold her gaze with the calculus laid bare: he had nothing to go back for. She did, and he did not share it, would not risk it. He tightened his grip on her hand, then she unlaced her fingers from his.

"I want to come back," she said. "I'd like to bury my parents here."

Gage hugged her.

Shooting stars streaked overhead.

Gage gave Adah his machete, saw them off at the road and returned to the gun safe. His hand flicked over its dial.

He assured himself Adah was smart. She knew when to run. She knew where her parents were. She'd waste no time. On clear roads, three hours separated Lost Pine from Portland. He eyed his watch.

Martin's and Sue's cocoons enlarged in his mind like flaring beacons.

He removed Sue's cocoon from the fridge, Martin's from the rain catcher, and dragged them to the yard out front. It pained him to think the water could now become tainted and his food would rot. But if the spiders came, he hoped they'd take what they wanted without damaging the house.

He returned to the gun safe.

Combinations tumbled in his mind and piled in a jumbled heap. Spindly yet gargantuan, Gage's imagined spiders climbed over them and into the dark, neglected territory occupied by his parents. He imagined his parents stacked with others inside a return ship, shooting through space toward a faint star, their thin cocoons cracking under the stresses of the journey. Deep down, like a fault line shifting along tectonic plates of guilt and regret, he felt responsible. But for what? Did Monk's stories reach at the truth? As cattle, those taken would prove old and mostly beyond breeding age. As pets, they'd act willful and uncooperative. As slaves, they'd fight. It didn't add up. Those left behind were the better choice. What else could motivate the aliens to take so much care to preserve lives they planned to displace to another world?

The daylight angling down the stairs into the cellar faded. Gage climbed to the roof to watch for returning headlights and found his eyes drawn toward the shooting stars. They numbered more than on previous nights. None seemed to reach the ground.

Gage worried Monk could have persuaded Adah into trouble neither could handle. Or the cocoons had been moved. Or someone wanted their truck. Or . . . Gage didn't want to think about it. In some ways, it felt better to believe Monk had duped them with theatrics and a fast tale and there were no aliens—Monk had kidnapped Adah. Even entertaining the idea sapped Gage of strength. Adah and Monk had left to fight something greater than them. He wanted to turn back time and have convinced Adah to stay. He murmured conversations he wished he had had with her. *Let the spiders take your parents; you and I are all the family that matters. Together, we'll make as large a family as we want. We'll be the parents that were taken from us. No, we'll be better. I love you.*

The longer the road remained dark, the angrier he was at himself for not saying what needed to be said, the deeper his fury at Monk burned for returning to Lost Pine. He imagined setting out after Adah on foot. Any way he looked at it, the road stretched too far, and he moved too slowly.

Unable to watch the dark road under the active sky, Gage returned to the gun safe. He made his way through the dark by muscle memory.

He tugged at the safe's handle in wild fits, screaming at it. He had dedicated everything to it. He blamed it for Adah leaving. He deserved its treasure. He told it he'd only do good with whatever it held, whether a single gun with a single bullet or a thousand guns with thousands of bullets.

Gage punched the safe for a dull, flat crack, and cradled his swelling hand in his lap. He threw his shoulder against it and kicked it until his toes felt like smashed masses, then kneeled and struck it with his forehead. A taste like iron shocked his sinuses and spread down the back of his throat, the taste of crud. He imagined if he broke himself against the safe, the crud would overtake him. So what if the spiders never found him and his cocoon was left behind? So what? Eventually, the crud would overtake him, regardless of how he felt about it, so why not just let what was planned happen? He had nothing more to lose in the terrible place the world had become. It was all he could do not to curl up and wait for the crud to take him when he heard clucking from the hens outside.

The hens knew nothing of the world. Everything living wanted to eat them. They wouldn't make it a week roaming free. Cooped up, they'd only last as long as their diminished feed held out, unable to forage for slugs and grubs. But what kind of life would that be, unable to escape, food dwindling, their waste mounting and always waiting for the door to open, hoping freedom wouldn't mean death? Small as his duty to them was, he couldn't abandon it. It was all either of them had.

He cooped them for the night and returned to the safe.

Listless, he dialed a combination and tugged on the handle. The safe opened.

As though watching himself from outside his body, he shut the safe door, his muscles so trained in pulling and pushing on it. Breath caught in his throat. Cold ran through his body. Turning the dial had been a wild, unthinking gesture, everything in him attuned against what hadn't worked. The numbers were a finger-painted mess in his mind, made messier the longer he groped for them. He trembled uncontrollably and backed away from the safe as if he could make it worse. Tears streamed down his cheeks. He whispered "No," reached out, then withdrew his hand. His legs gave out under him. He stared into the darkness.

Cold aches spread from his gut. He was sure it was the blow that would finish him—the crud would take him. He lay on the dusty floor, sniveling. Lost Pine, Portland, Adah, Monk, the hens, his obstacle course, the spiders, the crud, return ships, space, Gliese 876, all of it now as far away as a dream after waking. All of it insubstantial and meaningless.

A cold shiver spasmed his shoulders. Another. The cellar floor was cold. He was cold. His body wouldn't let him quit.

Slowly, he rose and approached the safe as though it could kill him if he startled it. He gripped the handle, gently turned it and pulled. It opened, the combination still set, the dial unmoved.

He leaned into the safe's dark cavity. Blubbering thanks to the safe, to God, to everything, he hugged the contents to his chest and frenziedly identified each item by touch. A smooth, slender barrel rang as he ran his hand from the muzzle's borehole to its stock, where the heady scent of gun oil had been rubbed into its crosshatched grip. A flimsy cardboard box hinged open, revealing the ridged butt-ends of organized bullets. Envelopes rattled with seeds. Odd-sized, tacky-faced papers cluttered a shoebox—photos. He pulled one out and stared at it, unseeing in the dark. He felt like he should apologize. Even at the end, whoever had stocked the safe thought to preserve their memories, and he had opened the door on them. Slowly, time and temperature and the air would erase them.

Gage returned the photo to its shoebox, closed it, and returned it to its shelf. After he had retrieved a candle and emptied the remainder of the safe, he closed the door and spun its dial.

With the contents of the safe arrayed before him, his body trembled and tears returned to his eyes. It was so little: two rifles, a shotgun, a revolver, ammunition, gun care kits and seeds. It could secure his present situation, but could not alter his course other than in the grimmest way.

His trigger hand swollen and aching, he carried the guns to the roof, where he loaded them and painfully fired at the shooting stars. Immaculately maintained, then untouched, they worked beautifully.

Night faded into day. Fatigue dropped on him like a net. Repeatedly, he told himself he saw movement on the road. Maybe Adah and Monk missed the covered entrance and drove by, the dash of movement he thought he saw not just a trick of his unsteady gaze searching through a thick forest brushed by breeze. Time proved him wrong. Heat shimmered from the roof. Gage found it best to remain still instead of pace the rough shingles his body didn't shade.

Continuously, he checked his watch until enough time had passed for the crud to have fully cocooned Adah and Monk had they been hurt soon after leaving.

He let the hens out, returned to the roof and restrained himself from looking at his watch but for every hour, then, as the sun passed midday, he considered only intervals equal to Adah's round trip journey. He dozed and woke with a cotton-mouthed start and urinated off the roof in a dark orange stream. He felt clumsy and stupid. He aimed a rifle at a hen as it dumbly scratched and pecked the yard, then tracked it until it rounded the house out of sight.

He climbed down to a rain catcher and drank and took the day's eggs from the coop. Feeling guilty, he ate all three raw, afraid of their shells' muck, yet hopeful it would do the harm to his insides he wasn't willing to inflict from the outside.

Slowly, he limped through the house. He felt the embossed fleur-de-lis on the hallway's wallpaper, ran his fingers down the staircase's smooth wooden banister to the carved pineapple finial crowning its newel post, and tapped the piano keys as Adah would've done. He pulled down the folding ladder to the roof and let it noisily retract into the third-floor ceiling.

He told himself he should've gone with Adah and Monk.

He found his lips forming the words "She will return." Over and over. His breath failed him when he tried to give them voice.

He found himself on the couch in the piano room, planning to crank the stove burners to high and blow it all up. But there was tomorrow. Tomorrow. Maybe. Tomorrow. He fell asleep.

Half in a dream state, the faint honking made no sense. Adah knew the safe route through the obstacle course. She wouldn't call him out. She'd come in. By inches, the incessant honking dragged him toward clarity, then it stopped, and he dropped back into the deep well of his fatigue. A scream tore him from it.

It was Adah.

Gage rushed from the house, his feet hardly touching the ground as he homed in on Adah's voice. No more than a hundred yards from the drive's entrance, she lay on her back, whimpering, an apologetic smile on her face, a huge log where her shin should have been. Her whimpering became sobbing laughs when she met his shocked stare, then her lips stretched over her teeth for a slow, restrained cry. Gage put his back to the log and rolled it off her. Where the log had been, Adah's shin fitted securely in a trigger hole. Broken cleanly, her shin hung at a right angle to her leg. With sharp, surprised cries, she freed it, and shuffled back. Gage rolled the log over the berm where it had rested.

Dumbly—he couldn't help himself—Gage asked, "What happened?"

Adah collected her breath, her face flushed of color, gathering herself for the pain Gage saw her adrenaline had held off but couldn't restrain forever. Wordless, she gestured in a way that encompassed her journey, the absence of Monk and her return. Her hand swelled, purple and broken. A gash rent her side. Dark blood pebbled in her hair. Old wounds. She knew the way through the obstacles.

She just hadn't had the strength. She had been hurt. Gage took her into his arms. She screamed from the jarring of her leg.

"Why didn't you wait for me to come out?" Gage asked.

"I thought . . ." she said, "I was gone so long. And you didn't answer."

"I'm sorry," Gage said. Tears rushed to his eyes and choked his throat as he carried her inside. The pain splinting his hand and toes faded from recognition.

On the couch in the piano room, Adah's breath came in swift, battling gasps, which she pressed through her teeth for words.

"They're not spiders anymore," she said. "It's only meteors now. They're getting big enough to reach the ground. There haven't been spiders touching down for at least a day."

"You're going to be all right," Gage said.

"We were wrong about the crud," Adah said, fighting for breath. "Wrong to fight it."

"You're going to make it," Gage said. "You're a survivor."

Suddenly, a numb look slackened her face. "They were right," she said. "It doesn't hurt." A yellow, viscous tear gathered in her eye and rolled down her cheek. "Don't touch me," she said. "Let it happen." Her heaving chest calmed. The hand Gage held became sticky. He unlaced his fingers.

It took less than twenty-four hours. Before the end, Adah removed her clothes in a fit of discomfort, then her strength left her. Crud thickened over her, lost its plasticity, and hardened. The roof drummed as though pelted with singular grains of hail. A window shattered inward. A puckered stone smoldered on the carpet amongst the glass. Outside, the hens raced about, clucking madly. Intermittently, something crashed in the forest.

The supposed mother ship, the massive moon-sized vessel hurtling in line behind the smaller objects before it, vanished from Gage's mind. It was not a ship. His desire and ignorance had let him see what he wanted to see when even sophisticated imaging only showed blips. It was nothing more than an unfeeling meteor led by debris, so large that insectlike efforts to move it failed to affect its attitude. He felt trapped. Suddenly, the spiders and their return ships seemed loving, the crud a plague of mercy—disorienting and painful in the short term, but in the long run, aimed at preserving humanity's best, its past, its knowledge.

Gage peered at Adah through her murky yellow cocoon and kissed the crud over her lips.

He holstered a revolver in his belt, strapped a shotgun across his back, pocketed ammunition, then carried Adah to the porch. Spread out before Martin's and Sue's cocoons, his obstacle course churned with ghostly motion set off by small meteors. His throat tightened. Pityingly, he looked at the hens, then started for the road. Metallic pings sounded from the propane tank beside the house. Heavy thumps pounded the earth. Dodging a springing branch, he toppled into a wooden spike, which gouged his thigh to the bone. Pain stole his breath. Adah fell from his grasp. The propane tank burst, sending a shockwave through the forest which set off all the triggers. Dizzy, Gage stumbled to his feet. Heavy, spiked objects he could not stop swung and rolled and dropped out of range around him. Fire had splashed the trees and bathed the side of Lost Pine. The rain barrels had broken. Their contents frothed and surged down the slope from the house toward the propane tank, but coursed under its support saddles. The fire blazed, rushing black smoke skyward. He heard no clucking. He heard nothing, a ringing so loud the only sounds to reach him beat his chest and reverberated up through his feet. A pair of hens lay burning in the yard, another above him, thrown into a tree. Adah's cocoon lay beside him. Seeing her, his purpose returned—get her to the spiders. With them, maybe, she had a chance under a different sun.

Adah's cocoon bit into Gage's shoulder as he limped through the stilled obstacle course. His leg felt wet, his foot sticky from the blood running down his thigh.

Panic crackled through Gage as he approached the rusted red pickup truck—had Adah pocketed the keys? He looked inside. They dangled from the ignition. Gage hefted Adah into the passenger seat and glanced at the truck bed for more fuel. His eyes watered from the rising mothball vapors. Five cocoons crowded each other, held in place with tension straps—Adah's parents; his parents; Monk. He swore at Adah for being so loyal, so thoughtful, so courageous.

The fire spread into the forest.

The truck started, and Gage peeled off toward Portland. His heart ached seeing the fuel gauge. It touched F. Adah had gotten fuel for another round trip. There was no telling what it had cost her, what it had cost Monk.

"You had everyone," he said. "You shouldn't have come back for me."

Smoking contrails scored the blue sky, falling, falling, then vanishing out of sight. Then a contrail rose, rose, rose. The spiders were leaving, their return ships ready.

Pits erupted in the road before him and pelted the truck with debris. Gage bucked against the raised shoulder, corrected away from the opposite side's dropoff, and veered onward. His mind dilated to the task, his every fiber clumsily imbued with muscle memory from when he had driven after the crud outbreak.

Gage passed turnoffs and skidded onto others and gritted his teeth. It was a convoluted route to Portland. Road signs had been scavenged for easily pliable metal. Gage told himself he still remembered the way.

The fuel gauge needle dipped. Explosions destroyed the road behind him. Meteors came in waves.

He crested a high hill, which descended into the valley and left the steep, twisting backcountry roads. Before him, smoky contrails arced into the sky from the horizon.

"They'll take you," Gage said to Adah. "I'll get you to them."

The speedometer needle trembled near 100. Gage's body fought between bracing and controlling, more aiming than steering. His gas pedal foot went numb, his leg like a paddle. Divots burst in the road. He aligned them between his tires. He touched his thigh. His hands felt sticky on the wheel. Blood? Only blood?

The gas gauge dipped below half. Like a flash of lightning, a meteor shot through the truck's hood, leaving a pebble-sized hole, which spat smoke against the windshield and clouded his vision. The engine roared, the steering wheel shook. The speedometer dipped to ninety, eighty, seventy, and came to rest on fifty, the accelerator rammed to the floor.

Gage screamed and coughed and slammed the steering wheel with a swollen fist. He punched the wound in his thigh and gouged it with a thumb. Pain quickened to his toes, curled hard against the accelerator. He smiled. His leg still cooperated.

"You can't do this to her and not take her," he said.

The rising contrails gained detail, small candle flames below slender bodies of such pure black they looked like silhouettes against the blue sky. The silhouettes gained detail and shape, not slender, but massive, sleek, elongated teardrops, falling upward.

Ahead, a murky yellow dot punctuated the roadside, a cocoon, one of those who had given up on life and walked away from Portland until dropping. Gage let up on the gas. Who was he to sentence someone who had suffered so much to obliteration? The truck sputtered. Gage's jaw tightened, and he trembled as he pumped the accelerator, hoping the truck wouldn't die. In starts and fits, he regained speed and sped past the cocoon. Another cocoon appeared ahead.

"I'm sorry," he said. "I'm sorry."

The cocoon disappeared in the rearview.

Another cocoon appeared ahead, then another, and another, closer together.

The road straightened after rounding a stand of trees, and Gage slammed on the brakes. A spider rushed at him. It straddled the road, its head a featureless BB the size of a basketball, its body an erector set of

411

trusses and chassis, housing an abdomen like a giant's freight container, which tapered to a point. It stood several stories high. A gang of crud-kids chased it, driving a pair of motorcycles and a truck. The road behind them churned from a scattering of meteors. The spider passed overhead, skidded to a stop and returned to the truck, where it maneuvered its limbs into a crouch over the truck bed.

Pops spider-webbed the windshield and confettied Gage with glass. He ducked into the cabin onto Adah, his gaze directed up through the back windows at the basketball-sized head as it emitted a blue light onto the truck bed. The light blinked twice. It swung the tapered end of its abdomen forward, under its head. An aperture irised open at its point. Deft, articulated metal arms emerged from the aperture and cut the tension straps.

A motorcycle squealed to a stop beside Gage's truck as the mechanical arms fed the first cocoon into the freight aperture.

A crazed male voice screamed. "It's better they die than you take them!" A gun blast punctuated the hate in the voice. As though bitten away by an invisible mouth, a chunk disappeared from the cocoon the spider held. Monk's head, peppered with buckshot, hung exposed. The spider tossed him aside. A puff sounded, and blood sprayed the driver's side window. The other motorcycle arrived. Gage's driver's side door swung open. With a sawed-off shotgun in one hand, a helmeted biker in weathered black leathers motioned for Gage to move out of the way of the cocoon on the passenger seat. The truck screeched to a halt nearby, the crud-kids in its bed hollering.

PAT R. STEINER

"Shoot the cocoons!"

"Take away its trophies!"

Gage peered at the biker's mirrored visor, and fired his revolver at his terrified reflection, the blast lost in the surge of gunfire.

Gage rose and emptied his revolver into the half dozen crud-kids piling from the truck, then slung his shotgun to his shoulder and pumped round after round at those who had tumbled to the road in surprise and fright. Return fire punched the door, raked through the window glass, and whined off the spider. A sound from the spider like a dismissive *pffft* ended the exchange. The crud-kids fell limp.

Gage threw himself onto Adah's cocoon, his hands probing it for bullet holes. When he looked out the window, the abdomen's aperture closed and the spider swung the container up into its secure housing. Something massive struck the ground nearby with a boom that jostled the truck.

"Stop!" Gage screamed. "Not yet!"

He threw the door open and jumped out. The spider swung its basketball-sized head toward him. A sudden exultant fear quickened through Gage, and he went lightheaded and rubbery. He threw his shotgun to the pavement, then dove back into the truck for Adah. When he dragged her out, the spider's head emitted a blue light, which blinked twice. It swung its abdomen down and took Adah's cocoon.

"Thank you," Gage said.

He searched it for understanding.

Its blue blight scanned Gage, blinked once, and the abdomen returned to its housing. The spider continued back in the direction from which it had come, its abdomen full.

Gage fell to his knees as the spider shrank into the distance. His body shook with tears for Adah, for Monk, for the cocoons along the road whose rescue he had greedily stopped.

In the distance, as if falling slowly, a huge meteor tumbled toward the ground and disappeared into the earth.

Nearby, a contrail elongated into the sky. The hushed shriek of its thrusters reached him moments later. They had taken Adah. They had taken Lost Pine, Portland and the unchecked wild in between. They had taken crud-kids and their parents, the struggle to survive, the flush that came before. Everything. Elsewhere, maybe, it had a chance. Adah was smart. She'd waste no time. She was a survivor.

A roaring gale bent trees and sent Gage sprawling.

Battered, he rose, turned his back to the cloud rising from the horizon and limped past cocoon after cocoon until he found himself alone.

It didn't hurt anymore.

A yellow, viscous tear gathered in the corner of his eye.

Advice for a New Illustrator

BY SHAUN TAN

Shaun Tan grew up in the northern suburbs of Perth, Western Australia, and began drawing and painting images for science fiction and horror stories in small-press magazines as a teenager. He has since become best known for illustrated books that deal with social, political and historical subjects through surreal, dreamlike imagery, such as The Rabbits, The Red Tree, Tales from Outer Suburbia *and the acclaimed wordless novel* The Arrival *that have been widely translated and enjoyed by readers of all ages. Shaun has also worked as a theatre designer, as a concept artist for the films* Horton Hears a Who *and Pixar's* WALL-E, *and directed the Academy Award-winning short film* The Lost Thing. *In 2011, he received the prestigious Astrid Lindgren Memorial Award, honoring his contribution to international children's literature.*

Shaun won the Illustrators of the Future Contest in 1992 (WotF 8) and has served as a Contest judge since 2011.

Advice for a New Illustrator

Illustration is a very diverse and scattered profession, a practice that takes many forms, sometimes even hard to define, and it's very unlikely that the careers of any two illustrators are alike. It's mostly freelance work where an illustrator moves from one opportunity to the next, often in an unpredictable way week to week and certainly unpredictable throughout a working lifetime. If nothing else, markets, technology, culture, personal skills and interests will change and develop all the time. That's the first thing to be aware of, especially when either giving or receiving specific advice—every artist's experience and circumstance is different. The most I can do is reflect on general principles gleaned from my own successes and failures over the years, tips that might be relatively universal, useful and encouraging.

Challenge Yourself

Perhaps the first and most important tip is one that applies to all work: enjoy what you do, to the extent that it is a pleasure to go beyond the call of duty. Creating work that is more than sufficient, that exceeds expectations and even the demands of the client, has always been something that I've not only tried to do but learned to *enjoy* doing. I rarely consider any job "run-of-the-mill" or just "bread-and-butter" if I can help it. Given time and energy (admittedly not always available!) I like to treat every creative task as a unique experiment and don't always go for the easiest solution, or the one most dependent on existing skills. Every piece of work should involve an element of innovation or novel difficulty. This is what I've come to understand as "doing your best." It's really about trying to do a little better than your best. I've always been surprised at the results, and that in turn has fed my self-confidence as an illustrator.

It also explains my success as a creator of picture books. When I first entered the genre, I was very interested in challenging both myself and this narrative form rather than executing good, safe and "appropriate" illustrations according to an agreed fee or royalty.

I was inspired by other artists and writers with similar intentions, creating artistic problems for themselves, and investing seemingly unnecessary hours for very little pay, sometimes reaching only a small audience, in a genre that's often critically overlooked and sometimes disrespected (true also of SF illustration from a mainstream viewpoint). That didn't matter: what most concerned me was the opportunity for some experimentation that may not have been possible at the bigger commercial end of the spectrum, where higher pay usually equals less creative freedom. For the same reason, I devoted most of my energy and passion early in my career to

419

small-press science fiction, because it offered the best opportunity for artistic development, weird visual challenges, and ultimately came to be the place where I could fine-tune my practical and conceptual skills as an illustrator in the absence of formal training. Making almost no money, mind you, although it's paid off in the long run. I've learned to be patient and stick with it!

So it's very important to pursue personally challenging work, and small jobs can be just as significant as high-profile ones for that reason. Although people are often impressed by an association with high-profile projects (especially film) perhaps my most significant achievements are modest landscapes and portraits painted in my parents' garage during my early twenties, work which remains unexhibited and unpublished. I still enjoy creating paintings that have no commercial concern or public dimension. I think it's very important to have this stream of work alongside commercial practice, a separate stream— again, it's all about strong personal development. A good artist is (I think) an eternal student, and even when most confident, never feels like a master. They are forever pottering in their backyard spaces, trying to explore their craft with modest integrity. That's how unusual and original work emerges, not by chasing markets or fashionable movements, or wanting to be conventionally successful.

Be Versatile

But speaking of chasing markets, for a practicing artist this remains of course an essential pursuit, if only to survive. It's the other, parallel course of creative practice: economic sustainability, making money. I think this area is the most difficult to cover with simple advice because there are so many types of working environment: adult, young adult and children's publishing, advertising, editorial and genre illustration, film design, animation, theatre, fine arts, games and other forms probably not yet invented. Most visual artists will cross over several of these, especially in a digital, multimedia environment. Therefore, versatility is paramount. That doesn't just mean being adept at working in known styles and media, but also unknown ones—you need to be able to learn and adapt, to remain flexible, diverse, open-minded.

Be Professional

The principle of versatility also applies to working with people, since nearly all commercial work is collaborative. Even if you are writing and illustrating a book in uninterrupted solitude, it's still a collaboration with an editor and other publishing staff. It's important to be reliable and easy to work with, as much as with any other job. This is the main reason clients will continue to give you work, and almost all of my early assignments came to me through the recommendations of others. A lot of preceding illustration produced for little payment in small-press magazines and anthologies proved to be worthwhile, both as training and exposure, a demonstration of my willingness to follow a project brief in a dependable and imaginative way. That's also true of one of my very first "jobs" as a teenager, an illustration for the Writers of the Future

421

anthology that needed to complement a story about a time traveler who kills kittens!

Be a Good Speaker

Communication is very important, even though so much time is spent working alone on what can otherwise seem an introverted profession. You need to be able to talk and write about everything you create in a clear and explanatory way to help others understand your ideas, especially when they are not immediately visible, especially to non-artists and the aesthetically blind. Empathy and patience almost always win the day, even in tough situations. You need to be open to discussion, revision and compromise, while at the same time maintaining your own artistic integrity—these are not necessarily incompatible, as so many people often believe.

Maintain a Broad Interest

Technical competence as an artist is of course essential, but this is only ever a tool for the realization of ideas; without a strong imagination, the display of skill is just that—and "style" is interesting only if backed up by content. Too much illustration looks great, but leaves little resonance in the mind; it's brilliant in style yet thin on conceptual relevance to real-life concerns.

It helps to remain interested in all forms of art and have a good grasp of art history as well as some knowledge of art theory, both past and contemporary. Understand the relationship between art and life. My own background is quite academic, and although I initially worried that studying art criticism might have been a bad choice (having no real idea what I wanted to do as a career), it's actually been very useful. A knowledge of history and theory, and interest in art beyond making attractive pictures: this can really boost your artistic thinking. Developing a visual sensibility and vocabulary, rather than just technical skills, means that you can be perspicacious enough to deal with many different projects and find original solutions.

Don't Despair!

As long as you are doing something, even if it isn't successful, you are not wasting your time. The greatest achievement of so much creative work is simply finding time and dedication to do it, especially when it seems difficult and less than enjoyable, particularly as almost every project seems to involve some kind of confidence-wounding "crisis." Good ideas and talent aren't worth much if they aren't put through the wringer of actual hard work. Ideas are not really ideas until they are translated into labor.

Pay attention to criticism, and don't pay attention to criticism! At the end of the day, you are the ultimate judge of your own work, so learn to be critical in an affirmative rather than negative way. All creators—if they are any good—suffer from periods of disappointment, even depression with their own achievements (or lack thereof); that's perfectly normal! Just keep going, if you want to cross that threshold. You also never find out if you've really failed until you actually *finish* a piece of work. Each

423

success, regardless of quality, will build confidence, and confidence is the key. You also need to protect that sphere of confidence from unwelcome opinions or minor setbacks.

Draw, Draw, Draw and Then Draw Some More

Finally, for anyone interested in being an effective artist, illustrator, designer, even a film director— you should really learn to draw well. It's a valuable foundation, something you'll always use, regardless of technology or genre. Drawing is more than just wielding a pencil with precision, it's a way of *seeing* well, something that takes several thousand hours of practice, and even then, never entirely mastered. Good drawing is a timeless skill, infinitely adaptable, and will never become passé. My entire career rests on my ability to draw well, to think effectively using simple pencil marks. All other visual skills and techniques, from oil painting to CG animation, are elaborations of this fundamental skill.

Tips on Getting Published

Being a competent artist is one thing; getting published represents a rather different set of problems. The most important advice I can offer is this: please consider the publisher. What can you offer them with your work? Research the area you are interested in and know what a prospective editor might be looking for, what other work is out there. A picture book text might be as brilliant as its potential illustrator, but if

424

it does not suit the list that a publisher is pursuing, both are quite likely to be rejected. Unfortunately, publishers do not exist to supply a canvas for free artistic self-expression—I wish!—they are primarily a commercial business. Many young artists don't pay enough attention to this important fact.

Be aware too that there is a "culture" of illustration in any genre that you need to be familiar with (which can vary from country to country). One good way of finding out about this is to study recent works that have won major awards and think about what they have in common. Recognize trends, but don't bend backwards to imitate them, or try to be something you're not. Rather, look for the point of *intersection* between your creative interests and the kinds of books that are being successfully published.

As a contemporary illustrator, you can accomplish a lot by having a very good website and a well-presented folio. I would keep both of these quite simple, showing only your best work; young artists always seem to err (as I did) on the side of excess. A good folio needs only about twelve pieces—be very selective. These should represent technical skill and diversity, color and monochrome, and especially anything featuring human figures, something editors usually look for. Where possible and appropriate, it is good to arrange a face-to-face meeting with a relevant editor or art director. I've personally found this very useful, to get to know each other as people rather than less memorable e-mail or web addresses. Success as an artist, especially in publishing, has much to do with warm relationships. But don't believe anyone who says "it's not what you know, it's who you know"—it's what you know *and* who you know.

And, last of all, good luck, but don't just wait around for it to happen: make your own!

Shutdown

written by

Corry L. Lee

illustrated by

GREG OPALINSKI

ABOUT THE AUTHOR

Inspired by a childhood spent reading science fiction, Corry L. Lee studied physics and applied mathematics in college while sneaking in writing time between classes and research. She went on to complete a PhD in experimental particle physics at Harvard University, taking a six-week break along the way to attend Odyssey, the Fantasy Writing Workshop.

Since completing her doctorate in 2011, Corry has been writing full time while contemplating her next move. Though she still loves big, fundamental physics questions, she's ready to tackle more applied problems—difficult issues in sustainable energy, perhaps? Until then, she channels her scientific background into her writing. Her current project is a series of novels set in an alternate 1890s, where the British Empire teeters on the brink of war with the Russo-Chinese Alliance. The first book follows a young lady inventor, a handsome aristocrat on the edge of financial ruin and a British spy crippled by his past.

Odyssey taught Corry a great deal about writing—including the value of community. She frequently attends science fiction conventions where she loves meeting other writers and talking to fans. When she's not writing or thinking about science, you're likely to find Corry hiking or rock climbing, enjoying a night at the opera, discovering new and delicious teas or reading a good book in the sun. That is, if she can find the sun. She lives with her husband in Redmond, Washington, and pines for the Colorado sunshine of her youth.

ABOUT THE ILLUSTRATOR

Greg began his artistic journey the way many others did. As a child growing up in Poland, he loved drawing, which contributed to many notebooks being filled with doodles and cartoons. In grade school his skills were quickly exploited by his classmates, who demanded drawings of their favorite characters from the television show DragonBall Z and others. Greg quickly realized that getting paid for drawing would be a great life. However, it wasn't until he came to the United States and attended the School of Visual Arts in New York City that he realized that there are people who actually do that. There he discovered old master painters, as well as contemporary illustrators who inspired him to take art seriously and commit to a life of creativity. His current plans are completing his undergraduate illustration study at SVA and transitioning to freelance work on books and advertising.

Shutdown

The alarm blared over the forest's metallic rustling, and my HUD's red warning light glazed the view through my faceplate. Ten seconds until the defense scan hit my position. Ten seconds until any motion, any electrical signature would whip vines down from the iron-cored trees, wrapping me as surely as steel cables, pinning me while cutter-bugs took me apart.

My muscles clenched, and I froze. The training sims hadn't prepared me for the terror twisting my gut, for the way my heart seemed to dance a *pas-de-bourrée,* its ballerina toes rapping against my ribs.

I didn't have time to panic. I chinned my skinsuit's kill switch and dropped to the forest floor. In the silence after the klaxon died, my breather hissed out one final gasp of oxygen. The red glow faded from my faceplate and the forest closed in, dark without the HUD's gain and unnaturally silent without the suit's audio pickups. Weak sunlight filtered through the thick canopy, yellowed by sulfur gas, enough to make out shapes, but not details. In sims, they'd cut our visual enhancement, but they must have extrapolated badly because the shadows had never been this deep, the shafts of sunlight never so diseased.

I crouched on a patch of dirt, crumpling fallen leaves, but avoiding the forest's ragged undergrowth. I folded my legs beneath me, splaying my arms for balance. My hands slipped on the metal-rich berries that covered the ground as if someone had derailed a freight train of ball bearings. I swept some impatiently aside and rested my helmeted forehead on the dirt. How much time had passed? Eight seconds? No time to worry.

Gritting my teeth, I stopped my heart.

A vise seemed to close about my chest. Sweat beaded on my brow as I dragged in one last breath, my body panicking, automatic reflexes screaming at me to fight, to struggle, to escape. I fought them as Sergeant Miller and Captain Johnston trained me, fought them and stopped breathing. My vision narrowed. My lips tingled and went numb. *Twelve minutes,* I repeated to myself as the forest grew dark and disappeared.

You'll come back. The words echoed in Sergeant Miller's clipped bark. Just a few minutes ago, he'd given me the thumbs-up after checking my suit's seals. He'd rapped his knuckles against my helmet for luck, and I'd stridden toward this forested hell.

So, Amaechi," Private Yaradua said as I topped my glass off from her flask. "If we were back on Hope's Landing, what would you do with your last night?"

"I'd go whoring," Obasanjo said. "Nice place in Makurdi where—"

"Wouldn't call it *nice,*" Tamunosaki said. "You mean cheap."

"No, not that place we went with Akpu-nku.

There's one uptown." Obasanjo shrugged. "Might as well spend all my money, right?" He said it like a joke, but nobody laughed.

Yaradua knocked her glass back, and Balogun focused on twirling her knife. We headed planetside at 0800 tomorrow, and MilComm gave slim odds that we'd make it back. The silence stretched, Obasanjo looking expectantly around for someone to agree with him.

Yaradua clanged her empty glass down on the table. "I didn't ask you, Obasanjo. I asked Amaechi."

"She'd probably go to the ballet," he said with a snort.

The corners of my glass dug into my palms; I wondered if I could squeeze it hard enough for it to shatter. The two missing fingers on my left hand itched. I twitched the stub of my middle finger and contemplated slamming my glass into Obasanjo's forehead. If it weren't for those fingers, I wouldn't be here. I wouldn't be about to land on a planet that would probably kill me.

"Obasanjo's an idiot," Tamunosaki said softly. "Ignore him."

"He thinks he's funny," Balogun said, like we didn't all know it.

"What?" Obasanjo said. "What'd I say?"

"Forget it," I said. I didn't want to think about the ballet. "I sure as hell wouldn't spend my last night watching those princesses stick their noses so high . . ." My teeth were grinding. "You'd think they were giraffes," I finished lamely.

"Screw that," Balogun said, jamming the point of

her knife into the table and letting it waver there. "This isn't my last night. I'm coming back."

"We all are," Tamunosaki said, voice loud as he tried to sound convincing. We all glared at him, then tried to pretend that we hadn't. MilComm had assigned him to penetrate only two shutdowns deep into the forest before returning to his lander. The rest of us were headed for the center and whatever might be hiding there. If anyone would make it back, Tamunosaki would.

A rushing sound like a raging waterfall. Colors and faces flashing past. A jumble of words. *Private Amaechi? Focus. Come back.* It sounded like Sergeant Miller, screaming over a buzz like Hope's Landing's insects at dusk.

My back arched. Shadows and shapes flitted behind my eyes: my squad members, mission briefings. Sergeant Miller was shaking me. No, I was shaking myself. Reboot convulsions. I gasped, and stale, humid air poured into my lungs. Nothing had ever tasted so sweet.

Panting, I licked dry lips. My vision stuttered in, grayscale. Motion out of the corner of my eye made me flinch. A fist-sized gather-bug skittered over on eight legs, gunmetal gray and dragging a mesh sack filled with fallen berries. Its mottled exoskeleton glinted in the jaundiced sunlight, its forelimbs in constant motion, spearing berries with sharp stabs of steel-tipped limbs.

My brain snapped out of the reboot haze. A green light winked in my periphery, and a knot in my throat loosened. My reboot seizures had started the suit and HUD reboot. I switched my attention to my environment. "Not a sim," I whispered as I assessed my physical condition.

I hadn't fallen out of my crouch during the seizures, so I scanned my surroundings without lifting my head, eyes darting in threat assessment, not wasting time interpreting details. The gather-bug skittered over my hand and I stiffened. I held myself motionless, expecting a sharp stab, expecting the rotten-egg tang of sulfur dioxide to poison my air. But the bug apparently found my skinsuit's carbon fiber uninteresting, and it marched on, spearing a berry next to my thumb.

My pulse hammered loudly in the enclosed helmet, and each inhale grew more labored as I depleted the bubble of stagnant oxygen. Each exhale fogged my faceplate, and the green light kept blinking. Was the suit's reboot taking too long? I could barely see through the fog.

This would be one hell of a time for the suit to crash reboot.

Sergeant Miller called me into his office after three grueling hours of weapons training. I'd joined MilComm a month ago and hated how Basic left me no time to practice my *pirouettes* and *soubresauts*. Hell, I rarely had enough energy at the end of the day to lace on my slippers and get up on my toes. I hated MilComm for that, hated the way my form was slipping. But mostly I hated myself for being so stupid, so distracted that I burned off two and a half fingers with a damn cutting torch.

To be a prima ballerina, you had to be perfect. And little Adanna Amaechi from Gwantu Village would

433

never be able to afford finger prosthetics on a factory worker salary.

When the MilComm fleet arrived in system and started recruiting, and rumors flew about them paying for high-tech implants, I figured them for my last chance. So far, though, they'd just driven me through grueling drills and stuffed my head with military propaganda.

"Take a seat," Sergeant Miller said.

I dropped my salute. Maybe this would be quick and I'd have time to practice a few *grand battements* before lights out.

"You used to be a dancer," he said, voice gruff like when he walked us through psych control drills.

I narrowed my eyes. He didn't say it like a question and I was pretty sure he didn't want to hear me say that, even though I wore damn combat fatigues, I still was.

"You've got excellent control."

That took me aback. "Sir?"

"Your regulation of breath, heart rate. You're leagues ahead of the other recruits." He fiddled with a stylus on his desk before deliberately placing it aside. "You've heard the latest reports from Helinski Five."

"The cutter-bugs?" They'd splashed the footage all over base: gleaming metal bugs hacking apart a recon probe that twitched helplessly beneath a tangle of vines. I wasn't sure if it was meant to scare us or motivate us.

"We're losing a war we haven't started fighting," he said. "To be frank, Amaechi, we don't even know if it *is* a war."

"So it's true then? There haven't been any survivors?" Five worlds had succumbed to the alien attacks, but the details were sparse and always distorted by speculation. I didn't have the faintest idea why Miller was talking to me, but the chance to get the story straight seemed too good to pass up.

"By the time our probes have arrived to investigate those worlds, they've already been terraformed past a human-breathable atmosphere. As far as we can tell, the aliens destroy all our electronics on their approach to the settled system. We've never received any transmissions about the attacks, and all colonial tech we've recovered has been slagged."

The reports I'd heard always painted MilComm in a more powerful light. They understood these aliens. They had a plan. Apparently, that was more propaganda.

"MilComm needs something to go on," he said, "and our best shot is that forest on Helinski Five."

"The one with the cutter-bugs?" My stomach twisted. Whatever point he was getting at, I wasn't going to like it.

He nodded. "It's roughly a hundred kilometers in diameter and radio opaque. We've sent probes in, but they've never returned. What Lieutenant Aldren's team found is that some sort of defense scan sweeps the area roughly every eight minutes. The scans short all active electronics and any motion attracts cutter-bugs."

The sinking in my gut worsened. He was going to send me into that hell.

"Aldren's team sent back detailed intel on the

first ten meters of the forest, but—" His jaw muscles worked and he took a minute before saying anything else. "—but once they started deeper, something got them."

I swallowed hard. "Dead?"

Miller nodded.

My jaw tightened, and I struggled not to run from the room. That forest had murdered a career MilComm team, so now they'd send the new recruits. The ones that didn't matter.

Could I quit MilComm? I could still dance in the cheap traveling productions the aristocracy put on as a token effort to bring culture to the masses. Commoners wouldn't care if a ballerina in the back was disfigured.

Miller ran a hand over his shaved head. "Captain Johnston and I got approval for a mission, but we need local recruits—without implants—to pull it off. We can teach you to escape the scans, which, at least at the forest's perimeter last a consistent twelve minutes each."

"You want someone who can hold her breath for twelve minutes?" Was this why he was talking to me? "I'm not an otter—sir."

A faint smile pulled at his stubbly cheeks. "We don't want you to hold your breath, Amaechi. We want you to stop breathing."

"And die."

"Temporarily."

I tried to come up with something to say. I didn't want to die. There still had to be a chance, somehow, that I could make it into the Abuja Ballet Academy.

Sergeant Miller must have taken my silence for confusion. "Soldiers have mastered the art of self-stasis before. But no one has revived without external stimulus."

Self-stasis was an awfully pretty word for death. "Stimulus like a defibrillator?" We'd learned how to use AEDs in the factory.

"Yeah." Sergeant Miller actually looked sheepish. I didn't know sergeants could. "But Johnston and I developed a new method. We'll start training on base, and as soon as MilComm gets a dreadnought resupplied, we'll depart for Helinski Five."

"I didn't join up to die, sir."

"You'll come back from these deaths, Private. And MilComm will pay big bonuses for solid intel on these aliens. We don't even know what these creatures look like—you could make a big discovery."

A few temporary deaths would be worth it if they got me into the Academy. But the footage of cutter-bugs chopping apart that probe still haunted me.

"Only a handful of the ten thousand grunts who lined up with you show any promise," Miller said. "We need you for this mission."

I rubbed my thumb over the scarred skin where the cutting torch had burned through my fingers and my carefully planned future. Sergeant Miller caught the gesture.

"That doesn't matter here. You've got seven and a half perfectly good ones."

"If I make it back with intel on these aliens, will MilComm pay for lifelike prosthetics?"

"Absolutely."

I took a deep breath and flexed the two and a half fingers on my left hand. I didn't care about aliens. I wanted my life back. "Then teach me how to die, sir."

With a faint hiss, my faceplate cleared. A heartbeat later, the HUD came online, brightening the gather-bug's outlines and transmitting the *scritch* and *crumple* of its steps across aluminum-plated leaves. Its sack of iron berries clacked like a child's bag of marbles.

"Alien defense scan has passed your position," the HUD said, its accent flat like Captain Johnston's.

"Roger." I leaped up and slipped through narrow gaps between hanging vines, keeping my steps as much on dirt and the uncertain footing of metal berries as I could. No one knew what foliage encompassed the defensive array. The other team had warned MilComm only of the vines, and I shuddered as I skirted some of the gray-green tendrils, imagining them pinning me while the cutter-bugs swarmed.

Step after step, I stole forward in my armored carbon-fiber skinsuit, wondering if the next defensive scan would come in eight minutes, or if it would strobe more frequently as I approached whatever lay at the forest's heart.

Had Yaradua, Balogun, Obasanjo and Tamunosaki made it through their first shutdown already? Were they seeing the same critters as we converged from our five points around the perimeter?

The HUD's alarm blared, and I dropped to the forest floor, heart hammering in an adrenaline burst I didn't clamp down on fast enough. My HUD shut down and the world went silent.

GREG OPALINSKI

As I stopped my heart, the shadows seemed to crawl with cutter-bugs poised to attack. *Make sure you come back,* Sarge had said as my feet hit the alien dirt and I glanced back at him silhouetted in the airlock.

"Yes, sir," I whispered before squeezing my eyes closed and stilling my lungs.

Kilometers bled past. My head grew fuzzy from too many shutdowns, and my chest ached each time I inhaled.

I checked the time; it felt like twenty minutes had passed since my last shutdown. It had only been five.

According to my HUD, I was coming up on my twentieth shutdown. Over six hours and fourteen kilometers had passed since I'd entered this hellhole. I slipped through some spiny shrubs and came out in a clearing. Exhausted, I sat cross-legged in the middle of it, sucking at my nutrient tube. My HUD counted down the minutes until the next anticipated defensive scan.

The backup scanner strapped to my calf felt like a brick weighing down my every step. I pulled it off, contemplating leaving it behind. The defensive scans had been coming like clockwork every eight minutes, so I probably wouldn't need it. I sipped water through another tube, beyond caring that it was recycled piss. Grimacing, I transferred the scanner to my other leg. Its crude circuits might survive if something took out my HUD, and I still didn't know what lay at the heart of this forest.

I hoped to hell that whatever it was, I'd find it soon.

I envied Tamunosaki, who was probably back on

the dreadnought already, kicking back with a pilfered glass of Yaradua's whiskey. I bit my lip. Were the others even still alive?

They had to be.

A metal-shelled creature the size of a dog scuttled past, and I reminded myself that everything I was seeing, everything my HUD was recording and writing to archaic plastic storage devices, was new intel. I had to make it out. I would get my prosthetic and be able to dance again.

But right now, that hardly seemed to matter.

My HUD blared its warning, and I killed myself again.

Up ahead, the vines thickened. I crouched low, sweeping foliage gently aside. Forward, ever forward.

The vines grew denser. I backtracked, cursing the extra distance as I sought a way around the thicket. But the tangle of vines stretched on. After wasting two precious minutes trying to go around, I steeled myself to go through.

My muscles quivered as I crawled on hands and toes through a narrow gap, feeling for solid footing through the thin fabric on my skinsuit's hands and feet, trying to disturb the vines as little as possible. I groped forward and the vines constricted. My pulse ratcheted up. They must have identified me as an intruder.

Somehow, I kept my wits and froze. Breathing deep, I studied the vines, arms shaking with the strain of holding myself still. They weren't moving. They simply grew close together, knotting and weaving around each other as though in a deliberate barrier.

My pulse still pounded in my ears, but now as I twisted my shoulders and hips, my heart hammered with excitement. I shimmied, pulled and wiggled through, anxious for sweet, bonus-worthy intel on the other side.

Another meter forward, and the light brightened suddenly. My HUD dropped its gain and I blinked past the spots in my eyes, confused by the open space stretching before me. Disbelieving after so many hours in the forest's close confines.

I craned my head to see the roof of the canopy arching high above, and for a moment, I forgot the protests of my muscles, forgot the vines gripping my ribs and tangling my feet. A dozen meters of open space stretched before me, ending in what I first took to be a building. As my gaze traversed it, I realized it was an enormous tree.

My neck began to ache from craning up, and my body rushed back to me, screaming protest at holding such an unnatural position after so many hours of travel.

I pulled myself forward and somersaulted, slipping my legs out from the vines and crouching, one hand on my slug thrower as MilComm training kicked back in. My eyes tracked the open space in automatic threat assessment, but soon I was gaping like a tourist.

The vines I had just pulled myself out of ended abruptly in what, as far as I could tell, was an enormous, gently curving ring, stretching off into the distance, fading into a yellowish mist. The thick tangle of vines climbed twenty meters into the sky. Above that, enormous branches arched outward from the forest I'd just escaped, forming a cathedral ceiling thousands of times bigger than anything on Hope's Landing.

Vertigo swept me, and I put one hand on the springy moss carpeting the open space, glad I hadn't stood from my crouch. I knew I should move on, should pay more attention to the tactical data scrolling in my periphery, but I kept staring upwards. The limbs from the trees behind me merged with those sprouting like spiky hair from the great structure in front of me, and I felt like an ant crouched between two skyscrapers. That analogy wasn't quite right. An ant in an inverted donut of skyscapers—forest to my back, the enormous tree in front of me, and a thin ring of open space between, fading away into the distance on my right and left.

The canopy wavered and shifted in a breeze I couldn't feel, and the sunlight, which had looked so sickly before, seemed suddenly beautiful. Gold glinted off aluminum-plated leaves, and I took a deep breath, somehow expecting the fresh scent of new growth.

The faintly metallic tang of my suit's air shook me, reminding me I was in hostile territory. I swept my surroundings. A few bugs skittered across the moss, absorbed in their own tasks.

I studied the enormous tree, its sides a familiar, mottled gray bark. The HUD used its faint curvature to calculate a diameter of 200 meters. It had to be a building; why else would it be so large, so isolated?

Whatever I was going to find, I would find it there.

I slipped the safety off my slug thrower and launched from my crouch like a runner from the starting blocks, beelining for the tree and hoping to hell that my sprint wouldn't trigger new defenses.

No cutter-bugs swarmed, and I pressed my back against the giant tree-building, scanning the way I had come. Time to stop being a tourist and become a spy.

I realized with a start that fifteen minutes had passed since my last shutdown. No other scan had taken so long. The hair on the back of my neck prickled, and I wondered if I'd made it past the scans. My stomach knotted in anticipation of what else awaited me.

I wouldn't come so far only to die.

Gritting my teeth, I slunk along the tree wall, seeking an opening. Ten minutes passed before I found it.

Three meters up from the ground, the HUD outlined a jagged shadow. Magnified, it resolved into an opening, and I couldn't help but smile. At least all those years drilling *soubresauts* would be good for something.

I holstered my gun and leaped, catching the fissure's lip and chinning myself up. I hung with just my eyes above the edge, toes digging into rough bark. An empty tunnel twisted into darkness, a meter wide at its center, three meters tall, narrowing to sharp points at ceiling and floor.

I heaved myself over the lip. Nothing rushed out of the darkness to attack me, so I pressed my back against the tunnel, one leg on the steep wall beneath me, the other angled out to the wall opposite. Slug thrower in hand, I scanned back the way I had come. No sign of pursuit.

After a few steps down the tunnel, I holstered my gun. I needed my hands to balance against the tunnel walls as I placed one foot in front of the other like a tightrope walker, struggling to step on the narrow crack where the sloping walls met. Whenever I stepped too far to the right or left, my ankles protested.

The aliens must not walk on the floor, I decided, because this tunnel was hell. The image of giant, sentient cutter-bugs skittering out of the shadows sent a chill down my spine.

Something was watching me, my hindbrain screamed, and my hand closed about the slug thrower. I squinted up into the darkness at the peak of the narrowing crevice, but even at full gain, my HUD failed to distinguish anything from the shadows.

Swallowing hard, I blamed the fear on shutdown stress. After a few deep breaths, I managed to holster the gun and keep walking.

The passageway darkened until my HUD failed to pick the merest outlines from the black. I wanted to turn on my headlamp, wanted to activate the suit's sonar. But those could trigger defenses, so I kept on, trailing my fingertips along the walls, groping forward with my feet. The tunnel branched, and I turned right then left, right then left, climbing and descending. My breath sounded loud over the breather's hiss, and the audio inputs amplified the scuff of my steps.

A faint *squelch-pop*. I froze, holding my breath. My hand dropped to my gun. *Squelch-pop*.

Squeezing my eyes shut, I concentrated on the sound, trying to pinpoint its direction, trying to imagine the creature that could make it. When I opened my eyes, a faint light shone down a tunnel ahead on my left.

I crept toward the glow, weapons holstered to keep my hands free for stealth and balance.

The tunnel opened into a lumpy, spherical room. Flattening myself in the shadows, I craned forward.

A bulbous creature with a dozen tentacle limbs clung to one wall, vines wrapping its body. The air before it shimmered and shifted—a display of some sort? I couldn't resolve what it showed and wasn't ready to waste time cycling my HUD through different EM frequencies. The scientists could sort that out later from the recording.

I studied the creature, but couldn't find anything on it I could call eyes. Maybe it saw through the puke-colored splotches the vines didn't cover.

Squelch-pop, squelch-pop. The sound came from above me. My head snapped up.

Another creature scuttled down from a fissure in the ceiling. A chittering screech emanated from it as it flowed down the wall and out of my line of sight. The vine-wrapped creature chittered back.

I leaned further into the room, hoping to see them interact. Was the new creature here to rescue the other from the vines, or had the first wrapped itself up intentionally? Had I stumbled upon a prisoner or bioengineered technology?

Several vines lashed out, wrapping the new arrival's limbs as it chittered away. A shimmer appeared before it, then widened, extending around the room to merge with the other's.

Suddenly, both fell silent. The shimmer disappeared.

My breath caught. Had they seen me?

Heart hammering my ribs, I flattened back into the shadows. Maybe I was overreacting. Maybe they'd responded to something else.

A vine whipped around the corner and lashed

about my arm. I yelped and jerked away, but the vine held. Without thinking, I grabbed my knife and hacked at the tendril. The blade bit, and I ducked another tendril as I sawed through the first. The vine tore loose, oozing grayish-white slime, and I stumbled back. More vines groped out from the room faster than I could retreat on that damn fissure floor. I slashed at one, but more flailed forward, whipping through the air around me and slapping my suit.

One caught me about the throat and yanked me forward. I hacked it off, but not before the tip of another wrapped my leg and jerked my feet out from under me. I fell hard, helmet cracking against the floor. But I was too desperate to register pain, and my fall loosened the vine's hold.

I kicked free. Knife in hand, I scrambled back on all fours until I could get my feet under me. My left ankle screamed in protest—I must have twisted it in the fall—but the vines no longer slapped my suit.

I edged backward. The vines still lashed the air, but could no longer reach me. Part of me wanted to hang around and learn more, but the aliens had clearly spotted me, and who knew what they would do next.

Suddenly, the vines retreated and three of the bulbous creatures scuttled into the tunnel, clinging to the walls. I picked up my pace, reaching for my slug thrower. One of the aliens clutched a dark, boxy device in a front tentacle, and before I could grab my gun, the boxy muzzle flashed, and something slammed into my chest, sending me sprawling backward while my HUD screeched alarms. The enhanced image flared white, then black.

I landed hard on my back. Impact drove the air from my lungs.

Through my faceplate, I saw only darkness. I chinned the HUD's reboot, but nothing happened. A bubble of silence quarantined me from the creatures' chittering.

Something rubbery grabbed my bad ankle, squeezing tight. I jerked and kicked, but a tentacle caught my other leg and pinned me. I struggled but another wrapped my arm, squeezing so hard the knife fell from my grip.

Before they could catch my other hand, I went for my gun. A sudden pain cut through my right thigh. I screamed and fought their holds, but more tentacles wrapped me, pinning all my limbs, squeezing so tight that my fingers tingled and went numb.

Lightheaded with pain, I stopped fighting. The moment I went limp, the aliens started dragging me somewhere.

The nauseating taste of rotten eggs turned my stomach as I banged down the tunnel on my back. As my vision adapted, I saw dim outlines of tentacled forms crawling over and around me. There had to be a dozen of them, at least.

Just like everyone had said, I'd joined MilComm to die.

Poor thing, they whispered when they thought I couldn't hear. *Lost the audition because she's disfigured.*

Pain twisted my vision as the creatures dragged me toward the room with the vines. I couldn't stop them.

I had danced as well as any applicant and better than most. One judge had taken me aside and told me I was the best she had seen. But she clucked her tongue and waggled her fingers. "You will never achieve true grace with such a handicap."

My eyes watered, burning from sulfuric acid and helplessness. Dark blood welled from a cut on my thigh. With my skinsuit compromised, I had maybe a minute to get to my patch kit before the atmosphere poisoned me. But pinned by the aliens, I was as powerless as I'd been after the audition.

My MilComm training was as useless as my perfect *pliés*. I flexed my left hand, my forefinger digging into my palm, the stub of my middle finger barely brushing it.

I opened my hand and lifted it slowly—the alien had relaxed its death grip now that I'd stopped fighting. My two and a half digits made an awkward silhouette in the dim room, and I remembered Sergeant Miller's gruff voice in that tiny office light-years away. "You've got seven and a half perfectly good ones."

I couldn't die here. MilComm needed the data I'd collected. And unlike on Hope's Landing, in MilComm, I had people who cared if I made it back. I wouldn't make Sergeant Miller blast back into orbit alone.

The aliens stopped dragging me. The creature holding my left wrist chittered loud enough that I heard it through the skinsuit; with another tentacle, it gestured with a blocky shape. I recognized that shape. That alien gun had slammed me to the ground and shorted out my HUD.

If I could bring the gun home, MilComm might unravel how the aliens slagged our electronics.

I twisted violently in my captors' holds and grabbed the alien gun with my left hand, two and a half fingers perfectly sufficient to wrench it free of the tentacle. The creature screeched, distracting the others enough that I jerked my other hand free and pulled the slug thrower from its holster. I pressed it against a bulbous body and fired.

"I'm going home," I yelled, rotten eggs thick on my tongue. I fired again, and the creature fell away. The tentacle around my right leg loosened, that creature reaching one arm out to its fallen comrade.

Had I killed it? The creatures screeched louder. I gripped the alien gun like a lifeline—MilComm needed this tech. Still firing, I kicked my legs free and stumbled to my feet. Agony shot down my leg.

An alien lunged down the wall, knife in its tentacle. My chest armor stopped the blade and I aimed dead center on its bulbous form and pulled the trigger. The creature fell from the wall like a heap of rubber hose.

I scrambled out of the room and down the passageway, firing over my shoulder as several creatures scurried forward. I tripped and slipped along the angled crevice, bracing my shoulder against the wall to stabilize myself when I fired. The air tasted worse and worse, but my faceplate wasn't fogging, so the weapon that shorted my HUD hadn't compromised my breather.

Alien screeches penetrated my skinsuit, but after I picked off a few more of them, they stopped advancing. I holstered my gun and ran, sealing the alien weapon in a pocket, then fumbling for the patch kit strapped to my side.

Teeth gritted with pain and lurching on the awkward footing like a crazed drunk, I grabbed the largest patch, tore off the backing, and slapped it to my thigh. My lungs burned, each breath searing like acid as I gulped poisonous air.

The passage forked and I turned right. Sprinting, I mouthed the words "Make it out, make it out" to the slap of my feet on the angled ground.

I pictured Sergeant Miller's pale face as he rapped his knuckles on my helmet for luck. The alien gun banged against my thigh, and I smiled through gritted teeth. That gun was intel gold.

If I made it out.

A quick glance behind me: no creatures. Had I scared them off? Were they too slow to give chase? I tried not to question my luck.

Another fork, turn left. The passageway descended, then climbed. Right then left, I retraced my route, fighting not to second guess myself or worry that I'd missed a turn.

More creatures appeared as I rounded a bend. I drew and fired, emptying my clip before one shot me in the leg. I turned the fall into a roll, hands already chambering another clip as I leaped to my feet. My aim would have made Corporal White proud as I brought down the one that had shot me, before picking off a couple of its friends. Still firing, I dove through the ambush, sprinting across twitching tentacles.

They must not have expected a fight, I decided, lungs burning as I raced back the way I had come. Blood slicked the inside of my skinsuit from the cut on my thigh, but I gritted my teeth and kept going, slug thrower in hand. I kept expecting another ambush, but it seemed I must have outrun them.

Daylight pierced the darkness as I rounded a bend, and seeing that sulfur-gas sunlight felt like winning the lottery. A muzzle-flash made me jerk to the side, and I stumbled. A handful of creatures blocked my exit. I kept running, firing as I did, their shots slapping me around like giant fists. But their weapons didn't penetrate my armor, and my slug thrower dropped them from the walls like rain.

Chanting a MilComm marching song under my breath, I sprinted past the ambush and leaped from the tunnel into open space.

I hit the ground with my hands, tucking around my gun and rolling to my feet, running for the vines. A few creatures streamed down the giant tree behind me, swarming across the forest floor. I holstered my gun and clawed through the thick web of vines at the forest's edge.

A tentacle wrapped my ankle, but I shot it and dragged myself fully into the vines.

When the vines thinned, I crouched, turning to face my pursuers. But no tentacles wavered through, and I didn't stop to worry why. I had the intel I'd come for.

My breath rasped in my ears as I pulled the backup scanner off my calf. I tore open its casing and stripped away the shielding, tossing it aside as I ran. Slipping on metal berries and tripping over vines, I pressed the scanner's power button. "Come on," I said as I shouldered through a thicket of yellow fronds.

A green light blinked on, and if it weren't for my faceplate, I would have kissed it.

I stopped, leaning against the rough bark of an iron-cored tree, chest screaming with every rapid breath. Pain lancing my leg, I glanced back the way I had come. Still no sign of pursuit. I held my breath, but couldn't hear anything through the skinsuit.

The scanner flashed red. I thumbed it off and dropped to my knees, arms and forehead resting on the ground. I chinned off my breather, sparing one glance back as I stopped my heart, wondering if I would come back from this shutdown, or if the aliens would lead the cutter-bugs straight to me.

Strong hands held me as I convulsed, and over the rushing in my ears and jumble of torn scrapbook images flashing past my eyes, Sergeant Miller smiled at me. Sucking air reminded me how dry my mouth was, and God did I feel like I needed to puke.

"How long?" I choked out. The ailing tree outside our practice room window wavered in the wind.

"Twelve minutes—exactly," Miller said, gruff voice at odds with the grin that split his face. "I knew you could do it."

I closed my eyes and took a deep breath, assessing my body the way Miller had taught us. My first shutdown, and I'd come back right on time.

A babble of voices burst over my tenuous understanding of the world, and more faces grinned at me past the wires and tubes sprouting from my body.

"Guess you won the bet, Amaechi," Obasanjo said.

"I was going to be first, damn you," Yaradua said, her voice light and her teeth shining white against skin almost as dark as mine.

"I guess we don't have an excuse anymore, do we, Sarge?" Tamunosaki said. "We can't let Amaechi show us up."

A waterfall roared in my ears. Reds and yellows, blues and purples flashed past my eyes. Faces fleeted by, and bulbous creatures scurried, chittering like insects.

I cried out and flailed back, away from the creatures. They retreated into the shadows. Panicked, my head whipped around, seeking pursuers.

But I crouched alone in that dimly lit forest. "Memories," I told myself, "that's all." The jumble of reboot.

Gripping the scanner, I punched its power button and chinned my breather on. Air hissed around me, tasting faintly of rotten eggs. I was alive. Somehow, the creatures hadn't followed me. The defenses must attack them, too. And who knew if they could shut them down—or how long that would take.

I didn't waste time thinking about it. I had to get out, get my intel to MilComm, get home. I remembered last night like it was an eternity ago, sitting around drinking with Yaradua, Balogun, Obasanjo and Tamunosaki. Had Tamunosaki gotten out after his two shutdowns? Had the others made it to the tree-building like I had?

I swallowed hard and prayed that I'd see their faces on the other side. With whatever bonus MilComm gave me, I wanted to drink with Yaradua and have Bologun teach me to throw knives. Even Obasanjo, who managed to effortlessly piss me off every time he opened his mouth—even him I wanted to see on the other side. I'd never felt like that about anyone on Hope's Landing.

Before MilComm, I'd pushed away everyone I knew. Other dancers were always the competition, and nothing mattered but dancing. To make it in that world, you couldn't care about anyone else.

I flexed the two and a half fingers on my left hand. Sergeant Miller had been right. Those fingers didn't matter. I had an alien gun in my pocket and a dozen kilometers to cover before I was back with the people I loved.

Screw dancing. I was Private Adanna Amaechi, and MilComm had worlds to save.

While Ireland Holds These Graves

written by

Tom Doyle

illustrated by

FIONA MENG

ABOUT THE AUTHOR

Tom Doyle grew up in East Lansing, Michigan, so when he attended the Clarion Writers' Workshop there in 2003, it was like coming home. His love of written science fiction and fantasy started in the second grade when he read The Andromeda Strain.

Tom lived in Japan for over a year and has traveled widely. In 2004, he visited Ireland for the celebrations of the hundredth anniversary of Bloomsday, and that experience contributed greatly to this Writers of the Future story.

*Tom won the 2008 WSFA Small Press Award for "The Wizard of Macatawa" (*Paradox #11). *He has published stories in* Strange Horizons, Futurismic, Aeon *and* Ideomancer. *His essays on science fiction and millennialism have appeared in* Fictitious Force *and* Strange Horizons, *and in the book* The End That Does. *He has recently completed a novel-length extension of "The Wizard of Macatawa." Paper Golem Press plans to publish a collection of his short fiction. This story is his third professional sale.*

Tom has appeared on the Hour of the Wolf *radio*

program and the Fast Forward TV show, and he has given a presentation on L. Frank Baum at the Library of Congress. The audio versions of many of his stories are available on his website.

Tom attended Harvard University and Stanford Law School. He used to work for an international law firm, but quit to pursue various dreams. Before focusing on writing, he traveled to Rio for Carnival, stayed in a Zen monastery, interned at the Center for Millennial Studies at Boston University, ran a marathon and formed a Guided by Voices cover band. He wants to continue to write full time in his spooky turret in Washington, DC. He holds a rock-and-roll jam session in his house each week, runs a lot of miles a day and listens to dozens of books a year.

ABOUT THE ILLUSTRATOR

Canadian artist Fiona Meng has always had a knack for drawing. One of her very first memories is waking up early on a beautiful sunny morning, still in diapers, filling the clean white walls of her bedroom with beautifully colored crayons. Though her medium of choice has changed, her love of art has not faded.

Working mainly with pen and ink and digital media, Fiona has always striven to push herself out of her comfort zone and create art that connects the viewer to a world beyond reality. It is her desire to create illustrations people may interpret with ideas and creative dialogues of their own.

Though Fiona chose to not study visual art in university and instead opted for general arts, illustration has always been her career of choice, on the side or as a full-time professional. She has an older brother, and an identical twin sister who is also an artist.

458

While Ireland Holds These Graves

Dev Martin surrendered his exterior electronic devices, then submitted to a scan of his head chip while it received the new cultural downloads. Exiting customs, he moved against the human tide of the Shannon Air and Compiler Portal. Around him flowed the fleeing hundreds—slow, wide, orderly, not panicked and poor like the North Korean Implosion, but of the same weary tradition. Their worldly goods, already shipped or decompiled, still seemed to weigh on their shoulders. The departing gazed at Dev with a disbelief and dark humor that assumed the new arrival didn't know what awaited him.

Dev could have told the refugees that he understood, that he had lost everything too, but they wouldn't believe him. They'd probably kill him. So Dev kept walking, avoiding their gaze, hoping that no one in this disconnected zone would recognize him.

A *Garda* officer stopped him. "Forget something?" she asked.

"I've just arrived."

"Haven't you already caused enough hurt?"

"Yes," he agreed. Shite, she knew who he was.

The big woman smiled like an Irish wolfhound at a hare. "Why don't you just turn yourself around then, before I tell these good people who you are?"

Dev pulled out some hard-copy papers. The *garda*'s brow furrowed, then she waved the papers away. "UNI can kiss my Irish arse. No one here cares anymore what they say, boyo." But she didn't tell him again to leave. "You know the terms of the Referendum?"

"Yes," he said, knowing that she would give him the bad news anyway. Some Irish just couldn't resist giving the bad news.

"Then you are aware that the final Cúchulainn Barrier goes up in three days, and entry and departure for Referendum Ireland will be sharply curtailed. If you decide to remain after that time, you'll be committing to stay for one year."

"Yes."

She studied his face. "You're not just here to write reports for UNI."

"I'm looking for someone."

She shook her head, but spared him most of that bad news. "Don't look for too long. You have three days."

"Right. Cheers."

"Oh, don't forget to turn on your Irish."

"Turn on my what?"

She tapped her head. "Language."

"Right." Dev told his head chip to switch to Irish Gaelic. He said "thank you" and out came *"go raibh maith agat."* Christ, what a gobstopper. He strode to the terminal exit, and Shannon kept flowing around him, an Irish wake en masse.

When he stepped outside, his head chip synced with the circumscribed Irish net. From overhead, a cry of challenge. A large dark bird, perhaps a raven, circled in the morning sky. *Just a bird,* Dev thought, somewhere between statement and prayer. *Not that AI goddess. Not the bloody Morrigan. Not before lunch.*

In Galway, Dev sat alfresco with his third pint and his untouched fish and chips. Seagulls and pigeons hounded him, probing for any opening, but no raven-like AI joined them. Dev should've been looking for Anna or leaving town, and shouldn't have been drinking, but he had ample time and means for his future failures, so he got pissed and took in the view.

The traditional music of an afternoon session cut through the other pub noise. Analog instruments and "one touch, one note" were again the rules. The biologicals and Personality Reconstructs mixed with easy familiarity: football-jerseyed drinkers laughed with baroque and Victorian PRs. The June sun and brisk breeze were busy drying the fresh paint covering all English language signs. A banner over Eyre Square declared in Irish that Galway/Gaillimh was "The Capital of the 2nd War of Independence."

With her unerring eye for the heart of the matter, Anna might be here if Galway was to be the new capital. Even if not, this protean town of gossip was a fine place to start hunting for his ex.

As Dev finally tasted a chip, nanobots slowly chewed

down global-style buildings they had fabricated only a few years before, their work sustained by generated energy fields in this often sunless city. Other nanobots were restoring castles, reroofing monasteries and extending the wall of the Spanish Arch; Galway had no room for nonfunctional ruins. The nanos were also busy redecorating any modern structures spared to accommodate the biological population. All buildings would be in Celtic harmony. Light gray flakes of nano-trash floated away from the sites and fell in small drifts.

"The newspapers are right: snow is general all over Ireland." A lanky-looking galoot with an eye patch and thin mustache wandered past Dev's table, swinging an ashplant walking stick. Dev about choked on his chip. "Jim?" The galoot walked faster. Dev got up and sprinted after him. "Jim. It's me, Dev Martin."

"My apologies, sir, I'm very busy right now with my work in progress. I'll have your money soon."

"Jim, what's feckin' wrong with you? You don't owe anybody shite. Though it's grand to hear you're writing again."

James Joyce stopped cold and slapped his forehead. His face seemed to ripple with the impact. The eye patch disappeared. "Shite and onions! I'm sorry, Dev. The new Sinn Fein have been at my inner organs again. It seems I'm not Irish enough for them."

"You never were. Why should you change now?"

Joyce whispered, "The revolution has plans for Dublin. They want to rebuild it as it was on the sixteenth of June, 1904."

The day of Joyce's *Ulysses*. "Bloody Bloomsday every day, forever."

"World without end amen," said Joyce. "I was just

feckin' joking when I said they could do it. If I fight it, they'll have me utterly domesticated, like poor Roddy Doyle. Or they'll set the Morrigan on me."

Dev winced. He wasn't sure which was worse. The revolutionaries kept the uncooperative Doyle PR confined to a working-class living room in front of an old-fashioned telly. Day after day, he spouted the Da's bits from *The Commitments*. The Morrigan would be quicker in objective time, but an AI could do almost anything with subjective time.

"Jim, have you seen Anna?"

"The mother of my resurrection? You can't find her?"

"I couldn't track her on the global, and the Irish net isn't cooperating. I need to find her. I need . . ." Dev opened his hands.

"My young father and artificer, I'll assist you, but," and Joyce lowered his voice again, "you must get me out of here. Even if they leave my ballocks attached, I'm cut off from the broadbands, and these other PRs—even you have no idea."

Dev nodded. "I'll do whatever I can." *Probably less than bugger all, sorry.* "As for the PRs, you're right, I don't have an iota of an idea—my access is desperate. For example, what are you doing here in the Wesht?"

"It's June, and I thought things were all up with me—I wanted to see Nora's house one last time."

"Oh, right. Let's go then." Dev wouldn't press the tetchy, deadline-adverse Joyce for an immediate response to his question.

They walked the short distance from the square to Nora Barnacle Joyce's childhood home. They passed tourist shops, shuttered since the Referendum. The irony that the PRs were designed to improve tourism was not lost on Dev, their codesigner.

Joyce stopped across the street from Nora's house and looked it over up and down. "It seems so small now." Two windows on two single-room floors, for a whole family. "Dev, I never asked you—why didn't you bring her back?"

Because I didn't think she was worth trying and trying again until we got her right? Now, having lost the love of his own life, Dev knew better. "What can I say? She didn't write literature. Anna and I tried a PR like that once, and it didn't work. I'm sorry."

"Barnacle. Stuck to me, all her life."

"You could, maybe, you know, do it yourself?" Dev felt like he was talking about sex and death with an adult son.

"No, you're right," said Joyce. "I've seen some of our solo efforts, like Swift's Stella. Poor ghosts. They don't pass the Joyce Test."

"The Joyce Test?"

Near tears, Joyce cackled. "You can't have a decent drink with them."

Dev laughed and wiped his eyes. This good friend could distract him for years, but Dev only had hours. "So, where's Anna?"

"I may have been addled by Sinn Fein attacks, but I'm certain your flower of the mountain left here after I arrived. She had been asking for Yeats."

"Which one?"

"She didn't seem particular."

Sligo was Yeats country. Dev couldn't know where Old Yeats or Young Yeats might haunt—the town, the old family house, anywhere. But Dev knew where Newly Dead Yeats was. Dev had put him there himself.

If Anna and the Morrigan had discovered the true reason behind Newly Dead Yeats, then Dev would soon join him in the grave.

Three years before, as a grad student in America, Dev pursued a dodgy thesis—that *Finnegans Wake* was the first cybernetic book, that its twentieth-century origin was like finding an integrated circuit diagram in an Egyptian pyramid. Everyone with the right language and literature enhancements understood and enjoyed the multi-/neolingual *Wake* now; few claimed to then.

To help argue his point, Dev decided to bring back Joyce. Of course, this had already been tried—in the earlier days of AI, almost everything had been done and done badly. Previous Joyce reconstructs could pass a full-sensory Turing Test, but they didn't have the distinctive responses of an *exceptional* human.

The traditional scholars sniffed that Dev hadn't "heard of the death of the author generally and of Mr. Joyce specifically." Undaunted, Dev started his design work, and ran immediately into two difficulties— money and ability.

For money, Dev found the Irish Tourism Board, one of the last vestiges of Irish national governance. To encourage people to visit Ireland physically rather than virtually, the ITB wanted more than Joyce—they wanted all the Irish greats. Greats to argue with in a pub or hang out with in a tower. Greats that would stay local.

For ability, Dev found Anna. She was playing violin in the quadrangle, alone and digitally unenhanced—a freak show to most. Dev bought her coffee and discovered a brilliant grad student in AI. Her full name was omen: Anna Livia Plurabella Vico (her Italian-American parents were *Wake* fans). With her long black hair and sea-gray eyes, Anna was an Irishman's dream of the Mediterranean.

Anna designed reconstructs, but she had run up against the limits of historical sources. Dev jived Anna about literature to interest her in Joyce and in himself. "What if every word choice in a text reflected the peculiar genius, the particular thought process, of the author? That's what great fiction is, and what makes it different from most speeches and letters."

This stimulated Anna to excited multitasking. One part of her brain investigated love with Dev; the other designed the fiction algorithm for converting analog source text to digital synapses and combined that algorithm with biographical data and Dev's unorthodox insights. Still, the process would not have worked, except Lingua, one of the great global AIs, took an interest. Lingua was short on human personality, but astronomically long on sheer intelligence and processing power. The AI had started as a translator, but enjoyed modeling other aspects of the human mind.

Thus, a trinity came together and made a baby: James Joyce. Snappers change everything.

Joyce was a hit, and the ITB ordered more literary figures for re-creation. Dev and Anna quit school. Business was grand; even minor authors were in demand. The first sign of trouble seemed more feature than flaw: the PRs had an unsettling way of reminding people of what it meant to be Irish as distinct from

WHILE IRELAND HOLDS THESE GRAVES

anything else. Some non-Irish even wanted to become Irish after listening to the "Returned," as they called the PRs. With global prosperity, parochial politics didn't seem rational, and Dev thought the fad wouldn't last.

Then, out of nowhere, Anna decided that they should recreate Maud Gonne, Irish nationalist and muse of W.B. Yeats. They had her autobiography and letters, but no literary fiction. As Dev expected, her PR came out physically beautiful but mentally thin, and even the Yeats PRs would have nothing to do with her. So, Dev boxed her with the other failures.

Anna took Maud's premature retirement hard, and Lingua seemed oddly disappointed as well. Thinking back on it, Dev wondered if he could have done something to change what followed. But he just went on to the next project.

Anna went back to work too, but she also had more frequent conversations with the Irish PRs already deployed. She asked Dev for countless details about being Irish, and suggested moving to Galway long term. Clearly, the PRs were getting to her as they had gotten to so many in Ireland. Ridiculous shite, and Dev said so, but seeing the effect of the PRs so close to home rattled him.

One day, the local United Nations and Intelligences office summoned Dev and Anna to a "program integration meeting." A UNI rep bristling with several generations of cyber-access nodes drew Anna into an extended discussion of the technical aspects of her work. Another rep, to all appearances unenhanced, sat with Dev over coffee.

"We've modeled your future," said the rep.

"Grand. Am I a very rich man?"

"We anticipate that one day soon, you'll want some insurance."

That was when Dev came up with Newly Dead Yeats.

Dev drove north with Joyce towards Sligo. Human-driven autos on killer narrow roads were a tradition and sport, so cars would continue to terrorize the new Ireland. Joyce hunted for music feeds and found "Irish rock," which amused, appalled and intrigued him all at once. "G-L-O-R-I-A, *in te domine,*" he quipped.

Dev didn't respond, too busy scanning the skies. He didn't stop at Sligo town, but went on to Drumcliffe, with its lonely churchyard just off the main road under bare Ben Bulben hill's head. Dev pulled into the small deserted parking lot. Again, with the deadline approaching, no more tourists for this attraction. One way or another, Dev's next stop was the grave.

"Wait with the car, Jim. Keep your ears open." Even at their best, the PR's authentically bad eyes weren't a match for Dev's chip-aided perceptions.

Dev paused at the gate. Too quiet—a steady stream of lyric poetry should greet any visitor. He switched his head chip to enhanced, and subjective time slowed as he walked towards Yeats' grave on the other side of the churchyard. The headstone had the same blue-gray shade as the local rock.

Finally, an otherworldly voice from the grave began to recite verse:

"Whether you die in your bed
Or my rifle knocks you dead,
A brief parting from those dear

Isn't the worst you have to fear."

Wait, thought Dev, *that's more a personal threat than the original.* From behind the headstone, a long metal tube swiveled towards him. Dev moved his head. A bullet cracked by his ear, the rifle boomed, the shot ricocheted off distant old stone. Definitely projectile—meant for biologicals. Dev hit the ground.

Newly Dead Yeats rose up from his grave. His nanoswarm body was, unlike Joyce's, translucent and spectral. Yeats' wild gray hair, beaked nose and black funeral clothes glowed with his rage. He pointed at the epitaph on his headstone. "'Horseman, pass by'— that means you, drunken lout."

"WB, it's me, Dev. I just want to talk."

Several more rounds passed over as Dev flattened himself. "I know who you are," said Yeats. "That's why I haven't killed you yet."

Dev scuttled back behind an old Celtic cross, hoping Dead Yeats wouldn't risk damaging it.

"Tell me what's the matter, Senator."

"You vainglorious bastard. Wasn't enough to have Young Yeats and Old Yeats; you insisted on Dead Yeats too?"

"You agreed to it!" That drew more fire, uncomfortably close. Probably the wrong thing to say.

"*They* agreed to it! Old and Young One could accept your conceit—they weren't buried here with the carcass. You said it would give me a cosmic perspective. You dull ass! It gave me endless tourists who haven't read a line of my work. When I cried for help, did you listen?"

"I'm sorry, WB. I had to do this because of Anna. That's who I'm here about."

"Was it Anna who stole my soul, bound it to this place, and prevented my reunion with the mysteries? No. She tried to free me."

So she had been here. But before Dev could ask more, Joyce walked through the gate, doubtless emboldened by the exclusive use of bullets. "Yeats, cut the mystical malarkey and occult shite . . ."

Dev's enhanced vision picked up the silent tracers of anti-nano weaponry before Joyce felt them against his shielded skin. So much for bullets only. Joyce crawled back behind the cross with Dev, and the Dead mocked him.

"What, you haven't fled to the continent again? Coward. Where were you when your country needed you?"

Joyce aimed his ashplant at Yeats and returned fire. Energy lightnings traced along the shielding around Yeats' grave, a gray mist drifted down. "Where was my country when I needed it?" he yelled. For a weak man, Joyce sure knew how to pick a fight.

"You can't keep that up for long on your own juice," noted Dev.

As if in response, Yeats bellowed, "I give you ten seconds to leave. One, two . . ."

"That's enough." From the shadow of the church doorway emerged a young man with full dark hair and spectacles. The Young Yeats. Dev did not relax one bit.

Dead Yeats sighed sepulchrally. "He has imprisoned me here forever."

"Are you going to risk crashing yourself again just to kill them?" Young Yeats turned towards the Celtic cross. "Tsk, tsk. Hiding behind the old god. It's a new age; come out and live it."

Dev stood up next to the cross, while Joyce kept him covered with the ashplant. If Dead Yeats had crashed, that confirmed that Anna had tried to free him. "Willie, where is she? Is Old Yeats still with her?"

Young Yeats smiled with his charming wistfulness and insufferable arrogance. "You realize, she's another Cathleen ni Houlihan, the Irish spirit incarnate, more so than even Maud was."

Dead Yeats snorted. "You mean she's crazier than Maud ever was."

"Silence, dead man." Young Yeats lacked Dead Yeats' perspective on how often Maud had frustrated him.

Dev pleaded, "Willie, for my sake, please."

"You're the least of my parents, Father. Anna is mother to us all, the maiden with the crone's eyes and the walk of a queen. The Golden Dawn predicted her and this Return."

Christ, the magical mystery tour. "Tell me where she is, and maybe we can try again to bring back Maud."

Next to him, Joyce flinched at this fib, but said nothing.

Young Yeats shook his head. "Anna already did."

She had tried again and again. Oh shite, not good. Dev came clean. "But there's not enough there for a full PR." No, more likely another mirror for Narcissus, another statue for Pygmalion.

"She looked pretty lively to me." Dead Yeats chuckled.

"Curse your eyes, cyber-carrion." Young Yeats

scowled. "Anna sought our help to enhance Maud. Maud is now a deep PR, though whether she's fully herself, I cannot say."

"Where have they gone?" asked Dev.

"I will not tell you."

"Was the Morrigan with them?" No one had mentioned the bird, which was damned quare.

In an instant, Young Yeats shed his Victorian manner and tone. "Right. This casual comedy is over." He turned and walked back to the church door. "Don't let the gate hit your arse on the way out."

"I'm sorry, sorry about both of you." But Young Yeats had shut the church door. "About all of you." Joyce walked back towards the car, ashplant over his shoulder.

Dev lingered. He wiped off the grass and gravelly dirt near his mouth with his sleeve and turned again to Dead Yeats. "Tell me where they've gone, and I'll free you." Letting Yeats loose was risky, but it was all Dev had to offer.

"But Anna couldn't release me," said Dead Yeats. "I crashed, and when I returned, she was gone."

All according to program. "I can," said Dev. "I will."

Yeats stared down at his translucent hands. Then, slowly, he said, "Gone off together, old self in tow, a Second Coming, not slouching towards Bethlehem, but Dublin."

"Dublin for Bloomsday. Grand." Dev's time was too short to search the city. "Any idea where?"

"They spoke of meeting the other Returned. That is all that I know."

"Okay." Dev had some ideas of where the PRs

might gather. A variable hole in Yeats' mind was Dev's key to his insurance policy, but which of the dozens of possibilities was now active? "Before I can release you, I need to run a check on your memory."

Yeats smiled thinly, eyes cold. "No need for that. I know what I've forgotten. I wanted to say something to Anna and Maud before they left—a poem, not mine, but an old lament that I once knew well. I remember everything about the lament, but I cannot remember any of the words."

"Is it Lady Gregory's translation, about losing everything for love?" Dead Yeats nodded. "Did you tell Anna about this?" If Anna knew, Dev would never make it to Dublin.

"No. Excess of love is bewildering them, and killing Ireland."

Yeats had guessed too much. "Don't worry . . ."

Like an impatient theater director, Yeats waved Dev's objection away. "Please, I know what I am, and what a blind spot like that might mean. You're here to tell us all those words. All I ask is that you say them with meaning."

"I will." Now to keep his other promise. "Do you recognize me as Dev Martin?"

"I do."

"*A terrible beauty is born.* Execute."

Instantly, Yeats became more substantial. "Thank you," he said. "Now, I think I shall take a long stroll up bare Ben Bulben's head. I have been under it long enough."

Not trusting his voice to stay steady, Dev said nothing and returned to the car. "Ineluctable modality

473

of the audible," said Joyce. Then he smiled. "No need to apologize, Dev. It's been brilliant, most of it at least. But once your quixotic quest is over, you will again try to restore Nora." Joyce tapped Dev's knee with his ashplant to emphasize his point.

Dev didn't know how to answer truthfully, so he changed the subject. "First things first. If UNI is still operating in Dublin, I think I can get you out."

"To Dublin town then," said Joyce.

"One thing before that."

They drove back into Sligo and stopped at a pub by the river, the Crazy Jane. At the bar rail, two men sat before their drinks, eyes like slates, jaws slack. "They look as if they've been thirsty too long," Joyce said, no doubt thinking of drunks past.

Dev shook his head, surprised at Joyce's error. "They're the Morrigan's regurgitated prey."

They were also Dev's predecessors. The two men had tried to hack the Referendum. When caught, they claimed UNI sanction, but UNI disavowed them. So they fell into the Morrigan's jurisdiction.

Unlike her mythic counterpart, the Morrigan's devastation was seldom physical. She had facility with the software of the human brain, and no amount of protection could keep her out for long. A terrible weapon, but only used to keep the fight fair.

As a warning to others, the Morrigan had left the hackers physically alive after wiping most of their minds. They would forever play the role of town drunks. Dev tried not to think about their blank eyes.

Over the last year, after Anna and Dev's summons to UNI, the changes in Ireland sped up. The Irish literary greats turned to writing aggressive speeches and manifestos. Nationalist PRs appeared and delivered the speeches. Up close, these thin and sometimes nutty PRs didn't socialize well, but they could sway huge crowds with the rousing words of their literary brethren.

The Irish revolution hinged on the paradoxes of the age. First, the global nano/info prosperity meant that even a single city could decide to go it alone. Fusion and solar power, a cornucopia machine and enough information flow to satisfy the watchful paranoids at UNI were all that were required. Second, with all information directly accessible through head chips, anyone could arbitrarily choose his or her language and culture. Irish could emerge from being a largely unspoken language of the schoolroom to become the living primary language of the nation.

So the revolution made its pitch: *let's leave UNI and this global homogenizer and again become really Irish, a particular people living in one place, speaking the Irish language, educated in the culture of the past and producing a new culture for the future.* All were invited, Irish ancestry or no. Global information flow would be narrowed. Entry to Ireland would be limited to those committing to remain for at least a year, which allowed for scholars, but not tourists.

This idea caught fire with the future-shocked citizens of the late twenty-first century. When UNI and the world corporations tried to reimpose global authority, a few AIs dissented and joined the demand for a referendum.

Anna asked Dev how he felt about the Referendum. Brilliantly thick until the end, he said, "It's bad for business. But we could use a vacation. Just us, without our artificial friends. Someplace warm would be nice."

Without saying goodbye, Anna left America and Dev. UNI accused her of helping the PRs design their nationalist siblings. Anna and Lingua spoke at monster-sized rallies in Ireland, announcing publically that they had joined the revolution. Lingua appeared as a raven, and called itself the Morrigan, the Irish goddess of sovereignty and slaughter.

Dev was gobsmacked. He had understood that he and Anna were a bit knackered and stressed with work, but he had assumed that their love continued despite the troubles. He took to drink, but slow self-destruction in modern times was surprisingly difficult and unromantic.

Officially to preserve the generation-long world peace, UNI allowed Ireland to hold the Referendum and, once it passed, let Ireland leave the global community. Then, seeing that Dev had an appropriate lack of interest in self-preservation, UNI sent him his papers and nudged him on his way.

That night, avoiding some heavy transformation along the other routes into the city, Dev and Joyce drove into Dublin from the north along Finglas Road. As they passed the iron gate of Glasnevin Cemetery, a dark corvine form shimmered overhead. Joyce shuddered. "The feckin' Morrigan. Death, death, death and more death."

Dev kept his head low, though that wouldn't do any good if the Morrigan chose to notice him. The AI that Dev had known as Lingua had been polite and pleasant to work with, but that had all been for show.

As Dev and Joyce approached the river Liffey, Dublin was slowly melting all around them, modern architectural travesties failing under the nanos' acidic assault. The people loved the dissolution, and the owners didn't squawk much, having negotiated a favorable restitution. Other nanos gave gray eighteenth-century houses a new shine. But the places Dev knew best all seemed to be gone.

Eventually they came to a roadblock barring their way to the UNI compound in the imposing old Custom House. Behind them, two plainclothes revolutionaries with paper notepads recorded their imminent passage from friendly ground. After fifteen minutes of apologetically holding assault rifles in his face, three UNI marines let Dev and his "AI-related object" drive through. Cut off from the frenetic transformation of the city, the UNI compound was under a polite state of siege. The city nanobots waited hungrily for their chance to restore the building to its full imperial glory.

Inside the Custom House, Dev and Joyce ran a further gauntlet of scanners, chaotic packing and courteous delay until they reached the office of the chief Dublin UNI representative, Thomas Kenny. Kenny appeared to be midway through a sleepless week. His reluctant handshake and his English accent by way of Trinity gave Dev an instant dislike for this south-of-the-Liffey poser.

Dev wasn't feeling very popular himself. Kenny's smile had less warmth than the most primitive PR's. "You have some nerve, Martin, showing up here. Returning to the scene of the crime?"

Joyce responded for Dev. "I wish to request asylum."

Kenny stared at Joyce as if he were a barking dog.

"If you don't mind, I would prefer to speak to Mr. Martin in private."

Joyce raised his stick, and Dev slapped it down. "It's okay, Jim. I'll get you out, I swear. Find someplace comfortable to connect and see if you can get us a room and some drink."

Joyce left without even a glance from Kenny. The rep poured Dev a whiskey, and then poured one for himself. "Charming. But at the next stage he could be a liability."

"Did you get him?"

"We've got him."

"And me?"

"And you."

Dev downed his drink in one. "Then all debts will be paid."

June 16, Bloomsday. Holo holy scenes from *Ulysses* played out about Dublin like ghosts in daylight. In the middle of O'Connell Street, humans dressed as Joyce characters enjoyed a breakfast of Denny's sausage and a pint of Guinness, some going whole hog with a bit of kidney. Sounds of celebration mixed with small casualty-free explosions, as holdouts struck the General Post Office and the Four Courts—the usual places.

Dev and Joyce walked across the river. They reached Davy Byrne's pub in time for lunch, which had to be the *Ulysses* gorgonzola sandwich with burgundy. The crowd couldn't tell if Joyce was a human actor, a recorded simulation or a full PR. Joyce found their confusion delightful.

Despite the celebration of their triumph, the major

PRs (besides Joyce) were nowhere to be seen on the streets. Rumor held that Anna, Old Yeats and Maud would make an appearance later, but in virtual.

"They're worried about something," said Dev.

Joyce tapped his ashplant. "The nationalists are great ones for security. Maybe the Morrigan is with them all."

"The cemetery." They had seen the Morrigan at Glasnevin. Sure, she could like a cemetery on its own merits, but so could Anna and Maud. Dev would search there next.

Crossing the river again, Dev noticed a hard-copy Referendum leaflet on the O'Connell Bridge. He bent over to grab and crumple it, then with an angry grunt threw it out over the rail at the wheeling gulls and into the Liffey. He stood silent and still, watching as the leaflet floated away. "Jim, are you sure you want to leave this again, maybe forever?"

"No, I'm not sure, but it's what I will do. What about you?"

"That depends on Anna."

They retrieved their car and drove back to Glasnevin Cemetery. At its gate, Joyce stood stately and rail straight. "Poor Paddies. As they are now, so once was I." He raised his hands over his head, as if giving a blessing or starting a race. "Finnegans! Wake!"

"Jaysis, Jim, not another joking word."

"What's eating you? Not the same thing that's eating them, I hope."

Dev fixed his eyes on the gate. He didn't want his friend to see what would happen inside. "I'm going in alone."

"I'm thinking not. I'm in this as much as you."

"Go back to the Custom House. Don't worry about what you heard last night; I already fixed it, and they'll get you out of the country." Dev patted the cemetery wall. "This is a private thing, between Anna and me."

"I'm thinking not. I'm thinking this involves all of us re-created bastards. And I don't trust that Kenny at all."

"Do you trust me, Jim?"

"Trust you? I like people, but I don't trust them."

"I don't plan on coming back out."

"If you don't come back, there'll be no escape or Nora, so I don't care if I survive."

"I do." Dev turned and offered his hand. "Farewell, Jim."

Joyce took Dev's hand in a superhuman grip. "I won't let you deny me, so you'll have to betray me." He closed his eyes and puckered up. "So where's the kiss, Judas?"

Dev couldn't help laughing. "Right, then. You'll get yours soon enough. Come on, help me over."

Joyce helped Dev over the gate, then squeezed his own more malleable body through the rails. Dev assessed the enormous forest of stone crosses. Pearse's old words mocked him. "They have left us our Fenian dead, and while Ireland holds these graves, Ireland unfree shall never be at peace." As if so many dead were some great benefit, when they made it bloody hard to find the right grave.

The one place at Glasnevin that stood out above the others was the tall round tower of Daniel O'Connell, the Liberator. While walking around the tower, Dev examined its wall in enhanced mode. He soon found the outline of a hidden door. "That was too easy."

"Must be trouble within," said Joyce. "We're bearding Circe in her den." He too couldn't resist giving Dev the bad news.

They entered the doorway and found granite stairs leading down and down, below the graves and the mortal world. Perhaps the Morrigan would be waiting for them in the dark. Nothing for it. They stepped down one, two, three steps . . .

And they were on the green hill of Tara, coronation site for the High Kings, open, sunlit, simulated. This beautiful holo-countryside held a crowd of sentients—AIs, PRs and biologicals. Around the Royal Seat and standing stone, four of the lesser AIs stood guard in their mythic manifestations—Maeve, Cúchulainn, Lugh and Finn MacCool. No sign of the Morrigan though, which didn't make Dev any happier.

On her Celtic Art Nouveau throne sat Queen Anna. Next to her, looking like her Irish sister, Maud sat as consort in her fully realized glory. Before them stood Old Yeats. The literal feckers had transformed him à la "Sailing to Byzantium" into a golden robot that sang poetic songs and bowed too much. He was deader than childish Dead Yeats, stiffer than stiff Young Yeats and sadder than the children of Lir. But Dev wasn't here to save Old Yeats.

Anna raised her hand towards Dev. "Welcome to the otherworld, Oisín."

"Don't let him speak!" Joyce had raised his ashplant and pointed it at Dev. "He spoke alone with Dead Yeats. I couldn't hear everything, but whatever he has to say is poison."

Anna held her hand up, and energy shimmered around Dev. Anna's words echoed at him from all sides. "Thank you, Jim, but as you can see, we have not forgotten the old times, when a bard could kill with his words. We modeled the possibilities and decided to contain Dev's sounds on a shielded delay until we root out what he's done. But we're glad you changed your mind and decided to work with us, Jim."

Jim nodded back at her, and Dev wanted to kill him. He hadn't realized that he still had things to lose, until this betrayal. But even if UNI's mission was going to fail, he'd say his personal words first, before he went down.

"Hiya, Anna."

"Dev. What took you so long?"

"I never took this blather seriously, until it happened."

"You've brought our firstborn."

"*Your* firstborn. I disown him." Joyce flinched at this, but said nothing.

"What do you want?" asked Anna.

"An impossible thing, macushla: I want you to come back with me. Your work is done; you can leave. We can be as Irish as you like somewhere else."

"Dev, this isn't romantic fiction."

"But that's what Ireland is. It's why you were able to bring back the nationalists with anything like verisimilitude."

"I've done more than that." She looked at Maud like there was a secret joke between them.

Dev shook his head hopelessly. "Grand. I understand completely. Oldest story in the world, falling in love with your creation."

"And you felt nothing for your precious pal Joyce?"

Right. Though he couldn't use the words he had learned from Yeats, Dev had some specific words for Joyce that they might not filter. *Usurper. Execute.* The words were quick and dirty; Joyce wouldn't know what hit him.

As if reading Dev's face, Joyce lowered his ashplant and tapped it against the ground. "If you've got something to say to me, say it."

He knows, but he's leaving himself open. Maybe he's still on my side. Maybe he'll let me pinch that stick of his. Dev dove for Joyce's ashplant.

Perhaps Joyce would have let Dev snatch it, but the energy field was having none of it, and it slid through his grip. Anna smiled. "Don't bother with that thing. I'm the only one here you could hurt, and neither of you would hurt me."

"I know," said Dev. He wiped his face with his sleeve and looked around at the assembly. "If you must stay, let me stay here with you, but away from all this software." The insult fell beneath the gathering's notice. *I must be that bloody pathetic.*

"Dev, it's too late for that. I belong to the nation."

"And I don't anymore." He had their attention, and with the feeds from here, he probably had the attention of all the PRs in Ireland. But he couldn't use it. "I just want to say goodbye."

"Goodbye," said Anna.

The room went silent. *If you've got something to say, Joyce, say it.*

Joyce cleared his throat. "Mother, I want my reward. Can you restore Nora to me? Now?"

"I don't know." Anna turned to Maud. "What do you say, macushla?"

Maud stood to her full six-foot height, narrowed her hazel eyes at Joyce and considered. Then she smiled like the Irish Mona Lisa. "In the old days, he could sing. Have him sing a traditional song of Ireland for us, and if it pleases, we'll give him back his beloved."

Joyce looked over at Dev, looked at everyone in the room, looked up at the holo-sky. "If you lend me your attention, I shall endeavor to sing to you of a heart bowed down." Then, slowly in his fine tenor, he sang "Young Donald."

Dev used biofeedback to keep his breathing and heart rate steady. Would they let Joyce finish, without delay?

After an eternity of verses and with his eyes full of tears, Joyce came to the final, shattering lines:

"You have taken the east from me,

You have taken the west from me,

You have taken what is before me and what is behind me;

You have taken the moon,

You have taken the sun from me,

And my fear is great you have taken Ireland *from me."*

Old Yeats smiled, for these were the words of loss that Dead Yeats had forgotten. Dev closed his eyes as if that would hide his thoughts. *Does he know how to say the final word?*

In a perfect simulation of Dev's voice, Joyce said, "Execute."

With that command, Joyce disappeared; his ashplant

clunked to the ground. He did not go alone. All the other PRs in sight vanished; Dev hoped the same held true everywhere in Ireland. The full PRs dissolved into puddles of nanogoop, while the holos faded to the flickering light of a filmless projector. The Old Yeats robot ceased its continual obeisances with a sigh. All gone, gone utterly, as if they were inhabitants of the faerie realm.

Maud was going slower; Dev could actually see her disintegrate. But as she burned away, another shape formed from her ashes. Like a phoenix from the flame, the Morrigan arose. So that was how Anna filled Maud out. The Morrigan stretched her wings, and cawed at Dev contemptuously. The other AIs stood ready for her order. Only then was Dev certain that he would never leave this place alive.

Dev spoke quickly, while Anna was still in shock. "I've a message from UNI. You're free to do this thing. Evolution is on the fringes and borders, and you will be a fringe and border to this world until that role can be assumed by other worlds. But not with the PRs. We leave you with the AIs for protection. Start fresh, without such an unbearable weight of dead, without such tempting toys."

Anna strode up to him and smacked him across the face. "Murderer." Overhead, a storm gathered with time-lapse abruptness. "Was there no other Troy for you to burn? You sabotaged my work, from the beginning."

"Our work." Dev's voice cracked with fear of the pain to come. "I'm a Joycean, which means I love people, but I don't trust them."

FIONA MENG

Before Anna could say she was done with him, and before the Morrigan could torture him for a thousand subjective years, Dev signaled his head chip. *Goodbye, Anna.*

In a flash, his chip fried his brain.

The Morrigan flew to the Custom House. To avoid embarrassing devastation, she did not allow her approach to be detected, save by the UNI rep. She dropped a small head chip on Mr. Kenny's balcony, then flew high above the Custom House and waited, and watched.

Mr. Kenny and his skeleton staff left the Custom House in a convoy of armored vehicles. Portal and air transport had closed, so the staff waited for the last ferry out of Dublin, an old vessel with an open deck. From high above, the Morrigan saw the tide of arriving thousands flow against the departing UNI staff. Hearing the Referendum's promise, they came by sea from other places that were no longer nations—Nigeria and Laos, Japan and Brazil, Australia and America. Like herself and her beloved Anna, they too could be Irish.

The UNI staff boarded the ferry. As the already lumbering ship approached the Cúchulainn Barrier zone, it slowed to drifting. The Morrigan circled, curious. They would want to study the barrier, of course, and this would be their best opportunity.

Kenny brought out the head chip the Morrigan had given him and two shiny metallic cubes. He placed the cubes on adjoining deck chairs, and placed the head chip next to one of the cubes. With a touch of his finger, he activated each cube, then strode away as if anxious to avoid words.

An image of Dev sprang from the cube near the head chip, and from the other cube emerged an image of Joyce. Energy and memory constrained them to holo mode; for now, they would remain two ghosts, talking.

Joyce looked about with theatrical emphasis. "You didn't get the girl?"

Dev studied his own translucent hands. "No, looks like she got me." His mission had succeeded, and he had failed. Anna was forever lost to him. "But I got you out at least."

"But what about you? Forgive me, but you don't seem to be all here."

Dev put his hand to his chest. "Oh, this? Second generation duplicate. I sent an organic copy to Ireland, and they scanned the copy's mind when they captured your data at UNI Dublin. Coming here was always something of a suicide mission. Assuming my original is still alive, I'll reintegrate, sorrows and all."

"No prosecution or protest about your demise?"

Dev gazed up at the black bird following, listening. "No harm, no foul. That's the official UNI line." His holo image gingerly touched his head chip, then shimmered, shivered.

"Some wee harm in that thing?"

"Just my last words and deeds after the UNI scan, along with synthetic memories of a millennium of torture. It's the Morrigan's warning to her former associates."

The Morrigan had known that the Dev who had

come to Ireland was a copy, as identical as it might have been. If one dared ask, she would have explained that it was too identical, quantum mechanically speaking. But she had not warned Anna.

"You completely fooled them, and me," said Dev.

Joyce raised his eyebrows. "You might have known. I was Ulysses and his Trojan horse in one."

"Thank you for saying the words," said Dev. "Why did you do it?"

"I didn't fight for Ireland before, so I fought this time. Those hard men and women would repeat a history that's the very opposite of real life, the very opposite of love. *Non serviam.* But it was a difficult thing, and I couldn't have done it if I thought any sentient beings would really be destroyed forever." Joyce turned to the ferry's bow. "Are they gone forever?"

"If I thought so," said Dev, "I couldn't have done it either."

The Morrigan cawed. Nothing was truly gone in this information-drenched world. Over time, Anna might figure out a way to bring back the PRs without attracting UNI's notice, but the Morrigan would not help her, and the AI would henceforth choose her own form rather than inhabit any of Anna's favorites.

"It's a small consolation." Joyce sighed without breath. "No Nora for me."

"Not for some time."

"Then we both lost the girl."

Dev nodded. "And her name is Eire." A barrier now stood between him and Ireland that he couldn't cross again. "By the bye, when you sang, how did you know to change 'God' to 'Ireland'?" As an extra layer of code, when Newly Dead Yeats generated a shutdown key, the user needed to change the last proper noun to 'Ireland.'

"I don't know," said Joyce. "I only remember up to our passage through the roadblock at the Custom House. I knew what words you'd need from overhearing you and Yeats' carcass, but I didn't know to say 'Ireland.'"

Maybe a not-so-little bird told him below his conscious programming. The Morrigan had been playing a double game. She needed to be an omnipotent protector, but the UNI models were right: too many Irish dead. But her unsettling projections were also right, and the world needed this fringe more than UNI knew.

Joyce considered a moment. "At least I'll have a friend in this second exile. I have the feed from Glasnevin, minus my poisoned poetry. What you said—maybe we need a fresh start. Gibraltar?"

"Why not? There, the sun may shine for us, instead of through us."

Joyce soundlessly slapped his friend on the back. "Young father, young artificer, stand me now and ever in good stead."

The Morrigan watched as the Liffey's ever-flowing waters carried the two friends past the crumpled Referendum leaflet, still afloat, and washed them out from her adopted home, out beyond the Cúchulainn Barrier, out to the info-permeated sea.

The Poly Islands

written by

Gerald Warfield

illustrated by

JAY RICHARD

ABOUT THE AUTHOR

Gerald Warfield was born in Fort Worth, Texas. He attended TCU, UNT and Princeton University, taking degrees in music composition. He taught music briefly at Princeton and the University of Illinois, and his compositions enjoyed modest success including performances by the Dallas Symphony Orchestra. His first taste of writing was in college where he reviewed music concerts for the Denton Record Chronicle. *He decided at that time that writing was not for him; it was too much work. His first nonteaching job was associate director of the Index of New Musical Notation, a research project at the New York Public Library, sponsored by the Ford and Rockefeller Foundations.*

In midlife, he went over to the dark side and began writing music textbooks and how-to books on finance and investing. This gave him the mistaken impression that he could write fiction. He lived in New York City for thirty years and moved to rural Texas in 2000, where he has served as chairman of the library board and president of the Mineral Wells Heritage Association.

Life began in 2010 when he was accepted by and survived the Odyssey Writers' Workshop, with Jeanne Cavelos as director. That same year, his short story, "The Origin of Third Person in Early Paleolithic Epic Poetry," won first prize in Grammar Girl's short story contest. His story, "The Poly Islands," constitutes his first professional sale in fiction.

ABOUT THE ILLUSTRATOR

Jay Richard is a graphic designer and freelance illustrator from the south coast of Massachusetts. He graduated from the University of Massachusetts Dartmouth with a BFA in illustration. He has done numerous designs for private clients including UMass Dartmouth's School of Law.

His artwork usually begins with a pencil, pen and marker base drawing with later digital manipulation in Photoshop or PaintShop. He also works in other traditional media including acrylic paints and watercolors. Besides illustrations, he sculpts horror and fantasy props for games such as Call of Cthulhu and Hunter: The Vigil.

Jay currently lives in Fairhaven, Massachusetts, with his wife Lisa and daughter Bria.

The Poly Islands

Liyang's hand hovered in the green glow above the instrument panel. Desperately, she wanted to activate the boat's running lights, but she did not dare touch the switch. She considered pulling back the throttle but pulled back her hand instead. Blind flight across the black swells was perilous, yet somewhere behind her, in the darkness, the thugs of the Old Buddha tong searched for her. If they caught her, she would not live long enough to return to Hong Kong Harbor. No. She would run in the dark at full throttle and risk that the debris was not sufficient to flip the boat or puncture the hull.

The plastic at the edges of the Patch was supposed to be small, free-floating particles, broken down from years of drifting in the Pacific. She had felt the increased drag on the boat as she entered the slurry of debris earlier that night. The bigger stuff, where she hoped to hide, was in the center, sometimes piled high like icebergs; at least that's what she'd been told. She imagined navigating amongst great mounds of plastic, perhaps lodging her boat beneath an overhang that would screen her from the air.

A crash at the prow caused the boat to lurch to

port. The motor screamed as its blades lifted from the water. She whipped the wheel, overcompensating, but managed to straighten the boat as it rocked once before leveling back. A wave of cold water and plastic particles washed over her feet, chilling them. She'd taken on water that time.

The thought of capsizing, of falling into the ocean at night, in black water filled with garbage, made her shrivel inside. Three days ago, hiding in a boat in the middle of the Pacific Patch seemed like a good plan. She was too tired, now, to tell whether the idea even made sense. Half the noise in her head was the buzz of sleep deprivation.

Within half an hour the overcast sky lightened enough for her to see the ocean's surface. As much as she had prepared for it, she was still shocked: the boat scudded across an endless mass of floating refuse. She had imagined bottles and objects of all kinds, and yet here there was nothing so complete. It was a thick stew of particles, washed-out, pale pieces of plastic, none bright, all faded together into a dull gray-white. The huge swells of the ocean rose and fell, but instead of waves of water they looked to her more like the undulations of an earthquake.

Her implant buzzed, shattering her thoughts. Who could reach her out here? With great reluctance, she punched the responder on her neck and heard: "Surface boat, you look like a WR300. Can you hear me?"

In English, and he knew the model of her boat. "Who is this?"

"You are about to be intercepted. Can you hear me? You are about to be intercepted."

"Who are you? I don't see any pursuit on my navs."

"The junk is blocking your navs. I can see their blip."

"Who are you?"

"Head for the cliffs. It's your only chance."

"What in the hell are you talking about?"

"Look west of you."

She looked through the salt-stained windshield. It was light enough to see that what she had taken for a cloudbank on the horizon was actually a pale cliff, not that far away. Who ever thought garbage could pile so high?

"Okay, I see the cliff. But you've blown my cover."

"They probably aren't monitoring phone frequencies. They don't have to. You've got a Wave Jack on your boat."

"How do you know?"

"I've got it on my screen." The implant was silent for a moment. "I used to install them."

Her heart raced. The boat had radar warp, but if there was a bug on board . . .

"Change your course. Head for the cliffs. Run your boat directly under the highest point. You hear? The highest point."

Frantically, she scanned the horizon. "I still don't see any interception."

"They're closing fast." He sounded exasperated.

"How do I know you're not setting me up?"

"On your present course, you'll find out in about three minutes."

The line went dead. She keyed the reset, but nothing.

Damn. She wasn't changing course for some

anonymous Good Samaritan. She had seen that game too many times. Still, why would he have told her about the bug? With an anxious glance at the debris through which she plowed, some of it now sizable, she set the boat on autopilot and dashed below, frantically opening cabinets and pulling out drawers. Her initial search had been thorough, but if the bug had been planted afterward, the dealer could have made a tidy sum selling the information to the Old Buddha tong.

The boat crashed, and the impact threw her to the floor. She felt the prow lift for a breathless moment, the engine scream and then the impact as the boat fell back into the water. On the floor of the cabin, on all fours, she thought she was going to be sick.

She scrambled back to the wheel. Lumps and piles of multicolored junk stretched in front of the boat. She also saw on her navs a green dot on an intercept course.

In cold despair, she turned the boat toward the cliffs. Okay, okay, she thought to her anonymous caller. You were right.

Why did she always have trouble trusting the good guys? If she had turned earlier, she might have made it. If that were a tong boat in pursuit, then they were equipped with shallow water torpedoes, and doubtless she was already in range. Even if she rammed the boat under the wall of garbage, they could locate her with the bug.

And what could her mysterious voice do about it? Where was his boat? She looked back at the navs screen. Fat chance of help.

The impacts on the hull were constant now. The

boat was taking a beating. A long trash reef floated directly ahead, like a giant caterpillar held together with fish netting. She'd have to go around.

A clap in the distance, and water spouted ahead. Artillery shells. They were trying to head her off.

She lost precious seconds skirting the caterpillar. Then the far end of the mass took a direct hit. Water and Styrofoam rained down on her boat.

"Aim north a few degrees. You'll see a cave."

She had left the line open. "They'll torpedo me broadside!"

"Not in that junk, they won't."

Weaving left and right she dodged the biggest pieces which lay strewn across the water like boulders on a valley floor. Another crack and an impact crater blossomed in the cliff ahead of her. She looked up. So they want me alive, she thought.

The boat lurched, and she barely kept her grip on the wheel. The solid wall loomed perilously close. Drawing herself up, she prepared to collide head-on when she spotted the cavern, more like a dark crevice that rose from the water in the side of the speckled cliff.

Without time to think, she corrected her course and held her breath that they would not shell the boat in the last moments it was exposed. Perhaps they thought she was trapped.

The cavern engulfed her. Half blind in the abrupt shadow, she peered ahead for passage through the mottled walls. Seeing none, she killed the motor and skidded across the calm surface. It was a dead end. The boat was going too fast. In her last moments, she searched for a sign of her mysterious friend among the crags and ledges of the chamber, but he wasn't there. She would be taken, after all, if the collision didn't kill her first.

She thought to reverse the motor, but there was no time. Gripping the wheel, she grimaced, and the boat smacked into the far wall. The sound was like a million plastic cups breaking at once. The steering wheel shattered in her hands and she flew forward against the shaft. Her head hit the instrument panel.

Silence replaced the roar of the motor. For a moment, she thought the shaft of the wheel had penetrated her chest, but it had gone between her right side and her arm. Her jacket was torn, and her side was hurt; how much, she couldn't tell.

Pushing herself back from the shaft, she blinked away the spots and saw on a sloping ledge near the boat a figure in what looked like a gray diving suit. He gestured with both hands, urgently. Unable to think clearly, she grabbed her backpack and windbreaker and stumbled to the side of the boat. She put her hand on the gunwale and tried to jump, though it seemed that she merely flung herself overboard, aiming for what looked like a solid surface.

Her feet went through the plastic. For a moment she felt as if she had jumped onto a cloud. Crying out, she threw her arms wide, grasping for anything, and felt the frigid water on her feet and legs. It was her arms that kept her from slipping down all the way into the sea.

A rope fell across her. Grateful for anything solid, she grabbed it, half climbed and was half pulled toward the ledge on which the figure stood.

The strange man reached down for her. He wore a skin of mottled gray plastic, a kind of camouflage that rendered him almost invisible except for his brown beard and goggles. A flat black case hung about his neck. Definitely weird, but what choice did she have? She gave him her hand, and he pulled her the rest of the way onto the ledge. The sensation was like being pulled up through a bakery crust.

"You're hurt," he said in English.

She looked down and saw the rent in her jacket under her right arm where she was bleeding and hoped she hadn't broken a rib. "I'm okay."

"Keep your arm pressed against it. We've got to move."

She looked back. "My windbreaker." The blue jacket lay sprawled on the plastic, half of it fallen in the hole where she had leaped from the boat.

"They'll think you drowned," the man said, rapidly smoothing with his gloved hands the gouges in the plastic she had made getting onto the ledge.

The roar of a motor sounded outside the opening.

"Quick. Keep hold of the rope in case you fall." He turned and sprinted with a kind of hopping motion up a path through a narrow crevice. His shoes were big platter-like things, resembling pictures she had seen of snowshoes.

Liyang followed, gripping the rope with one hand and the backpack with the other. The ground wobbled, the result of her sea legs, and she threw her arms about, but she did not fall.

He shouted down, "Try not to catch yourself with your hands or touch the walls."

Behind them, through the tunnel, she heard the rumble of a powerful motor and voices shouting in Chinese, but she could not make out what they were saying.

She managed one foot in front of the next through mushy debris that often broke at her touch. The passageway meandered. They circumvented a smooth gray boulder, jumped a fissure and crawled beneath the drape of a fishing net. At last, a light appeared above them.

The man held up one hand and they stopped just as an explosion rocked them from underneath. Air and debris shot up the tunnel. Liyang steadied herself against the wall, despite the warning, and hoped the tunnel would not collapse.

"Too bad," her companion said. "We could have used that boat."

"Why would they blow it up?" In her long, desperate race to the Patch, she had bonded with the small cabin cruiser and now felt an odd sense of bereavement.

"They know there are people out here. They don't want to leave us anything."

"It could have been towed, or . . ."

He shook his head and motioned her forward.

They emerged onto a bizarre snowscape made up of a jillion faded colors. Solid outcroppings thrust into the sky like miniature mountains while cracks and holes perforated the surfaces below. A few ragged sea birds perched atop some of the mounds. She had seen pictures of arctic wastes. That was what the scene before her resembled except for the colors, and, of course, it wasn't cold.

Sweating from the climb and weak in the knees, she sat heavily, catching her breath. The ground was more solid than she expected.

The man squatted in front of her. "Adam," he said, proffering a gloved hand and grinning as if the whole incident had been contrived for her amusement.

"Liyang," she answered, gasping for breath and taking the hand. "I had no idea."

"No one does. Welcome to the Poly Islands."

"Poly Islands?"

He spread his arms as if encompassing the whole of the island. "Polyethylene, polyvinyl, polypropylene, polystyrene, polycarbonate—need I go on?"

"It's amazing. What holds it together?"

"Actually, it's *not* held together very well, but in answer to your question, it's bound by government bungling."

Liyang gave him a blank look.

"Do you remember the short-lived nation of California, the one that was going to address all the ecological problems of the planet? Among their more modest projects was cleaning up the Pacific Ocean. They dropped hundreds of small buoys into the Patch, each one transmitting a type of velox wave that was supposed to cause the polycarbonates to release their lighter gasses and sink. What happened, instead, was that in this environment the molecules became excited and polymerized further, binding them closer to one another. By the time they realized their mistake, they had been conquered by the Alaskan Coalition, which wasn't about to waste a cent on the environment. And so the little buoys were left in the ocean, beeping away. The nation of California may be no longer, but these islands live on, monuments to their good faith and incompetency."

"You sound like a professor."

He inclined his head and waved an arm in a mock bow. "Guilty as charged. And this is my new nav-com by which I located your boat," he said, tapping the flat case that hung by a strap from his shoulders. "It's been rigged to run on static electricity which, I might add, we have here in abundance."

"But you look like a lunatic."

He threw back his head and laughed. It was a natural laugh that, for all his posturing, seemed genuine and uncomplicated. She tried to make out his face, beyond the beard and goggles, and wondered if he could be trusted.

"You're a bit banged up, but your side doesn't seem to be bleeding anymore."

"No. It's not bad."

"That's a pretty good bruise on your forehead."

She felt her right temple. "I've had worse." And then she felt the hard spot on her neck. "My implant seems to be okay."

"Not on the plastic. It's useless here."

She sighed. "Other than that, I'm okay."

"Very well. I'm on my way somewhere. You'll have to come with me."

"Have to?"

"Ah, do not leap to conclusions, my dear. I assure you, it is for your own good. You cannot survive in the wild Polys by yourself."

"Where are you going? A research station?"

"You could call it that," he said with a subdued

grin. "But I'm late, now, so we'll have to hurry. Just step where I step. Sorry, I don't have an extra pair of snows. And don't touch the plastics unless you have to. You don't have a P-suit on, so you can cut yourself. For instance, don't sit down like that. Those trousers won't last the day."

She got to her feet. He extended his hand in an offer to carry her backpack, and she reflexively clutched it to herself.

"Sorry," she said, embarrassed by her obvious gesture. "It's all I have left."

He eyed the pack. "Your survival, now, will depend on others. You'll have to give them something."

Her grip tightened on the strap.

He spread his hands. "I'm just telling you so you won't be caught by surprise. It would have been better if we had saved your boat. Still, Crab will expect presents."

"Crab?"

"Come on."

Following in Adam's footsteps, she quickly adjusted to walking on the jumbled surface. Only once did her foot punch through, cutting the fabric of her trousers, but not her leg. They soon came to a compacted trail where the "ground" was smoother, if not flat. Adam took off the snowshoes and strapped them on his back. The surface here had the feel of something hollow. It was, she imagined, like walking on ice.

As the traveling eased, she considered the loss of her boat. It was a blow, yet she had successfully evaded capture. Better still, they thought she had drowned, and there would be no further pursuit. *And*

GERALD WARFIELD

she still had the chips. Having come ashore on what seemed like another planet, if she could just survive long enough to get those chips to a black market, her plan still seemed feasible.

The path wound through debris, skirting the highest outcroppings. Her guide seemed to be heading toward a smokestack-looking spire, plastic she assumed, that leaned at about forty-five degrees. Sure enough, a makeshift stairway, cut into the plastic, opened at its base.

"We call these 'hatch caves.'" He started down the irregular, hard-packed steps. "Again, don't touch the walls unless you have to. There are sharp particles embedded in the plastic."

Sunlight sparkled through the plastic fragments and gave her the feeling of descending into a glacier. Yet the passageway soon narrowed, giving her a rush of claustrophobia. She hurried down the last few steps. At the bottom, the stairs opened into a big oval chamber with a flat wooden floor, and she gratefully stepped onto its smooth surface. They had, apparently, descended onto the deck of a boat.

Walls of debris hid the edges of the deck, even the ship's railing. They crossed the wooden floor to a doorway, a metal oval beyond which a second pair of stairs led down into the ship's interior. Adam wiped his feet on a large mat just inside the door, and Liyang did likewise. As they descended, she heard a voice below in English.

At the bottom of the stairs another oval doorway opened into a long room lighted by electricity. Men and women sat on tatami mats in rows on each side of a center aisle facing one another. She stepped

504

inside, and the odor of unwashed bodies struck her with physical force. Everyone was naked, or near naked, wearing what appeared to be only underwear. Their clothes, suits like Adam wore, were folded next to them. They sat in the "perfect" posture, some in a full lotus.

In front of each person, or to one side, sat a plate with knife and fork and an empty wine glass. Some of the plates were still half full. They had just dined on fish—raw fish.

The scene confused her. While it had the look of an ashram meeting, the wine, even the raw fish, were not traditional Hindi.

"Om, Crab," said Adam, placing the palms of his hands together and bowing to a wizened old man sitting at the far end of the room. His skin was a rich brown, but at first, Liyang couldn't tell his ethnicity, perhaps Southeast Asian, perhaps Indian. His loincloth and turban definitely said Indian.

"Ohm shanti," he responded. "You have a companion, Adam."

"Yes, Crab. This is Liyang. She was pursued all the way to the cliffs. They got her boat."

A general groan at this news. She noticed that everyone was thin and pale.

"They did not see you?"

"No, but there was no time to salvage. My regrets."

"Take your place and introduce your guest," said the old man with a wave. He spoke in a detached manner, as if her presence was unimportant, but, as she walked with Adam down the middle aisle, she felt the intense stares of the others.

One of the Chinese, a young man with a smooth

round face and an unruly shock of straight black hair, smiled and shifted his position. The gesture was subtle, but Liyang read in it an invitation. She was suddenly aware that all the Chinese sat on one side of the room, and the rest, various ethnic groups, sat on the other. Torn for a moment, unsure whether to join the Chinese or follow Adam to the other side, she realized that her future in the group would be determined by her decision. After a pause, she placed her hands together and bowed, and followed Adam.

A plate of sliced raw fish sat at his place, a wedge of lime and a glass of white wine, about a third full. A few condiments that she didn't recognize also rested on the plate. But instead of sitting down, Adam peeled off his plastic suit. Liyang looked at him and then at the others.

General laughter. "Don't worry, dearie," said a woman in Chinese. "You don't have on a P-suit. You'll want to strip naked after a day in one of those." Liyang had not noticed her before; she was the only fat person in the room.

Adam was down to baggy underwear when he sat. His body was better proportioned than she thought, though she tried to show no interest.

"She's just off a boat," said Adam, "and hasn't a clue what we're about."

Crab stroked a stringy goatee. He was quite thin, though not emaciated, and wore a white diaper-looking loincloth. His eyes remained half lidded as if falling asleep. "What has she brought us?" he asked, his gaze falling on the backpack.

"Ah, I haven't had a chance to explain that to her." Liyang's pulse quickened. Her gun, a necessary accoutrement of life in the tong, was in the bottom of her backpack and could not be quickly reached. How could she have walked into this situation unprepared? Had she grown up in the Old Buddha tong for nothing? Assessing the strengths of the individuals, particularly the Chinese, she remembered Adam's warning. She would need help, perhaps the help of these very individuals, in order to survive.

"They blew up my boat. All I have is what's in my pack."

"You may present it to us." No mistaking the old man's command. He gestured to the spot in front of him, yet he did so with an indifference that quieted her alarm.

"Do you have any food?" asked the fat woman, this time in English.

"I'm sorry. Nothing but some energy bars."

It seemed to her that everyone in the room leaned forward.

"We accept your energy bars and any other edibles you have." He waved again to the spot on the floor in front of him.

"You are welcome to them, Crab, and I have some mints, too." Reluctantly, she placed her pack on the floor where he indicated. Then she knelt on the other side of the pack, not wanting to get too far away from the chips.

Crab reached forward and dragged the bag into his lap where he released the catch and lifted the flap. One at a time, he removed the energy bars and lined them up in front of him.

"Oh, God, I hope they've got chocolate on them," said a woman's voice from farther down the room.

507

"Draw," said one of the men.

"Divide," cried several others in a sudden cacophony of English and Chinese.

"I will decide," said Crab in a louder voice than before, bringing out two little plastic boxes of mints and placing those next to himself.

Next, he withdrew a notebook, which he placed on the floor by Liyang. Then he withdrew a battery pack. "One of our members no longer has batteries."

"Thank you," said a middle-aged woman sitting to Liyang's right.

Crab continued to bring out the items of her pack, placing them next to himself or indicating to whom they would go, or placing them next to Liyang. Finally, only two items remained in the bottom of the bag: her box of computer chips and her revolver.

He lifted out the long box and held it in the air for a moment. His half-lidded eyes flickered as if in recognition.

"Honorable Crab," she said, deferentially. "Those are my computer chips. They are the only way I have to start a new life."

Crab flipped the latch and raised the lid so that he looked down on the individual chips, each one in its own transparent case. "What kind are they?"

"Genji480s."

Crab only stared at them.

"They could bring high price in Hong Kong or Okinawa City," said a voice behind her in English. Liyang recognized the fat Chinese woman who had spoken before.

"Valuables are kept in my safe," Crab said, placing the box next to himself. "They can be a source of conflict."

Liyang felt a rush of heat to her face. Her hands twitched. He had taken her chips—or had he? Her eyes flashed at Adam. His brow was wrinkled, but otherwise she couldn't read him. Did Crab know what the chips were? They had appeared on the Chinese market not two months ago. Perhaps he was faking.

He lifted the bag and placed it next to her. He had seen the gun at the bottom. She knew he had seen it, and yet he did not acknowledge it. That gave her hope that he was not confiscating the chips.

"Thank you, honorable Crab," she said, bowing her head. She had studied yoga in a college class, but could not remember the proper phrase of obsequence.

She put the few items he had returned to her back in the pack. As she stood, a voice said in Chinese, "Your place is on this side." She turned, but could not tell who had spoken. It was a man's voice in the Shanghai Mandarin dialect. The words had been stated as fact, not as command, and no one moved to make room for her. Crab said nothing; she couldn't even be sure that he heard, or that he understood Chinese. Acutely aware that all eyes were on her, she bowed in the traditional manner, her mind in turmoil, and then returned to the place on Adam's mat.

When she sat, Adam smiled, his eyes sparkling, as if he were proud of her. It made her angry. Her whole future had just been plopped into the lap of an old man who probably didn't know what computer chips were. Yet, she was also pleased, a bit, with his regard for her.

The Chinese across from her stared expressionlessly. The faces of the others, on her side of the room, she could not see. When she glanced back at Crab, he proceeded as if nothing had happened, placing the bars, their wrappers off, on a wooden slab. He brought out a knife.

"This will seem strange to you, Liyang," he said without looking at her. "We have plenty to eat; it's just that we do not have a great deal of variety. Certain highly refined food products, for instance, are extremely rare and highly prized.

"Drawing for them has produced too much conflict, and so my ruling is that we divide. Each bar will be divided into six pieces. There are nineteen of us, but Liyang will not get a piece. The mints will be distributed at our next meeting."

At that, he cut the energy bars, carefully, not touching them with his hands. He leaned over them, his nostrils expanding, although how he could smell them over the odor of his body Liyang did not know.

"You may now approach. Come in your designated turn."

Liyang watched in rapt fascination as the members of the group approached the old man, knelt to the floor, bowed their heads and held out a hand. Crab lifted each piece with the knife and deposited it into the waiting palm. He mumbled as he did it, although Liyang could not hear what he said. The ritual had the look of a Christian communion, a few of which she had seen before.

None ate their piece until they returned to their mats. There they nibbled, took small bites and closed their eyes. A woman wept. When Adam returned with his piece, he offered to share, but Liyang shook her head. Adam chuckled. "Take it. In a few days you'll wish you had."

"Honorable Crab," said the Chinese woman again. Crab nodded to acknowledge her.

"In another week, rotation of the gyre will be putting us out of range of Hong Kong. Perhaps one of our poor boats could be repaired enough to make one more run for . . . serious supplies."

"What kind of supplies do you need?" The tone of Crab's voice gave no indication of interest.

"We must think of the future. One day, gyre will bring us directly across from Kamwome Island. It could be easily taken, even with few boats. Most of the Marshall Islands have been abandoned since the Kiekie incident. People live in palm huts. They will be easily defeated. I have been there. It is my vision that our days of living on floating garbage will end."

There were murmurs of agreement from the Chinese. Those on the opposite side sat silently. Crab appeared to be asleep. Liyang could not help but notice that the woman had said "one more" run to Hong Kong. Perhaps they weren't as isolated as Adam said.

"Meantime," Madam Woo said, "the Genji chips would give us enough yuan to buy necessary guns and ammunition, and many comfortable things. To sell them would be a benefit to all."

Liyang straightened her back and started to respond, but Adam placed a hand on her arm.

"I know that some have doubts." The woman raised a hand as if reprimanding the non-Chinese who faced her, "but you will see. Put feet on solid sand instead of plastic that shreds your skin. I ask you to consider how different life will be on Kamwome. You will see I am right." She nodded and squinted at the assemblage.

Crab looked up and blinked. "Each of us is free to act upon his or her own conscience. We are not a force to be marshaled like an army. I am reminded of the lessons of Lord Krishna as he spoke to Arjuna before the battle of Kurukshetra. He said . . ."

Crab quoted from the *Bhagavad Gita.* Liyang knew it from a class at the university. As his response droned on, she fell asleep in her sitting position.

The trail they followed took a steep decline into a narrow valley. Enough white was contained in the plastic to reflect the light off the walls, and Liyang saw the necessity of Adam's goggles. But the faded particles also contained many other colors, giving an overall mottled appearance. Some of the individual particles were recognizable: the arm of a doll, the handle of a soap dispenser. The trail and the floor of the little valleys through which they passed were brown and dark, as if dirt had washed in and settled in the low places.

"I have to get those chips back."

"You didn't seem terribly anxious, falling asleep and all." Adam's lips turned up ever so slightly. Liyang imagined his eyes twinkling behind the goggles.

"The *Bhagavad Gita* is boring."

"How discerning of you. Your education does seem a bit beyond that of our ordinary inhabitants.

"Accounting at Hong Kong University. The tong

needed a high-powered accountant to deal with the government."

"They teach Hindu mythology in Accounting 101 these days?"

"Those were electives. I took many, many electives. But right now, I need to know what happened back there. Will I get my chips back?"

"Crab is always fair."

"That's not what I asked."

"To be frank, he's never confiscated something like that. Usually he divides things up or assigns them according to need. Just how valuable are they?"

"Very."

Something moved on the mound next to Liyang, causing her to jerk away.

"Crabs. Real crabs," said Adam. "An amazing number of things manage to eke out a living on the plastic." When Liyang did not respond, he continued. "That meeting was strange in several ways. You missed the second glass of wine. Crab is usually quite stingy with it. He must have thought that we needed a balm after Madam Woo's declaration of war on the Marshall Islands."

"I sensed that people were shocked, especially the people on our side of the room."

"That's the first time anyone has ever gone against Crab, and the first time anyone has ever admitted trips to the mainland."

"Who are all those people?"

"To wax poetic," he said, "you could call them the flotsam and jetsam of the world. Appropriate, don't you think?"

"You mean, like the scum of the earth?"

"Ah, I see that poetry doesn't appeal to you."

"Actually, it does, and that's an apt metaphor."

Adam bowed.

"But I need to know what's going on."

"We're a diverse group, actually, but we do share the common trait of having, shall we say, failed at our last venture."

"But what are they all doing here?"

"The same thing you are."

She thought it best not to respond to that. "I take it we're not trapped? That woman talked about a boat making a run to Hong Kong."

"Various opportunities arise for departure," Adam said, "but few of us take advantage of them although there are some, I believe, waiting for the gyre to bring us close to Hawaii. We were near Indonesia for months which accounts for the Indonesian contingent. All of us, I believe, are hiding, some from justice—some from injustice."

Liyang wanted to know more about the rotation of the gyre, but she felt it best not to show interest at this point. "Are you hiding?"

"Of course."

"But why?"

"My dear, in Poly Island Society that question is considered very impolite. It's obvious enough that we are here. Do you imagine that anyone of sane mind would remain in such a hostile environment of their own volition? Besides, that wasn't exactly a vacation cruise that brought you to our sterile shores."

"Fair enough. But what about Crab?"

"Crab. Ha! He's been here the longest, before

514

anyone else. He figured out the P-suit technology that's kept everyone alive. Prolonged exposure to the plastic wears away the skin. Everyone knows they are dependent on him for survival. He's probably working on a suit for you right now."

"He hasn't got some kind of hold on people?"

"There are rumors about a conflict with earlier inhabitants. Every once in a while he shows a kind of scientific side, but then he lapses back into this guru thing. You know, he makes predictions about the bergs based on their sound. During a storm he listens to the creaking of the plastic. That's what those drawings were about—oh, you were asleep. He's predicted where the next rupture is going to be."

"What's that?"

"The islands are a kind of a loose aggregate of plastic bergs. Sometimes they break apart and then rejoin in another couple of months. The worst is when they turn. If one of them turns, and you happen to be on it, then you'll find yourself in the ocean with a very big chunk of plastic on your back."

"That sounds scary," Liyang said, looking around her.

"Come. I can show you where the next partition will be—according to Crab."

They followed a ridgeline north and then west to a broad hill. The wind smelled of salt, and in the far distance they saw a blue line of ocean and, to her surprise, several patches of green.

"Dune grass?"

"Why, yes. Small amounts of soil have blown onto the island. Crab even has a few pots of it. He raises miniature lime trees.

"There." He pointed to a wide mound north of them. "The next break should be along that line and to the east."

She looked at him pointedly. "It occurs to me to ask where we are going after this."

He gave a devilish grin. "Why, to my boat, to see my etchings, of course."

"Why don't you all live together? This is a dangerous place to be by yourself."

Adam laughed. "Some of the Chinese do live together. Madam Woo has her enclave on a distant barge."

"Is she the one who wants my chips?"

"Ah, yes. Very enterprising, that one."

"Who is she?"

"As far as we can tell, she was ousted from the Shanghai cartel, a gang or a tong I guess you call it."

"You don't get fat on raw fish; she's got to be getting calories somewhere."

"Obviously. It's because of her that I saw your boat."

"Remind me to thank her."

"That nav/com unit I showed you was actually from parts Crab gave me. He asked me to keep track of boats that come and go from here. Madam Woo ran a boat until recently. Four of her men are missing, and it's my guess that they got caught, or perhaps they ran out on her."

"Got caught doing what?"

"Stealing or hijacking. There's no money here, so her men have to simply take whatever they come across. Anyway, her wings have been clipped, and she's chafing at the bit."

"I see you mix your metaphors, too," said Liyang.

"Only for appreciative audiences."

It was her turn to bow.

"I must admit that I'm pleased you decided to . . . remain with me, but I fear that you are now on the wrong side of the second most powerful person in the Poly Islands."

The wind gusted, lifting Liyang's straight black hair.

Adam raised a finger. "Ah, the wind is up and when that happens the plastic tends to move a bit more. You can hear it creak, and at night, when it moves enough, it produces the most beautiful sight you will ever see: St. Elmo's fire. Have you heard of it?"

"I don't know much about Christian mythology."

"St. Erasmus was the protector of sailors, definitely a minor saint. But the phenomenon named after him is truly remarkable. We call it just 'fire.' It's a kind of static electricity that travels along the ridges at night and gathers at the hilltops, creating a spectacular display. On a windy night, it's an awe-inspiring sight."

Magic fire. What a strange place she had tumbled into. Perhaps her situation was not as dire as it seemed. Her chips were, for now, safe, the world was magical and her guide was—interesting.

For the last two days they had fished at West Cove where the plastic sloped down to the level of the waves. They both had tethered themselves to substantial mounds in case an accident should send one of them falling into the slurry.

It was difficult, close to a "beach," to tell if a smooth patch of ground were solid or "quicksand," as they referred to it. Adam's method was to use these quicksand patches to push a baited hook on the end of a long plastic pipe into the water below the debris. It was like ice fishing, he had said, except one stuck the pole into the water.

The late afternoon stillness inside Adam's boat was a welcome relief from the blustering wind that had raked West Cove. Roomier than Liyang had expected, the interior space had been enlarged by removing the walls so that one large room stretched from port to starboard. She had anticipated small staterooms of the sort that triggered her claustrophobia. However, like Crab's boat, Adam's small trawler was completely trapped in plastic. The keel no longer even touched water, he said.

Much floor space was taken up with Adam's collections, bits and pieces he had found in the plastic. His biggest collection was heads: dolls' heads, dummies' heads, even a large plastic face of an Egyptian Pharaoh. These he mounted on the wall. With a tube of Super Glue he managed to cover most of a bulkhead. The faces, protruding from the walls in the dim light of the oil lamp, made Liyang feel queasy.

"You might as well talk, my dear." Adam's face reflected the golden light of the lamp as it flickered on a low table between them. "You are looking decidedly contemplative, and there's nothing else to do. My library is quite limited, and I'm afraid the bookmobile hasn't been by for years."

Liyang looked puzzled. "A truck that carries books?"

"A library on wheels," he answered.

Her bed was across the room from his. He had made it clear that she was quite safe. "I would like us to get along," was the only thing he had offered in the way of explanation.

She had been relieved that she was not expected to enter into a relationship. But now . . . "My head's a jumble." She folded the pillow behind her and leaned back.

"What was your plan, arriving here in a cabin cruiser? Surely not poaching salmon," he said with a chuckle."

"You said, yourself, such questions are impolite on Poly Island."

"Ah, but not between intimates."

"We are not intimate, and why should I trust you?" She immediately regretted the words. Her voice sounded harsh, and she wondered if Adam would take offense.

"Because, Liyang, I can help you."

It was the first time he had addressed her by her name, and she found that it pleased her. "I'd planned to hide among the mountains of plastic I'd heard about, and then, when they quit looking for me, to continue across the Pacific to the Baja Peninsula, south of California."

"I'm afraid there aren't many marinas between here and southern California. Even with an alpha engine, it's unlikely you could have carried enough fuel."

"I brought a sail and some rigging."

Adam laughed, though good-naturedly. "It's hard for even real sailboats to do what you were planning. Probably a good thing that you ended up here."

"I didn't have a lot of time to plan. It was . . . urgent that I get out of Hong Kong."

519

"That wasn't the harbor patrol pursuing you. I assume one of the cartels?"

"The old Buddha tongs."

He nodded his head. "I don't think we have any representatives from that group."

"I don't know what to do now." She meant to sound objective, detached, but she heard the edge of fear that crept into her voice.

"I believe your best choice is to stay here."

"I thought you said you'd help me."

"I meant only for now. You see, the Poly Islands are moving in the Pacific gyre. In a month or two, we'll be near Japan, and after that, Hawaii, and after that, at least closer to Baja. If you could manage to scare up a boat in those intervening months . . ."

"I see what you mean."

"Did you steal the chips?"

The directness of the question caught her off guard. "No. Yes. I mean, they aren't the reason I was running."

"What did you do?"

"I was just a bookkeeper," she said with bitterness that surprised her. "I grew up in the Buddha neighborhood in Hong Kong. I never did anything important. It didn't even feel like I was working drugs. But one day I came across a large payment that wasn't accounted for."

"Aha, are you rich, now?"

"That's the stupid part. I gave most of it away, assigned it to an untraceable account. There was a woman I was very close to, an older woman, a prostitute. She wasn't able to work much longer, and there is a place in Hong Kong, a rather nice place, actually, that takes care of older women—of her sort."

"But they'll trace the transfer."

"No. That's why they spent such effort looking for me. Not only my life, but hers, would be forfeit if they caught me."

"You are a faithful friend. But why Baja?"

"My family left Hong Kong for two years when I was a girl; we lived in Baja. I loved the place. I see it in my dreams. It comforts me when I am lonely, like now."

Adam watched her with a strange look of innocence as she rose and went to his bed.

Liyang."

She turned to see Lu Ping approaching on the other path. She had noticed him at Crab's weekly meetings, and, although they hadn't spoken of it, he was the one who had subtly offered her a seat at her first meeting. His round cheerful face and bushy black hair had stood out amongst the somber men of Woo's retinue.

"What have you got?" she asked. He carried an oversized spool, a pole with a hook on it and what appeared to be a wind-up mechanism.

"I'm going fishing in West Cove. We've been having terrible luck around Madam Woo's Barge of Heavenly Bounty." He fell in beside her, and they continued toward Adam's boat.

"I've only used a long plastic pipe to fish with. I caught a saury, and some others I didn't know what they were."

"You cannot catch the big ones that way. Tuna dive deep under the plastic."

He spoke Cantonese like her mother's family, and she easily fell into its tones. "Aren't you afraid to hook something that size? If you got pulled in . . ."

"That's what the rigging is for. I drive some cables into the plastic in case I get a big one. I can show you. Why don't you come with me? I could use some help with the gaff."

"I'm working with Adam on the salt water filter. Sorry. I was just picking up some electrical tape at Crab's."

They rounded one of the higher mounds, one that Adam had christened Poly Peak.

"You know, you shouldn't keep yourself away from the other Chinese. We're your people."

"I appreciate what you say, but Madam Woo's designs on my chips have made me cautious."

"You are direct for a Chinese. I like that."

"Did Woo set you up to speak to me?"

He didn't answer for a moment. "I volunteered." He laughed nervously.

They came to the fork in the trail, one way which led to the West Cove. Lu Ping looked into her face. "Adam is a good man. I like him. Are you . . . fond of him?"

"Yes. We seem well suited to one another."

"You are lucky," Lu Ping said. "But you do have other options, even among the Chinese."

"What do you mean?"

"Madam Woo leads only the Kumas." He paused to let that sink in. "I am Shen."

Of course. She should have realized that gang structure would persist, even in this remote place. "I've never heard of those tongs."

"They're not mainland. It's why I invited you to sit with me. There are fewer Shen. We need members."

"You were recruiting?"

"There were other reasons. You are a beautiful woman, Liyang."

She grunted.

"You have a classic Chinese face, like you stepped out of a painting by Qi Baishi."

"Nice try. Qi Baishi didn't paint people. He painted frogs and shrimp."

Lu Ping lifted his hands and laughed. "Well, if he *had* painted people . . ."

Liyang laughed, too. "Thanks, anyway, Lu Ping. I must go. You can report back to Madam Woo that I like you."

He grinned. "It would be better if you went fishing with me."

"I hope you catch something."

He inclined his head and turned down the path to West Cove.

Two weeks later, Liyang stood with Adam on the deck of Crab's boat along with twenty-seven inhabitants of the Poly Islands. The body of an American—they had known him as Stephen—was wrapped in cloth and tied securely. It lay on a gurney that was harnessed to a winch. An anchor rested at his feet.

Almost no light penetrated the mass of plastic above them, so the ceremony was conducted by the glow of little oil lamps that rested in niches carved into the plastic walls. Someone, Liyang saw, had carefully lined the niches with something, apparently nonflammable, so that the plastic would not ignite. The golden orbs of illumination gave the setting the appearance of a Buddhist grotto, like one she had occasionally gone to in Hong Kong. Liyang took Adam's hand.

More Chinese had recently appeared, and they now outnumbered all other groups two to one. Liyiang noticed that the division among the Chinese was more obvious. Madam Woo's Kuma tong, the largest, stood together with arms folded defensively. A smaller group of Shen clustered around Lu Ping. The remainder, Indonesians, Caucasians and two blacks, stood deferentially near Crab.

A man named Saurington, who had been a friend of Stephen's, operated the winch which lifted the gurney and moved it over the rail. The sides of the plastic cavern in which the boat was entombed pressed so close that a large niche had been hacked out in order for the body to be hauled over the side.

"We have before us the body of Stephen which we commit to the sea." At a nod from Crab, one end of the gurney dropped and Stephen's body—led by the anchor—fell into the slurry at the side of the boat. Crab spoke again with resignation. "We shall retire and reflect on this man, Stephen, that his life not yet disappear from the world."

Crab's words were curious. Liyang had assumed him to be an Indian guru of some kind, perhaps fallen from an ashram, but his words reflected no Hindu theology she knew of. Was he making this up?

They filed down into the familiar meeting room where everyone, including Liyang, stripped off their

P-suits and sat in their appointed places. At Crab's request, they ate in silence. She had spoken a few times to the man Stephen. He had seemed particularly close to Crab.

By the end of the meal, a tension permeated the room. People seemed to be watching one another, perhaps calculating. Sweat ran down Liyang's back, and the odor of the fish was not appetizing.

At last Crab spoke. "The voices of the plastic have changed. I hear in them a new sound, one that speaks of a different fracture likely to cross this part of the island. We must begin scouting, now, for new locations to the east where it is more stable."

"We venerate honorable Crab," broke in Madam Woo in English. "But we see his interests diverge from our own." The faces of the Chinese remained expressionless, but the others stared in surprise. There it was, thought Liyang, the challenge. No one had ever interrupted, much less contradicted Crab.

Madam Woo sat in a huge overstuffed chair that her men had brought in for her. Her hair bunched on her head in the traditional Han style. Her thong, her only article of clothing, was almost subsumed in rolls of flesh. She resembled statues of Neolithic goddesses Liyang had seen in the Hong Kong Museum. In contrast to the others—who were, for the most part, skin and bones—her bulk was overwhelming.

"One may hear sounds of plastic in different ways, not always warning of disaster. My men tell me plastic is too thick in this part of island to break. It is my decision," Madam Woo said, using the same expression that Crab often used, "that the Chinese not waste time

525

finding new places to live. We stay here; we conserve energy for more fruitful pursuit."

Crab showed neither surprise nor anger but merely nodded and said nothing else. Eventually, everyone filed from the room in silence.

Liyang followed Adam back to his boat on the now-familiar path, but even so, the plastic could be treacherous at night. Shadows hid holes and weak spots, and twilight impeded depth perception. Yet, despite the dangers, it was Liyang's favorite time to be on the surface. The stars, even without the moon, cast enough light to turn the world's garbage heap into a landscape of fantasy and imagination.

Abruptly, Adam stopped. "I've got something in my foot."

"What do you think's going to happen?" Liyang said as he found a smooth outcropping on which to sit. "Madam Woo's tong outnumbers the rest of us, and we aren't united. With poor Stephen gone, we're even fewer."

She squatted in front of him and batted his hand away and then unzipped his foot cover herself.

"Adam, did I ever tell you that you had good feet?"

"Why, no, my dear, we haven't discussed my extremities—any of them."

She laughed and then lifted out the piece of plastic she found in his foot cover.

"I smell trouble," she said.

"Not my feet?"

"Do you think Crab understands the tong system?"

"I don't think *I* understand it, but Crab isn't a fool."

"Do you think the island's really going to fracture?"

"It has in the past. Madam Woo knows that, and it surprises me that she's ignoring his warning."

"It's about power," Liyang said.

"Ah, you're back on the tongs again."

"I think she sees herself as Queen of the Poly Islands."

Adam laughed. "I think you're right. It reminds me of her boat, *The Barge of Heavenly Bounty*. I almost laughed aloud when I heard that one."

"As much as I want to reach dry land, I wouldn't want to be there under her." She zipped his foot cover closed.

"I don't think you have to worry. Even with an alpha motor, I can't imagine she's got the fuel to make it all the way to the Marshalls."

"Adam, it's time we left."

"Shall I call a taxi?" he said, getting up.

"Why couldn't you have found a boat that wasn't entombed in this . . . this crap?"

"Ah, I can always tell when you are really upset. You resort to colorful language." A moan of gusting wind made him look up. "But now we need to get below."

"Adam." She put her arms around his waist and pressed her pelvis to his. "Let's sleep out here."

He shook his head and laughed. "These are the highest winds we've had."

"I'm serious. Let's bring the tarp out."

"In this wind?"

"Don't you want to feel the breeze—in every crevice of your body?"

"If there's a shift . . ."

"We can watch the fires tonight. They'll be strong. The plastic's moving."

Liyang brought out the tarp and their only blanket rolled up in her backpack. The wind had risen, and she could feel the gentle undulations of the island as it rode the giant swells beneath them. By the time they lay naked next to one another, the wind whistled off the higher mounds, scooping into their little valley to lift strands of Liyang's straight black hair. She sat up to feel the wind caressing her skin, and it sensitized her to Adam's touch.

Never had she experienced so vividly the space beneath the stars, the feeling that her body belonged to the universe, and that as she partook of that universe, they merged into one being. Adam trembled, and it was then she saw the blue fire, glowing, dancing on the heights of the mounds. The rising wind swept over them, stronger, and the blue fire danced. It traversed the rills and sparkled on the highest mounds, encircling their world.

Amidst the groans of the plastic and the gasps of Adam, she raised her arms again, and the fire was upon her. She saw Adam's chest covered in blue light. She thrust her hands higher and the fire of St. Elmo leaped into the sky, ejecting itself into the wild wind as if to reach for the stars themselves.

Strangely, the fire ebbed with their passion spent. Their perspiration, sucked away by the wind, left them cold, and they sank into one another's arms for warmth.

Crab, I want my chips back."

The old man sat in the full lotus, his eyes closed. His brown skin looked leathery and seemed to sag on his bones. The creases in his face were deep. She wasn't sure he heard her.

"If you don't give them to me, I'll take them." She had walked into his chamber without the usual obeisance, sat in front of him and made her demand. She did not believe in gurus and pushed aside the feeling of disrespect that she, nevertheless, could not help.

His eyes opened, and he stared at her. "What will you do with them here?"

"That doesn't matter. The point is they're mine."

"The point is that I am keeping them, not from you, but from others."

"You are losing control. You may be a wise man, but you have no experience with violence. You . . ."

"When I came here, I killed the men who were living on these islands and the first three that came afterward."

In the long pause that followed she wondered if she had miscalculated. Her hand drifted to her pack where her revolver was stowed, but she sensed no threat from him.

"Why?"

"They would have taken my boat. All they wanted was to escape this place, and they would have done anything to that end."

"Escape? Are we your prisoners?"

"Of course not. Anyone may leave, but not with my boat."

"Still, I don't believe you understand Chinese tongs."

"Why don't you enlighten me?"

JAY RICHARD

"In the Chinese view, there are three tongs on this island: the Kumas, led by Madam Woo, the Shen, led by Lu Ping and the 'Others,' led by you."

"Go on."

"No two tongs are equal. They will always fight until a hierarchy is established. You are on top now, but you are outnumbered. The Kumas will overwhelm you, and Madam Woo will take what she wants, and she wants the chips."

"She's smart enough to know that if she kills me, she could probably not get the chips."

"Is this boat seaworthy?"

"It was. Although I don't know if it can break out, now."

"Why don't you try? Why don't you leave this hellish place and take those of the Others who want to go with you? This is not the only spot in the world to hide, although it's got to be the most uncomfortable."

Crab's face broke into a smile. "You are the only person who's tried to reason me into leaving in a long time. And for your consideration, I owe you an answer."

He broke his position, got to his hands and knees and then stood. "Come, I want to show you something."

He walked to the door at the back of the room, a door that Liyang had barely noticed before, but now realized was the only other exit from the room and, presumably, the only entrance to the rest of the ship. He took a key from a small pack at his waist and unlocked the door. Beyond, in the small room, Liyang saw, to her surprise, a stairway leading up.

They climbed the spiral staircase to a long narrow room with a number of monitors, apparently computers, and other machines that she did not recognize. A few ancient office chairs sat in front of the monitors. The windows were covered with the usual plastic debris, and a fan came on for ventilation. She assumed they were still entombed in plastic. Crab punched a few buttons, and the monitors came to life.

"Where do you get the power for these?"

"Batteries. Argon batteries."

"But you have to charge them."

"Static electricity. It's a charger of my own invention. Not particularly original, but no one else would need to avail themselves of such a meager power source. Static electricity is one of the few natural resources of this place."

Crab stood proudly as if he had cast off the skin of the humble yogi. The central monitor at his side displayed a grid speckled with dots and columns of numbers beneath. "Surely, you've heard of the buoys that created these islands."

"Adam said that they had malfunctioned, and the plastic didn't sink like it was supposed to."

He motioned to the monitor. "These are the buoys, or rather displays from the buoys. Two hundred and forty still operational, but over a hundred down. I'm fairly frantic."

"I thought they were malfunctioning in the first place. Wouldn't it be good that they all stopped?"

"It's true; we didn't expect the polymeyers to bind. I wasn't in charge of the project then, but it killed Dr. Stroud, who was. I had come on a reconnaissance mission in this very boat to observe the phenomenon, to investigate how we might reverse the process. I was returning home when the Cal-Alaska war broke out. After I was declared a public enemy—it's a long story—I decided to abscond with the boat and hide in the Patch."

"That's been a long time ago. You could probably return to California at this point."

"There I'm afraid you are misinformed. The Alaska coalition is not forgiving, and they have a long memory. One of my colleagues was executed only last year. I'm still very much on the wanted list. And so I continue my labors here. So far, I'm able to keep the majority of the buoys running."

"That's what I don't understand. Why keep them running at all? The experiment failed. Let them go."

Crab looked weary. "Do you realize what would happen if the buoys stopped broadcasting? These bergs would begin to disintegrate again. Eventually all the plastic would be released back into the Pacific. You see, this is one of the most spectacular failures from which the earth has ever benefited."

Liyang looked at the windows of the little room as if she could see beyond the plastic to the ocean. "I'm beginning to get the picture. These bergs are like giant magnets, gathering up the garbage from the gyre."

"Precisely." His eyes flashed for the first time. "It would be better that there were no pollution at all, but, given that there is, it's a vast, vast improvement for it to be gathered together into inert masses like these."

Liyang put her hand on one of the monitors and watched the display. "Then what you are doing here . . . is saving the ocean."

He sighed. "How sweet your praise. I've received little enough of it. But now . . . now I'm afraid my equipment deteriorates. The buoys have broadcast far beyond their life expectancy. Components fail. One by one, the buoys fall silent from the want of parts."

Liyang studied him for a moment. "My chips."

"I'm afraid so. Not only would they keep the buoys going, the preprocessor would increase their efficiency by a hundredfold."

The morning sun did not reach into the gullies and fractured valleys of the plastic wasteland where three figures trudged, single file.

"If I can just repair the buoys along the fault line," said Crab, in the lead, "I can keep the island together."

"Liyang, " Adam gestured with his free hand, "I can't believe that you've come along and in just a few months found out more about Crab than I've learned in the past three years."

"She is resourceful," said Crab.

"I had something he wanted." Liyang carried the ropes and climbing equipment. "And let me clarify again, this is a reciprocal agreement. For his five chips we get a boat and enough petrol to reach Okinawa City as soon as it's in range."

"I couldn't have thought of a better plan, myself," said Adam.

"Don't go pinning a medal on me," said Liyang, carefully stepping where Crab had just placed his feet. "I'm a selfish woman who knows what she wants. The other 195 chips are coming with me when we sail away into the sunset."

"I'm not complaining," said Adam. "It's a wonderful arrangement for Liyang and me except, what are you going to do, Crab, after we're gone? How are you going to manage the Woo contingency?"

"I'll make do. Perhaps Lu Ping and the Shen will help me. Madam Woo, of course, will be furious that you've gotten away with the chips but my ship is fairly impregnable if she tries an all-out assault. The more difficult thing will be managing the buoys. Unfortunately, I can no longer service them on my own. That's why I took Stephen into my confidence, because he was strong."

"It's strange that he died."

"Yes, I've thought of that, but I could find no signs of foul play." After a long pause in which the only sound was the crunch of their footfalls, Adam spoke again.

"There are a few other things I am curious about, Crab, or perhaps I should call you Dr. Rajkrab, now. What about this whole Indian guru thing? Was it for real?"

"If you mean, am I a guru? The answer is no. I *am* Indian, but I was born in Santa Monica. My goal, in adopting the guru posture, was to keep from having to kill. You see, at first, I shared all my knowledge and resources with the people who were already here, and they very nearly killed me for my boat. It was the same with the few people that came afterward. There seemed to be only two strategies that made any sense, killing everyone on sight who arrived here or befriending them and helping them survive, physically, emotionally, and at the same time, hiding my resources and my true purpose. Obviously, I preferred the second. Stephen was the only one I felt I could trust, before Liyang and you."

Adam stopped. "I say, is it my imagination or is the plastic softer here?" They tracked the wastes north of Crab's boat. No paths had been trampled, and the surface was rough and irregular. The peaks were small, and some of the debris was actually loose and lay on top of the other pieces.

"It's not your imagination. This is the area around the buoy that's been down the longest. The plastic that bonded here is becoming undone."

"I'm wondering if we shouldn't be roped together in case one of us falls through," said Liyang.

"No need. We're here," said Crab, looking at his locator screen. "The hatch cover should be right about here."

They found a domed lid camouflaged with various pieces of plastic waste attached. "This stuff is stuck on to make the lid look natural," said Crab. He tried to lift the lid. After several grunts, he jerked it up with a cracking sound.

"Ah! I've broken it. I'll have to glue this back together while Liyang is replacing the chip. We can't risk the access tube filling up."

Adam shined his light directly into the hole. It extended at a steep angle down into the plastic. "I can see the end."

"It's about twenty-five, thirty feet. Stephen was able to lower me to the service panel with no problem and pull me back."

"Then let's get on it," said Liyang as she dropped her backpack and began taking off her snowshoes.

"You're sure this is safe," said Adam.

"You can't be sure of anything here, but I made it fine the two times I went."

Crab looped the rope around both Liyang's legs.

"I wish there were some other way," said Adam. "Hanging upside down in that pipe, she could black out."

"There's no room to turn around at the bottom. Believe me, I tried it."

"Let's get this over with." She strapped the light onto her forehead.

"The tool bag has only the things you'll need. I don't want to weigh you down," said Crab. "If you need anything else, you can shout up and we'll slide it down to you."

She crouched on her knees before the hole and then crawled inside. The slant was sharper than forty-five degrees, and she would have slid down but for Adam holding her feet. At least it wasn't straight up and down, she thought. She turned on the light on her forehead to reveal a round, cream-colored tunnel that gradually narrowed to a dark point below.

"Let's go," she cried, more cheerful than she felt. It was, she thought, like being lowered into a claustrophobic nightmare, but she shook her head and blinked it away.

The pipe was smooth and the joints well fitted except that in the middle she encountered a rupture, a long, jagged crack that she had to get across.

"Hold up," she shouted. "Let me pull. I've got to crawl over a crack."

The crack was sharp and almost a third of the length of the pipe. She could easily cut her hands on it or rip her P-suit, though, once past it, the pipe was smooth again to the bottom. The top of the buoy was more than a meter wide and round. It reminded her of the old-fashioned mines placed in harbors in earlier years.

Debris, probably from the crack, covered most of the small hatch door, but she was able to scrape it back and stuff it around the edges. The buoy seemed to be firmly embedded in the plastic.

She heard water surging below her and gasped. The image of the tube filling up with icy water gave her chills, and it was all she could do to keep from crying out for them to raise her back to the surface. Gritting her teeth, she inserted the key into the cover slot.

With several strong twists, the watertight cover lifted off. She was able to get it out of the way by wedging it above her.

The air was beginning to get stale, and she was anxious to be finished and pulled back to the surface. The port for the chip was vacant, as Crab said it would be.

She had to take off her gloves for this part. Removing the case from her pack, she opened the cover and lifted out the tiny chip. It sparked as she fitted it into place. It seated. Then she removed a round, flat battery and inserted it into the battery port. A tiny pilot light blinked.

She pulled the buoy cover down and turned it into place, patting it for luck. It made a hollow sound.

"Okay. Done!" she shouted up the hole.

"Okay," came the faint return. She was zipping up the tool bag when she heard something that she didn't understand: a pop.

She wrinkled her brow. Then she heard it again, a shot. Her pulse jumped from fright. What's happening up there? Voices. Instinctively, she turned off the light on her head. Plunged into total darkness, she tried to force her ears to the surface, listening, hardly daring to breathe.

A clunk as something was thrown into the pipe. She heard it slide down and braced herself, not knowing what it was. Then she heard it catch at the break and stop. She had to get out of there. She hoped Adam and Crab could hold off their attackers, but she had a bad feeling about that. Perhaps, she thought, she could pull herself up with the rope.

A loud shot rang in the pipe, and she jumped. The bullet barely missed her, crashing into the buoy below and bouncing into the plastic. She was too frightened to scream. They were shooting down the pipe at her. No, she wailed in her mind. Not to die like this! Shot upside down in the dark in a damn pipe. She clinched her fists. Buddha help me! she cried in her mind.

More voices, but no more shots. She strained with all her might to hear. Then she heard something else thrown into the pipe and felt a coil begin at her feet above her. They had thrown the rope into the pipe. No. It was all she could think. This could not be happening. And then the sound she dreaded above all others: the grating of the hatch cover as it was replaced on the pipe.

The blackness was filled with the sound of her breathing. They were leaving her to die upside down in the pipe. Her eyes wide, seeing nothing, she pressed with her arms against the walls that held her as if she could spread them apart. Her mind churned. She had to resist panic. Think. There must be a way out.

She turned the light on her forehead back on. The close surroundings seemed to leap into her face. What did she have with her? Nothing but the tools. With a rotosaw she could cut handholds to push herself up, but she had only screwdrivers, chip tools, a spare battery, the bag and the rope. She felt back for the plastic length coiled at her feet and pulled some of it to the front of her. Something else lay on her leg. It was the other object that had been thrown into the pipe, dragged down, now, by the rope. She felt back behind her for it. Not a tool. It was soft and mushy. She brought it to the front of her. No, not a tool. A tube of old-fashioned Super Glue.

The meeting chamber on Crab's boat was partly filled. The "Others," as the non-Chinese had begun to be known, sat despondently on the floor and were guarded by the Shen, under Lu Ping, with guns drawn. One by one the members of the Kumas tong entered the room with their prizes, first Adam, disheveled and with a swelling, black eye, then Crab, carried by two of the Chinese. They propped him up where he stood, mostly on one leg, the other bleeding from the thigh.

"Now, Crab," Madam Woo said. "I'll have the chips."'

"No," he said.

One of his guards raised a hand to strike him, but Madam Woo stopped him with a gesture.

"I do not know what games you play with your little experiments, but are they worth your life?"

"If you kill me you will never find the key to that door, and, believe me, you won't open it without the key or a bomb."

"On the contrary, I'll open it with a single bullet or, perhaps, three or four. Is it worth it, Crab, to see all your friends die, one at a time? I will bring each one before you and explain to them that you could save them, merely by producing a small key. Then I'll put a bullet in their head and bring the next one before you—until you produce the key and the chips."

"For God's sake, give her what she wants," said one of the Indonesians. "What can be so important that we all die?"

"You see, your friends understand the wisdom of my position."

"No, they don't," said Crab.

"Oh, I think they understand all they need to. They will die because of your stubbornness."

"The chips are not his to hand over," a loud, ragged voice said from the doorway.

"Liyang!" cried Adam.

All eyes turned to her. She held her revolver extended in front of her with both hands, which were skinned and bleeding. Her hood was missing, and her hair was wild. Her P-suit was torn. She panted for breath.

"Move out of the way, Crab," said Liyang.

"I'll kill him," said Madam Woo, pressing her pistol against the back of Crab's head.

"I am an expert marksman," said Liyang, her voice trembling with emotion. "I am so angry, I could kill you no matter what happens in this room. You left me to die like a rat in that pipe."

"But look around you. All our guns, against yours."

One of the Kumas turned his gun on her, but Liyang's shot rang so quickly that it seemed her gun never left Madam Woo.

The man fell, a bullet in his head, and everyone seemed to hold their breath.

"Shen tong! Guns on the Kumas!" It was Lu Ping, and almost half the Chinese turned their guns on the members of the Kuma tong. The Kumas wavered, not seeming to know where to point their guns.

"It seems the Shen want to play, too." Liyang's voice was stronger than she felt. "Back off. Take your men with you."

"You should have been on my side, Liyang. I saw you were strong from the beginning."

Crab finally spoke. "None of that matters now. It is abundantly clear that both Madam Woo and I will die if there is an exchange of gunfire—along with some of you. Perhaps we should all simply back away."

"No." Madam Woo's jowls quivered as she raised her chin. "You have something I want. I have something you want." She shoved her gun again against Crab's head. "We make exchange, then back away."

"You monster!" Liyang was nearly screaming. "There is no exchange for what you did to me. I could kill you right now."

"There are too many of us," said Madam Woo hurriedly. Her voice took on an edge of fear. "If we all fire, there will still be Chinese left who will take your chips."

"I don't bluff," said Liyang, "and it doesn't matter how many are left. You won't be among them."

Liyang's mind tumbled. She both sensed that she

was out of control, but at the same time calculated that her wild looks and near hysteria might be enough to frighten Woo.

"Do it," said a subdued Woo.

Liyang turned so that she could see everyone in the room. "All right, both tongs start backing off. Madam Woo will be last."

Madam Woo nodded.

Lu Ping nodded.

Slowly, and with extreme caution, the Chinese began backing toward the door. Those on the far side of the room carefully stepped over the body of the Kuma member Liyang had shot. In the silence, it seemed as if the least noise might set off a deadly chain reaction. Long minutes ticked away as one by one the Chinese reached the stairs and began their ascent.

Then Lu Ping reached the door.

"I go, now, too," Madam Woo said. She released Crab, lowered her gun, and defiantly turned her back on Crab and the others as she walked away.

"Lu Ping," said Liyang, making eye contact with him. She nodded slightly.

Madam Woo looked up, realizing her peril too late. Lu Ping shot three times in rapid succession. Madam Woo jerked with the first shot, clutched her chest and then fell forward to the floor.

Lu Ping didn't move, his gun still pointed at Madam Woo. "Thank you, Liyang," he said and looked up. "Crab, there is much to settle. You have been good to us. I grant you one boon of the tong."

"I don't know . . ." stammered Crab.

"If I may," said Adam.

Crab looked at him.

"We should divide the island. Neither of us will cross the central ridge without the consent of the other."

"Agreed. I'll send men for the two bodies." And with that he turned and disappeared up the stairwell.

"Liyang," Adam said. "I thought it was you who shot her until I saw his gun recoil."

"No, it is how the tongs work. He had to kill her. It was the only way."

Dec. 10, 2109. OSLO, Norway—"Your Majesties, Your Royal Highness, Distinguished Members of the Norwegian Nobel Committee, citizens of the world:

"Before I present the award, I am pleased to announce that at 2:00 AM this morning, Norwegian time, the final anchor was set for Crab's Island. It now resides north of the Bering Strait in international waters where it joins with real icebergs but, itself, remains inert. In two years, Adam's Island will be berthed off the shore of northeast Greenland, and two years after that, by international agreement, Liyang's Island will be berthed in Ross Sea, Antarctica. It is estimated that sixty to seventy percent of the oceans' plastic will be contained in these three masses.

"Seldom can a few people, without the help of governments and huge subventions, make a dramatic difference in the world. The pollution by plastic of the oceans, considered at one time to be unsolvable, has been largely reversed by the dogged persistence of these three individuals. Braving threats to their persons, dangers of nature, chemical hazards and years of extreme isolation, they persisted in the dream first laid out by Dr. Param Rajkrab, and realized by his followers, Dr. Adam Thompson and his wife, Liyang Thompson."

After the applause, Liyang stepped haltingly to the podium. Her shoulders were bent, her white hair pulled back in a bun. Her eyes were alert, although her voice trembled.

"I am so sorry that Adam and Crab did not live long enough to see this day. They are the ones who deserve to receive this prize and not posthumously. I was the least of them. As a young woman, I started out a member of a Chinese drug cartel, and forty-five years later my journey has brought me here. No one is more amazed than I."

Insect Sculptor

written by

Scott T. Barnes

illustrated by

JOHN W. HAVERTY JR.

ABOUT THE AUTHOR

Born in San Diego, California, Scott T. Barnes spent most of his early life working on the family farm in the mountain town of Julian, raising apples, cut flowers (lilacs and lily of the valley) and beef cattle. Most of these products he sold from his family's roadside produce stand.

Scott wanted to be a writer from an early age and wrote his first 60-page "novel" about skeleton warriors and a flaming sword at age 11 on an old manual typewriter. He has photos of evening typing sessions in his pajamas to prove it, though the original manuscript has been lost.

On her thrice-yearly shopping trips to San Diego, Scott's mom would leave him at the mall bookstore for hours, knowing she could later find him in the science fiction section reading everything he could reach. Scott spent his twenties and thirties getting a BA in journalism and Spanish and an MBA and working in such disparate places as Mexico City, Mexico and Paris, France. He spent far too much time studying flamenco guitar and kenjitsu rather than writing.

Now settled in Orange County, California, Scott finally developed the discipline to write every week come rain, shine or children. His first goal was to be accepted into Odyssey, the Fantasy Writing Workshop, which he accomplished in 2008. That program helped develop his writing to the point where he could accomplish his second goal, win the Writers of the Future Contest.

Today Scott is a stay-at-home dad with his children Elizabeth, 3, and Kaylynn, 1. He edits the online magazine NewMyths.com and recently completed the fourth-grade illustrated reader Rancho San Felipe with award-winning illustrator Sarah Duque, to be published by the Wieghorst Western Heritage Center in September 2012.

ABOUT THE ILLUSTRATOR

John W. Haverty Jr. was born October 2, 1986, in Boston, Massachusetts, and grew up in Marion, a small town on the state's south shore. He studied and earned his BFA at the University of Massachusetts Amherst.

Before reaching his twenty-third birthday, he managed to visit and experience thirty-four countries spread throughout five continents. These experiences abroad helped shape and influence the diverse body of work that he currently illustrates and paints. Since receiving his degree, Haverty has lived and worked on painting in Martha's Vineyard and Memphis, Tennessee. Lately, his larger-than-life illustrated works are being exhibited in a number of galleries throughout the United States. Haverty now resides in the historical city of Savannah, Georgia, where he is earning his MFA in painting at the Savannah College of Art and Design.

Insect Sculptor

I arrived at the Hive cabaret in Abidjan, Côte d'Ivoire an hour before my audition. My only luggage, a day bag, leaned against the silver valise-insectarium marked Adam Clements. The sidewalk whirred with native people, legitimate businessmen, pickpockets, whoonga pushers barking in French and tourists of all stripes. Music blared from a divertissquirt shop. The chaos reflected perfectly my mood.

Anxiety.

I had been rehearsing the interview ever since I left Vancouver, B.C.—twenty-nine hours with layovers. I worried through another hour in an old 2038 BMW taxi that coughed at every intersection.

What would the Great Gajah-mada, the greatest insect sculptor in the world, want with me? More importantly, how could I hide the fear-wall that denied my progress?

A charming outdoor café sat opposite the performers' entrance. Further down rue Gagous the Hive's curved-glass front bordered a fine plaza where two-meter-long bronze scorpions shot water from their claws into shallow pools. Children played in the water. Mothers in bright sarongs gossiped.

549

SCOTT T. BARNES

I finished my gin and tonic and ordered another, courage in a glass. My father's voice sounded in my head. "The Clements have always been engineers. Just get the degree."

No, I would not be shackled by a nine-to-five. I would return home triumphant, free from my father, free from mediocrity.

A grifter in a white shirt rolled up at the elbows picked up his coffee and sat down next to me. His arms were chocolate, his face tanned to black coffee. "You are waiting for her? And so handsome. I know I have no chance. And yet I wait."

At five-foot-nine with mousy hair and features characterized by my sister as "knobs and bumps," I rarely thought of myself as handsome. At one time, perhaps, I imagined my gray eyes resembled Humphrey Bogart's. But at twenty-six, I had lost many illusions.

Three Vespas whined by. The grifter slurped on his coffee. "I cannot afford to see her inside the club. A month's salary for one show!"

His words began to intrigue me. Who had he fallen in love with? A waitress, I decided. They would be gorgeous and willing to indulge this gray-haired slouch for a generous tip. Poor soul. I signaled the waitress and bought him a coffee. "I am a sculptor. I seek an apprenticeship for the winter season."

"Show me something. It will help pass the time until she comes."

"You have seen the Great Gajah-mada?"

He looked surprised. "No one sees the Great Gajah-mada. But I have seen his best work. Many times."

I did not know how to take this. But I hoped the demonstration would divert me from my inner

550

turmoil. I put the diadem-like control circlet upon my head, plugging the computer-amplifier into the socket behind my ear. My termites immediately took note, lining up at the insectarium's door.

I linked.

My mind loosened from its moorings, the neo-cortex's logical prison, and became a blue mist above collections of insect will. My subconscious imagery portrayed these collections as vibrating, sea-green gel caps. If I descended a little further, if I wrapped myself around those gel caps I could lose myself. Indeed, rapture is the biggest danger of insect sculpture—to fall so deeply into the insect consciousness that you have no desire to leave. You become a worker, a soldier, a queen. Pheromones become gods.

I approached the gel caps. A rumble filled my ears, a wall of mental noise between gel caps and mist. My deepest consciousness—deeper than the cerebral peduncle that interfaced with the bugs—feared rapture beyond all things. That was my weakness, my fear-wall. Unlike the best performers, I could not smell through the termites' antennae. I had never experienced multifaceted vision.

The other patrons shuffled their chairs into a semicircle. I snapped open the insectarium's insulated door and my termites crawled onto the table to seek the configuration I held in my mind.

An elephant.

The brown winged termites crawled over each other like Keystone Cops, building, climbing, falling and building again until the sculpture rose eight inches. They settled. They smoothed their wings. The men around me stopped talking.

I had the elephant turn its head and wiggle its ears, and balls of insects threw themselves out of the trunk like balls spit from a clown's mouth. I did not try to make the elephant walk. That was beyond my skill.

"It would be fine work anywhere else," the brown-armed man said, as the termites returned to their home. "But here in Abidjan . . ." He placed a consoling hand on my shoulder. "If Isabella teaches you, you could be great. Oh, look."

The woman paused at the doorway: long legs, green-and-white sun skirt swishing against them, a white blouse, a stylish straw hat with yellow ribbon shadowing her face, her braided hair spilling out the back. She paused with one hand over the door's reader, turned and crossed the pavement with a confident stride. She looked every inch a model . . . or a Maasai warrior.

Her eyes, topaz and delicate like lacewings, flirted with mine. "Mister Adam Clements, I recognize you from your brochures. You took an early flight."

My companion held his breath, but those lacewing eyes did not even flicker in his direction.

She took my hand in a firm, dry handshake. The bumps on her face (measles? chicken pox?) did little to diminish her allure. "I'm afraid I'm at a disadvantage."

"Isabella Mada, the Hive's director. Come with me."

I followed Isabella across the street, rolling the insectarium, wondering how I had gotten my day bag in my hands. I could have easily left it behind, so intoxicating did I find her. I glanced at the man who had shared my table and he looked back sorrowfully, scooted his chair and shuffled down the street.

JOHN W. HAVERTY JR.

In the open door, I looked back again. Every table was deserted, half a dozen men disbursed, fading into the asphalt. A minor play finished. They, too, had been waiting for Isabella.

The nondescript side door led directly into the black box, a sound stage with black walls roughly 150 feet long by 75 wide—the same dimensions as the theater's main stage.

We passed through double doors into an empty corridor, then into the stage shop where half-repainted props, cans of paint and a pile of lumber attested to preparation for the coming show. One of many doors led to Isabella's office. She held it open.

Her warmth radiated through her thin cotton blouse as I squeezed past. An expansive walnut desk with a glass top dominated the room. Monitors above the door showed the empty main stage and dining area of the cabaret with its red décor and circular tables.

A black leather and wood armchair beckoned. I sat with my back to the door.

Seeing the plaque on her desk I read, *"Theater Director.* But what of the Great Gajah-mada?"

"He is the chief attraction, but I am the director."

"Won't I see him?" I shuffled my feet.

"We are here to see what you can do, Mister Clements. Afterwards your questions."

I swallowed my disappointment. He had been my hero since I was a boy, and now I might not even get to see him.

We discussed my background and my work for the British Columbia Repertory Theater. But of course, the demonstration counted for all. On the glass-topped walnut desk, I created several works, including the elephant. Each time I began, Isabella's beautiful brown eyes grew wide, hopeful and then narrowed as I failed to deliver. My chest sagged as the minutes toiled by.

Finally, she put both hands palm up on the desk in invitation. "Adam, stop holding back. Art is about releasing your inner self."

She sees through me. She knows I am afraid.

I clenched my jaw until my teeth hurt, using the pain to get centered. I dropped my palms into hers, feeling a roughness that told of a life not always in the arts. Her bones settled into place, her grip firmed up and then within my circlet I felt a warm, lilac presence.

But not a woman's presence. A multiple of intrusions, as if Isabella herself were compartmentalized. The termite minds quickened, became more eager.

"Your best work, Adam. Breathe deeply."

I created a "green man" image, bearded wise man with billowing robe, leaves in his hair and snarled roots for feet.

My ears buzzed softly as the fear-wall tried to assert itself.

"Adam, do you believe insects subservient to their handler?"

It was difficult to hold the image and talk. Had she so mastered the insect psyche as to be indistinguishable from it? I managed, "Yes. Yes, I suppose. They do what I tell them."

"Each with its role, like cells in a body."

"Yes. Exactly."

I could feel her probing the gel caps, the clusters

of insect consciousnesses manifesting in the circlet. Everything felt . . . paired. We descended closer and closer, beyond my normal limits.

My fear grew to a rumble. The more I tried to banish it, the more assertive it became. My concentration wobbled. Isabella tightened her grip.

"You tell them exactly where to go? How to link their legs with their neighbors' legs and flutter their wings so that the hair seems alive?"

The termites began to move their wings until it appeared that wind whipped across the green man. Wave followed wave. The hair and beard danced. I had never before seen such unity of purpose.

I looked from the startling image to Isabella. "Yes, yes."

The fluttering became fierce and chaotic. A gale. It roared through the room.

No, not through the room. Through my head. My fear-wall battered the mist of my concentration.

Isabella's temples tightened. "This is incorrect. You must understand that insects follow because they *want* to follow. They thrill to touch the sculptor's mind, which must be as great to them as God's mind is to our own. The *master* forces his insects to work." She withdrew her hands. The fluttering stopped. "The *performer* rejoices in them."

Embarrassment flooded my cheeks. I wanted to retort, to stomp out, to hide my face . . .

I kept my expression neutral and sent the termites back to the insectarium. *If Isabella can do this, what can the Great Gajah-mada do?*

She watched the emotions flicker behind my irises.

"You have come a long way, Adam. I'm sorry it won't work out."

I stuttered. My father reared up in my mind's eye, waving a diploma. "I—I came to apprentice to the Great Gajah-mada. I will apprentice to him or not at all."

You can't destroy my dreams like this!

Her left index finger tapped the glass desktop. I heard props being moved in the scene shop, low voices speaking.

Slowly, deliberately, she took an envelope from the top drawer and passed it to me. "I'm afraid that is impossible. Come to the show tonight as my guest." The door opened behind me and a silent workman took me by the arm. "You have talent, Adam. But we seek greatness. I'm sorry."

The worker led me through the black box and outside. In the sunlight on rue Gagous, I opened the envelope to find a ticket to the night's performance.

Folded around it a typed note read:

Thank you for your interest in this position. After careful consideration, we have determined that your qualifications do not match our needs.

—The Great Gajah-mada.

The room recalled an old-fashioned cabaret: deep red curtains, elaborate wooden chairs around tables with red velvet tablecloths, a wall of expensive bottles backlit in soft light behind a polished mahogany bar. The waitresses wore silver-lined flapper dresses cut unevenly to the knee, suggestive (incorrectly) that there might be paid ladies waiting upstairs.

557

This was not a theater but rather a cabaret where audience participation was encouraged. Fried calamari and skewered beef were served. For a thousand francs, giant aphids would solicit patrons to lick a honey-like paste from their posteriors.

I had hoped for a room full of morose applicants. Instead, the patrons squealed when someone tried the aphids, or a fried scorpion or any of a dozen bug-themed delicacies. They giggled with anticipation.

It can't be that good.

Most wore the silk shirts and European-cut dresses de rigueur for the nouveau riche. The tourists, dressed in wrinkled casual dress, pointed and gossiped in eager bunches. Two or three white-haired ladies flirted shamelessly. Most were native African.

Only one person appeared out of place, a chocolate-skinned lout at the bar carefully enunciating compliments at each waitress who passed. He spoke far too loudly.

I raised my hand for another gin and tonic.

Isabella, now in a topaz sheath dress, appeared from the wings. She sparkled. I couldn't decide if I were angry or infatuated with her. Her rejection was nothing personal, of course—my failing. The fear-wall defeated me.

She shook hands and greeted acquaintances. Jealousy flashed through me each time she kissed a man's cheek. I caught her eyes. She waved discreetly.

I set both feet flat on the floor. My knees bounced. I hoped she would make it to my side of the room . . .

The lights dimmed. Cello music murmured.

And then a scream cut across the audience. The lout at the bar had pulled a waitress onto his lap. Her legs flailed above her head, bright red panties flashing in the strobes. I stood, knocking my chair over backwards, and began clawing between the tables to free her when the woman's chest collapsed beneath his hand. Her head slumped forward, melting like chocolate in a microwave. The drinks she carried on a tray clattered to the ground as she dissolved into a gigantic swarm of bugs which flew, crawled and scuttled backstage.

The lout fell back in shock, bellowing like a wounded bear. Bouncers dragged his limp form out. I had nearly the same reaction, reaching the scene with a look of abject astonishment. Other souvenir hunters had arrived before me. I reached down and snatched the only remaining article of clothing—her bright red, lacy panties. A spotlight found my dumbfounded expression, eyes glued to this undergarment, and I became the laughingstock of the room. My ears warmed.

The performance began. Uncountable cockroaches poured down the center stage and began building a living city, a replica of Abidjan. A waitress helped me regain my seat. My eyes took in the performance, and yet my mind cycled.

The waitress—a construct.

Impossible. How could she hold together?

The man in the café outside: *I have seen his best work. Many times.*

What artistry. What mastery!

I searched the room. Isabella had departed. Still, I felt her presence, her watchfulness, as though our sharing of the circlet hadn't quite ended.

There was no question. I would return.

It took four days for me to find the makeup, wig and materials I needed to perform my "bearded Dutchman" routine. Insect sculptors love practical jokes, and I had learned a thing or two over the years. I glued cuttings of donkey hair to the wings of my termites, a decent facsimile for salt-and-pepper hair. I painted my insectarium blue and bought a loud red leather jacket to attract the eye. I practiced.

Each day at three, I waited at the outdoor café. The applicants arrived universally on time. In the evenings, I walked the quay on the beautiful Baie du Banco, marveling at the orange sunset rippling on the water. I inhaled the sea breeze, the smell of charcoal fires, the freedom of the moment.

On the fifth day, I knocked on the performer's entrance at ten minutes to three. A worker opened the door.

"I have an interview with Isabella Mada."

He looked at his watch, nodded and led me through the black box and scene shop. Isabella's door stood open. She turned to greet us.

I held out my hand. "Hello. I'm Frank van Straalen. I have a three PM appointment. I apologize if I'm early."

She tried to glance at a list on her desk, but I held firmly to her hand. "You said your name was . . . ?"

"Van Straalen. I flew in from Denmark this morning. No problems, I hope. It was a horrible flight. The child next to me barfed from all the turbulence. I had to buy a new shirt on the way over. And my termites didn't like it either." I patted my insectarium. "Well, let's get started?"

I dropped the case on the desk—covering her list of candidates. "You'll want to see a demonstration. A lifting of the mask, so to speak." I judged my cover nearly blown. And so, at my mental command, the termites comprising my sideburns, mustache and beard climbed to the top of my head. There, they formed a green man, obese from donkey hair.

I smiled my best Humphrey Bogart.

"The eyes." She tilted her head. "I should have recognized the eyes."

I returned the termites to their home, removed the wig and held it in both hands, projecting humility. "Well?"

"You have a long way to go, Adam. A long way." She smiled.

"Good. That is why I came to the Hive. But I have another thing to tell you. I intend to do more than just apprentice. I intend to court you."

Isabella introduced me to the cast: eight dancers, three insect sculptors and nineteen crew. Many more worked in Gajah-mada's laboratory across town, providing genetic engineering and breeding facilities for the Hive and supplying GM bugs all over the world.

Hans Wasserman, the chief sculptor, clapped his hands. He stood six four, an imposing Afrikaner with crew cut and square jaw. He wore black sweats and a white polo shirt. "Good. He can start with me this afternoon. I could use the help."

"Adam will not be working on the show. He is not qualified."

561

Wasserman's slack jaw reflected my bewilderment, if not my embarrassment. "Then what is he doing here?"

"Learning." Isabella turned heels and strode away. I hurried after.

"I wish you hadn't done that."

"You needed it. And Wasserman did as well. Now he won't be bothering you all the time."

We descended the stairs into a large basement atelier broken up by hydraulic lifts and machinery, metal trees rising to the stage above. Pallets of honeycomb containers stood ready to lift insectariums into the stage's wings. Workers vacuumed up fallen performers. Laboratory technicians in white smock coats and hairnets hustled to and from the incubator wing.

Everything smelled of insects which, when dead and dry, smell like the interior of a vacuum bag, but when active smell of pumpkin bread. This room held something of both.

"I still intend to court you," I warned.

"And I will play hard to get."

She led me to a short overweight man in blue overalls and a white T-shirt. He looked vaguely familiar. His overalls sported a badge. *Dieudonné, chief mechanic.*

"You will be working together until Dieudonné decides otherwise," Isabella said. "You must learn to mesh insects with robotics until the beginning and end cannot be perceived."

I bowed slightly. "Adam Clements, enchanté."

Dieudonné frowned. "Monsieur. I believe you have something that belongs to Eve." He gestured to the manikin he had been polishing with a white cloth, a buxom woman of semicircular aluminum tubes. Louvers created the outline of a pretty face.

I circled it, noting tiny hinges at the joints, smelling machine oil on its hinges.

Dieudonné removed a touch-screen device from his breast pocket and tapped with his fingertips. The robot drop-folded onto the floor, taking up no more than a foot square by six inches tall. Wheels emerged and it scooted away.

After a second of incomprehension, I burst out laughing. This hollow frame was the "waitress" from the show! I stuck out my hand, which startled him, but he shook it. "I'm sorry, but I left the red panties in my hotel."

"She loses one an evening. Such a slut!"

And then I recognized him—the lout from the cabaret. I took an instant liking to him.

"Good. Adam knows nothing of your art. See that he learns." Isabella winked at me. "Good luck."

Dieudonné's eyes followed her swaying departure. "If only I could create such perfection."

I, too, watched. "Is she single?"

At this Dieudonné lifted his gold necklace. The chain supported a fig beetle with green metallic wings encased in plastic. Looking closely, I saw that it had one solid wing. Useless. Fused with genetic engineering. I noted the shape, the ridge . . .

A fingernail.

"Did you get one of these?" Dieudonné asked.

I ran my tongue around my teeth. "No."

"Well, play your cards right. She has nine more."

His brown eyes did not mock me. "She has false fingernails?"

"She is a construct, as sure as the sun rises."

"I can't believe it. Impossible."

He placed a thick hand on my shoulder, as if I had joined some sort of club. "We all love her. But take my advice, my friend. Do not believe she loves you in return. She is incapable of love."

A shell of genetically engineered bugs, with proper studio lighting and theatrical diversion, could mimic a waitress. But it wouldn't fool people for long. Isabella was too perfect, from her teeth and gums down to the Achilles tendon that stretched against her high heels as she walked. No one could maintain that kind of control over the insects without descending irretrievably into rapture.

And yet . . .

And yet I half believed him. Her sense of humor could be borrowed. Her intelligence might be Gajah-mada's intelligence. Her lilac presence inside the circlet had meshed so intimately with the insects.

Was she Gajah-mada's greatest creation?

My jumbled emotions made progress difficult. The fear-wall blocked it entirely.

I learned other things, however. The Great Gajah-mada lived in an apartment above the theater. Few performers had ever seen him.

The show was faltering, but not from lack of popularity. Indeed, they sold out months in advance. The problem lay in Gajah-mada's wavering control. Rumors abounded that he had finally succumbed to rapture. Or Alzheimer's. Or both.

Wasserman tried to take up the slack, but the locusts escaped his control. Twice. Dinner was spoiled, tickets refunded.

The cast resented me. They refused to eat with *le Canadien*, as they called me. I burdened Dieudonné. I didn't pull my weight.

They were right.

Every time I coordinated Eve's termite shell beyond a couple of steps, the insects emitted floral-like pheromones more attractive to my cerebral peduncle than opium. The aroma bypassed logic, appealing directly to desire. They wanted me to meld. The nearer I approached, the more difficult the invitation became to resist.

The roar crescendoed until I could not think. Like a man plagued by vertigo, I dared not descend the stairway.

We managed to make Eve walk and talk, even carry drinks. But the termites sat on her with all the aplomb of flies on dung.

"It is time to present Eve to Isabella," Dieudonné told me. "The season is half over."

"I'm not ready."

He shrugged. "You have stopped making progress."

After a minute, I nodded.

She came with Wasserman, he showing the fatigue of the season, sunken eyes, slack shoulders and limp spine, she looking so hopeful it broke my heart.

We did our best. A "naked" Eve cantered around Isabella and Wasserman, grinning, spinning and finally collapsing into a square and rolling away as the termites fled to their insectarium.

A mud-man would have looked more alluring. I lost

control from the start. The termites clung together in lumps. Bare aluminum flashed. Some termites took refuge inside the metal frame and got caught in the moving parts, their extinctions jolting my consciousness like an electric shock. I nearly loosed my bowels as Eve collapsed down, squashing hundreds.

I would have done anything to avoid the inverted smile on Isabella's visage. I picked lint from my trousers, waiting for somebody to fire me.

Wasserman cleared his throat. "He needs your help, Isabella." His head sat jauntily on his neck. A grin pulled his face upwards.

He doesn't want Isabella to hire anyone else. He sees in me a rival to set up to fail.

My stomach knotted.

Isabella rubbed her right triceps with her left hand, her arm crossed under her breasts. Her cheery blue jean jacket bunched at the shoulder. "There's not enough time."

Dieudonné was shaking his head.

"You've spent so much on him already," Wasserman insisted. "He knows how to coordinate with the robot. He lacks finesse, true. But you can teach him the finer points . . . or no one can."

My cheeks tightened. Never had Wasserman's six-foot-four seemed so intimidating . . . and so in need of a wallop.

Dieudonné stepped between us. "This is deeper than coordination, and you know it, Wasserman. He can't get past his fear."

"I should have listened to my instinct," Isabella muttered, as if unaware everyone could hear.

I stepped around Dieudonné. "I can do it, Isabella. If I don't succeed in five weeks, fire me."

Wasserman laughed.

"Take my money, my life savings. Here. It will cash in a Canadian bank." I pulled my wallet from my back pocket. I always carry one blank check there, and I wrote it out to the Hive for $28,300 dollars, all the money I had in the world. If I lost this, I would own a credit card, a plane ticket home and nothing else. I handed it to Isabella. "If I don't break through the wall in five weeks, my savings are yours."

Dieudonné stared into headlights, eyes flipping from me to Isabella.

Isabella folded the check and slipped it into her jeans. "Let's get started."

We made for the stairs.

Wasserman chuckled behind our backs.

A maze of four-inch-diameter, white plastic PVC pipe sprawled over Isabella's desktop. Every few inches a T-joint covered in plastic wrap faced skyward. This provided light for the bee inside. There was one entry, one exit and many dead ends.

A new hole had been drilled in the side of one of the PVC sections from which a black electrical cord led to the wall.

I tried to smile. "A bug light?"

"I'm not joking. I had Dieudonné fit it into the pipe."

"I didn't suppose you were." Four weeks had passed, time for desperate measures. My eyes roamed from the pipe to Isabella, attracted and repulsed at the same time. I adored her Ivory Coast accent and shiny black skin. Her braided hair and slinky legs. Her personality. Her confidence.

Whose confidence? The Great Gajah-mada's?

A Mary Shelley creation or a woman?

Under normal circumstances, being asked to work with a single bee would have been an insult. But not here. I could not see the bee. I had to guide it through the maze by using its own senses. No cheating. No going halfway.

The fear-wall rumbled.

Isabella reached out. "If you walk the bee into the bug light, it will be electrocuted. That won't be pleasant—for either of you."

"I know." My throat dried. *If this bee dies with me sharing its consciousness, I could go insane. My heart could stop.*

"Adam, I'm sure you've heard the rumors about the Great Gajah-mada. They are true, in essence. I fear he won't live much longer. Wasserman is good, but he can't hold the show together without help. If you don't succeed, I must begin training someone else immediately."

"I know, I know. Thanks for putting me at ease."

"Just remember, this is your twenty-eight-thousand, three-hundred-dollar try." She took a deep breath. "Let's make sure this bee doesn't die, shall we?"

My fingers trembled. *If Isabella is a construct, what will happen when Gajah-mada dies? Will she dissolve like the wicked witch? If Wasserman takes over, will she acquire his personality?*

I couldn't bear that. "I'll do this alone."

I plugged the circlet into the socket behind my ear, finding the bee in a dead end, confused by footprint pheromones left by previous bees.

We walked blind, careening off the walls as if in a stupor. I brought my consciousness-mist as close as I dared to the single pulsating gel cap that represented the bee's mind. In the distance a white disk beckoned—the bee's view of the world.

I dared not access it.

The urge to fly grew harder and harder to resist. What a glorious feeling, to fly. But that would only speed my demise. The legs moved, the abdomen rocked against the thorax.

"Describe what you see." Isabella's voice came from far away.

"A circle of light above my head." I lied. I saw nothing.

"What is written on the pipe?"

My palms dampened. The fear-wall thundered like a train. *Now or never.* I gulped a breath and wrapped my mist around the gel cap. The world turned white. I thought I had gone blind until I realized that I saw the PVC pipe from the inside.

I saw.

"Red marks on the wall. They look like they're made of coins." My voice sounded garbled and distant. I could barely understand it.

"Read it."

"Can't."

"Adam Clements." Her voice stern. "Read the writing."

I peered until it came into focus, multifaceted

coin-like images sitting around my eyes rather than flat in front of them.

1 + 1 = 2.

Mary had a little lamb.

Isabella brushed sweat from her eyebrows with her right index finger. I could see from the bee—and from my own eyes. We were paired.

I laughed aloud.

My legs moved. I detected a tar-like odor on the ground, a footprint pheromone a bee had left in an earlier visit.

Joy! I resisted the urge to fly. I deposited a marker of my own. I navigated two more corners and read two more English expressions scrawled on the interior of the PVC pipe. They tickled my neocortex, reminding me of my dual nature. And then . . .

. . . a corpse. The bee Isabella and I had worked with the week before, starved to death. It reeked of vacuum bags.

I skittered around it. Far away, Adam Clements felt sad. I did not.

Electricity crackled. My stinger poised, I crept around a bend.

I will die to protect the hive.

A violet light surrounded by some kind of mesh half blocked the pipe, casting a pattern of bars on the walls. Static charged the air, as if a lightning storm approached.

I remembered something about this, something off, even though I didn't smell warning markers.

No pollen, not a food source.

The roar of the fear-wall intensified.

The violet light shone like a beautiful flower.

Something pressed me forward, a niggle to my consciousness. I slicked a warning pheromone onto the ground. My gait became stilted. I cantered up the walls, slid down, tried again and climbed partway.

Stay as far away from the mesh as possible. Don't panic. The thought came from far away.

The static tickled as I passed. My wings fluttered. And then I could see through the smooth eyes once more. I had breached the fear-wall from both directions. I listened from Adam Clement's ears. Joy filled my thorax, as if a new queen were born.

I heard human screaming.

The monitors over Isabella's desk showed panic in the cabaret. The clientele bolted for the exits. A black tide of cockroaches wept from the stage.

Where is Isabella?

Groggy, I reached to my ear and jerked the plug from its socket.

I became Adam Clements once more.

Isabella lay slumped over the desk. Her face rippled. The bugs comprising her skin had lost cohesion. I grabbed her by the armpits and helped her from the leather armchair to the floor.

She breathed . . . or at least her chest moved. "Heart attack."

I put my hands together over her cotton shirt to begin CPR before I realized the absurdity of the notion.

Isabella was a construct.

"Whose heart attack? The Great Gajah-mada's? We've got to help him."

"Help Wasserman."

"Forget Wasserman. The Great Gajah-mada is in trouble." *You are in trouble*.

"Gajah . . . is . . . fine. He has a nurse. Wasserman won't be able to handle the bugs alone."

"No. If we can't help the Great Gajah-mada, everything else doesn't matter. The show will die." *You'll die*.

Isabella put her fingers on her temples. Cohesion returned to her beautiful black skin. "Yes. Right. Help me up."

She led me to the glass-walled atrium. Patrons scampered in every direction, jamming the exit, pressing to get out the single open door. Yellow and blue butterflies filled the space to its third-floor ceiling. One of them caught in Isabella's hair. Two men grabbed armloads of programs. In the plaza outside, a mob of passersby stared through the glass.

We made for the elevator.

On the second floor, we sprinted through the upstairs lobby. Beside the restrooms sat a nondescript door I had assumed to be a closet.

Isabella unlocked it to reveal the Great Gajah-mada's suite—private kitchen, bathroom, nurse quarters and bedroom. His room could only be described as a hospital room, white and chrome and blinking lights, the sort of place where one fears to touch any surface. A half bottle of Purell hand sanitizer beckoned on a shelf next to the door.

Wrinkles deformed his mouth. His eyes stared at a point on the far, white wall. A circlet sat catawampus on his head, partially covering his right ear. But his thumbs skated across a touch-screen remote—a mirror of the one Dieudonné used—with the adeptness of an adolescent playing VGs.

Medical machines beeped. A printout folded onto itself in an endless stack. A sixty-something nurse stood over a gray Formica counter preparing an IV. She glanced up at our arrival.

"The Great Gajah-mada." Isabella curtsied and bowed, right fist over her heart.

His thumbs paused. She froze.

The thumbs resumed . . . and she rose.

A ghost whispered through the room.

"He needs rest." The nurse spoke in a stern bass, startling me. I had forgotten her. "His heart rate dropped suddenly. I've already given him one IV to raise his blood pressure."

"We won't be long." Isabella walked to the far side of the bed and knelt there, taking his left hand in both of hers. White tape secured a cannula to the back of his wrist. She bowed her head; her braids dropped forward, curtaining her ebony face.

Not knowing what else to do, I introduced myself.

"The Great Gajah-mada has forgotten how to talk in this way." The nurse put the IV on a chrome stand and wheeled it to his side. "But he understands everything."

Isabella said, "Take his hand. He enjoys the contact with human flesh."

His tongue probed his lips, the gap where his front teeth used to be.

Human flesh.

I knelt.

"Isabella thinks highly of you." Isabella spoke in the third person.

Gajah-mada's right hand dropped the remote and extended toward me. I grabbed it with both hands. The soft freckled flesh smelled of baby powder.

Isabella's braids came to a complete rest.

"Sir?"

"She doesn't really think, you know, not in the way you and I do, though she has achieved some degree of independence." My bones chilled to hear that flat version of Isabella's voice with no accompanying movement of mouth, throat or jaw, no faux intake of breath, no rise and fall of her chest.

Whir, click, whir, click went the machines, the endless folds of paper.

"Isabella must replace two hundred thousand insects a week. Such short life spans. If insects lived longer, then yes, I believe I would have created a new form of intelligence entirely. That is why the Hive and its breeding facilities must be maintained. Her life depends on it."

"Very interesting." I couldn't bring myself to look at the beautiful . . . woman . . . kneeling across from me, uttering the Great Gajah-mada's words without movement.

"Her hair sprouts from genetically altered bumblebees. I developed them myself. I was a geneticist before becoming a sculptor. Most of the later refinements have come from others. Our labs. The Thai. The Thai make great skin, don't you think?"

"Beautiful. Mister Gajah-mada, sir, what will happen to Isabella if Wasserman takes over?"

"I did not believe you could do it, Adam. I argued with Isabella. I told her to find someone else, but she refused.

"You have a rare gift. You can reach deep into the insect psyche and return. Very few can return. For me, it was a one-way journey. My motor skills have been reduced to what it takes to manipulate the controls and the involuntary processes needed to keep this frail body alive.

"I haven't much time. Pledge to me that you will take over where I leave off. Wasserman doesn't have the strength. He will descend into rapture as I did. And then he will die."

The nurse slid the needle into the cannula. "It's time to go."

I stood and released the hand.

"Pledge to me, Adam." The hands found the remote again. Isabella stood in one fluid motion. "Pledge to me!"

I mumbled something, turned and fled out of the suite, across the lobby to the elevator, hitting the button multiple times. Isabella hurried after and entered behind me. I wondered if it were Isabella again or the Great Gajah-mada. I wondered how much strength her robot frame had. Could she become violent? Could the insects swarm me?

The door closed. She backed against the wall, looking anywhere but directly at me. She seemed . . . embarrassed.

"Isabella, I—" I did not know how to end my sentence. My thoughts collided like bees in a jar.

The weight returned to our knees. The elevator opened. A giant empty space greeted us, the deserted atrium with its glass walls dominating rue Gagous. The real world.

Tourists, pickpockets and whoonga pushers milled

SCOTT T. BARNES

about, oblivious. Isabella remained in the elevator, obviously intending to go down . . . or up. Time ticked.

I couldn't let her go. Not completely. "Give me something of . . . of you."

Her lips turned wistful. She plucked something from her scalp and placed it in my hand.

A black bumblebee sprouting a three-foot-long braid.

Here, let me help you."

Isabella adjusted the knot of my red cravat. I had never been good at them. In the mirror over her shoulder, I watched her back muscles flexing beneath the blue scoop dress. She popped my fedora on, hiding the circlet and completing my gangster look. "There now, grifter."

I dipped into Isabella's consciousness—synaptic-like signals moving from insect to insect, gel cap to gel cap. There resided a lilac presence inextricably linked with my own.

I love you, Isabella.

A hard pinch to my cheek brought my attention to the now. "I want you here. Did you turn off your remote control?"

"Dieudonné is in charge for the soirée. We can enjoy the cast party."

Isabella kissed my lips chastely. "Good. Traditionally, I am the last one to leave."

The Great Gajah-mada passed away a fortnight ago. We haven't told the media. My inclination is to simply take on his name. After all, I have taken on his greatest creation.

And I love her.

576

The range of the Hive's circlet amplifier is two blocks. If I leave it, Isabella Mada will cease to exist. Although most of the creatures that comprise her live only a few days, Isabella will live as long as I do. Longer, if I can find an apprentice who defies rapture. I will not pass on the legacy to anyone too weak to handle it.

I am now a prisoner. Willingly.

The Year in the Contests

This is the year that Eric James Stone took home his Nebula for the novelette "That Leviathan Whom Thou Hast Made" (*Analog,* September 2010).

The list of 2011 Nebula Award Nominees has seven Writers of the Future alumni listed, more than any prior year: Carolyn Ives Gilman (WotF 3) and Ken Liu (WotF 19) for Best Novella. Brad R. Torgersen (WotF 26) for Best Novelette. Tom Crosshill (WotF 26), Aliette de Bodard (WotF 23), David W. Goldman (WotF 21) and Ken Liu (WotF 19) for Best Short Story.

Nnedi Okorafor (WotF 18) has been nominated for the Andre Norton Award for Young Adult Science Fiction and Fantasy Book.

The list of 2011 Hugo Award Nominees included several entries of writer and illustrator winners as well as judges: Nnedi Okorafor (WotF 18) for Best Novel. J. Kathleen Cheney (WotF 24) for Best Novella. Eric James Stone (WotF 21) and Aliette de Bodard (WotF 23) for Best Novelette. Mike Resnick (WotF judge) for Best Related Work. Shaun Tan (WotF 8 and IotF judge) for Best Dramatic Presentation, Short Form. Bob Eggleton (IotF judge), Stephan Martiniere (IotF judge), Shaun Tan (WotF 8 and IotF judge) for Best Professional Artists for which Shaun took home the trophy.

We are excited to welcome our newest contest judges: Writers of the Future judge Todd McCaffrey and Illustrators of the Future judge Gary Meyer.

As a reminder, Author Services has a special room dedicated to the Writers and Illustrators of the Future Contests where past winners are encouraged to send copies of their published books. To date we have recorded 822 novels and 3,550 published short stories and we highly recommend that past winners send us copies of their published works so that we may include them in the library. And as an invitation, please come by Author Services and visit our Writers of the Future hall to see not only the library, but also photos and works of our contest judges and images of past awards ceremonies.

And, in very sad news, we had to say goodbye to beloved judge Anne McCaffrey in 2011. She passed away in Ireland on November 22 and left behind a popular legacy of fiction as well an unwavering commitment to help new writers. Each year, when her health permitted, she attended the Writers and Illustrators of the Future awards ceremony and spoke at the writers' workshop. She touched the lives of everyone who knew her or read her fiction. We miss her already.

For Contest year 28, the L. Ron Hubbard Writers of the Future Contest winners are:

First Quarter

    1. Marie Croke
    OF WOVEN WOOD

    2. Gerald Warfield
    THE POLY ISLANDS

    3. Harry Lang
    MY NAME IS ANGELA

Second Quarter

    1. William Ledbetter
    THE RINGS OF MARS

    2. Nick T. Chan
    THE COMMAND FOR LOVE

    3. Corry L. Lee
    SHUTDOWN

Third Quarter

    1. William Mitchell
    CONTACT AUTHORITY

    2. M. O. Muriel
    THE SIREN

    3. Jacob A. Boyd
    LOST PINE

Fourth Quarter

    1. David Carani
    THE PARADISE APERTURE

    2. Scott T. Barnes
    INSECT SCULPTOR

    3. Tom Doyle
    WHILE IRELAND HOLDS THESE GRAVES

    Published Finalist: Roy Hardin
    FAST DRAW

For the year 2011, the L. Ron Hubbard Illustrators of the Future Contest winners are:

FIRST QUARTER

> Hunter Bonyun
> Greg Opalinski
> Carly Trowbridge

SECOND QUARTER

> Mago Huang
> Jay Richard
> J. F. Smith

THIRD QUARTER

> John W. Haverty Jr.
> Fiona Meng
> Pat R. Steiner

FOURTH QUARTER

> Emily Grandin
> Paul Pederson
> Rhiannon Taylor

Our heartiest congratulations to all the winners!
May we see much more of their work in the future.

WRITERS' CONTEST RULES

1. No entry fee is required, and all rights in the story remain the property of the author. All types of science fiction, fantasy and dark fantasy are welcome.

2. By submitting to the Contest, the entrant agrees to abide by all Contest rules.

3. All entries must be original works, in English. Plagiarism, which includes the use of third-party poetry, song lyrics, characters or another person's universe, without written permission, will result in disqualification. Excessive violence or sex, determined by the judges, will result in disqualification. Entries may not have been previously published in professional media.

4. To be eligible, entries must be works of prose, up to 17,000 words in length. We regret we cannot consider poetry, or works intended for children.

5. The Contest is open only to those who have not professionally published a novel or short novel, or more than one novelette, or more than three short stories, in any medium. Professional publication is deemed to be payment of at least five cents per word, and at least 5,000 copies, or 5,000 hits.

6. Entries submitted in hard copy must be typewritten or a computer printout in black ink on white paper, printed only on the front of the paper, double-spaced, with numbered pages. All other formats will be disqualified. Each entry must have a cover page with the title of the work, the author's legal name, a pen name if applicable, address, telephone number, e-mail address and an approximate

word count. Every subsequent page must carry the title and a page number, but the author's name must be deleted to facilitate fair, anonymous judging.

Entries submitted electronically must be double-spaced and must include the title and page number on each page, but not the author's name. Electronic submissions will separately include the author's legal name, pen name if applicable, address, telephone number, e-mail address and approximate word count.

7. Manuscripts will be returned after judging only if the author has provided return postage on a self-addressed envelope.

8. We accept only entries that do not require a delivery signature for us to receive them.

9. There shall be three cash prizes in each quarter: a First Prize of $1,000, a Second Prize of $750, and a Third Prize of $500, in US dollars. In addition, at the end of the year the winners will have their entries rejudged, and a Grand Prize winner shall be determined and receive an additional $5,000. All winners will also receive trophies.

10. The Contest has four quarters, beginning on October 1, January 1, April 1 and July 1. The year will end on September 30. To be eligible for judging in its quarter, an entry must be postmarked or received electronically no later than midnight on the last day of the quarter. Late entries will be included in the following quarter and the Contest Administration will so notify the entrant.

11. Each entrant may submit only one manuscript per quarter. Winners are ineligible to make further entries in the Contest.

12. All entries for each quarter are final. No revisions are accepted.

13. Entries will be judged by professional authors. The decisions of the judges are entirely their own, and are final.

14. Winners in each quarter will be individually notified of the results by phone, mail or e-mail.

15. This Contest is void where prohibited by law.

16. To send your entry electronically, go to:
www.writersofthefuture.com/submit-your-story
and follow the instructions.

To send your entry in hard copy, mail it to:
L. Ron Hubbard's
Writers of the Future Contest
PO Box 1630
Los Angeles, California 90078

17. Visit the website for any Contest rules updates at www.writersofthefuture.com.

ILLUSTRATORS' CONTEST RULES

1. The Contest is open to entrants from all nations. (However, entrants should provide themselves with some means for written communication in English.) All themes of science fiction and fantasy illustrations are welcome: every entry is judged on its own merits only. No entry fee is required and all rights to the entry remain the property of the artist.

2. By submitting to the Contest, the entrant agrees to abide by all Contest rules.

3. The Contest is open to new and amateur artists who have not been professionally published and paid for more than three black-and-white story illustrations, or more than one process-color painting, in media distributed broadly to the general public. The ultimate eligibility criterion, however, is defined by the word "amateur"—in other words, the artist has not been paid for his artwork. If you are not sure of your eligibility, please write a letter to the Contest Administration with details regarding your publication history. Include a self-addressed and stamped envelope for the reply. You may also send your questions to the Contest Administration via e-mail.

4. Each entrant may submit only one set of illustrations in each Contest quarter. The entry must be original to the entrant and previously unpublished. Plagiarism, infringement of the rights of others, or other violations of the Contest rules will result in disqualification. Winners in previous quarters are not eligible to make further entries.

5. The entry shall consist of three illustrations done by the entrant in a color or black-and-white medium created from

the artist's imagination. Use of gray scale in illustrations and mixed media, computer generated art, and the use of photography in the illustrations are accepted. Each illustration must represent a subject different from the other two.

6. ENTRIES SHOULD NOT BE THE ORIGINAL DRAW-INGS, but should be color or black-and-white reproductions of the originals of a quality satisfactory to the entrant. Entries must be submitted unfolded and flat, in an envelope no larger than 9 inches by 12 inches.

7. All hardcopy entries must be accompanied by a self-addressed return envelope of the appropriate size, with the correct US postage affixed. (Non-US entrants should enclose international postage reply coupons.) If the entrant does not want the reproductions returned, the entry should be clearly marked DISPOSABLE COPIES: DO NOT RETURN. A business-size self-addressed envelope with correct postage (or valid e-mail address) should be included so that the judging results may be returned to the entrant.

We only accept entries that do not require a delivery signature for us to receive them.

8. To facilitate anonymous judging, each of the three photocopies must be accompanied by a removable cover sheet bearing the artist's name, address, telephone number, e-mail address and an identifying title for that work. The reproduction of the work should carry the same identifying title on the front of the illustration and the artist's signature should be deleted. The Contest Administration will remove and file the cover sheets, and forward only the anonymous entry to the judges.

9. There will be three co-winners in each quarter. Each

winner will receive an outright cash grant of US $500 and a trophy. Winners will also receive eligibility to compete for the annual Grand Prize of an additional cash grant of $5,000 together with the annual Grand Prize trophy.

10. For the annual Grand Prize Contest, the quarterly winners will be furnished with a specification sheet and a winning story from the Writers of the Future Contest to illustrate. In order to retain eligibility for the Grand Prize, each winner shall send to the Contest address his/her illustration of the assigned story within thirty (30) days of receipt of the story assignment.

The yearly Grand Prize winner shall be determined by the judges on the following basis only:

Each Grand Prize judge's personal opinion on the extent to which it makes the judge want to read the story it illustrates.

The Grand Prize winner shall be announced at the L. Ron Hubbard Awards Event held in the following year.

11. The Contest has four quarters, beginning on October 1, January 1, April 1 and July 1. The year will end on September 30. To be eligible for judging in its quarter, an entry must be postmarked no later than midnight on the last day of the quarter. Late entries will be included in the following quarter and the Contest Administration will so notify the entrant.

12. Entries will be judged by professional artists only. Each quarterly judging and the Grand Prize judging may have different panels of judges. The decisions of the judges are entirely their own and are final.

13. Winners in each quarter will be individually notified of the results by mail or e-mail.

14. This Contest is void where prohibited by law.

15. To send your entry electronically, go to:
www.writersofthefuture.com/submit-your-illustration
and follow the instructions.

To send your entry via mail send it to:
> L. Ron Hubbard's
> Illustrators of the Future Contest
> PO Box 3190
> Los Angeles, California 90078

16. Visit the website for any Contest rules updates at www.writersofthefuture.com.